DEAD
for a SPELL

Raymond Buckland

BERKLEY PRIME CRIME, NEW YORK

THE BERKLEY PUBLISHING GROUP
Published by the Penguin Group
Penguin Group (USA) LLC
375 Hudson Street, New York, New York 10014

USA • Canada • UK • Ireland • Australia • New Zealand • India • South Africa • China

penguin.com

A Penguin Random House Company

Berkley Prime Crime Books are published by The Berkley Publishing Group.
BERKLEY® PRIME CRIME and the PRIME CRIME logo are trademarks of
Penguin Group (USA) LLC.

Library of Congress Cataloging-in-Publication Data

Buckland, Raymond.
Dead for a spell : a Bram Stoker mystery / Raymond Buckland.—First edition.
     pages cm.—(Bram Stoker mystery ; 2)
     ISBN 978-0-425-26803-2 (paperback)
1. Stoker, Bram, 1847–1912—Fiction.   2. Murder—Investigation—
     Fiction.   3. Mystery fiction.   I. Title.
PS3552.U3378D43 2014
813'.54—dc23
2014021984

PUBLISHING HISTORY
Berkley Prime Crime trade paperback edition / October 2014

PRINTED IN THE UNITED STATES OF AMERICA

10 9 8 7 6 5 4 3 2 1

Cover illustration by Bill Angresano.
Cover design by Diana Kolsky.
Interior text design by Tiffany Estreicher.

To Tara and in loving memory of "Tish"

ACKNOWLEDGMENTS

I thank my wonderful agent, Grace Morgan, for her constant enthusiasm with my work. She is a gem! I cannot thank enough my talented editor, Berkley Prime Crime's Michelle Vega, who has the ability to pick up on my very thoughts! Thanks also to Marianne Grace for her excellence in copyediting, and to artist Bill Angresano and designer Diana Kolsky for the beautiful and eye-catching cover. I am extremely grateful to Natalee Rosenstein and all the wonderful family at Berkley Prime Crime who have contributed to the production of this book. Such a pleasure to work with them all.

Thanks also to Barb Lang, Ed Schrock, and all the other enthusiasts of the Killbuck Valley Writers' Guild, who have listened to me read and have given constructive criticism throughout my writing. Finally, very special thanks to my wife, Tara, for her constant encouragement and always brilliant critiquing of the book.

Chapter One

I got up from where I sat, near the door, and moved around to stand facing the boy. "So what makes you think that she's missing?" I asked.

"We was to meet for breakfast, Mr. Rivers," he said. "We always do; every mornin'. At the 'ot chocolate stand on the corner down the road. Just a cuppa and a slice of bread but, well, it was a start to the day, you might say."

"All right, Billy. Take it slowly and go over it one more time," said Stoker, studying the young man who sat on the edge of the straight-backed chair in front of his desk.

Abraham "Bram" Stoker was theatre manager of the Lyceum Theatre, and I, Harry Rivers, was stage manager. I was also a personal assistant to Mr. Stoker, running any number of errands for him, Lyceum business and otherwise.

"It's Nell, sir. Nell Burton." Billy Weston ran a dirty finger around the frayed neck of his collarless shirt. "She's done mostly crowd scenes since she's been 'ere, which ain't long. She's one of the Players in Act Two of 'Amlet. But, sir, she's gone missin'."

Mr. Stoker gave me a quick glance, one eyebrow raised.

"After last night's performance she 'urried away; said that she 'ad a *most important* fing she 'ad to do. She wouldn't say what it was, but I took the thought that it was somefin' for the Guv'nor; for Mr. Irving, sir."

"Of course." Stoker nodded understandingly. "So Miss Burton did not appear this morning?"

"No, sir. She ain't never missed before, and she said as 'ow she'd tell me all about last night's 'adventure'—that's what she called it, sir, an adventure—when she saw me this mornin'."

"She was most likely delayed in some way, Billy," I said. "I think it may be a little soon to start worrying."

"No, sir! . . . Beggin' your pardon, sir. When she didn't come to meet me I went 'round to 'er lodgings. Old Mrs. Briggs on West Street. She said as 'ow Nell 'adn't come 'ome last night. She 'adn't seen 'ide nor 'air of 'er."

Stoker glanced at me again then back to the young stage-hand. "Is there anyone she might have gone to? Any close friend, or a relative, perhaps?"

Billy Weston shook his head. "She ain't got no relatives, sir. She's an orphan, or so she says. And I'm 'er closest friend, so she would o' come to me, wouldn't she?"

I could see that Stoker was concerned, but he tried to ease the boy's mind. "I think you can leave this with us for now, Billy. Mr. Rivers, here, will look into it more thoroughly. I'm sure there's just some misunderstanding. You let Mr. Rivers know if you hear of anything else, and he, in turn, will get back to you."

"All right, Billy." I opened the door and held it as a signal that the boy should now leave. With a last pleading look at both of us, he went out, and I closed the door behind him.

"What do you think, sir?" I asked, taking Billy's place on the seat in front of Stoker's desk. "Not very encouraging, is it?"

Stoker shook his great head, the sunlight streaming in through the small window catching the red, along with the silver, in his auburn hair. He sat back and steepled his fingers, his elbows on the arms of his chair.

"There are gangs about the London streets that will abduct a young woman and sell her to traffickers in the white slave trade, Harry. I'm sure you know that. I wouldn't want to think that a young woman of our Lyceum family had been so interfered with. What do you know of this Nell Burton?"

"Not much, sir," I said. "She joined us a month or so back, when one of the female extras had to leave because of family problems. Miss Burton had come to London from up north . . ."

"Like so many," sighed Stoker.

". . . seeking fame and fortune," I continued. "She had little experience but seemed to take to the boards very quickly. She'd done a few walk-ons at the Theatre Royal, Nottingham. I think she actually came from Derby; close by there. John Saxon noticed her and drew my attention to her. I was watching Miss Burton with a view to possibly bringing her to your attention at the end of the *Hamlet* run."

"Our Mr. Saxon always notices the young ladies." Stoker pursed his lips and sat in silent thought for a moment. "We cannot afford to lose good young material, Harry."

"What would you like me to do, sir?"

"You might take a walk around to this Mrs. Briggs and question her, Harry. Young Mr. Weston was obviously too upset to get all available information. See if there is any clue as to where this mysterious assignation was to take place yesterday evening."

"I know of Mrs. Briggs," I said. "She runs a respectable boardinghouse used by girls from both here and other theatres in the central London area."

"You might, then, see if any other of our extras board there. I find it difficult to believe that this Miss Burton knows no one—other than our young stagehand, of course."

I nodded and then hurried off. At twenty-two, I, Harry Rivers, had been delighted to obtain employment at London's famous Lyceum Theatre, home of England's prominent Shake-spearean actor Henry Irving. I had dabbled in stagecraft during my education at the Hounslow Masonic Institution for Boys, which I attended courtesy of the Honorable Gregory Moffatt. I should explain that I am not of that class, by any means, but my father, a blacksmith, had done a great deal of work for the Hon. Mr. Moffatt (third son of Baron Runny-mede), and that gentleman had looked kindly upon me.

My mother died trying to bring my brother into the world, and my father passed soon after that, so, at the age of fourteen, I was forced to come to London to seek my for-tune. After a few rough years as crossing sweeper, errand boy, newspaper seller, and cab driver, I met the owner of the small Novelty Theatre on Great Queen Street, Lincoln's Inn Fields (he was one of my cab fares), and I obtained the job of theatre doorman—so much preferable to sitting up at the back of a cab in all sorts of weather. When I later heard that Mr. Irving was to take over the running of the Lyceum—a much more prestigious theatre—I applied for a position there. Apparently Mr. Irving had brought over from Ireland a Mr. Abraham Stoker, a theatre critic who had written very favorably of Mr. Irving's performances in that country. Mr. Stoker became the Lyceum's business manager, and I became stage manager . . . a job with which I fell in love.

I worked closely with Mr. Stoker and also became a per-sonal assistant to him. I came to admire him a great deal, although even after three years I could still be caught off guard by some of his idiosyncrasies. He was not afraid to display his emotions and, despite a fine business sense backed by years at the best Irish university, was easily swept up by tales of ancient Irish lore and legend. He openly believed in ghosts, sixth sense, and even "the little people," and spent what spare time he had writing his own stories. I must admit, however, that I would not change my employ-ment for any other.

It didn't take long to find out that several of the Lyceum's young ladies boarded with Mrs. Briggs. In fact, Miss Tilly Fairbanks was Nell's roommate. I found Tilly sitting in the greenroom by herself, studying the *Hamlet* script. She was young—about five years younger than myself—and not unattractive. Her dark brunette hair reminded me of my inamorata, Jenny Cartwright, though Tilly's hair was shorter and, at this moment, in some disarray. She sat with the fingers of one hand tugging on a ringlet. For whatever reason I was suddenly conscious of my own carrot red hair.

"Oh, hello, Mr. Rivers," she said, glancing up. "Just looking over my lines. Sarah Jenkins is off with a sore throat, so I'm doing the Player Queen for a bit."

"I'm sure you'll do the part proud, Tilly. I just wanted a quick word with you."

"Nothing wrong, is there, Mr. Rivers?" She looked worried.

I shook my head. "I hope not. I understand you room with Nell Burton?"

She nodded. "Why d'you ask, Mr. Rivers?"

"Haven't you heard?" I said. "Nell seems to have disappeared."

"Disappeared?" she echoed.

"Did she return to your room last night?" I asked. "I understand she went out somewhere in the late evening. What time did she get back?"

Tilly turned very red. She brought her script up to cover the bottom of her face, as though she wished she could hide behind it. There was a long silence before she replied.

"I—I'm sorry, Mr. Rivers. I . . . I mean . . . You see . . ." Then, in a rush, "I didn't sleep at home last night, Mr. Rivers! I don't make a habit of it. I'm not a bad girl. It's just that . . . well, last night me and my young man—Sammy Cooper. You know him. He works the curtains. Well me and him has been stepping out together for some time and . . ."

I held up my hand. "You don't have to tell me, Tilly. You

know as well as I do that you're on very dangerous ground there. But I'm going to ignore it for now because there are more important things to look at. You are saying, then, that you don't know when or even if Nell Burton slept in your room?"

She nodded mutely, still clutching the script in front of her.

"It seems unlikely that she was up to the same shenanigans that you were, since it was her young man who reported her missing." I had a sudden thought and looked hard at Tilly. "By any chance does Nell have more than one young man? Would she be likely to . . ." I didn't get a chance to finish.

"No!" Tilly sounded shocked and almost dropped her script. "No, Mr. Rivers. Nell is very serious with Billy. She wouldn't be untrue to him. Her and Billy and me and my Sammy, why, we often go out together. None of us would ever deceive the other."

"Thank you, Tilly," I said. "You don't know, then, where Nell might be?"

She shook her head. I turned to leave.

"Just behave yourself," I said over my shoulder.

"Yes, Mr. Rivers."

By rights I should have reported her impropriety to Mr. Stoker, but I decided to overlook it. There were times when I had extremely strong feelings toward my Jenny, but, thankfully, I had so far kept them in check. I could, however, acknowledge and understand such feelings in others. I headed for West Street.

Jenny Cartwright was a housemaid in the home of the Guv'nor, Mr. Henry Irving. I had met her quite by chance when I had been sent to the residence to collect a book belonging to Mr. Irving. Somehow Jenny and I had taken a shine to each other, and I had, on more than one occasion, met with her on her afternoon off and we had spent a few precious hours together.

As a youngster at school the other boys had teased me about my red hair, calling me "Ginger." Also, my ears were a little prominent, and I had to endure endless jokes about being cautious in a high wind in case I was lifted off the ground. My freckles did not go unnoticed, either. But I had survived the ragging of my fellow students and found that such idiosyncrasies were not dwelt upon in the adult world. Jenny seemed not to notice them at all, or if she did she was too kind to comment.

I thought her extremely beautiful and had not been slow to tell her so. She had blushed with pleasure and denied the charge, though she was obviously secretly pleased. I looked forward to the coming weekend when we had planned to take Jenny's aunt Alice to Kew Gardens, now that the weather was a little less cold. Miss Alice Forsyth had raised Jenny when her parents died, and Jenny was very fond of her. Aunt Alice had been instrumental in getting Jenny placed in the Irving household. I had not yet met the lady and looked forward to it. But Sunday was still several days away, and I had work to do.

I focused my attention on the immediate problem, the disappearance of Nell Burton. I approached the front door of Mrs. Briggs's establishment on West Street. It was a plain-looking house typical of the area. A black-painted wrought-iron fence stood around the basement; the front doorsteps had been scrubbed clean and whitewashed—a good sign of pride of ownership on Mrs. Briggs's part—and the brass door knocker gleamed in the sunshine that fought its way through the ever-present traces of fog coming off the river. I walked up the steps and knocked.

A tiny, frail-looking lady with wispy gray hair escaping her cap opened the door and appraised me. She wore a high-neck black dress that, although somewhat worn and faded, was obviously clean and smartly pressed. A cameo brooch sat in the center of the neckline; her only adornment. She looked up at me. I am but five feet and six inches of height, so this attested to her slight frame. She squinted slightly as her eyes studied my face. I wondered if she needed spectacles.

"Good morning," I said, smiling and raising my hat. She did not return the smile. "Mrs. Briggs?" I asked.

"What do you require, young man? I will have no callers for my young ladies at this hour of the day."

"Oh no! No, Mrs. Briggs, I am not here to call on any of your tenants. At least, not directly."

"What are you blathering about? Oh, come in! Come in. We can't have you standing on the doorstep inviting talk from the neighbors. Come on inside and explain yourself."

She turned and led the way into the house. I followed, looking around in the dark hallway. The walls were vaguely discernible in the dim light, covered with ancient flock wallpaper. There were a number of small colored prints of country scenes in gaudy gilt frames, together with matching framed silhouettes of a man and a woman, and an overlarge etching of a stag at bay. A massive walnut Renaissance Revival hallstand projected from the wall into the hallway and had to be carefully negotiated. It was festooned with ladies' coats, and its outer arms held an assortment of umbrellas on cast-iron drip pans. Mrs. Briggs hurried on, opening a door and ushering me into the parlor.

The parlor furniture was dark—mahogany and darkened oak; I got the sense that the whole house was dark if not dingy—and overfilled with chairs, tables, and potted plants. I ducked around an aspidistra and found myself facing Mrs. Briggs as she stood in front of the imposing marble fireplace. There was no fire burning in the hearth, but the heavy curtains pulled only slightly apart at the windows seemed to keep out much of the cold. A single gas lamp burned low over the mantel shelf. My eyes were drawn to an ornate clock with two overly pink cherubs supporting it, one on either side, the small hands permanently pointing to two of the clock. The timepiece itself rested between two large glass globes covering dusty and mangy-looking stuffed birds, once colorful.

"Now, young man. Your name and business."

"Of course." I fumbled for a calling card but couldn't find one. "I, er, I am Mr. Harold Rivers, stage manager and assistant to the Lyceum Theatre manager, Mr. Abraham Stoker."

"I know the gentleman." She nodded her head. "I have a number of Mr. Stoker's young ladies who reside here. Have been suffering them for many years now."

"You have one named Miss Nell Burton," I said.

"A model young lady . . . or was until today. I do not stand for my young lady tenants who play it fast and loose. She did not return to her room last evening, as was the case with her roommate Miss Fairbanks. I shudder to think where they might have been. This will be their first warning—each young lady receives only three warnings before she finds herself out on the street."

Mrs. Briggs's lips were pressed together in a tight, thin line. She may have been small, but she obviously ruled her house with a will of iron.

"Miss Burton apparently is missing," I informed her. The tight lips remained. "We—Mr. Stoker and myself—have some concern regarding her safety." The lips relaxed a trifle. "I would be greatly obliged if you would allow me to see her room, in case there be any clue there as to her present whereabouts."

"Miss Fairbanks . . ." she started to say.

"Her roommate has agreed to it," I said. "She is as concerned for Miss Burton as are we all."

It was with grim determination and obvious disapproval that Mrs. Briggs preceded me up the staircase to the second floor, where she selected a key from the large key ring at her waist and unlocked one of the doors on the left.

"I should stay and watch you, Mr. Rivers, but I have work to do. I hold you and Mr. Stoker responsible should anything later be found amiss in this room."

She looked at me sternly, her eyes still squinting slightly, her head tipped back that she might look me full in the face.

"I thank you, Mrs. Briggs, and I assure you I shall merely look and take note. I will not be removing anything, however slight its value, from the room."

"Hrrmph!" She snorted and then turned and retraced her steps down to the lower level.

I looked about me. The room was small, with two iron-framed beds side by side filling most of the space. Both beds were neatly made up. A worn wooden chest of drawers stood against the wall at the foot of the beds, and a washstand bearing washbowl and jug was on the adjacent wall, next to the door through which I had entered. Two small, framed watercolor pictures of birds and flowers were hung, one over each bedhead. A tiny window looked out over neighboring narrow backyards, and even with the window closed as it now was, I could detect the faint smell of the privies lining the ends of those yards.

I hesitated a moment, feeling uncomfortable examining the bedroom of two young ladies. But Mr. Stoker had sent me to do a job, and I would not fail him.

I saw that one of the young women had apparently taken off her clothing—in a hurry, I would guess—and simply dropped the garments on the floor. Her underthings were there also, and I was aware of myself blushing as I glimpsed them, although I was alone in the room.

I turned to the chest of drawers and gently opened and closed each drawer, trying not to disturb the intimate apparel within. In one drawer, lying atop the obviously well-worn blouse bodices, was a bundle of letters tied up with a red ribbon. They were addressed to Miss Tilly Fairbanks.

There was no sign of any other correspondence; nothing addressed to Miss Nell Burton.

I returned down the stairs and found Mrs. Briggs in her kitchen, stirring the contents of a large cast-iron pot with a wooden spoon. The smell issuing from the pot made my mouth water.

"I like to have a good offering of soup for my girls when they come home," she said. "Poor twists! A pair of them are only at gaffs, so you know they don't have much money for eating."

I began to see a softer side to Mrs. Briggs's stern exterior.

"What can you tell me about Miss Burton's coming back from the theatre last night?" I asked.

She stopped her stirring for a moment and screwed up her face in thought. Then she started stirring again. "I remember now. There was a dress—a white dress—that was dropped off here for her yesterday. In the late afternoon. I guessed as how it was for some play your theatre must be doing?"

I shook my head. "Nothing that I am aware of. Who delivered this dress?"

It was her turn to shake her head. "Just some street boy who'd been given a ha'penny to bring it. He didn't know anything—I asked him."

Mrs. Briggs was nobody's fool.

"Oh, and one more thing," she said. She stopped stirring again and looked at me intensely. "Miss Burton must have changed into the dress right away, when she came back from the theatre, for she came running down the stairs in it and out the door. I had to shout after her to shut the door behind her, but she didn't hear me. I went to close it and would you believe, there she was getting into a hansom. It must have been waiting for her."

"Getting into a hansom cab?"

"As I live and breathe."

Chapter Two

"Mr. Rivers!"

I had returned to the Lyceum and reported my findings to Mr. Stoker. I was then approaching my office when I was accosted. It was Edwina Abbott, one of the extras. Miss Abbott was a reliable young actress. She would never rise above bit parts and crowd scenes, and I think she knew it, but she seemed content just to be a part of the theatre and especially one of the greater Lyceum "family," as both Mr. Stoker and the Guv'nor termed it.

My so-called office had walls on only three sides, the fourth being open to any and all who passed by. In truth, it was no more than a large closet with no door and no privacy. Mr. Stoker was always talking of finding me better quarters, but there was not a great deal of available space in the theatre, especially close to the stage, as I needed to be. I had contemplated taking possession of the properties room and swapping contents, but I realized that the properties needed to be somewhere that could be locked securely. With a sigh—which I invariably gave when considering my office space—I beckoned Miss Abbott to follow me in and find a seat as close to my desk as the piles of assorted props, scripts, set layouts, and books would allow. I turned up the single gas jet that protruded from the back wall, the electrification of the theatre not yet having reached my humble quarters.

"Now, Miss Abbott?" I said, sliding a pile of papers off my chair and sitting. I glanced down at the desktop in front of me to see the cold remains of fish and chips that had been resting there since the previous night. I vaguely remembered abandoning them when some small crisis occurred toward the end of last evening's performance. I swept the newspaper-wrapped bundle into the rubbish bin.

"Tilly Fairbanks suggested I come to see you, Mr. Rivers." She spoke hesitantly, obviously unsure as to whether or not she was doing the right thing.

I nodded and tried to look welcoming, even though I was aware of a hundred and one things that cried out for my attention. "My door is always open, Miss Abbott," I said, and then smiled at the literal meaning of my words.

"It's the cards, sir."

"I beg your pardon?"

"The cards." She dug into her reticule and pulled out an ancient deck of playing cards, which she set down on the edge of my desk. "They was given to me by my aunt Jessica, God rest her soul. She had 'em from a French sailor, begging your pardon."

"Cards? French sailor?" I felt as though I had landed in the middle of a pantomime scene at the Princess's Theatre.

"They're tarot cards, Mr. Rivers. Not found a lot on this side of the Channel, as I understand it. My aunt used to say that the Froggies was into them a lot. O' course, she weren't really my aunt, you understand. Just took me and my kid sister in when things was rough."

I held up my hand to signal silence and reached out to

take the cards and examine them. They were well-worn, obviously having been used a great deal. One or two were missing corners, and a few were torn, but I recognized them. Tarot cards were used for telling fortunes and—so it was claimed—for seeing into the future. I recalled Mr. Stoker describing them once to Miss Ellen Terry, when she was reading a play by Molière. I didn't remember much about them except that there were far more of them in a deck than would be found in regular playing cards.

I fanned them and saw mysterious scenes, along with symbols of swords and cups, coins and cudgels. I stopped at one of the more colorful cards depicting a skeleton wielding a scythe and slicing heads that protruded from the ground like so many cabbages. It was titled *La Mort*. I glanced up at my visitor, but her face was serious, her eyes locked on the pasteboards I handled.

A large moon with a grotesque face looked down on two foxes standing one on either side of a river. An ancient tower rose behind each of the canines, and a crustacean of some sort menaced them from the waters. I studied a harlequin juggling two large coinlike balls embossed with multi-pointed stars. On one card a hand floated in midair wielding a sword; on another an ancient crone staggered out of a forest weighed down with fagots. A windmill struck by lightning spewed forth the figures of the miller and his wife, and various knights on horseback wielded swords, cudgels, large coins, and goblets.

"What do you want me to do with them?" I asked.

"Nothing. No, Mr. Rivers. I just sometimes read 'em for the girls backstage, when things is quiet. Just funnin', you know?" She looked anxious.

I nodded for her to continue.

"Well, Tilly said as how Nell has gone missing, and Janet Broad said why didn't I ask the cards where she might be."

"You thought they could tell you?" I tried not to sound as incredulous as I felt.

She nodded. "I done a quick reading . . . I'm not good at this. My mum was, God rest her soul. So was my auntie Jessica. You should have seen her. Anyway, I done a five-card spread and the two ending cards was these." She reached out and took up the deck. Quickly she shuffled through them . . . I could tell she was more familiar with handling them than she was willing to admit. She stopped and put one of the cards down on the desk in front of me, followed by a second. I stared at them.

The first depicted a young woman standing bound and blindfolded in the midst of a large number of swords stuck into the ground. The other card showed a large red heart with three swords sticking through it. Blood dripped from the heart to the ground beneath. Neither of the cards could be viewed as propitious, in my humble opinion, though I knew nothing of tarot card interpretation. I decided to play dumb.

"So what do you see these cards as meaning, Miss Abbott? And how do you attribute whatever it is to our missing Miss Burton?"

Her mouth gaped. "Ain't it obvious?" she cried, and then cupped a hand to her mouth. "Oh, I beg your pardon, Mr. Rivers. It's just that . . . well, to someone as reads these cards on a regular basis—well, occasional, p'raps I should say—it's as though these pasteboards are screaming out to me. That's why Tilly says I should come and see you." She was silent a moment, and then, with her face growing red, she reached forward and started gathering up the cards. "I—I'm sorry, Mr. Rivers, sir. I shouldn't have come and wasted your time. I can see . . ."

"No!" I held up my hand to stop her. "It is I who am sorry, Miss Abbott. Edwina, isn't it?"

She looked at me from beneath lowered brows and nodded.

"Edwina. You are obviously something of an expert with these cards, compared to myself. I can see that what you have recognized as being represented here is important to you."

"Nell was our friend, Mr. Rivers."

"Yes. Yes, I'm sure." I got to my feet. "Come with me, Edwina. I'd like you to repeat what you have said, and shown, to Mr. Stoker. He is far more attuned to such arcane lore than am I. I think he would find this well worth his attention."

I took her to Mr. Stoker's office and tapped on the door.

"Come!"

I eased open the door and peered inside. I was relieved to see that he was alone. I advanced inside, beckoning Miss Abbott to follow me. Stoker raised his eyebrows, slid an account book to one side, and nodded toward a pair of chairs facing his desk. We sat and I quickly explained why we were there.

"May I see this tarot deck?"

Edwina Abbott produced the cards, handed them to me, and I passed them across to Stoker. I watched his face closely as he examined them, looking through them and pausing from time to time to study a particular card more closely.

"These are very old," he said, without looking up.

"Yes, sir. My old aunt gave 'em to me and she said as how they had belonged to some French lady who had 'em from a sailor."

Stoker nodded without comment.

"There's two cards missing," added Edwina.

He stopped shuffling through the deck and looked sharply at her.

"The Four of Cups and the Nine of Coins."

He nodded. "Unfortunate but not disastrous."

"No, sir."

After a few more moments of studying the cards, Stoker

laid them, faceup, on the desk in front of him and sat back. He steepled his fingers as he now studied the young actress.

"What was this spread you used, Miss Abbott? Just five cards, I understand?"

"Yes, sir." She seemed to lose some of her nervousness and sat forward on the edge of her seat. "It's one my auntie showed me for what she called a quick reading. One for the person; one for strength; one for weakness; one for 'working,' as she put it; and one for the climax."

"The climax?" I said.

Stoker nodded. "What the others were leading up to." He fastened his attention on Edwina. "The first three are immaterial right now. What were the other two?"

"As I showed Mr. Rivers, sir. Number four was the Eight of Swords and number five was the Three of Swords."

He pursed his lips but said nothing, his eyes returning to the cards.

Edwina looked at me, her eyebrows raised. I tried to indicate that we should wait and see what my boss might say. He finally looked up, first at Edwina and then turned to me.

"This is somewhat disturbing, Harry."

"It is?" I was surprised.

"Indeed. You did right to bring this to our attention, Miss Abbott. Harry, I want you to get onto this right away. See if you can contact that wretched policeman who kept hanging around us last month. What was his name?"

"Sergeant Bellamy, sir. I'll track him down. You think this is that serious?"

He did not immediately reply but got to his feet and moved across to remove his topcoat from the mahogany clothes tree by the door. As he struggled into the garment he spoke.

"Thank you, Miss Abbott. We are obliged. You may take your cards—remarkable deck, if I may say so—and return to your duties. It is possible I may have to call upon you in the future." Edwina took up her cards and, tucking them into her reticule, scampered out of the office. "Forget Bellamy for the moment, Harry. This is urgent. Come with me."

"I'll just get my coat," I said.

"I shall be outside hailing a cab. Don't dawdle, Harry."

As the hansom rattled over the cobblestones, Stoker refreshed my memory on the tarot cards.

"Almost certainly brought into Europe by the Roma—the Gypsies—since the tarot first appeared about the same time as did those nomads. The cards have been known in England since the time of King Edward IV. He, however, forbade the importation of them, and they have ever afterward been difficult to find in these Isles."

"Why was that, sir?" I asked.

"Why did he forbid their use? I imagine that he felt—as did others, especially leaders of the Church—that they were instruments of the Devil. He was afraid of them."

"Afraid?"

"People are always afraid of that which they do not understand, Harry. Remember that. The more you study something, the more you come to understand it, ergo the less you find to fear in it. But the tarot cards are innocuous in and of themselves. They are simply tools. In the right hands they can be valuable . . . and revealing."

"Revealing, sir? Are you saying that you believe they can show the future?"

"I cannot explain—and I have yet to meet the man who can—exactly how it is that a fall of the cards can indicate all that it does. And yet I have found the tarot to be amazingly accurate in many ways, Harry. Not so much in predicting the future, for the future is not cast in stone, yet able to indicate the forces at work in a given situation . . . the energy that inclines us in various directions. You might do well to peruse what this Madame Blavatsky is promoting in her new Theosophical movement, though her focus is not on the tarot. You might also take a glance at Shelley, Blake, and even Swedenborg."

I glanced out of the cab. "Where are we going, sir?"

"Scotland Yard."

It took me a moment to take in what he said. "Scotland Yard? Why is that?"

"I have grave concern about our missing young lady. Appraising what you gleaned from her landlady, and then considering what was indicated in the tarot by Miss Abbott, I believe it to be vital that we demand immediate action by the Metropolitan Police . . . if it is not already too late."

"Too late?" Was I missing something?

Stoker continued. "Our Miss Burton was enticed away and instructed to not reveal where she was going. She was provided with a gown—presumably appropriate for a particular occasion; I suspect a ritual of one sort or another—and transported in a cab provided by her abductors."

"Abductors?" I was unsure of the word's import.

"Don't keep repeating what I say, Harry. Although it would appear that Miss Burton left of her own volition, I am of the opinion that she was lured away and for no good purpose. I fear she may be in extreme danger and only pray that we are not too late to rescue her."

I almost repeated his last few words but managed not to do so. The hansom turned into Scotland Yard, and Stoker thrust coins up through the trapdoor into the cabbie's hands before leaping from the vehicle and striding ahead of me into the police station.

"Mr. Stoker, as we live and breathe. And Mr. Withers."

"Rivers," I corrected. I was surprised to see a familiar figure standing at the far end of the enquiry desk. Sergeant Samuel Charles Bellamy, his beady brown eyes gleaming.

"Our apologies. What brings you gentlemen to Scotland

Yard, might we ask? Not another human head rolling out of your scenery, we trust?"

A burly constable seated behind the well-worn counter chuckled behind his copy of the *Police Gazette*.

"Sergeant Bellamy?" said Stoker. "We had occasion to mention your name less than an hour ago. How fortuitous that you are here at Scotland Yard."

"Fortuitous indeed, sir." He inclined his head but continued to stand with his feet apart and with his thumbs tucked into his waistcoat pockets. "And we would make so bold as to correct you and tell you that we are now *Inspector* Bellamy and have been moved permanently from C Division to the Yard."

"Well, let's hope you are up to the task," said Stoker. Before Bellamy could bristle he added, "We need a competent police official to locate a missing young lady. One whom I very much fear is in imminent danger."

To his credit, Bellamy extracted his thumbs from his pockets and moved briskly past the end of the counter to usher us down a short corridor and into a small office.

"Please be seated, gentlemen."

We took the two plain wooden chairs in front of the desk, which the inspector sat behind. I glanced about me and noted the inevitable framed portrait of Her Majesty on the wall behind Bellamy together with a decidedly smaller photograph of the police commissioner, Sir Edmund Henderson.

"Now sir," said the inspector, addressing Stoker and studiously ignoring me. "Who is this young lady? Let us have the full facts. What crime, exactly, was perpetrated upon her?" He flipped open a notebook that lay on the desk. It looked to me to be the same one he had used in his days as a humble sergeant. As he licked the end of his pencil I got the impression that he was overeager to record details of any improprieties that might have been committed.

"The young lady is missing, Sergeant . . ."

"Inspector!"

Stoker merely waved his hand. "As yet we are unaware of any harm done to her, but then that is why we are here."

"We don't quite under . . ."

"Time is of the essence, man!" snapped my boss. "Every moment that passes increases the possible danger. You must rally your troops—or whatever you have to do—and we must get out after her and find her. I have the strongest feeling that . . ."

"Whoa! Hold on there, sir." Bellamy held up his hand as though halting traffic. "You have a 'feeling'? You are unaware of any harm done? You want us to have our men go running off in all directions just on a whim? We don't think so, sir."

"A whim? A *whim*?" Stoker came to his feet, his face red. "You incompetent fool! You are as stupid as you ever were as *Sergeant* Bellamy! Promotion did not bring brains. Come, Harry!"

He stormed out of the room, leaving Bellamy spluttering. I ran after him.

Chapter Three

"So what now, Mr. Stoker?"

I studied my boss's serious face as we strode along Whitehall. He had been too angry to stop and signal a cab and had muttered something about "walking it off."

"I'm giving it thought, Harry," he said, his head down and his stride diminishing so that I might keep up. "I am positive that our Miss Burton is in very real danger and we need to find her as quickly as possible . . . but how? Where did they take her?"

"Perhaps if we could find the cabbie," I started to say.

Stoker stopped abruptly, causing a tall, thin, military-looking gentleman striding along behind him to almost lose his footing as he avoided running into Stoker's back. Muttering and glaring at my boss, the colonel—or whatever rank he was—sidestepped neatly and then, dodging around us, slid back into step and continued on along the pavement.

"Well done, Harry. Yes, of course. We have to find that cabbie."

"There are an awful lot of hansom cabs in the city," I said. "Talk about your needle in a haystack."

"But all needles can be traced. Get yourself round to Mrs. Briggs again as quickly as you can. Find out all you can about the hansom that picked up our girl. Did Mrs. Briggs notice anything in particular about the driver? What color was the horse? Anything—*anything*, Harry—that may help you find that needle! Mrs. Briggs is on West Street, is she not? There is a cab rank on the corner of Monmouth and Long Acre. Enquire there. Ask every cabbie you can find."

I flagged down a passing hansom and jumped in.

"Don't worry about me," said my boss, waving me off. "I have some leads I will follow up myself. Just find that cab driver and discover where he took Miss Burton. Let us pray we are not too late."

"Goodness me, Mr. Rivers! It was dark, you understand? Miss Burton had just returned from the theatre, and you know full well when that turns out."

"But you did see her get into the cab?"

"Yes. Yes, I did."

"Think, Mrs. Briggs! Please think. Cast your mind back. Miss Burton's very life may well depend on it! Was there anything, anything at all, that you noticed about the cab or its driver? No matter how small a thing. Anything at all?" I implored.

The old lady pressed her thin lips together and knitted her brow. I waited, holding my breath.

"He was a stocky fellow, the driver," she said, speaking as the thoughts came to her. I slowly let out my breath, not daring to interrupt her. "Wore a top hat, not like so many of 'em these days as sports a bowler. Oh, and he had near-white sideboards. Bushy muttonchops. Bit old-fashioned now, I suppose. I remember thinking he was getting on a bit to be driving around late at night."

"Anything about the cab itself, Mrs. Briggs? Or the horse, perhaps?"

"Yes! Yes, of course. As he pulled away the cab passed under that new gaslight they put up last December. We really needed that, I can tell you. Nothing to light the pavement from here to the corner."

"The horse, Mrs. Briggs?"

"Yes, yes. I was coming to that. A piebald it was. Don't see many of them pulling cabs. Nearly all black or brown. Occasionally dappled gray. Hardly ever see a piebald."

"Piebald." I was delighted. A black-and-white horse was certainly distinctive. "Anything else?"

"No. No." She shook her head. "No. That was it, Mr. Rivers. Does that help?"

"Oh yes! Yes, thank you, Mrs. Briggs. You've been a *great* help!"

She looked pleased and a tiny smile crept onto the thin lips.

I wasted no time in hurrying off to the corner of the street. I turned right and ran the block to the corner of Long Acre.

There was only one hansom at the rank, waiting for a fare. The driver was a thin fellow with a scraggly, drooping mustache stained from food or beer. He wore a brown bowler hat, the side of it boasting a dent.

"Ev'nin', sir," he said when he spied me. "Where to, guv?"

"Not just yet, thank you," I said. "I'd just like to ask you a couple of questions."

He looked anxiously about him. "'Ere! Wot's this then? You a copper? I ain't done nothin'. Wot you want wif me?"

"It's all right," I assured him. "No problem. I just need some information. I need to locate another cabbie."

"Wot's wrong wif me, then?"

"No." I tried to be patient, though I was very much aware of the urgency that Mr. Stoker had placed on the situation. "I'm trying to locate a cabbie who was in this area last night. I wondered if you knew him?" I repeated Mrs. Briggs's description.

"Piebald 'orse, you say?"

I nodded.

"Was it a green cab?"

"I have no idea," I said. "I assumed it was black, like so many others."

He nodded, removed his hat, and scratched the top of his head. "Dark green," he said, carefully replacing the hat. "Looks black at night. They all do."

I took his word for it. "You do know the cab, though?"

"Ho, yes. Buster Wilkins, that was. 'E's that fond of that old nag of 'is. Too old, really, for this lark . . . both the 'orse and old Buster, if you ask me." He broke into a fit of coughing, and I waited till he finished.

"Where might I find this Buster?" I asked.

He scratched his head again. I wondered if that activated his thinking.

"'E mostly sticks to the Trafalgar Square to Westminister district, I fink. I'm surprised he was up at West Street. Must 'ave been called for, I reckon."

"Yes," I agreed. "I believe it was arranged for him to go there." I had a sudden idea and started to climb into his cab. "Why don't you take me down to that Westminster area? Perhaps you'll be able to spot him for me. There's a half sovereign in it for you if you can help me locate the man."

He needed no urging. We were soon trotting at a brisk pace around Trafalgar Square and then along Whitehall.

It was an hour later that we spotted our quarry. We had been up and down Whitehall half a dozen times and driven along Victoria Street, Victoria Road, and back along Birdcage Walk. It was as we approached New Palace Yard for the twentieth time—or so it seemed—that my cabbie let out a shout.

"Hellooo there! That's 'im!" He opened the trap and shouted down to me, nearly deafening me. "There's old Buster. Just coming off the bridge. Lor'! 'Oo would 'ave thought it? I didn't know 'e ever went Lambeth side."

"Can we stop him?" I asked. "I have to question him."

"You leave it to me, guv. I'll stop the old nag."

He spun the hansom around in a tight circle, causing cries and shouts, curses and blasphemy. Cutting across a line of traffic going in the opposite direction, he hauled his own horse to a stop only feet in front of the primly trotting pie-bald as it came off the Westminster Bridge. The other cab's driver—whom I recognized from Mrs. Briggs's description—waved his whip and shouted at my driver, bringing the dark green hansom to a halt half on and half off the pavement.

I jumped out and ran toward the old cabbie in the top hat.

"'Ere! Wot about my fare . . . and the sovereign as you promised?" The driver who had brought me there sounded understandably angry.

"Hold on just a minute," I shouted over my shoulder. "I'll be right back."

There was no passenger in the green cab, and I jumped up on the step in order to be closer to this Buster Wilkins.

"I would have stopped, if all you wanted was to change cabs," said the old man, eyes wide in astonishment. "No need to cause a barney right outside the Palace of Westminister!"

"This is an emergency," I said, trying to sound official. It wasn't hard to mimic the manner and inflections of Sergeant-now-Inspector Bellamy. I quickly explained to the flustered old man what I needed to know. Where had he taken the young lady he had picked up on West Street late the previous evening? He remembered her quite well.

"Pretty young thing," he said. "In a white gown. Thought she must be going to some party. Lots of them debitats go running off to 'em, you know. Bit early in the season, though, I thought."

"Do you remember where you took her?" I asked.

"'Course I do! I'm a cabbie, hain't I? I allus remember me fares."

"Can you take me there . . . now?"

"Reckon so," he said. "Mind you, it weren't nothin' like I was hexpectin'. Not 'xactly a fancy house."

"No matter," I said. "Wherever it was, I want to go there. Wait just one moment."

I jumped down and returned to my first cab. I held up two sovereigns. "Here, my good man. The first is for your excellent tracking. The second is for my fare plus a second job I have for you."

He bit into the sovereigns to be sure they were real and then looked at me all attention.

"Go as fast as you can—without causing any accidents— to the Lyceum Theatre. Ask for Mr. Abraham Stoker and bring him to this address." I then shouted across to old Buster. "Where is it we are going?"

"Down by the river," he called back. "It's off the Strand, between Duchy Wharf and Savoy Wharf. A big old ware-house right on the water. Tell 'im to turn down Savoy Street and then make a right on the first wharf."

"Did you get that?" I asked.

The cabbie nodded.

I was soon in the green cab, behind the piebald as it plod-ded along Charing Cross and turned onto the Strand. I sev-eral times urged Buster Wilkins to make more speed, but it seemed that was more than his old horse was capable of doing. I bided my time, tapping my foot on the floor of the hansom. At this rate, Mr. Stoker would get there before me!

Eventually, after what seemed like an hour or more,

though was probably considerably less than that, we turned down a narrow cobblestone lane. I could see ahead of me the masts of a number of ships, together with the red sail of a Thames sailing barge, moving majestically downriver. At the Duchy Wharf we turned and squeezed between large bails stacked ready for moving into one of the many warehouses. Mr. Wilkins brought the cab to a stop outside a dilapidated building that abutted the side of the wharf and that stretched down and out over the water itself. At the opposite end of the wharf the dark shape of Waterloo Bridge towered over everything, stretching off into the mist that rose from the murky waters.

"'Ere we are, guv. Made good time, I reckon."

I was not about to argue.

"This is where you brought the girl last evening?"

He nodded. "Pretty little thing, all in 'er white gown and all. Wot's going on 'ere, then?"

"Did she go into the building?" I asked, ignoring his question.

"That she did, sir. Broke into a bit of a run, too. Seemed real eager to get in there."

"Was there anyone to meet her here?"

He shook his head. "Not a bleedin' soul, beggin' yer pardon, sir. I wouldn't 'ave gone in there meself, but she seemed to think as 'ow she was hexpected."

"I see. Thank you."

I paid him. He reversed the cab, shook the reins, and the piebald walked slowly away. I made my way up the few wooden steps. Paint peeled from the sides of the building and from the double doors. The wood of the steps felt none too secure, bowing under my slight weight. The entrance was not locked but called for a determined thrust on my part to open just one of the doors.

The inside smelled of damp and rotting timber. Abandoned piles of rope, cast-off clothing, burst bags of unknown ballast; the flotsam of the wharves was scattered about the place. I made my way carefully toward the stairs leading to the upper floors. Outside, seagulls screeched and the occasional steam whistle from a merchantman echoed off the walls. What on earth had Nell Burton been doing in this place? I wondered.

The floor above was slightly better. It looked as though it was used, if only on rare occasions. Like the ground floor, it was divided into a number of rooms along one side, leaving a main open area that ran the full length of the building. None of the rooms had doors, reminding me of my humble office back at the Lyceum. There were one or two tables plus a few chairs in some of the rooms. Two of them contained high accounting desks, drawers hanging out or completely missing where the local mudlarks had ransacked the place. I moved on up the stairs to the top floor.

Here there were no small rooms, just the full open area with the raftered roof above. Suddenly it became clear to me. This was one of the many available buildings along the river used as rehearsal rooms by London's theatrical fraternity. Plenty of space and availability. On the floorboards near the top of the stairs I saw chalk outlines to indicate the placement of scenery and furniture. There were other chalk groupings off to both far ends of the building. A few old chairs were scattered about, and there was an ancient sofa with its horsehair stuffing protruding from a variety of well-worn spots.

So that was it! Nell Burton had been drawn here for a tryout. But for what? She was a member of the Lyceum family and firmly ensconced as a character in *Hamlet*. Had some other theatre taken note of her and enticed her here for an audition of some sort? I pondered. But what talent did she have that would lead to that? In all fairness, there was none of which anyone at the Lyceum had been aware. She was a walk-on; a crowd scene character. Like so many young hopefuls she had little chance of even playing speaking roles in these, her early years. It was true that John Saxon had noticed her, and made mention of her to me a time or two, but I had not seen any extraordinary talent there myself as of yet. Perhaps with some personal coaching and some elocution lessons, but the same could be said of several of the young hopefuls. Besides, John might well have an ulterior motive in trying to advance a pretty young girl and have her beholden to him.

I began wandering around the ill-lit loft, peering into corners, but stopped when it occurred to me that I had not given the ground floor a thorough investigation. I should do this systematically so as not to miss anything, I determined. I started down the stairs again. As I reached the bottom I heard noises outside on the wharf. There were shouts and the sound of wheels. A horse whinnied. I hurried to the door and tugged it open.

Outside I found an active scene. A cab—the very one I had earlier used and sent off to the Lyceum—had just discharged Mr. Stoker. He paused to look back at the vehicles behind him. A second hansom bore Inspector Bellamy and a sergeant, and behind them a police growler was emptying out four other policemen.

"This way!" shouted Stoker, and then turned and made for the steps.

"Mr. Stoker, sir!" I cried. "You made excellent time. But what's happening? How did you get Scotland Yard to pay attention?"

"It was the Guv'nor," he said, breathing heavily as he came up the steps. "I complained to him and he—as you may or may not know—is a good friend of the police commissioner. I don't think our friend Inspector Bellamy was overjoyed to be told to get down here with all possible speed."

As he finished speaking, the inspector himself came blustering over to the warehouse.

"All right then! Where's the body? You do have a body, we hope, to make all this fuss?"

"I sincerely hope we do *not* have a body," said Stoker grimly. "But it will be no thanks to you if we do." He swung back to me. "Lead on, Harry. I take it you've had a look around?"

"There's not much to see," I said, as I returned inside with my boss and a goodly number of the Metropolitan Police Force behind me. I quickly ran over what I had observed on the upper floors.

"Let us proceed to the top floor," said Stoker. "The chalk markings, as you say, Harry, would seem to indicate that space has recently been used."

When we reached the large open area the police fanned out and, as I had done earlier, started peering into every dark and dingy crevice.

"Looks empty to me," muttered Bellamy to his sergeant.

"Yessir!"

"But not to me," said Stoker. He had looked briefly at the chalk outlines at one end of the space and then proceeded to the far end—the one closest to the river. "Look at these markings, Harry."

I did. They didn't tell me anything in particular, although they did seem far more complicated than the other ones I had seen.

"Describe what you see, Harry," Stoker urged.

"Er—large circles, one inside the other," I said hesitantly.

"Concentric circles," Stoker clarified.

"And there is some writing between the lines," I added. I leaned forward and peered down at what had become smudged by the boots of the policemen. "Can't make out what it says," I continued. "But it looks like Latin or some such to me."

"Correct," said Stoker. "Latin. The Words of Power."

"Excuse me?" Bellamy came and stood beside us as we looked at the markings on the floor. "Here! Sykes!" He called to one of the constables. "Get your bullseye over here sharpish. Let's have a good look at what Mr. Stoker thinks to be so important!"

The policeman hurried across and shone his lantern down on the floorboards. The light showed a large rectangle drawn with the corner points hitting midway along the sides of a larger rectangle that enclosed it. The corner points of the larger figure touched the inside of the first circle. The "Words of Power," as Stoker termed them, were written between this first circle and the larger outer circle encompassing everything.

"It doesn't look like a layout for scenery or stage furniture," I hazarded.

"It is not," said Stoker.

"'Ere!" Another constable let out a shout. He had been shining his own bullseye lantern along the end wall and looking at the solitary window that faced out onto the river. "Hinspector! Don't this 'ere look like blood, sir? 'Ere on the windowsill?"

As Bellamy, Stoker, and myself moved to look, the sergeant, who was left where Bellamy had been standing, gave another shout.

"Looks like blood here, too, sir. Lots of blood."

"Well this is a rum do," muttered the inspector.

Indeed, we had been so taken with interpreting the chalk design on the floor that we had failed to notice the large, dark reddish stain in the very center of the inner rectangle. Bellamy had been standing on it.

Chapter Four

"There is indeed a lot of blood," said Inspector Bellamy. "Well soaked into these ancient and dry old floorboards," agreed Stoker. He turned away. "Damnation! I feared we would be too late!"

"Down in the water, sir!" sang out the policeman who was leaning out of the end window. "Somefink's down there. Floatin' in the tide. Could be a body, sir."

We all rushed over and squeezed together to stick out our heads. The constable was right. Something white—like a woman's dress—was gently swaying back and forth in the tide. It looked as though it was caught up on a metal spike protruding from the side of the wharf. As one we turned and started for the stairs.

"Dickinson! Martin! You stay here and see what else you can find. Don't touch anything, just make note of it." Bellamy had suddenly become efficient, I thought.

The warehouse jutted out adjacent to the wharf, though there was an eight-foot gap between the two. The body—if body it was—was caught up at the corner of the building. Bellamy sent off one of his men to find a boat hook. When he returned with one there was much fishing and tugging to get what was indeed a body free and draw it in to where we crouched.

"Must have thrown the body out of the window hoping the tide would carry it away," observed the police sergeant. "Didn't reckon on it getting caught up."

"It's her," I said, as the now-obvious body nudged the wharf side. "It's Nell Burton."

"You're certain?" asked Stoker.

I nodded.

"Damnation!"

It was unlike my boss to use such language. Now he had done so twice in ten minutes. He was obviously greatly moved.

As the dead girl was brought ashore a gasp issued from several of the men. One policeman—a younger man— turned away and was violently sick over the edge of the timbered wharf side. I almost followed suit. Nell's head flopped backward, a dreadful gash slicing across the once-delicate female neck. She had had her throat cut, and savagely at that.

Abraham Stoker stayed for over an hour, making a sketch of the chalk markings on the floor, with notations about the blood and the disposition of Nell Burton's body. He sent me back to the theatre, since it was getting close to time for the evening's performance, assuring me that he would be returned before curtain-up. He also said that he would personally break the news to Billy Weston. I was grateful for that.

News of the death spread rapidly through the theatre after Stoker returned. People moved about in silence, seemingly nervous and jumping at any sudden noise. After curtain-up things progressed in a more normal fashion, though there was an indefinable lack of sparkle about the whole presentation of the play. So much so that, after the final curtain, the Guv'nor called everyone onstage as soon as the audience had vacated the theatre.

Henry Irving stood center stage and gazed around at the assembled cast and crew. He seemed to meet every eye. I stood in the prompt corner but felt the draw of his magnetism as his gaze swept over me. It was a little like being back in the Hounslow Masonic Institution for Boys when I was a youngster. I remember a time when the whole school was assembled and the headmaster, Dr. Birch, similarly cast his beady eyes over us all, after some minor breach of discipline by a few. We all felt incredibly guilty then, and I felt the same now. None of us at the Lyceum had done anything wrong, of course, but I think we all felt as though we had been brought up on the carpet.

"The loss of one of our number," said Irving, in his tragedy voice, "affects the whole family. Those both onstage and off; in the orchestral pit or up in the flies. Those who work so diligently behind the scenes and those who expose themselves to the theatre audience . . . all are equally vulnerable. It is like losing a loved one, even to those of us who never had the fortune to actually meet with Miss . . ."

"Nell Burton," murmured Ellen Terry, who stood slightly behind the Guv'nor.

"Indeed!" Irving's gaze once again ranged around those crowded onstage. "But we are actors!" He seemed to stress the last syllable for some reason. "We are servants of our audience. We are here to give of our very best . . . or we should not be here at all." He gave one of his dramatic pauses before continuing. "Tonight's presentation was woefully inadequate. Woefully inadequate!" Again the piercing gaze at all assembled. "I do not say that we may not mourn our fellow actress. Indeed, it would be sinful not to do so.

But, we must mourn in our own time, and not onstage during the performance of the play."

This last was said in a rush. I glanced about me to see how the Guv'nor's words were being taken. I was surprised to see Billy Weston at the back. Mr. Stoker had told me that he had suggested the boy take some time off, but that Billy had insisted on staying, saying that he would rather keep busy. I admired him for that. It seemed to me that I saw the glint of a tear in Billy's eye, and there I knew he was not alone.

"It is my understanding," continued the Guv'nor, "that the Metropolitan Police—indeed, Scotland Yard—are now investigating this tragedy. We must leave them to do their job even as we continue with ours. Mr. Stoker has requested that all make themselves available to any member of the constabulary who may need to ask questions. Thank you, everyone. Please carry on."

He turned on his heel, almost colliding with Miss Terry, and strode from the stage with her trotting behind him. I almost applauded, such was the impact of any speech from Mr. Henry Irving. I returned to my office and had a last look around, then shrugged into my topcoat, ready to return home to the minimum "comforts" of Mrs. Bell's establishment on Chancery Lane.

"Mr. Rivers, sir?"

I looked up. It was Edwina Abbott—she of the tarot cards—who peered nervously around the corner, obviously uncertain whether or not to delay me.

"Miss Abbott," I said. "What can I do for you?"

There was a long, awkward pause before she said, "It were just like what the cards said, Mr. Rivers, weren't it?"

I wasn't sure how to respond.

"In a sense, Edwina, yes. I suppose it was. Either that or coincidence, of course."

"Coincidence? Do you really believe that, sir?"

I shook my head. "No, I suppose I don't."

"Nor me, sir." She looked at me for a moment and then turned and went out. "Good night, Mr. Rivers."

"Look at this, Harry."

I had only just arrived at the theatre. My boss was already there. Mr. Stoker had spread a copy of the *Era* across his desk. The weekly newspaper was regarded as the Bible of the theatrical profession. Started just over forty years ago, it was then a general newspaper, but since being taken over by Frederick Ledger and then his son, Edward, it now dealt mainly with the London theatre scene, Freemasonry, and sport.

"What is it, sir?"

"That young upstart Reginald Robertson. His company is opening in Oxford with *Coriolanus* of all things. No great soliloquies for him there, I think. But see here what he has the effrontery to say to the newspaper."

I leaned forward to read over his shoulder, but Mr. Stoker insisted on reading it aloud.

"*With this pivotal role I feel I will finally establish myself as the equal, if not the superior, Shakespearean actor of these British Isles. Perhaps it is time for others, who have trod the boards for too long, to slip away into retirement and allow the younger generation to carry the banner.* Ye Gods, Harry! If that isn't a direct slap at the Guv'nor I don't know what is!"

"It is a trifle strong," I acknowledged.

"The man is obviously perfectly cast as Coriolanus!"

"Sir?"

"Coriolanus is proud, immature, stubborn, and inflexible. But that is beside the point. To publish such a comment in the *Era* is an insult. I think an apology is called for; nay, demanded!"

I could see that Mr. Stoker's Irish temper was up. He was devoted to the Guv'nor. So were we all in our way, though nowhere nearly as staunchly as my boss.

"Surely it's just hot air, sir. No one could take him seriously, comparing himself to Mr. Irving."

"This is the way rumors get started, Harry. You mark my words. The gossipmongers will sink their teeth into this."

"Who is this Reginald Robertson anyway, sir?" I asked. "I've heard his name mentioned in connection with provincial theatre, but he's never played London, has he?"

"No. No he has not, now that you mention it." Stoker seemed to calm a little. "Good point, Harry. Young upstart!"

"What do you know of him?"

Stoker sat back and gazed thoughtfully at the ceiling. "His father was the old character actor James Robertson. His mother was Cynthia Ecclestone, so he came from good theatrical stock. But young Reginald has never been a forerunner. He put his so-called company together on a shoestring. Against the advice of his father, as I understand it. Got most of his bookings by occult means."

"By occult means?" I echoed. "What exactly do you mean by that, sir?"

"His grandmother, on his mother's side, was supposed to have been a witch, so rumor has it." Stoker's gray green eyes came down to look into mine. "He himself consults with an astrologer to set the major dates for his performances." He shook his head. "Lot of nonsense, if you ask me."

I never thought I'd hear my boss pooh-pooh the occult. He who believed in good luck charms, vampires, zombies, fairies, and the like.

There was a rap on the door.

"Come!" shouted Stoker.

The door opened and Edward, Miss Terry's nine-year-old son, the Lyceum's callboy, poked his head in.

"Mr. Thomas says that the Scotland Yard inspector wants a word, sir," he said.

"Send him in."

"Yes, Mr. Stoker." Edward's head disappeared.

"I suppose it was inevitable that the inspector would show up."

"Yes, sir," I agreed. "He must have a hundred questions."

"Well, I'm as anxious as he is to find who murdered our young lady. I'm thinking that there is a lot more to this than meets the eye, Harry."

I had to agree. Why had Nell gone to that riverside warehouse? Were there auditions being held there? Why late at night, after the theatres closed, and not during the day? Why the secrecy? And who could have murdered an innocent young woman so viciously? I hoped Inspector Bellamy would have some answers.

"Mr. Stoker, sir."

Bellamy did not remove his bowler hat when he came into the office and barely nodded to acknowledge myself.

"What may we do for you, Inspector?" said Stoker. "Have you found the killer yet?"

"Bit early for that, sir. But he won't get far, believe me."

"Oh! So you know it to be a man, do you?" Stoker looked surprised.

"What? What d'you mean? Do you think it was a woman that did it, then? Bit extreme for the fair sex, wouldn't you say?"

I barely caught the glint in my boss's eyes. If there were any hint of a smile it was well hidden beneath his bushy red mustache. "Just trying to keep to the facts," he said. "And incidentally, was it not less than ten years ago that Mary Ann Robson Cotton was hung for murdering her three husbands, a lover, and a dozen children? Less than twenty years ago did not Frances Kidder hang for killing her eleven-year-old daughter? I mention these members of the 'fair sex' merely in passing, Inspector."

Bellamy pulled himself up straight. "As I recall, *Mister* Stoker, sir, they were all poisonings. A far cry from the throat slashing that we have here . . . if I may say so, *sir*? Perhaps we should allow Scotland Yard to get on with its job?"

"Touché, Inspector!" Stoker looked pleased. "I am delighted to see that you are well up on your work. I was beginning to wonder."

"Just what have you learned, Inspector?" I asked. I could not contain myself. I hoped that some very real clue or clues had been uncovered.

"As it happens, Mr. Stoker," he said, addressing my boss as though it were he who had asked the question, "we have found something relevant. Caught up in the rubbish and jetsam that seems to accumulate around piers, we salvaged a black robe similar to the white one worn by our victim. It was at the foot of Waterloo Bridge."

"And you associate it with this case?"

"As we say, sir, it is a similar robe and it is also covered with blood, as may be expected from creating such a wound."

"Slashing the throat?" I said.

He looked at me with his beady little eyes before turning back to Stoker and ignoring me again.

"We were wondering if this might all be connected in some way with a theatrical production," said Bellamy. "We understand that these warehouses, with their large floor space, are attractive to you people for practicing your plays. We wondered if, perhaps, this was a case of such a practice session gone wrong. Some actor who perhaps got carried away with his part. You see what we are saying, sir?"

"I do indeed, Inspector." Stoker came to his feet and stood looking down on the slightly shorter figure of the policeman. "We term these 'practices,' as you call them, rehearsals. And no, I do not for one moment endorse your theory. Firstly, no actor—no matter how involved in his part—would go that far, even in the heat of an actual performance in front of a theatre audience. And secondly, at no time would props—weapons, to you—be used that could do any real harm. No, Inspector, the suggestion is untenable."

"Hmm." Bellamy rubbed his chin as though unconvinced, looking Mr. Stoker square in the eyes. "Well, time will tell, sir. Time will tell."

"It will indeed," responded my boss. "Meanwhile, may I suggest that you bring this robe—in fact both robes, if you'd be so kind—here to be examined by our wardrobe mistress, Miss Connelly. She will be able to ascertain whether or not these are, in fact, theatrical costumes."

"A good idea," acknowledged Bellamy. "We will see to it that they are delivered here as soon as we have finished looking at them ourselves. Now, sir, we would like, if we may, to speak with your people. In particular we would like to ask a few questions of those young ladies who were close to the murdered girl."

"Of course. We were expecting you to do just that. Harry, take the inspector backstage, would you? The cast should be arriving shortly for today's matinee. The inspector can use the greenroom to conduct his enquiries."

I returned to my boss's office for a moment, after depositing the inspector among a group of *Hamlet* extras. They included both Tilly Fairbanks and Edwina Abbott, though I hoped the latter would not get into discussing tarot cards with the policeman. I didn't think Inspector Bellamy would be as fascinated as Mr. Stoker or myself.

"Was there something, Harry?" Stoker had a pile of correspondence in front of him and, although always open to any queries I might have, looked as though he would much prefer to be left to complete his own work.

"Sorry to trouble you, sir," I said. "I can come back later if you'd prefer, though I thought that with the matinee this afternoon . . ."

"No, no, Harry. Come on in." He waved me toward the chair in front of his desk. "Another problem?"

I shook my head. "I was just wondering about those chalk

markings, in the warehouse. You spoke about 'Words of Power,' if I remember correctly. I was wondering just what they might be and how they connected with Nell Burton's murder?"

"You do remember correctly, Harry. What I recognized, drawn in chalk on those floorboards, was the so-called Sun Pentacle for compelling spirits. In the rites of high magic it is used to connect with honor, kingly power, and glory. The words written around and between the circles were the names of the genies of the Lower Orders who are called upon by ceremonial magicians. There is Astaroth, war god of the ancient Semites . . ."

"Excuse me, sir," I interrupted. "But did you say 'magicians,' as in conjurers, prestidigitators, and all that hocus-pocus?"

"I did indeed say magicians, Harry, but not—I venture to say—as in legerdemain and the like. No. Far from it. These are serious workers of true magic. Ones who have almost certainly studied the arcane arts for many years and are dedicated to their own particular goals."

"But . . ." I started to say. Stoker held up his hand.

"In the Middle Ages this art, or science, was at its height, Harry. It is still prevalent today, in certain circles. It is a belief that there are certain *spirits*—for want of a better term—who are able to influence our thoughts and actions. If one is able to prove mastery over these spirits then one is able to command them to do whatever one desires."

"To make things happen?" I hazarded.

"Precisely. And that is one concise definition of magic . . . to cause change to occur in conformity with will. In other words, to make something happen that one wishes to happen."

I shook my head in disbelief. "No one can do that," I said.

"Have you ever been to a church, a Roman Catholic church especially?" he asked. "And have you not observed there a number of candles burning, not just on the altar . . . ? The practice of candle burning is not restricted to that particular denomination."

"Why yes. Of course." I nodded. "You mean votive candles?"

"Exactly. These are frequently lit as a form of prayer; an appeal for a higher power to intervene in the case of, for example, the illness of a loved one. Basically, working magic. Making something happen that is desired by the petitioner."

"But—but that's talking to God," I protested.

"I am not particularizing the source of power," continued Stoker. "Merely drawing a parallel so that you may understand the actions of these ceremonialists. The power, or powers, they address are of a far lower order yet can exhibit tremendous influence, if properly approached. Magicians of this ilk believe that they can invoke these infernal spirits and dominate them to grant the rewards they seek."

"So what does this have to do with Nell Burton?" I was still somewhat bewildered.

"I would suggest that someone is seeking to bring about some calamity. This was no audition that Miss Burton believed she had been invited to, Harry. This was a well-organized group of devil worshippers with one goal in mind, although exactly what that goal might be we have yet to determine. In order to gain their desire, to be granted their boon, it would be necessary for them to give of something in return. Since they were asking for something major, they needed to offer something major. A sacrifice, if you will. Miss Burton was lured there to be that sacrifice."

My hand went instinctively to my heart. "A sacrifice? You mean . . . they killed her—cut her throat—as part of some macabre ritual?"

"My guess—and probably theirs also—is that Miss Burton was a virgin. Such is the required form of sacrifice for the major rites of these salacious ritualists."

I could think of nothing to say. The whole thing made me think of what we termed the Dark Ages. To think that such practices were still performed in this modern day, in the eighteen hundreds, left my mind in a whirl. Human sacrifices? Was that possible? Yet I knew that Abraham Stoker knew whereof he spoke.

"How were the chalk drawings tied to this sacrifice?" I asked.

"They would have been drawn as part of an elaborate ritual," he responded. "Words and actions—*legomena* and *dromena*—would be performed as the squares and circles were drawn and the Words of Power written. A makeshift altar would be placed in the center, on which our young lady would be laid. I think I noticed an old table pushed to the back wall. We should have thought to examine it for blood."

"I'll make a note to tell Inspector Bellamy," I said.

He grunted and nodded. "Do that, Harry. Yes, she would have reposed on that. Possibly drugged by that time, so that she would not protest. Then the leading ritualist would have flourished the sacrificial knife and, as the high point of the ceremony, shed the blood that they see as power."

"How many of them were there, sir?"

Stoker looked thoughtful, his brows knit and his lips pursed. He placed a forefinger alongside his nose, as he was wont to do when thinking.

"We do not know, Harry, but it would be to our advantage to find out; to see what are the odds against us. There could have been as few as two or three, though for such a major undertaking I think more would have been called for. Perhaps as many as a dozen."

"That's a lot of people," I said. "Surely somebody would have noticed them?"

"Good thought, Harry. Alert our police inspector. He should have the manpower to get out there and ask questions. We have other clues to follow."

"We do?" I said. "What are they?"

Chapter Five

"Before we do anything else, Harry, I have to meet with the Guv'nor, Colonel Cornell, and Mr. Booth and thrash out a schedule for *Othello* rehearsals."

America's premier Shakespearean actor, Mr. Edwin Booth, had earlier in the year arrived in England ready to treat London to a taste of the Bard as enacted on the far side of the Atlantic Ocean. He was accompanied by his manager, Colonel Wilberforce Cornell. They had been enticed here by the proprietor of the Princess's Theatre, on Oxford Street, who thought that Mr. Booth would be a big draw. Regrettably the manager's mind was more on the box office potential than on production values, and Mr. Booth arrived to find that he was expected to play melodrama rather than drama, and to work along with pantomime acts and other such nonlegitimate spectacles. A month or so back Mr. Irving had come to Mr. Booth's rescue, in effect, and invited him to play at the Lyceum. They chose *Othello*, with Booth in the title role and the Guv'nor playing Iago.

"It seems that Mr. Booth is becoming quite restless," continued Mr. Stoker. "According to his manager, 'he is at his best when busy.' Is that not the case with us all?"

It seemed to me that my boss was not overly enamored with Colonel Cornell. I felt the same way. The man was overbearing and seemed to consider Mr. Booth a cut above anyone else, including the Guv'nor. Needless to say this did not sit well with anyone at the Lyceum.

"Do you need me there, sir?" I asked, hoping that the answer would be in the negative. I was out of luck.

"It might not be a bad idea, Harry. You have a better grasp than I on what we can do and when; on the use of the theatre and rehearsal rooms. Yes, I think it would be a good idea to have you there. Come along with me this afternoon. We'll be meeting at Mr. Irving's home at two of the clock. You know the way. I will see you then."

I did indeed know the way. My heart skipped a beat. I now did not mind in the least having to attend the meeting. My inamorata, Jenny Cartwright, was a housemaid at the Guv'nor's home. It would be like a beautiful break of sunshine in a cloud-covered sky. I went out to lunch fully anticipating a wonderful afternoon.

The Druid's Head was a favorite watering hole for Lyceum workers. It was an ancient Elizabethan inn ruled over by the tavern keeper John Martin. John was a giant of a man with a deep rumbling voice that could fill a theatre, if he should ever feel inclined to tread the boards. But overseeing the distribution of ale and the serving of some of London's finest roast beef was more to his liking. And to that of his customers.

I slipped into a corner near the massive fireplace and waved to Penny the serving girl. She gave me a cheery smile and quickly delivered my usual tankard of porter.

"Thanks, Penny," I said. "Let me have a roast beef sandwich, please. How is it today?"

"Same as all'ers," she said. "Best in Lon'on."

Penny was from the West Country—Devon, I believe—and her soft voice always helped soothe the customers of the Druid's Head and settle them in their seats. We always had that same exchange, and she was right; it was the best food for miles around.

I could see John up at the bar, cutting thick chunks off the joint, while young Samuel, his son, slapped them between slices of homemade bread still steaming from the oven. Penny soon returned with my order, having taken just long enough for me to drink my ale down to the level where I would need to order a refill.

I eventually sat back, patting my stomach, and looked about me with satisfaction. Penny brought me my pipe, and I stuffed it with tobacco, taking up one of the tapers to light it from the logs burning in the fireplace. Life was good, I thought.

"Well, if it ain't the ginger man from the bloody Lyceum!"

I knew immediately who that was, and I almost revised my thoughts on life being so good. I looked around to spy Bartholomew Nugent grinning at me through the blue haze issuing from my pipe. I hated people calling me "ginger" and had since I was a child and was so taunted on the school playground.

"What do you want, Bart?" I said. "I didn't know you were out again."

Bart Nugent spent almost as much time inside Newgate Prison as he did out of it. He was a petty thief and pickpocket, and I had once had the pleasure of catching him red-handed stealing a gold half hunter watch from one of our theatre patrons. He had done hard labor for that and had sworn he would get even with me. I was not pleased to see him on the loose again.

"Jus' bein' civil like and sayin' 'ello, *Mister* Rivers," he said, still grinning. His mouth was nothing but crooked, blackened teeth with great gaps between them. "'Ow's it goin' then? Business good, is it?"

"What do you mean?"

"I 'ears as 'ow your Lyceum is losing its pretty gals." He tut-tutted. "Narsty business that, I'm finkin'."

I felt a flutter in my stomach. "What do you know about that?" I demanded.

"Jus' what's in the noospapers."

"And since when have you been able to read, Bart Nugent?"

"Oy! You!" John Martin's deep, powerful voice stilled all the conversation in the crowded room. You could hear a farthing drop. Nugent looked around, for the first time the smile on his face faltering. John gestured toward the exit. "We don't want none of the likes of you in 'ere," he said, waving the meat cleaver and jerking his thumb in the direction of the door. "Git out!"

Bart Nugent gave a nervous laugh, glanced at me again, and then turned away. "Jus' the start of the season, ain't it, Mr. Rivers? Jus' the start."

He gave another laugh and went out.

I took the omnibus to the corner of Bond Street. The Guv'nor's rooms were just around the corner at 15a Grafton Street, over Asprey's Jewellers. I raised the polished brass knocker on the gleaming black door and let it drop. Almost immediately the door was opened by Timmy, the fourteen-year-old serving boy. He greeted me and led the way up the stairs inside.

"Mr. Irving and Mr. Stoker is both 'ere, Mr. Rivers," he said. "Just waiting on the American gents, I think."

"Timmy, you mind your business!" Mrs. Cooke, the housekeeper, appeared at the top of the stairs. "Just you take the gentleman's coat and 'at."

Timmy dutifully did as he was told, and I followed the

short, stocky housekeeper as she led the way down the passage to the library. I looked left and right in the hopes of spying Jenny, but she wasn't to be seen.

"In 'ere, sir."

I found Mr. Stoker and the Guv'nor standing side by side, with their backs to the fire, warming themselves. They were deep in conversation and nodded to me, Mr. Irving indicating a chair. I sat down and looked about me.

I had not been into this room before. On my previous visit I had spent my time in the study, searching for a copy of the *Hamlet* script that the Guv'nor needed back at the theatre. This room was much larger, though overfilled with furniture: comfortable chairs and couches, occasional tables, cabinets, whatnots, and pedestals, in a mixture of styles and periods. A variety of potted palms, aspidistras, and other plants filled in the spaces between the furniture. Mr. Irving had an eclectic taste, it seemed. A Renaissance Revival tripartite sofa sat sedately beside a Rococo Revival gentleman's chair, while a lady's rosewood parlor rocker rubbed elbows with a caned Grecian rocker that more fittingly belonged in a bedroom. But the one thing that the pieces of furniture had in common was that all appeared comfortable and well appreciated.

I had hardly sat when it was necessary to rise again as Mr. Edwin Booth and Colonel Wilberforce Cornell were shown in. We had all met before, so introductions were not necessary. The Guv'nor and Mr. Stoker moved across to sit on either side of the American couple.

Mr. Edwin Booth I thought an interesting gentleman. He was not quite as tall as Mr. Stoker and the Guv'nor—both of whom reached to six feet and two inches—yet was an imposing figure. To one of my slight build, all were "tall gentlemen." In his youth, Mr. Booth had been described as possessing extraordinary beauty. At forty-seven years of age, he was still handsome, though one would hesitate to use the word "beautiful." His eyes were dark and striking, but his hair had somewhat receded and was brushed back and parted to the left. To my mind his nose seemed prominent and slightly bulbous over a weak chin. I had heard tales of his gentleness and generosity. It seems he had little business sense and partly because of that had, eight or nine years ago, lost his own theatre in New York to bankruptcy. I could understand why he needed the firmer hand of a manager such as Colonel Cornell. Our own Guv'nor might have taken a similar path had it not been for the steadying and controlling presence of Mr. Stoker.

Colonel Wilberforce Cornell was almost as tall as the others. He was completely bald (I suspected that he shaved his head), counterbalanced by a longish dark beard and mustache, the latter drooping down on either side of his tightly held mouth. Somehow I could not imagine the colonel laughing, nor even smiling. He had a monocle firmly gripped in his right eye, and the light reflected off it as he turned his head, peering about him in every direction.

There was a tap at the door, and when it opened my heart skipped a beat. Jenny came in and bobbed a curtsey. She caught my eye and blushed but addressed herself to Mr. Irving.

"Mrs. Cooke asks if you would like tea served, sir?" she asked.

"Indeed," responded the Guv'nor, glancing at the rest of us. We all nodded our heads. "We might as well make this as painless as we may." We all laughed dutifully, though I noticed that the colonel did not join in. "Bring it in about twenty minutes please, Jenny."

Jenny bobbed another curtsey, risked a quick half smile in my direction, and went out, closing the door behind her.

"Now then," said Irving. "I thank you all for coming. As you know we have a play to put on in just six weeks. A tight schedule but one that we have all dealt with before, I am sure. Happily all the principals are thoroughly familiar with the piece."

"If I may interject, Henry?" said Booth. "Although this

is not a great problem for us actors, I do wonder about your stage staff? That is not a great deal of time to construct the sets. Of course, you know of what your people are capable better than I do, but . . ." He left the sentence hanging.

"Mr. Booth is accustomed to the very best in stage settings," added the colonel. "He would not want any slipshod . . ."

I couldn't let that go, and apparently neither could Mr. Stoker. He broke in, beating me to it. "The word 'slipshod' is not in the Lyceum's vocabulary, Colonel Cornell. I don't know to what standards the American theatre holds . . ."

"Gentlemen! Gentlemen!" The Guv'nor held up his hands. "Please. Let us not get off on the wrong foot. I am sure we all want nothing but the best, and it is to that end that the Lyceum is dedicated." He spoke to Mr. Booth, more or less ignoring the colonel, a fact that I know my boss recognized. The colonel looked annoyed but contented himself with harrumphing, which we all disregarded.

"We did both approve the set designs a week or so ago, Edwin, I am sure you recall," continued the Guv'nor. "You may now put any concerns regarding that aspect of the production out of your mind. Let us concentrate on our part in all of this. We are here to draw up a schedule for rehearsals. We have merely to bear in mind that our present production of *Hamlet* has the usual two matinees a week, Wednesdays and Saturdays, so we must work around those. The run will terminate with the evening performance on the twenty-third of April, so we will have a full week for stage set and dress rehearsals before opening night on the second of May."

"You have not had very good preproduction publicity, if I may say so," put in the colonel, glaring at Mr. Stoker.

"You are referring to the murder of one of our girls?" Mr. Irving sounded annoyed that the subject should have been brought up.

"Indeed I am," responded Cornell. "Not an ideal thing to focus on just before a new production, I would think."

"*Othello* is, as I have just pointed out, six weeks away, so this unfortunate affair is hardly a preproduction focus, would you say, Edwin?" The Guv'nor's speech was clipped.

Mr. Booth looked uncomfortable. I got the impression that he allowed his manager to manage not only his theatre life but much of his private life as well. "No. No, you are right, Henry. But it was most certainly unfortunate."

"As is any murder," I couldn't help saying.

"The police are on top of it," said Mr. Stoker. He turned to the colonel. "By the way, Colonel, when was it exactly that you and Mr. Booth arrived here in England? I was just trying to remember."

"The first of February," came the response.

"That's when we got to London," corrected Booth. "We actually docked at Liverpool the morning of the day before, but Wilberforce insisted we take a day to recuperate from the voyage and not proceed here right away."

"Very wise," said the Guv'nor. "I would need more than a day myself, to recover from such a long ocean voyage."

"Especially since we were two days late in docking," said Booth. "They said it was one of the roughest crossings in years."

"I understand it has been a very bad winter for the transatlantic trade," observed Mr. Stoker.

"Most of December and all of January," agreed the American. "I tell you, I was not sorry to reach Liverpool."

We were interrupted by Jenny and Susan, the other maid, bringing in the tea. They poured and distributed the cups, together with an assortment of delicate sandwiches and petit fours, before retiring again. The atmosphere seemed to ease with the tea, until the colonel commented on a preference for coffee. However, he then declined any change in what was before him. I noticed that the Guv'nor's mouth was unnaturally tightly drawn, and I heard Mr. Stoker sigh.

From then on we seemed to make headway, and a little over an hour or so later the meeting broke up. Timmy was sent out to call up hansoms, and I soon found myself sharing a cab with my boss, rattling over the streets on our way back to the theatre.

"What did you make of our American cousins?" Stoker enquired.

I hesitated.

"Be honest, Harry," he added.

I took a deep breath. "Well, sir . . . I think I liked Mr. Booth. He seemed to be all business, which as we know is what the Guv'nor appreciates. But as for his manager . . ." I let my voice trail off.

Stoker chuckled. "Yes," he said. "He does rather take some getting used to, does he not? I don't know if this is typical of American businessmen, but he has an eye for details."

"And he certainly looks out for Mr. Booth."

"He does that, Harry. But then, that is his job."

We continued in silence for a while, and then I had a thought.

"Oh, by the way, sir. I had an unexpected encounter at lunchtime, just before our meeting." I went on to tell him about Bartholomew Nugent.

"That man is poison," said Stoker. "I thought he'd been put away for longer than this."

"He certainly should have been," I said. "And I don't know how he knew about Nell Burton. The man is illiterate, so he could not have read about it. And what business is it of his, anyway?"

"Keep an eye out for him, Harry. Keep an eye out."

Two days later I was accosted by Billy Weston, as soon as I entered the theatre.

"Mr. Rivers, sir. Might I 'ave a word?"

"Yes, of course, Billy. How are you holding up? Everything all right?"

"Well, yes, sir, and no, sir, as it were." He looked uncomfortable. "It's summat I found out about Nell."

"Something about Nell? The police . . ."

"No, sir. Nuffin' the police 'as to know. Not yet, anyway."

We were standing outside my office. I beckoned him inside. Open as it was, it was still a little more private than standing in the passageway with stagehands and actors squeezing past all the time.

"Here. Sit down, Billy. Tell me all about it."

He perched on the edge of the chair and scratched the top of his head. He made a face as though uncertain of what he was doing and then tugged on his ear. "There's this . . . this Ben Gossett." He paused.

I was puzzled. I knew of no one by that name associated with the Lyceum. I was about to ask who he was, but Billy suddenly continued, the whole story pouring out at once.

"It seems as 'ow Nell 'ad this 'ere 'young man' when she lived up north. Not to really be steppin' out wif 'im, like, but just to know. She told me about 'im once. Nufink special, she says. I fink 'e lived next door to 'er, there in Derby. 'E was a bit older than 'er. Anyway, 'e suddenly turned up 'ere and 'e said as 'ow they 'ad been goin' to get married, but then she got bitten by the playacting bug and took off for London. Of course, she'd done a bit of that stuff at the Nottingham Royal, but nothin' real serious like."

"Whoa! Slow down, Billy," I said. "You are saying that this Ben Gossett claims he was engaged to Nell before she came here?"

"'Sright, accordin' to 'im! But she weren't never engaged to 'im, neither. She was frightened of 'im."

"She told you this?"

"Hoh yes! She said as 'ow 'e 'ad threatened 'er. Said as 'ow if 'e couldn't 'ave 'er then no one could!"

This sounded serious. Serious enough that I thought perhaps Inspector Bellamy should know of it. "What is he doing here?" I asked. "You have seen him, I take it?"

"You might say that." Billy scowled. "'E grabbed me by the coattails as I come out of the Red Lion one night, and waved 'is fist in my face."

"This was before Nell . . . before she was . . ."

"Afore she was done for, Mr. Rivers, sir. Yes."

"Why didn't you let me know this earlier?" I asked.

"Never thought no never mind. Jus' 'im blowin' steam, I thought. It was a week or more afore what 'appened. Then I kinda forgot all about 'im what wif Nell gettin' . . . you know."

"Yes. Of course," I said. I thought for a moment. "Is he still about? Still in the area?"

Billy shrugged. "Dunno. Ain't seen 'im since then. I just suddenly thought of 'im and 'ad to tell you. You know, just in case, like?"

I knew exactly what he meant. "I'm glad you did, Billy. Let me speak to Mr. Stoker, and then I think it might be a good idea to let the police know." Billy started to protest, but I stopped him. "No. This is important, Billy. Let's see what Mr. Stoker has to say. I'll get back to you as soon as I can."

Inspector Bellamy dropped a brown paper—wrapped package onto Abraham Stoker's desk. My boss looked at it then up at the policeman.

"And this is . . . ?"

"The two robes, Mr. Stoker. One white; one black. Both heavily bloodstained. You did say that your costume lady might be able to help."

"Miss Connelly. Yes. Our wardrobe mistress. Harry, would you get these to her right away, please? Meanwhile, I will apprise the inspector of this recent turn of events you learned from Billy Weston."

I took the package and went backstage and downstairs. Next to the greenroom, in Wardrobe, I found Miss Connelly in her usual position behind the very latest sewing machine. As always, she was surrounded by yards of fabric, ribbons, lace, reels of thread, balls of wool, and assorted shears, tape measures, chalk, pins, needles, and all the many accoutrements of the theatre costumier.

"What have we here, Mr. Rivers?" she asked, peering at me over the rims of her pince-nez spectacles.

I explained. "Mr. Stoker thought that maybe if you examined these robes—and we do apologize for the condition in which you will find them—you might be able to make a guess as to who it was who made them. Or where they came from. One was worn by Miss Nell Burton. Perhaps you can tell if they both were made by the same person? Or were they made for some production that we might be able to pinpoint?"

She drew the package to her and began untying the string. "One was worn by our Nell, you say?"

I nodded.

"So sad," she said quietly, and sighed. "Well, if I can help bring her killer to justice, Mr. Rivers, it will be as much as I can hope for."

She stood up and cleared a space on the big wooden worktable. Drawing out the two robes, she pushed the bulk of each away temporarily so that she could examine the bottom hems. She pursed her lips and nodded.

"Yes. Handmade and no mistake. Nice stitchwork. Flesh basting."

"Were they both made by the same person?" I asked.

"Oh yes. No doubt about that, Mr. Rivers, sir. Now let me think. I know this diagonal stitching." She squinted up at the gas mantle above her head, her brow wrinkled, slowly shaking her head. Suddenly, she stopped and turned to me, her eyes bright behind the lenses. "Old Penelope Proctor!" she cried. "As I live and breathe, I'd know her stitching anywhere. Lor' but I thought she was dead and gone these many years."

"You know her?" I asked.

"Knew her," she corrected me. "She was wardrobe mistress at the old Elephant and Castle Theatre a lifetime ago. I worked there with her for a brief period before I went on to the Princess's and then from there to here at the Lyceum. Last I heard she had retired."

"But both these robes were made by her?"

"I'd swear to it," said Miss Connelly. "She did this fine fore-stitching on her hems. No one else would take the time, especially since it was for stage work. But she was proud of it. And so she should be. Beautiful work it was."

I reported the identification to Mr. Stoker. "Should I let the inspector know?" I asked.

He did not even pause to consider. "No, Harry. Not right away, I don't think. Plenty of time yet. We don't want to interfere with Inspector Bellamy's questioning of the staff. I think that perhaps we can first investigate a little further ourselves . . . just so that we will be able to present him with a more complete picture, of course."

"Of course, sir," I said, a smile creeping across my face. "So you want me to follow up on this and track down Miss Penelope Proctor?"

"You are very good at mind reading, Harry. You should be on the stage." He chuckled at his own joke. "Yes. Pop down to the Elephant and Castle and start there. You know the way, as I recall."

It was little more than a month ago that I had visited that theatre trying to trace an elderly actress who had thoughts of blackmailing the Guv'nor, so it was a strange sensation when I once again boarded the light green omnibus and paid my fourpence fare. Alighting at the Elephant and Castle Hostelry, I hurried around the corner, tugging my topcoat close about me as a cold gust of wind blew down the New Kent Road as though aiming directly for the old theatre.

The theatre had been badly damaged in a fire some three years ago and still awaited repairs and renovations. I pushed past the unlocked stage door, sagging on its hinges, and found my way to the manager's office.

"Hello! Ain't I seen you afore?" The little figure, in his shirtsleeves and waistcoat, no jacket but sporting a bowler hat, looked up from where he sat behind a well-worn desk, covered with papers. His striped shirt looked clean but it was minus the collar. His sleeves, as the last time I encountered him, were pulled back with black armbands. Most of the papers on the desk, from where I stood, looked to be unpaid bills. He made no attempt to hide them. "Don't tell me," he continued, pausing to chew thoughtfully on his straggly mustache. "Ain't you the gent from the Sadler's Wells?"

"The Lyceum," I said.

"That's right. You was here after one of our young ladies."

"Enquiring," I said. "And she was far from young!"

"Oh yes." His face broke out in a grin. "Our Miss Daisy Middleton. I remember. Is that who you want this time?"

"No, thank you."

"Don't blame you. Anyway, she's moved on. Given up treading the boards and is now treading the pavement full-time, if'n you take my meaning."

I decided to come straight to the point. "I have been led to believe that you have, or had, a wardrobe mistress named Miss Penelope Proctor?"

"*Mrs.* Proctor." He stressed the title. "She never liked to be called Miss, though I came to find out that she'd never actually been married. Just thought it made her sound more distinguished or something, I think."

I nodded. "Is she still employed here?"

"Lor' no! She retired a goodly time ago. Just afore the fire, I think it was. Good thing, too, if you ask me."

"Why is that?" I asked.

"Well, it was the wardrobe room where the fire started, wasn't it?"

I shrugged my shoulders. I had no idea. "So do you know where she is now?" I asked.

"She was always talking about buying a nice little cottage down at Margate or Ramsgate or one of them seaside places. A lot of old actors and theatre folks do that, as I'm sure you know. But it weren't to be for old Mrs. Proctor."

"Oh?" I was beginning to feel the effort of drawing out all these facts and wanted to get to the final curtain, as it were.

"No. Had a nephew what ran off with her savings, poor old dear. She had to start taking in sewing work to makes ends meet."

"Could she not have come back here?" I asked, even though I knew I was prolonging the story.

"We'd already filled her place, hadn't we?"

I wished he wouldn't keep asking me questions like that. I sighed. "So where is she now?" I asked.

"Newington Butts, or just off it."

"I don't understand," I said.

"There's a graveyard alongside Newington Butts, just south of here. Mrs. Proctor is planted there."

"She's dead?"

He laughed. "I hope so. Otherwise there'll be hell to pay with the gravediggers!" He laughed at his joke.

I moved forward and slapped my hand down hard on his desk. He looked startled.

"This is no laughing matter. When did she die?"

"All right, all right! No need to get shirty." He started sorting papers into piles as though he had no more time to spend with me. "Just a few days ago, as it happens. She was hit and run down by a brewer's dray that came out of George's Road faster than he should have done. Made no effort to stop, from what I hear."

Chapter Six

It could not have been a nicer day to spend with Jenny and her aunt Alice. Miss Alice Forsyth was from Bermondsey, on the south side of the River Thames, and she informed us that not since the days of her youth had she visited Kew to enjoy the nearly three hundred acres that comprised the Royal Botanic Gardens, generally known simply as Kew Gardens. There we found swathes of immaculate lawns dotted with rare trees. Although it was only the end of March, the sky was clear and the sun shone down. However, it had little warmth so we all sported our topcoats.

I found Aunt Alice to be a delightful lady; short and plump, with rosy cheeks and gray hair pulled back in a bunchignon. She obviously adored her young niece, and I saw no reason to argue with that. Aunt Alice did not ask a lot of questions but seemed most content to simply smile and nod and look around her with inquisitive eyes that blinked behind a firmly held tortoiseshell-framed lorgnette.

We admired the Pagoda, designed by Mr. William Chambers, and spent quite some time touring Mr. Decimus Burton's Palm House: 363 feet long, 100 feet wide, and 62 feet high. It was spectacularly made of iron and curved sheets of glass. A new Temperate House was in the process of being built.

We were in awe of the most beautiful tropical plants, astonishingly flourishing here in England—ferns, fruit trees, and cacti—with flowers, shrubs, and trees of every imaginable sort. Such was the tropical temperature maintained in the hothouse that we all were obliged to remove our outer garments, though we hastily donned them again on emerging from the building.

We proceeded to the refreshment pavilion, close by the Winter Garden. There we were able to procure a table overlooking the arboretum, an area of 178 acres that extends down to the River Thames. It is intersected in every direction by shady walks and avenues. I noted that the famous Kew Gardens' rhododendrons, at the Hollow Walk, would not be in flower until May and June, according to the brochure we had acquired on entering the Gardens, and vowed to bring back both ladies to view them at that time. I ordered tea for all of us, eschewing the popular ices and instead indulging in scones and strawberry jam with Devonshire clotted cream.

As Jenny and her aunt caught up on each other's activities, I perused the people making the most of the unexpectedly glorious March day. A familiar figure suddenly appeared coming from the direction of the Pagoda. It took me but a moment to place him. It was Colonel Wilberforce Cornell, and he was accompanied by two other men. He himself was obviously an American, affecting the wide-brimmed hat of the western section of that country, and wearing a large-patterned coat with big fur collar such as you would never see worn by an English gentleman. His companions were more traditionally attired, with bowler hats and well-worn coats, one sporting an Inverness cape.

They paused under the branches of a huge cedar tree, and

the two men, both shorter than the colonel, seemed to be listening carefully, eyes fixed on him as he gave instructions. From where I sat I could see that he frequently waved his cane to emphasize what he was saying and at one point seemed very angry, causing the shorter of the two men to flinch and take a half step backward. Then the colonel reached into his pocket and gave the men what I presumed to be money. They both touched their hats respectfully before turning and hurrying away. It was as the men turned that I recognized the taller and thinner one in the Inverness cape as Bart Nugent. What the devil was he doing with Colonel Cornell? I wondered.

The colonel looked about him, and I pulled back a little so that I was shielded from view behind Aunt Alice's large hat. He took out a cigar, lit it, and after standing a moment, apparently in thought, himself strolled away in the direction of Lion Gate, which opens onto the Richmond Road.

"My brother always loved the theatre, Mr. Rivers," Aunt Alice was saying brightly. "I think he had a secret yearning to appear on the stage."

"You never told me that, Auntie," cried Jenny.

"Oh, and please call me Harry," I said, bringing back my full attention to my two companions. "Tell me, what was your late brother's background?"

"Charles—my brother—was a coachman at a large house in Putney. I was a parlor maid there. He used to save up his money to go to the Drury Lane Theatre and get a seat in the pit. Saw a lot of Mr. Edmund Kean, I seem to remember."

"How wonderful," I said. "But he never trod the boards himself?"

She shook her head, the flowers on her hat bobbing vigorously. "The closest he came was to become one of them Freemasons," she said.

"I didn't know that," said Jenny.

"Mr. Irving plans to join that fraternity," I said.

"Brother Charles felt that he almost had to."

"Had to?" I couldn't think what she meant.

"Oh! It was just silly of him." Aunt Alice smiled and refilled our teacups from the pot on the table. "He would talk of our ancestor, Mr. Thomas Potter, who was a member of Sir Francis Dashwood's organization back a century ago."

"And that was . . . ?" I asked.

She shook her head. "I'm no good at names, though he did mention it many times as though everyone should know it. Hotfire Club or Hamfire Club." She smiled. "Quite different from the Freemasons, I gathered, but not something that stayed in my head, I'm afraid."

"It was a theatrical endeavor?"

Again she shook her head. "He always spoke of it as though they performed, but, again, I do not know the details. However, it seemed it made a big impression on Charles, and he felt he should try to follow in Mr. Potter's footsteps, however belatedly."

I resolved to ask Mr. Stoker about it. If anyone would know, it would be my boss. I turned and smiled at Jenny, who seemed to be delighted with the way the day was going.

I hadn't realized that the police worked on Sundays. For some reason—I suppose I had just never really thought about it—I assumed that they all took off the Sabbath. Apparently I was wrong, for on Monday morning, Inspector Bellamy once again turned up at the Lyceum with the fruits of his previous day's labor. He appeared in Mr. Stoker's office bearing a brown paper–wrapped parcel, this one much smaller than the previous one.

"Another robe, Inspector?" asked my boss.

"Far from it, sir. We are happy to report that we have recovered the murder weapon." I thought he sounded justifiably proud.

"Have you indeed? Well done," responded Stoker. "Where was it, might I ask?"

"Oh, it was not easy to find, we can tell you, sir." Bellamy seemed to stand up straighter and throw out his chest. "It took our men most of yesterday morning to recover it. Thrown down into the river, along with the victim, as it happens."

"In the Thames?" I said. "I'm surprised you found it, with all the mud and heaven knows what else that must have been down there."

"It was not easy, as we said, sir. Took five of our men groping about in ice-cold water for several hours." He paused. "But we do not give up. When Scotland Yard is on a case, we are . . ." He seemed at a loss for the appropriate word.

"Tenacious?" supplied my boss.

"That's what we are," he said, as though he had come up with the word himself.

Mr. Stoker carefully unwrapped the package. As he pulled aside the brown paper and revealed the contents, he and I both gasped. His eyes quickly met mine. Neither of us spoke.

"Ugly-looking instrument, is it not, Mr. Stoker? Can't imagine who would own something like that."

Perhaps the Scotland Yard inspector could not, but Stoker and I most certainly could. The ornate, decorative, curved-bladed dagger that lay on the brown paper was owned by none other than the Guv'nor himself, Mr. Henry Irving. It was a most unusual knife that had been presented to him by the Spanish ambassador a year or more ago, and it normally hung on the wall of the Guv'nor's dressing room. He had used it once when playing Shylock in *The Merchant of Venice*. It was one of his proud possessions. Neither Stoker nor myself said a word.

"Looks to us as though it might be some sort of playact-ing artifact," continued Bellamy, "which is why we brought it around for you to see. Would make sense, since you say that they were practicing—rehearsing, you call it—in that warehouse. We expect you see a lot of this sort of weapon with all your plays and things, but we thought you might possibly be able to identify it or have some idea as to where it might have come from and who might have used it."

Stoker got up from his chair and, apparently examining the dagger, moved over to stand in the light of the window that looked out over the small courtyard between the theatre and the back of the Wellington public house on the Strand. He stood as though scrutinizing the knife, though I could tell that his mind was racing over how it had come to be where it was discovered. I kept quiet and waited for his lead. Eventually he turned back to the policeman.

"It is an unusual property, Inspector, even for the theatre. I would like to hold on to it for a while, if I may?"

Bellamy was about to protest, but Stoker quickly continued.

"I am sure that within a relatively short space of time Mr. Rivers here—our property manager, who deals all the time with such weaponry, among other things—will be able to track down the origin of this particular piece."

"I am sure I could, Inspector," I quickly added. "As Mr. Stoker says, it is an unusual piece but most certainly theatrical in its origins."

"We will, of course, keep you apprised of our progress," said Stoker, and handed me the knife as though the matter were settled.

Inspector Bellamy stood with his hands out as though to retrieve the dagger but finally lowered them and apparently resigned himself to the situation. He grunted. "You will appreciate the urgency, Mr. Stoker, we are sure. Police work is ever under pressure. We do not have the luxury that a theatre has in preparing its presentations, you know?"

"Of course. Of course, Inspector. So I am sure you have much more to get on with, and the sooner we can start our own enquiries, the better. Good morning, Inspector."

Bellamy stood a moment before, without a farewell, he turned and went out. For a long time we said nothing, and then Stoker spoke.

"You do recognize it, of course, Harry?"

"Oh yes, sir. No doubt about it. I'm sure there are not two like this in the whole of London, probably not in the whole British Isles."

"So how did it come to be used to slash the throat of one of our young actresses?"

"It's as though someone stole it and is now using it to incriminate the Guv'nor," I said.

"Precisely my thinking, Harry."

Other than confirming that Mr. Irving's knife was indeed missing from its place on his wall—Mr. Stoker took care of that, and said that the Guv'nor had not noticed that it was gone—there was not much I could do right away. I did, however, make a few enquiries around the theatrical property shops and warehouses, as to the possibility of there being other knives available of this ilk. It seemed that this one was, as we thought, a unique form of weapon.

On examining the knife I did notice that its normally dull blade had been sharpened, apparently by an expert, and now sported the razor-keen edge that had done such damage to Miss Burton's throat. I reported that to my boss.

"There is where we might start our enquiries, Harry," he said. "As you say, the blade must have been sharpened by someone who knew what he was doing. Probably not by one of the usual itinerant knife grinders who push their carts around the West End and offer their services for tuppence a blade. No. This dagger has been ground and honed and brought to a fine edge, without nicks or roughness."

I had a sudden idea. "One name springs to mind, sir.

Nicholas Lang. He's on Ludgate Hill, and I happen to know that he is employed, among others, by some of the fencing clubs and private gentlemen who collect knives and swords and the like. I've known Nick for a couple of years. I'll go and have a word with him."

"Excellent, Harry. The sooner the better, I'm thinking. Our Inspector Bellamy is not long on patience, it would seem."

I set out right away, eschewing an omnibus and hailing a hansom. I was lucky in finding Nicholas in his shop when I got there. His was an establishment on Ludgate Hill and the corner of Creed Lane, with a small entrance on the Hill.

"Young Harry Rivers!" cried Nick, when I entered. He always referred to me as "young" Harry Rivers, even though he was no more than a year older than myself. "What brings you to this part of the world?"

He was polishing a fine-looking saber that, to judge by its crested hilt, belonged to an officer of Her Majesty's Household Cavalry.

"I have a question for you, Nick," I said, unfastening the leather pouch I had brought with me and extracting the deemed murder weapon. "Have you seen this dagger before?" I placed it carefully on the table in front of him.

Nicholas laid down the saber and peered at the knife. He slowly nodded his head, taking his time looking at it in situ before picking it up.

"Oh yes, Harry. Where did you get this? I haven't seen it for a few days, but yes, it has been in my establishment before."

"Did you sharpen it?"

Again he nodded. "Not simple, curved as it is. Too easy to end up with a series of short, straight sections instead of following the smooth curve of the blade. And that's Toledo steel, Harry. Not one of your cheap Birmingham blades or something picked up in Houndsditch Market or over on

Cheapside. No! That's quality, Harry, or I wouldn't have touched it. I have a reputation to maintain."

"I know it, Nick," I said, mollifying him. "That's why I came to you. Now the thing is, who was it that had you work this for them? This is important."

He looked hard at me, and I think he saw the resolution in my eyes. "As I recall, it was brought in and later picked up by a young boy—street arab. But I should have a note of the owner. Just a moment."

He turned to a shelf of thick ledgers and pulled down the end one. He flicked back the pages and then suddenly stopped.

"What's wrong?" I asked. A frown had creased his brow, and he turned a page or two back and forth.

"That's strange! Some deviltry! Someone has torn out a page from my account book!"

"So that was something of a dead end," said Stoker, when I reported back.

He had just finished his Indian clubs exercise regimen and was standing the heavy objects in the corner. I was happy that I hadn't arrived any sooner. Mr. Stoker whirling clubs about his person always unsettled me. I had visions of him losing his grip and allowing one of them to go flying off through the air to land I knew not where.

"So far as tracing the person who had it sharpened, yes," I said. "Though Nick said he would keep an eye out and see if he could spot the street urchin who brought it to him."

My boss nodded, pursing his lips and squinting up at the overhead gas mantle. "Harry, it may be as well to acknowledge to Inspector Bellamy that this was somehow stolen from the Guv'nor's dressing room. At least we may then have it returned to him. I'm sure that even Scotland Yard would not entertain the possibility that Mr. Henry Irving slew one of his own actresses."

"You don't think Bellamy might view it as a terrible accident that we were trying to hide?" I suggested.

"Possibly." His auburn head nodded up and down. "But I think we can dissuade him from that line of thinking."

"So what is our next move, sir?"

"We obviously need to find who murdered Miss Burton and their objective in doing so. And we also need to discover why—if such be the case—they are trying to implicate the Guv'nor, if that is in fact their intention."

"The cast and crew have been talking of nothing but the murder since it happened," I said. "John Saxon is of the opinion that the killing of Miss Burton is somehow linked to that recent report about Reginald Robertson's regrettable comments. John, Anthony Sampson, and Guy Purdy see it all as part of a plot by Robertson to destroy the reputation of the Lyceum and of the Guv'nor in particular."

"Yes, well we both know how much thought John Saxon puts into anything, don't we, Harry? If it's not wearing a skirt then his mind won't focus on it for more than ten minutes. And as for Tony Sampson and Purdy, well, they are two of a kind and we both know what kind that is."

I had to admit that what he said was true. Messieurs Sampson and Purdy were "very close friends," as Miss Connelly phrased it, and were easily led by the masculine energy of John Saxon.

"But is there any possibility of Reginald Robertson actually being involved, sir?" I asked.

Stoker thought for a moment. "I rather doubt it, Harry. He's busy with his troupe up in Oxford. It's one thing to make contemptible remarks to the newspapers but quite another to actually put words into actions, especially when immersed in a theatrical production of his own."

"I suppose so," I said, though I was not entirely convinced. After all, Oxford was only two and a half hours away by the Great Western Railway.

Two days later Inspector Bellamy visited again, to see what progress we had made on the murder weapon. Mr. Stoker told him of the dead end we had reached on following the blade-sharpening route and then acknowledged that the knife did in fact belong to Mr. Henry Irving. He convinced the policeman that the weapon, as a theatrical prop, had long been discarded and forgotten about and that Mr. Irving was as surprised as we were to find it suddenly turn up under such disconcerting circumstances. The inspector, after much hemming and hawing, accepted that no one at the Lyceum seemed to be involved in the actual murder, though he did insist on retaining the knife for the time being, as part of the ongoing police investigation.

"This spurned boyfriend of the victim would seem to merit further investigation," said Bellamy, as he hovered in the doorway of Stoker's office. "Young Mr. Ben Gossett seems to have disappeared. We did find where he had taken rooms, but he has subsequently fled them—also leaving his unpaid account—and gone off without providing a forwarding address. Not an encouraging sign, we would say, sir."

"Indeed," agreed Stoker. "Quite the contrary, I would imagine. But the actual conduct of the crime would seem, to my humble mind, to be somewhat beyond that of a spurned would-be lover, especially one of such tender years."

The inspector raised his eyebrows and waited for my boss to further expound. As did I.

"The setting for the murder," continued Stoker. "It was in the rehearsal hall, with chalked signs and symbols on the floor. Most decidedly ritualistic, to my mind. Not at all the action of an impulsive youth."

"We see what you are saying," agreed Bellamy. He stroked his beardless chin and then scratched his bushy sideboards. "Not unlike the case we had up in Warrington, it turns out."

My boss's eyes widened with interest. "A similar case, Inspector? When was this?"

Bellamy seemed to suddenly realize that he had spoken out of turn. "We should not be speaking of it, sir. Our mistake."

"But there are similarities?" urged Stoker.

"Well, yes, sir," the policeman acknowledged, obviously reluctantly. "It would seem to have been, as you put it, a ritual type of killing—once again."

"Can you tell me more, Inspector?" Stoker was obviously very interested. "As you know, I do have a certain expertise in this field. Perhaps I can be of assistance?"

Bellamy came more fully into the room. He had been preparing to leave, but now he purposefully closed the door behind him. He glanced at me and seemed to recognize that I was part of Mr. Stoker's furniture, in a manner of speaking.

"Warrington," he said.

"Lancashire?" I asked.

He nodded. "A young woman—not of the theatre, I hasten to add—was murdered in an old stone barn. Also with her throat slashed. And also amidst a number of strange symbols crudely written, again in white chalk."

"You have note of these symbols?" asked Stoker.

Inspector Bellamy pulled his notebook from his pocket and turned several pages to find what he was looking for. He then opened it wide and laid it on the desk in front of my boss. I moved around to be able to see it clearly.

"Aha!" murmured Stoker.

"Sir?" asked Bellamy.

"You may not see the similarity, Inspector, but I do. I can assure you that these glyphs were part of a scenario not unlike that acted out for Miss Burton's demise."

The inspector looked blank.

"The Words of Power were slightly different, as I would expect," continued Stoker. "And of course the symbols were in a unique configuration. But the intended purpose was the same."

"The intended purpose?" I asked.

"And what would that be?" asked Bellamy.

Mr. Stoker ignored our questions and put one of his own. "What was the date of this murder, Inspector?"

Bellamy turned back a page in the notebook. "We estimate it as having taken place on the last day of January, sir. The thirty-first of that month."

Stoker nodded. "Of course. As I suspected."

"Would you care to elaborate, sir?"

I could hear that the Inspector's patience was wearing thin. I think my boss knew that also.

"Let's just say that, based on the dates of these two murders, we might expect there to be a third such sacrifice," he said. "And if my suspicions are correct, it will take place on the thirtieth of April."

Both my jaw and that of the inspector dropped.

Chapter Seven

Mr. Stoker had refused to elaborate on his prediction of a third ritual slaying, and Inspector Bellamy had left in a huff.

"It is too soon to state categorically that such will occur," Stoker had said. "I personally believe it to be a strong possibility, but we will first need to do more investigating."

"Well, you let us know just as soon as you can, Mr. Stoker. And just where you think this murder will take place. We must prevent it, if at all possible." So saying, the inspector had hurried away.

"You really believe there will be another one, sir?" I asked, when we were alone again.

Stoker's great head nodded up and down. "Oh yes, Harry. I have no doubts. But I don't yet have enough evidence to give details to Scotland Yard." He paused for a moment before adding, "I may have to ask you to go up to Liverpool and take a look around for me."

* * *

I didn't fancy leaving the theatre in the middle of a production and going north to Lancashire. It wasn't my favorite part of the country at the best of times. And besides, I thought, what good could I do? I wouldn't know what to look for; how to recognize clues if they were there. But I had faith in my boss and presumed he would give me full instructions when the time came.

On my way back to my office I met Miss Edwina Abbott; she of the tarot cards. I smiled and nodded and moved to pass her but she reached out and grasped my arm.

"I'm sorry, Mr. Rivers, sir, but I need to speak with you. Urgent like."

Her eyes were big and round and, I thought, pleading.

"Of course," I said. "Come into my office."

She followed me in, and, not for the first time, I wished I had a door to close. I waved her to the chair in front of the desk and, squeezing around behind it, sat down and cleared a space on the desktop.

"Now, what can I do for you, Miss Abbott? Is it the cards again?"

She nodded and produced them from her reticule. "I was doing a reading for Tilly Fairbanks. Just funnin', you know, sir. I told Tilly it was too soon—you have to wait a bit between readings 'cos the forces takes time to move, if'n you follow me, sir? Best to give it at least a moon's span."

I nodded, even though I was not too certain about what she was saying.

"Well, sure enough, as I was trying to do her cards—Tilly's—I got this stuff that was about someone else."

"Someone else?"

She nodded. "The struck tower, it were. Calamity. It's really a windmill on the card but the name is the Tower."

I recalled the picture I had seen the time before, when

Edwina first showed me her cards, of the figures being thrown from the windmill.

"Someone done to their death," she continued. "In some sort of old building, I reckon."

I thought of the woman Bellamy had mentioned, murdered up near Liverpool. "Let me ask you something, Miss Abbott. If what was shown to you in your cards was something that had already happened—perhaps as much as a month or more ago—why would it suddenly appear now? And why in someone else's reading?"

She shrugged. "I wouldn't know *when* it happened, if'n it *has* happened, sir. I can only tell you what I seen. I knows it wasn't Tilly's stuff, 'cos she was all about lovey-dovey over this boy she's wantin'. Then this Tower card suddenly drops in. Here!" She looked up at me as a thought suddenly struck her. "Now as I think on it, the Tower *did* come up inverted. Upside down. I wondered about that. P'raps that was to show it was already done for?"

"Perhaps," I agreed. "Though you would know better than would I. Thank you, Miss Abbott. Thank you very much. I will pass on this information to Mr. Stoker."

Friday morning I sat in the second-class compartment of the London and North Western Railway carriage bearing me north to Liverpool. It seemed to me that I had left Euston Square station at an ungodly hour and was suffering a seven-hour journey costing the Lyceum Theatre twenty-one shillings and ninepence each way. Mr. Stoker had insisted that I go and speak with the local police in Warrington and glean all that I might about the murder that took place there on the thirty-first of January.

Inspector Bellamy had initially been strongly opposed to what he termed "interference in the affairs of Scotland Yard" but had finally acceded that Mr. Stoker's special expertise might help break what was turning out to be an insoluble case for the Warrington police.

The train proceeded by way of Rugby, Crewe, and Stoke-on-Trent. At Liverpool I had to change onto the Cheshire Lines Railway to Warrington. It seemed to me to be a far cry from the backstage of the Lyceum Theatre, and, more importantly, the trip meant that I would be unable to meet with Jenny on this weekend. I sighed. The things I did for Mr. Abraham Stoker!

The train sat for a lengthy stop in Stafford, affording me a fine view of Stafford Castle, situated on a hill overlooking the countryside. Stafford is on the River Sow above its junction with the Trent. Its claim to fame is the manufacture of shoes and boots and as the onetime residence of Izaak Walton. I was not sorry to hear the plaintive whistle of the locomotive and to suffer the lurch as the train once again moved forward, gathering speed as it hurried toward the Potteries and Stoke-on-Trent. Soon chimneys rose in all directions, with furnaces, warehouses, and drying houses for the pottery industry.

I must have dozed off but awoke to the changing rattle of the wheels as the train started across the long iron viaduct over the River Mersey. Shortly afterward the locomotive passed through the deep cuttings in the red sandstone and steamed, breathing heavily, into the Lime Street station where, with a long, loud sigh, it came to rest at platform three.

Clutching my portmanteau, I escaped the confines of the carriage and consulted the listings to find the branch line to Warrington. I discovered that I had a wait of a little over an hour for my connecting train and sought refuge, and refreshment, in the station waiting room. I sat nursing a cup of weak, lukewarm railway tea and nibbling on a digestive biscuit, and thought back to Edwina Abbott and her tarot cards. If, as seemed faintly possible, the emergence of the Tower card in the midst of Tilly Fairbanks's reading had a connection with the crime I was about to investigate, why had it suddenly turned up now, two months after the actual murder? Miss Abbott had not seemed surprised, telling me that the tarot revealed its secrets when they were most needed. Some divine hand, presumably, was dealing the cards.

Warrington is a busy little town on the right bank of the Mersey. It is a town of some antiquity, dating to Roman times when it was a major crossing point of the river. Today it manufactures cotton, iron, and glass. After making my connection and then finally arriving, I walked the half mile along to the Patten Arms, an ancient oak-beamed tavern with gleaming polished brass proclaiming a pride of ownership on the part of the landlord. I secured a room for a couple of nights and decided to wait till the following morning, a Saturday, to pay my respects at the police station.

Apparently Scotland Yard had originally been called in to investigate the murder of Elizabeth Scott, a local girl who had scraped together a living selling flowers in the market square. Her brutalized body had been discovered on the floor of a hayloft in a barn alongside the parish church. Inspector Bellamy's predecessor had been in charge of the investigation but, being on the eve of his retirement, had not pursued matters as thoroughly as Bellamy felt he should have done. However, Bellamy himself had visited the site only briefly, due to his recent promotion to inspector and to the inherited workload at Scotland Yard. I had been told that the case was very incomplete. Mr. Stoker was intrigued that the pattern of the murder seemed to follow so closely the ritual slaying of Nell Burton, and had Lyceum business allowed it, I know he would have come to Warrington himself. I felt proud that he had entrusted the investigation to me, but nervous that I might not ask all the necessary questions nor get all pertinent information.

The Patten Arms provided a most satisfactory evening

meal, and I sat at a table close to the hot, if slightly smoky, log fire that filled the enormous fireplace. My knife and fork rested on my plate in the midst of a steak and kidney pie, with peas and carrots, flanked by a tankard of their best porter. I eased my belt out a notch and smiled about me. There were two taverns in Warrington: the Patten Arms and the Lion. I had been advised by my host that the Patten Arms was by far the superior of the two, and from the crush of customers I could well believe it. Three bosomy serving wenches moved rapidly around the big dining room, ensuring that no one waited on food or drink. Mr. Peregrin Atherton, the portly landlord, stood at one end of the bar, puffing on a churchwarden pipe and smiling around at all and sundry. Suddenly I didn't miss my little theatre office at all.

B right and early Saturday morning I presented my credentials at the Warrington police station and found myself facing an Inspector Whittaker, a bald-headed, red-faced gentleman no taller than myself but full of self-importance. He read the introductory letter from Bellamy three times, holding his steel-rimmed spectacles at various distances from his face as he screwed up his eyes to focus. I saw that one of the earpieces had broken off the spectacles, which was why he held them rather than wore them. He finally paused in his perusal, looked up, and sniffed.

"Scotland Yard thinks itself to be so much cleverer than the provincial police force, does it not?" he said.

I opened my mouth to respond, not quite sure what to say. I was saved from comment by his continuance.

"They come running in here when there is an unusual murder, as if to say that they are the only ones capable of solving it. And what do they do?"

This time I waited. Sure enough he went right on talking as though I wasn't there.

"Nothing! That's what. Have they solved the crime? Do they have the murderer safely under lock and key? May Warrington—nay, all of Lancashire—breathe easily again? I think not! And now, after leaving everything sitting for weeks, they send some *civilian* . . ." He pronounced it as though it were a dirty word. "Some civilian here to pry into what should be *our* case, and ours alone."

He sat up in his high-backed wooden chair and pressed his lips tightly together. He was without facial hair and had a receding chin that almost disappeared as he glared at me over the wavering spectacles.

"I—I do apologize, Inspector Whittaker," I said. "I'm sure you must think . . ."

"I must think, must I?"

"No, sir." I hastened to explain myself, but he would have none of it.

"Scotland Yard has spoken!" He tapped the letter with his spectacles. "I might as well be a mere constable on the beat, so far as they are concerned. 'Afford Mr. Rivers every courtesy,' they say. 'Every courtesy.'" He paused briefly to take in a deep and noisy breath. "They'll be telling me to offer you a cup of tea next."

I cleared my throat. We were not getting off to the friendly cooperation for which I had hoped. "Again, I apologize, sir. But we do have a very similar murder in London, and I—we—were rather hoping that . . ."

"Aye! Aye!" He sat silently for a long moment, staring off in the direction of an ordnance survey map of the area, drawing-pinned to the wall close to the door. I swallowed and again prepared to speak. Again I was beaten to the post. "Well, Mr. Rivers, it is no fault of your own, I suppose. High-handed of Scotland Yard, but I expect no more from them. All right."

He rose to his feet and came out from behind his desk. He put on his cap and tucked a short baton under his arm.

"Come!"

He marched out of the room, and I had to break into a run to keep up with him as he moved briskly along the passageway and out past the sergeant at the front desk. We emerged from the police station and stood for a moment on the topmost of the five stone steps leading up to the double doors. Whittaker pointed his baton in the direction of the church, visible at the far end of the road off to our right.

"Saints James and John," he said. "Did you know those two always go together?" I shook my head. "Heaven knows why, but they do."

"Is that where the girl's body was found?" I asked, feeling it was time I made my voice heard.

"There is a barn close by the church—you cannot see it from here—and that's where we found the body. Aye." He seemed to have mellowed very slightly, I thought, now that we were outside and on the case.

"Might we proceed there, that I may view the site?"

He mused for a moment, once again gazing off into the distance, tapping his baton on his gloved hand. Finally he turned back as though to return into the police station.

"I have work to do. Important work. I shall have Constable Hudson escort you to the murder scene. You will interfere with nothing, of course. Merely observe—make notes if you so wish—and return here if you have any questions. Do I make myself clear?"

He disappeared inside, through the doors, before I had a chance to respond. I stood there for a long moment, wondering if I had been meant to follow him. Eventually, one of the doors opened again, and a large-girthed police constable emerged, carefully positioning his helmet on his head.

"Constable Hudson?" I asked.

"P.C. Hudson it is, sir. Am I to understand correctly that you was wantin' to be escorted to the Scott crime scene, as it were, sir?"

I smiled and nodded. "You are correct, Constable. Thank you."

"Follow me, sir."

He labored down the steps and then set off at a leisurely pace along the road. I matched strides with him and tried to engage him in conversation, hoping for greater success than I had had with his superior. He seemed to be of a friendly disposition, stroking his large black mustache and beard as he walked and nodding in friendly fashion to occasional passersby.

"You are a native of Warrington?" I hazarded.

"Hoh yes, sir! Born and bred, as they say. Man and boy. Twenty-nine years come Michaelmas."

"And did you know the murdered girl?"

"Most everyone knew Lizzie," he said. "Been selling 'er flowers in the square as long as I can remember." He shook his head sadly and let out a long sigh. "I swear as 'ow I don't know what this country is coming to, sir, I don't. 'Ad 'er throat slashed from ear to ear. 'Orrible, it were. Like a pig as 'ad been bled, sir. She din't deserve that an' no mistake. I mean, 'oo does deserve something of that sort? Must 'ave been some pervert from Liverpool, if'n you ask me, sir."

"You think it was someone from Liverpool?" I said.

"Stands to reason, don't it?" He pointed to a gate into the church graveyard. "We'll cut through 'ere, sir. Save us a bit." He let me through first then made a point of closing the gate behind us. "'Ave to keep this closed, sir, so the hin'abitants don't get out." He chuckled at his own cemetery humor. "Now then, where was we? Yes, it 'ad to 'ave been someone from the big city. I mean, no one around Warrington would ever do a thing like that, would they? I mean, what would be the reason?"

I nodded agreement and followed as he led the way between the gravestones, around the end of the church, and out of a side gate into a field beside the church. A large, dilapidated stone barn with half of its roof fallen inward stood a short distance away. It seemed an unusual shape, with the end rounded and the broken top rim jutting up higher than I would have expected. I commented on it to the constable.

"Aye, well it would, wouldn't it, sir," he said enigmatically. "Stands to reason. It used to be a windmill, you see. O' course, the sails is long since gone and most the top part's fallen in'ards."

He led the way there, through nettles, dock, and bracken struggling to emerge from months of stifling snow. *A windmill*, I thought. *Just as on the tarot card.*

"Watch where you walk, sir," he cautioned as we entered the structure. "'Ooever did the deed picked out the only solid floor for their devil's ritual, so mind you don't go fallin' through any rotten boards."

The place smelled of stale, musty hay and rotting wood. One or two pieces of rusting farm machinery stood in the corners. A mouse scampered away from our feet as we walked across to the wooden steps leading up to the hayloft. Constable Hudson made a point of testing each step carefully before placing his not insubstantial weight on it. We eventually emerged on the upper floor, with the weak sunshine poking fingers through a multitude of holes where slates were missing from the roof. Up the far end from where we were was the milling machinery, or what remained of it; great wooden-toothed gear wheels above massive granite millstones.

"This is it, sir. What there is to see. Don't know what you'll be able to make of it. Hinspector Whittaker didn't seem able to make much of it even when it was fresh, if'n you ask me."

I moved forward slowly, studying the floor. A large upturned tea chest sat in the middle of the storage area. The constable indicated it.

"That's where they found the body, sir."

I nodded. It didn't take me long to be able to make out

the chalk designs on the rough floor, though they had been well trampled over.

"She was all laid out with 'er arms crossed on 'er chest just like she was peaceful sleepin', only she'd 'ad 'er throat cut somethin' cruel." He turned his head away as though he could still see her lying there.

"They was drawin' pretty pictures, as you can see, sir." He continued after a moment. "What sort of a . . . ?"

"Yes. Thank you, Constable," I said. I needed time to think. I pulled out the notebook I had brought with me and spent some time copying the designs, as accurately as I could. I could hear P.C. Hudson shifting his weight from one foot to the other, obviously ill at ease as he waited on me.

"If you'd rather, you can wait for me downstairs, Constable," I said.

"No, sir. Thankin' you. But the hinspector said as 'ow I weren't to leave you 'ere alone, sir. Beggin' your pardon."

"Of course. Sorry to take so long."

"No, you go right ahead, sir. I'd rather be 'ere waitin' on you than filin' reports back at the station."

I made a note of the layout of the barn and its north-south alignment, just in case that was important. I paced around the hayloft—mindful of the rotting floor—to get some perspective. One thing that did strike me was what looked like the word "*primus*" chalked at the top of the stairs. I seemed to remember that there had been a similar, if not quite the same, word as we had entered the rehearsal warehouse where poor Nell Burton's body had lain.

It was nearly an hour later that I returned to the police station with Constable Hudson. He had been very patient, I thought, as I had carefully checked and double-checked everything, measuring and sketching all that seemed in any way connected to the crime. I knew there would be no opportunity to return here, so I didn't want to leave anything to chance. I thanked the good constable and asked the desk sergeant if Inspector Whittaker was available. He shook his head.

"Saturday, sir," he said.

"Er, yes. Yes, I'm aware of the day, Sergeant."

"Saturday the inspector goes into Hoylake, just outside of Liverpool, to the golf club there. The *royal* golf club, as he likes to point out, sir. Has done for over a year now, to my knowledge."

"Golf?" I had heard of the game, but I had not realized its growing popularity. "So he won't be back today?"

The sergeant shook his head. "You might catch him tomorrow, sir," he suggested. "Sometimes looks in for a half hour or so on his way back from church."

"I see. Thank you, Sergeant."

So much for the Warrington police extending to me every courtesy . . . and the inspector's "important work." Just so long as it didn't interfere with his leisure time, it seemed.

I thought it might be prudent to speak with the local vicar, but I found that he, too, was away, tending to his flock, for the rest of the afternoon. I determined to catch him immediately after the Sunday morning service, before I went to speak with the inspector. I didn't fancy sitting through a full Warrington church service, so I planned to mingle with the crowd as they exited the church and introduce myself to the vicar at that time.

Chapter Eight

It was a small group that emerged from the church on Sunday morning. Inspector Whittaker was not among them. As I stood in the shelter of an ancient yew, with rainwater pattering onto my raised umbrella, I heard the swell of the organ music as the service came to an end, and then I saw the vicar emerge and take up his place just inside the open doorway, ready to bid farewell to the faithful. The congregation was comprised of what looked to me to be elderly farmers and shopkeepers and their wives. I saw no young people, though the vicar himself was fresh faced and pink skinned and apparently still full of the fervor of the seminary.

I kept expecting to see Inspector Whittaker, but the trickle of worshippers eventually petered out with no sign of him. As the vicar waved farewell to the last of them and turned to go back into the building, I moved forward and hailed him.

"Good morning, Vicar," I said.

He turned and smiled, a quizzical look on his face. "Good morning to you, too, my son. I don't recall seeing you . . ."

"No. I'm afraid I was not at the service." I shook his hand. I explained who I was and why I was there. He introduced himself as the Reverend Prendergast.

"I expected to see Inspector Whittaker here," I said. "Did he not come to the service?"

The reverend's smile remained. "Ah! I have already learned not to rely on the appearances of local constabulary. The inspector is a busy man. I see him or I don't."

"His duties keep him away a lot?" I asked.

His smile became even broader. "Duties most often, but we cannot discount this modern game of golf. The inspector is a convert to that, and it is not easy to discipline such conversions." He laughed. "Time will tell, I am sure. I have a feeling that this game of golf is but a passing fad. Tell me, is there anything I can help you with? You say you are investigating that most regrettable murder of Miss Elizabeth Scott?"

I nodded. "I wondered if you could tell me anything of which the police might not be aware. Anything that perhaps you have remembered in recent days?"

Reverend Prendergast's face became serious as he slowly shook his head. "Believe me, young man, I have searched my very soul for the minutest of details that might help bring this monstrous person to justice. The good inspector and his men have done their best, I know, and we have even had Scotland Yard come up here from London. But to no avail. You say you are part of some further investigation?"

I explained more fully the similarities between the two murders and the interest and knowledge of my boss.

"Ritual killings?" The vicar beckoned me inside the church. I folded my umbrella and gratefully followed him in, as the light rain had swelled to more of a downpour. "The Scotland Yard man—and the second one who came more recently—was very closemouthed about exactly what it was that they had found here, but I did hear something about mystic markings and rumors that poor Lizzie was not simply murdered but was killed as part of some strange rite, or so it was hinted. I know not how seriously. I was questioned on that score, but I am afraid my seminary training did not extend in that direction."

"I was wondering, Vicar, if you had heard of any similar activity—not including actual killings necessarily—anywhere in the area? Any individual or group that was into that sort of thing?"

We sat down at the end of the last pew. He ran his finger around his clerical collar as though to ease it, while he seemed to ponder the question.

"You know, I was not asked that before. But now that you mention it, I do recall my predecessor once complaining about some minor desecration of the graveyard. Overturned gravestones and that sort of thing. It was before my time and was put down to juvenile high spirits. I have only been here since the end of last year. I was called in on the third Sunday of Advent, when my predecessor had a heart attack. But now that I give it some thought, I do recall that the Reverend Swanson claimed there was what he termed 'satanic activity' in the area. Very old-school, was the Reverend Swanson." He chuckled and shook his head. "Very superstitious, if I may say so." The smile returned to his face. "Of course, I suppose we are in the business of superstition, are we not?"

"I would like to speak further with you on this, if I may?" I said.

"Of course. Of course, my son." He looked about him at the empty church. "I have some clearing up to do, but I'd be happy to spend some time with you this afternoon. Come along to the vicarage. About two of the clock?"

It was Tuesday before I, thankfully, got back to London and to the dear old Lyceum Theatre. I made my report to my boss, and he seemed to think that I had done excellent work. I was pleased. He sat and studied the diagrams I had made and asked me several times to read aloud from my notes . . . perhaps my handwriting was not all I had thought it to be.

"So the Reverend Prendergast had heard reference—if only vague—to a satanic group in the area, Harry?"

I nodded. "Heard mention of it from his predecessor," I said. "He had no details when I first asked, but he was kind enough to dig back through the church records for me when I visited him at the vicarage. It seems the older vicar had been long plagued with doubts about some of his flock. There was never any positive proof, but the Reverend Swanson suspected a link to an old club run by Sir Francis Dashwood in the last century. The young Reverend Prendergast did not concur and put down any shenanigans to exuberant and misguided youth."

Stoker pursed his lips. "Hmm. I don't think I would be so quick to dismiss events." He did not expound on his thoughts.

"Just what was this club, sir?" I asked, thinking back to my day out with Jenny and her aunt. "Jenny's aunt Alice mentioned something like it, though she couldn't recall the exact name. And something about an ancestor named Potter who was a member. I looked in a couple of books and found something called the Hellfire Club. Could that have been it? I must admit the name sounds oddly familiar, but I have no idea of any details."

"Aah!"

There was a wealth of meaning in the sound that issued from Bram Stoker. I settled back in my chair and waited.

"The Hellfire Club it was, or that was its common name. And a Mr. Thomas Potter was indeed a member at one time. He was a politician and a well-known rake, though I'm sure Jenny's aunt Alice is unaware of that fact! Sir Francis Dashwood was a young buck of the last century. At the age of sixteen, on his father's death, he inherited a large fortune. Like many a young man in such circumstances he went a little wild, though to be honest he had been pushed from the straight and narrow a year or two earlier."

"Oh?" I was intrigued. I knew my boss loved to tell a good story, and it didn't take much to get him going. I tried to show my interest, which I most certainly had.

"He had done the usual grand tour of Europe, as all well-bred young men did. With his tutor he had visited Paris, Geneva, Barcelona, Florence, Rome, Venice, and so on. However . . ." Here Stoker made a dramatic pause. I couldn't help but think how much of the theatre he had absorbed without actually treading the boards. "It was in Rome that the telling event took place."

"Yes?" I sat forward in my chair. It was so easy to get caught up in his storytelling.

"Late one night, after an evening of carousing and debauchery, young Sir Francis retired to his chamber and fell into a deep sleep. But it wasn't long before he was awakened. To his bleary eyes there appeared two demons crying out and fighting for possession of his very soul."

I took a deep breath.

"But even as he watched," continued Stoker, "an angel dressed all in white entered the room and chased away the demons."

"Wonderful," I murmured.

The big head nodded. "Indeed."

"But?" I said. I knew there had to be a "but."

"Ah no! Do not be too dismissive, Harry. The whole affair had a profound effect upon young Sir Francis. He returned immediately to England and became most religious and devout. He donated money to hospitals and paid for the installation of stained glass windows in more than one church."

"But?" I persisted.

A smile slowly but surely spread across Stoker's face, and he nodded.

"But it was not long before the true story of what had taken place emerged. In no time Francis found himself the laughingstock of London."

My mouth hung open.

"It seems that his tutor, the person in charge of this young man, merrily explained to all who would listen that in fact, on that fateful night, it was two mating cats not two devils on the rooftop outside Sir Francis's window, responsible for the yowling and screaming."

"And the white-clad angel?" I asked.

"None other than the tutor himself, in his nightshirt, who shooed away the creatures disturbing his master's sleep."

I couldn't help laughing.

"Yes," said Stoker. "All of London was soon laughing, too. Consequently, Sir Francis changed overnight. He cursed the Church, as though it was their fault. He turned away and, to show his contempt for religion, gathered his friends about him and formed the Friars of Saint Francis of Wycombe, better known as the Hellfire Club. They would frequently hold their fiendish rites perhaps fittingly beneath the ground in the caves of West Wycombe."

"And what was their purpose?" I asked.

"To ridicule religion." The big man got to his feet and moved across to look out of the small window of his office. "He restored the old ruined Medmenham Abbey—putting in stained glass windows depicting himself and his 'apostles' indulging in various lewd acts—and developed satanic rituals for the club members. They held what were termed 'Black Masses' with women of a certain type, hired for the occasion, dressed as nuns and brought by ornamental barge to the abbey by way of the river."

I didn't know what to say.

"A variety of notables were members at one time or another," continued Stoker. "Including your Mr. Thomas Potter. But eventually, over the years, Sir Francis and the other principals died and the club, supposedly, faded away."

"Supposedly?"

He turned to look at me, his bright, gray green eyes overlarge and his head with something of a halo effect from the backlighting of the window. "Whether directly descended from the original Hellfire Club or not, there have been episodes brought to the attention of the police where devotees of Beelzebub have performed Black Masses and even made sacrifices, usually of young virgin women. The cult—for that is how I see it—has cropped up around these Sceptred Isles and even reared its ugly head across the broad Atlantic. I doubt there is a county in all of England that is free of some sort of association with this corruption. And from what I have heard, America is just as bad. I believe this incident outside of Liverpool that you were kind enough to investigate for me, Harry, may well have been one such example of our home variety."

"And our own Nell Burton also?"

"Again, I believe so."

There followed a long silence while we both absorbed all that he had said.

"Why do you think there will be a third such ritual, sir?" I asked.

"The dates, Harry. Now reinforced by a clue that you have just brought to light."

I sat up straight. My boss continued.

"In the ancient pagan calendar, certain dates were celebratory, just as they are in today's Christian calendar. Indeed, many of the latter were borrowed from the former, but that is neither here nor there. Two of the major ancient celebrations took place at February Eve, known as *Imbolc*, and at May Eve, known as *Beltane*. Halfway between those was the spring equinox, *Ostara*, which was a third slightly lesser celebration. The slaying of the Liverpool young lady took place at Imbolc. That of our Nell at the equinox. It seems highly likely, then, that a third might well occur at Beltane—would you not agree?"

He was right, as he always was, it seemed to me. If there was such a bloodthirsty group operating, then odds were they would follow that ancient calendar. It was certainly well to be aware of the possibility and to take whatever precautions we may.

"The Germans refer to this coming date as *Walpurgisnacht*," said Stoker. "Some consider it the most important of the dates, on a par with our All Hallows'. Incidentally, the very first meeting of the original Hellfire Club was held at Sir Francis's home in West Wycombe on *Walpurgisnacht* 1752."

"Have you apprised Inspector Bellamy?" I asked.

Stoker seemed to shake himself and moved back to his desk, sitting and shuffling papers on its surface.

"I somehow doubt that our good inspector would take a great deal of notice until the dreadful deed has been done. No, Harry. I think it will be up to us."

"You said that I had revealed a clue, sir?"

"Ah yes, Harry. Indeed you have, and I am grateful to you. In your notes on the Liverpool murder, you mention— and show in your meticulous drawings—that there was a particular word written in chalk at the top of the stairs, where one enters the ritual area. That word was '*primus*.'"

His meaning was no clearer. "Sir?"

"Latin for 'first,' Harry. Now—was there not a word written at the top of the steps into Miss Burton's ritual area?"

"Er—I believe so, sir, but don't ask me what it was."

"It was '*medius*,' Harry. Meaning 'midway.'"

"Midway?" There I was echoing him again.

"Midway. So if we have a 'first' and then a 'midway,' must we not later come to a 'last'? Confirmation, I think, of my supposition that there will be three such sacrifices."

It seemed to make sense, as did all my boss's suggestions.

"I had wondered about that word '*medius*,' at our site," Stoker continued. "To write 'midway' at the top of the stairs did not seem to make a lot of sense by itself. Now it does."

I frowned. "But . . . if there's to be a third murder, we don't know who might be involved; what other young lady will be threatened. We don't even know whereabouts in the whole country the group will act."

He threw a glance at me. "You are catching on, Harry. But that doesn't mean we can ignore it, does it?"

"No! No, of course not, sir."

He directed his attention to his papers, and I rose, realizing that the interview was over. I left and returned to my office feeling far from happy.

Wednesday morning's *Era* sported another headline proclaiming Reginald Robertson's belief that he was the Crown Prince of Shakespearean theatre in Great Britain and that all "pretenders"—obviously alluding to Henry Irving—should run into the wings of their respective theatres never to reemerge. Unfortunately, at the foot of the same page there was a brief review of Robertson's *Coriolanus* suggesting it was under-rehearsed, poorly staged, and lacking any sparkle of creativity.

"Henry is determined. He has made up his mind."

It was Miss Ellen Terry's dulcet tones that broke into my thoughts later that day. I had been through the properties room and inventoried items that would be required for the upcoming *Othello* production. Some things needed to be painted or repaired, and one or two I felt should be replaced. It was a long time since we had last done this favorite of the Shakespearean repertoire, but most of the props were still to hand.

"Then there's nothing anyone can do or say, it seems to me."

I recognized the second voice as that of Miss Margaret Grey. Currently playing Queen Gertrude in *Hamlet*, Meg Grey spent a great deal of time trying to convince the Guv'nor that she should be considered for younger roles. Neither he nor anyone else could see her so cast. Word was that she would play Emilia, wife of Iago, in *Othello*, though almost certainly she would prefer to be Bianca. Miss Terry would, of course, play Desdemona.

"I really can't see the point," continued Miss Terry. "Oh, I know that most of the notable gentlemen—'anyone who is anyone,' as Henry puts it—are Freemasons, but one wonders why."

Just then I came out of the properties room to find the two ladies standing at the foot of the stairs leading up to the star dressing rooms.

"Ah! Mr. Rivers," cried Miss Terry. "The very person, I do believe. You have a firm grasp on most things, or so Henry believes."

I was pleased to hear of the Guv'nor's view of me but was somewhat trepidatious as to what knowledge I was about to be asked to divulge.

"Tell me," she continued, "what is the point of Freemasonry? Oh, I know it's a nice excuse for the men to get away without female attachments on occasion, but surely there must be more to it than that? I would have thought that Henry would have enjoyed a break from the theatre, but is not this Freemasonry all ritual and stagelike presentation?"

"You must excuse me, Ellen," put in Miss Grey. "I have a costume adjustment I need to pursue with Miss Connelly. I will leave you in Mr. Rivers's capable hands, my dear." So saying, she scurried away.

I cleared my throat. "I don't know that I'm the best person to elaborate on this, Miss Terry," I began. "Needless to say, Mr. Stoker is far more informed than am I. But . . ."

"Are you yourself a Mason?" she asked.

"Er, no. No, I am not. But . . ."

"Is Mr. Stoker?"

"I'm not really sure. He certainly is . . ."

"Take me to him, please. I believe in going directly to the source. If you want to know something then . . ."

"He may not be in his office," I interjected. "I know he has a lot to do before curtain-up tonight."

Miss Terry smiled as she advanced on me. "I admire your loyalty to Abraham, and your attempt, feeble as it is, to protect him from the ramblings of a madwoman, Harry, but I am determined. Lead on."

It was not often that Miss Ellen Terry called me by my first name. I felt myself blush and turned to lead her to my boss's office, hoping that the redness I felt on my face did not extend around to the back of my neck.

"Welcome, welcome!" cried Bram Stoker, when we arrived in his office. "Always such a pleasure to see you, Miss Terry."

He hurried around to arrange a chair close to his own, beside the desk. To my surprise he produced a cushion for the hard wooden seat and placed it for the actress's comfort. A cushion! I was astounded. I had never seen one in his office before. He certainly never offered me one! From whence it came I had no idea.

"Harry, make yourself useful and see if Bill can produce a pot of tea for us."

"You are sweet, Abraham." Miss Terry sank down onto the plump cushion, and I went out to find Bill Thomas.

I couldn't help thinking of how Mr. Stoker always seemed to charm the ladies. Perhaps it was something to do with his Irishness? As I understood it, he had snatched his wife, then Florence Balcombe, away from her former suitor, Mr. Oscar Wilde. Florence was a great beauty, and Stoker and Wilde, who had been college students together, had vied for her hand for some time before Bram Stoker won the day. Mr. Wilde had been upset by Florence's decision but apparently had finally accepted it with good grace. Yes, I reflected, there was a great deal more to Mr. Abraham Stoker than was visible on the surface. I chuckled to myself as I watched Bill brew up the pot of tea, and I bore the tray back to my boss's office with a smile on my face.

"So, it is like a fraternity of older, generally successful gentlemen who meet together to act out ancient magical rituals?"

Miss Ellen Terry was, apparently, summing up Mr. Stoker's explanations.

"More or less, yes," agreed my boss. I felt that he was trying to appease the lady without going too deeply into greatly detailed explanations.

"How do you know of these rituals if you are not yourself of this fraternity, Abraham?"

Stoker gave one of his deep sighs and, opening a drawer in a cabinet behind him, pulled out a small blue clothbound book. He placed it on the desktop, turning it so that Miss Terry might read the title.

"*Freemasonry Exposed* by Capt. Wm. Morgan," she read. She looked up at him, eyebrows raised.

"It was privately printed some fifty-odd years ago. There are virtually no copies of it still available; I just happen to have one of the only ones to be found."

Just happen to? It was my turn to look at him, but his eyes were on the book.

"Explain yourself, Abraham."

"When a person becomes a Freemason," he said, looking her full in the face, "he takes an Oath of Secrecy; a promise to keep the confidences of the organization. This is not uncommon with the majority of secret societies and extends back to the days of the mystery religions of ancient times."

Miss Terry nodded. "So I understand. Go on, please."

"The penalty for breaking this oath can be very severe. In fact, the penalty for the Freemasons is spelled out. The 'Entered Apprentice,' as he is termed, at his initiation will declare that he is 'binding myself under no less penalty than to have my throat cut across, my tongue torn out by the roots, and my body buried in the rough sands of the sea at low water-mark, where the tide ebbs and flows twice in twenty-four hours,' if he should break his oath."

"My Good Lord," murmured Miss Terry, her hand going to her heart. I joined her in the sentiment.

"Unfortunately," continued Stoker, "our Captain Morgan—filled with the excitement of his newfound fraternity—desired to share his wonderful knowledge with one and all. He therefore produced the book you see here, detailing all of the secrets of the Freemasons. To pay for his perceived sins, on the eleventh day of September 1826, he was kidnapped and carried away from the village of Batavia—in America's New York State, I believe—by a number of fellow Freemasons and cruelly murdered. All known copies of his book were gathered up and destroyed."

"All except this copy?"

Stoker smiled. "There may be just one or two others somewhere, but they would be very difficult to locate."

"Excuse me, sir," I said. "But, 'may my throat be cut across,' or whatever the words you said, is that not reminiscent of the murders of our Miss Burton and Liverpool's Miss Scott?"

"Indeed it is, Harry," agreed Stoker. "However, the major difference is that they were both of the female gender, and Freemasonry is only available to the male of the species. The ritual nature of their murders is certainly reminiscent, as you say, but I can see no direct connection."

"So this is the sort of company into which Henry Irving is wanting to insert himself?" Miss Terry sounded alarmed. "Are you going to permit that, Abraham?"

Stoker shrugged. "Regrettably, Miss Terry, I have no influence over the Guv'nor one way or the other. If he has made up his mind then there is nothing I, or anyone else, can do about it. However . . ." He gave another of his calculated dramatic pauses. "I would assure you that the Brotherhood of Freemasons, with the exception of the Captain Morgan incident a half century ago, has an exemplary record, encompassing virtually all of the leading figures of today's society, not least being the prime minister himself, Mr. William Ewart Gladstone."

Miss Terry sniffed in a most unladylike manner. "That gives me small consolation," she said.

Chapter Nine

"I don't know what has happened to Billy Weston," I said to my boss just before Wednesday's matinee performance. "I had told him you felt that he should take off some time, after what happened to his young lady, but he had decided to work through it. He said it was better if he kept his mind busy."

Stoker nodded. "Quite right. That is exactly what I would have done. So what do you mean, you don't know what has happened to him, Harry?"

"Just that, sir," I said. "He didn't come into the theatre for Monday night's performance, and there's been no sign of him yesterday or today."

Stoker was in a hurry to get to an appointment and had no time to dwell on it. He left the matter in my hands, saying that he had every confidence that I'd find the young man and set him to rights. I wish I had as much trust in myself as he seemed to have in me.

None of the backstage staff seemed to know anything,

except that Billy had left them shorthanded. I checked with everyone. It was old Rupert Melville, the scene painter, who gave me my first clue. We were both in the Druid's Head, taking a quick lunch.

"Billy Weston? After the Saturday matinee I saw him duck out," Rupert said.

"You mean he wasn't around for the Saturday evening performance?" I asked. I had not noticed the absence, but it helped explain the annoyance of the other stagehands; there was always plenty to do backstage.

"Reckon not, Harry." The scene painter tucked into a large helping of shepherd's pie.

"He should have reported to Mr. Stoker or myself if he was going to be away for even one performance," I said, not a little annoyed that I had overlooked his absence. "If he missed Saturday evening and then hasn't been here since, I wonder if he was at his digs at all over the weekend?"

"He's a good lad. Not one to avoid his responsibilities. But I do recall overhearing him talking to some street arab at the stage door right after the final curtain of the Saturday matinee. I think he was being given some sort of information he'd been waiting for, and he wasn't too happy about it."

"What do you mean? What sort of information?" I asked.

Rupert shrugged. "I don't know. I assumed he'd paid the street urchin to find out something for him and he was getting what he'd asked for. As I say, it wasn't something that cheered him up at all."

"Did you hear him say anything?" I quizzed. "Any clue of any sort? Think back, Rupert. After what happened to Nell Burton I think it's important we check on anybody going missing for any length of time."

Rupert put down his knife and fork and stroked his grizzled chin. He always looked as though he was in the process of growing a beard, but in the two or three years I had known him it had never fully materialized. His long, stringy hair was a dirty brown color, but the whiskers on his lower jaw were distinctly white. His tall, skinny frame did little to present his well-worn clothes, but I knew he had an active mind, and as an artist, he paid wonderful attention to detail of all sorts.

"He was talking more to himself than to the street arab, it seemed to me. Said something about 'that damned'—pardon my French, Harry—'that damned Ben Gossett.' I think that was the name. Said something about 'getting him' and 'making him pay for what he did.' Any of that make any sense, Harry?"

He looked at me through red-rimmed eyes, his eyebrows raised as though in surprise.

I felt suddenly uneasy. "Yes. Yes, Rupert. I think it does." I got to my feet, leaving my pork pie and half-drunk porter on the table. "Thank you. Thanks a lot. I must go."

I hurried back to the theatre.

Billy had said something about Ben Gossett claiming that if he couldn't have Nell then no one could. It seemed highly likely that Billy was taking that as evidence that Gossett was responsible for Nell's murder—something Mr. Stoker and I did not believe. My boss was convinced that the murder showed far too much sophistication to be the hasty action of a spurned adolescent. But if Billy believed it strongly enough, he might well do something he would live to regret. I had to find him and stop him. The life of a simple stage manager was never truly simple, I was coming to realize. I sighed and headed for Scotland Yard.

"Ben Gossett," said Inspector Bellamy, his mug of tea halfway up to his mouth. I waited till he had taken a mouthful, cursed the fact that it was almost cold, and then drunk half the mug.

"You said that you had learned that he'd fled his lodgings, bill unpaid, and disappeared. Have you done any further investigation on him, Inspector?" I asked.

Bellamy set down the mug and leaned forward, peering into it as though he might learn the reason for its lack of warmth. He looked up again, almost as though seeing me for the first time.

"Mr. Rivers." He sat back and contemplated me. I began to grow impatient.

"One of our young stagehands—the one who was walking out with Nell Burton, the murdered girl—has now gone missing," I said. "I am a little concerned."

The policeman got to his feet and crossed to a set of shelves at the rear wall of his office. He moved aside some papers and dragged out a file, bringing it back to his desk.

"Your theatre certainly keeps us on our toes, Mr. Rivers, does it not? You could almost believe that we exist only for your entertainment, rather than the other way around."

He grunted, and I couldn't tell if it was an attempt at a laugh at his own joke or if it was a sound of annoyance and frustration. I had a feeling it was the latter.

"Another missing person is a reason for concern, I would have thought," I said, forcefully. "Even for the likes of Scotland—"

He held up his hand as though stopping traffic in Westminster Square. "Grant us some ability, Mr. Rivers. We are sure you are adept at your profession, so please return the compliment where police work is concerned. Your view of the police is largely shaped by the presentations of Mr. Gilbert and Mr. Sullivan a year or so ago, but . . ."

It was my turn to interrupt. "The Lyceum does not indulge in musical farce, Inspector. Mr. Irving's company presents the works of the Bard. Whether or not a policeman's lot is or is not a happy one is of no concern of ours." It seemed that the popular comic opera, performed so successfully about London, had hit a sore spot where the Metropolitan Police were concerned. "May we stay focused on the mysteries at hand and especially on this latest disappearance? I am trying to locate our young Billy Weston before he becomes another statistic in your files. I suspect that he has gone chasing after Ben Gossett with a view to doing him harm."

Bellamy slammed his fist down on the file in front of him. I think it was the first time I had ever seen any real emotion in him.

"And you think we don't care? We will have you know, Mr. Rivers, that we have spent some considerable time on this case and have by no means written off your Mr. Gossett. The fact that this Billy Weston is now very much in the picture is, of course, of interest to us, and we thank you for advising us of it. But now would you please leave the work of detection to the professionals and get back to your stage-managing duties?"

We sat for a long moment glaring at each other before I came to realize that there was much truth in what he said. It was his bailiwick, not mine. I think I had the grace to be the first to back down. I reclined in my seat and spoke softly.

"You are right, Inspector. My apologies. I hope you can understand the emotional stress that is placed on our whole theatre when one of our own goes missing, especially in this case where it may be that the young man in question is possibly placing himself in harm's way."

Bellamy grunted, and his fist relaxed into an open hand on the file in front of him.

"If there is any way . . ." he started to say. I jumped on it.

"Would you be kind enough just to let me know where you think Mr. Gossett might be? Just for information's sake?" I forced a smile at him.

He grunted again and flipped open the file. He scanned the information on the top sheet and then relayed it to me.

"Our last investigation showed a strong possibility that the young gentleman in question had almost certainly returned to his hometown of Langley Mill." He looked up again and held my gaze. "We do not, however, Mr. Rivers, want to learn that you have gone running off up north after him. We will take advisedly the report of your Mr. Weston now being missing and proceed with our own investigation. But as we said before, leave these matters to the professionals."

I thanked him and made my departure. *Leave it to the professionals?* I thought. *But they were the ones who were unmoved by the disappearance of Nell Burton. They were not directly responsible for her murder, but they certainly did not hurry themselves to search for her, initially.*

I made my way back to the Lyceum and to Mr. Stoker's office, determined not to sit back and wait for Scotland Yard to solve the case of the missing stagehand.

"It's ludicrous!"

It was seldom, though not completely unknown, that Mr. Stoker became angry, but I found him in a surly mood when I returned to the theatre.

"What do you think the Guv'nor has decided, Harry?" Before I could hazard a guess he told me. "He has acceded to Mr. Booth's request. Actually, as I understand it, it was his manager Colonel Cornell's request."

"And what was that?" I managed to ask.

"To take on a completely untrained actor. Oh, just in crowd scenes I grant you; no lines or anything likely to befoul a scene, but still . . ."

I could understand my boss's feelings. There were plenty of seasoned performers who would love to work in the Lyceum company. Why hire an amateur?

"Who is this person?" I asked. "Why does Mr. Booth want him aboard?"

"The colonel said something about making Mr. Booth feel 'comfortable,' whatever that is supposed to mean."

I shrugged. "So is that so terrible?" I asked. "Perhaps Mr. Booth just feels happier with another American in the cast. Granted, it's unprofessional, but perhaps that's how they do things on the other side of the Atlantic Ocean."

"Well, this is *this* side of the Atlantic Ocean, Harry. We play by British rules."

"You say the Guv'nor has agreed to it?"

He nodded resignedly. "I think there was some sort of a deal. The colonel is apparently a Freemason, a member of that fraternity, and has agreed to coach the Guv'nor on all their shenanigans in return for us broadening our crowd scenes."

I looked up sharply. "The colonel coaching the Guv'nor? I wouldn't think Mr. Irving would need coaching in anything."

"Oh, they have all sorts of secret handshakes, grips, and so on," he said, offhandedly.

"Is this a good thing?"

Stoker's expression darkened, and he peered at me from under his bushy eyebrows. "That is not for you nor me to say, Harry. All I know is that I have a bad feeling about this. My old granny always told me to pay attention to my feelings. She had the sight, did I tell you?"

"Actually, several times, sir."

He ignored me. "She had the sight just like her granny before her, or so she told me." He nodded, in agreement with himself. "We must stay on our toes, Harry."

"Yes, sir." I waited to see if there was more to come, and then, when it seemed there wasn't, I told him of my visit with Inspector Bellamy.

"The man is an ass, Harry. Don't forget that."

"No, sir."

"Young Billy has not reappeared?"

"No, sir." I told him of the observation made by Rupert Melville. Stoker looked concerned.

"Where exactly is Langley Mill?" he asked.

"I looked it up. It's between Derby and Nottingham."

"And young Nell Burton had come from Nottingham. Leastwise, she had done some work at the Theatre Royal there. Hmm." He tugged on his ear and screwed up his face, as he did when thinking things through. "Harry, *Hamlet* is running smoothly—as it should be after all this time. I would like you to go up to Langley Mill and see if you can intercept our Billy Weston before he does something foolish."

"Up to Derbyshire, sir?" I had visions of missing yet another weekend with Jenny, but then chided myself for putting my simple pleasures before consideration of Billy's possible predicament.

"I know. I know. You've barely got back from Liverpool, and I hate suggesting you leave again."

"That's all right, sir," I mumbled, unconvincingly. After all, it was only Wednesday. I might even be able to make it back by Sunday, if I could locate Billy quickly enough. "You are certain this is necessary?"

"I am, Harry. I am. I think it will be for the best. Again, I hate to ask it of you."

I didn't mention that Inspector Bellamy had expressly forbidden me to go north in search of Billy. Then I comforted myself in the fact that the inspector had actually forbidden me to chase after Ben Gossett, not our Billy. Splitting straws, perhaps, but one does what needs must. Or as the Bard says: "He must needs go that the devil drives."

I put my head around the corner of the greenroom. Act Three had not yet been called. The young ladies who made up some of the Players were huddled in a corner. Arthur Swindon, the Ghost of Hamlet's Father, sat alone in another corner draining his flask and studying, with bleary eyes, the paint flaking off the wall next to him. I approached the group of girls.

"Miss Abbott?"

"Oh! Mr. Rivers. Yes, sir. We haven't been called yet."

"I know," I said. "I don't mean to interrupt your short break but, er, I was wondering . . ."

"You want me to read the cards, Mr. Rivers?"

The other girls giggled. I ignored them.

"It's just that . . . well, I have to go somewhere for Mr. Stoker and I wondered . . ."

"Say no more, Mr. Rivers. Here! Make room, you lot."

The other girls pulled back. I saw that Edwina already had her cards out; she was probably reading them for one of the group. I felt bad for interrupting, but I did not have a great deal of time. Miss Abbott scooped up the cards, shuffled them expertly, and then fanned them out and offered them to me. I hesitated a moment, my hand hovering along the display, and then I pulled one that seemed to beckon to me. She put aside the others and lay down the one card, faceup, on the small table in front of her. The girls all leaned inward, and there was a collective gasp.

"What? What is it?" I was suddenly concerned.

"Oh, don't pay them no nevermind," said Edwina. "They get excited no matter what the card."

We all looked down at the pasteboard, which depicted five swords; nothing more. *What did they mean?* I wondered. I looked up at Edwina.

"Five épées," she said. "That's what Auntie Jessica called them."

"So what do they mean?" I had difficulty containing my curiosity.

"Well, first of all they're in the Minor Arcana. Don't ask me what that means, but it's just that they ain't court cards, if'n you take my meaning."

"But they are significant?" I asked.

"Oh yes. They are *all* significant. But the thing with these here Minors is that it means there ain't no big forces at work. Nothing major, Auntie would say."

"I'm still not sure . . ." I began.

"Forces change around us all the time," explained the girl. "But with big forces, like the Major Arcana, there really ain't *no* changing them. What you see is what you get. With these little ones, you can do things to make changes happen. Do you follow me, Mr. Rivers?"

I was not sure. "I—I think so," I said. "You mean that with the court cards it shows what is set in stone, as it were, whereas with these smaller ones, things are still fluid; still changing."

"That's it! You got it, Mr. Rivers."

"Well, that's good . . . I think. But then what do the five swords actually signify?"

Her brow wrinkled as she studied the card. "The card is upside down. It's not easy to see with these Minors, but I can tell you it's not right side up."

"Is that bad?"

"Needn't be. Hmm. It says that there's a possible problem, a misfortune, that could happen to a friend." She looked up at me. "You got someone as you are worried about, Mr. Rivers?"

I nodded. *Billy Weston*, I thought, though I didn't say his name out loud. "What can you tell me about him?" I asked.

"Draw another card," she said and, picking up the rest of the deck, fanned them again.

I ran my fingertip along the backs of them, dithering over the choice.

"Beginners, Act Three!" came young Edward's voice, as he moved past the greenroom door.

Edwina scooped up the cards and slipped them into a pocket in her skirt. With the rest of the girls, she ran out of the room, calling back over her shoulder: "Sorry, Mr. Rivers. Mr. Irving doesn't like us to be late."

They disappeared toward the steps leading up to the stage. I had no idea what that next card might have been.

I saw that Arthur Swindon was slumped in his chair, snoring. I didn't think he was needed onstage, so I left him.

Chapter Ten

Langley Mill is a small village in the Amber Valley. To the left, as the train chugs into Langley Mill, may be seen the ruins of Codnor Castle, a desolate site on a hill surrounded by wheat fields. The village is right on the border of Derbyshire (of which it is a part) and Nottinghamshire, and is on the River Erewash. It has little to commend it, to my mind.

It was noon when I disembarked at the railway station. I was beginning to hate rail travel. I had left London's St. Pancras Station before the morning had fully arrived and then suffered a hard seat on a slow-moving train of the Midland Railway's L.N.W. route. The stop before Langley Mill was Derby. I would have preferred to have done my investigating in that city, with its large hotels and restaurants, but Inspector Bellamy had assured me that Ben Gossett had gone to earth in Langley Mill, so that was where I needed to be. That was where Billy Weston would be drawn.

In the village there were but two rooms offered at the

Black Swan Inn, locally referred to as the Muddy Duck. I was lucky to find one of those rooms vacant.

After a surprisingly edible ploughman's lunch at the inn, I set off along the High Street in search of my prey. When I had queried the landlord, he had assured me that he knew the Gossett family but had not seen Ben for a few weeks. The boy, he said, had lived with his aged mother and an aunt and had scraped a living doing odd jobs.

"Never amounted to much," he said. "Not surprised 'e went off to London."

"But I hear he has returned," I said.

He sniffed and concentrated on slicing cheese. "I ain't seen nothin' of 'im, if'n 'e 'as," he said.

So I passed along the High Street in the direction the landlord had indicated. The Gossett farm was a half mile beyond the last house in the village, and I found it to be in very run-down condition. I presumed there were no longer animals there, since the barn roof had fallen in and the chicken house leaned at a precarious angle. I was surprised, therefore, to hear sounds coming from the dilapidated pigsty.

It took a number of raps on the farmhouse door to elicit a response. Finally, an elderly lady dressed all in black, stooped and obviously arthritic, squinted at me from red-rimmed eyes, one of which was white and cloudy.

"'Oo is it?" she demanded.

I introduced myself. "I was wondering if young Mr. Ben Gossett was at home?" I said. "I believe he has been away in London, but I have been led to believe that he has recently returned here."

"What?" she said, cupping a hand to her ear.

I sighed and repeated myself, leaning in toward her and raising my voice a little.

"Ben?"

"Yes, ma'am. Ben Gossett."

"You'd best come in and speak to his mam."

She turned and shuffled away back into the darkness of the passageway. I stepped inside and followed, closing the door behind me. This left me in almost total darkness, despite the brightness of the sun outside. I could make out the woman's white cap as she moved away, and I followed it. She led me into the parlor, where a small amount of light fought its way into the room through heavy, dark-colored curtains that almost entirely covered the window.

A second elderly lady, looking much like the first, also dressed in black but with bright, intelligent eyes, sat in a rocking chair knitting something large and multicolored. The click-clack of her needles did not pause as she acknowledged my presence with a bob of her head.

"Young feller says it's about our Ben," said the woman who had led me in.

Another bob of the head.

I looked about me but could see no empty seat—I believe there were one or two chairs, but each supported a cat—so I remained standing.

"Yes, ma'am. I understand that Ben has newly returned from London?"

The bright eyes looked at me, and she smiled; the needles continued their tattoo.

"Is that correct?" I pressed.

"She don't 'ear too well," volunteered the first lady. "Best if you talk to me."

I was bewildered. Hadn't she just told me to speak to Ben's mother? Yet here Ben's mother couldn't, or wouldn't, speak. I mentally shook myself and counted to ten. I smiled.

"Of course. Forgive me," I said. I took the liberty of shooing an overweight calico cat off the nearest chair and sitting down. The ladies didn't seem to take it amiss.

I told my story of needing to contact Ben and of the possibility of Billy following him and wishing him harm.

The aunt—for that is whom I took the first lady to be—

repeated my tale, sentence by sentence, to the mother. It seemed to me that she did not speak any louder than did I, yet the mother appeared to hear and understand her. Least-wise, the mother kept nodding her head and smiling as she worked her knitting needles.

"So is Ben here?" I persisted. "May I speak with him?"

"He'm out and about," said the aunt. "Best you leave it with me. I'll let him know you was askin' after him."

I was more than "asking after him"; I was there to warn him of a possible attempt on his life. I did not feel comfortable just "leaving it" with her. But what was I to do? I got to my feet. Ben's mother's head bobbed as she smiled at me.

"When do you think he will be back? I really would like to have a word with him myself."

"Of course you would," agreed the aunt, but she made no suggestion on how to proceed.

"Look," I said, "I am staying at the Black Swan, in town. Would you please ask Ben to come and see me there? And I'll come back here tomorrow just in case. Is that all right?"

"He'll be out and about," said the aunt agreeably, start-ing to struggle to her feet, ready to see me off.

I held up my hand. "Please don't trouble yourself. I can see myself out. I hope, perhaps, to visit with you tomorrow." I gave a half bow and then turned and left, the sound of the knitting needles fading away as I exited the house.

"You won't get nowhere with Mam and Auntie A," said a voice.

I looked around. A tall, thin young man with an unshaven chin and straggly attempt at a mustache stood leaning on the top rail of the fence around the pigsty. He looked as though he hadn't washed in two or three days and I noticed that his fingernails were black with grime.

"Are you Ben?" I asked.

"That's what they call me. And 'oo might you be?"

I moved forward, resisting the impulse to extend my

hand to shake his. "Harry Rivers," I said. He remained slumped forward on the fence rail. "I'm from the Lyceum Theatre in London. I came here . . ."

"Aye. I know all about that. I've 'eard of you."

"You have?" I was surprised. I didn't think my fame had spread so far. In truth, I didn't think I had any fame! "Might I ask, from whom?"

"Billy," he said. "Billy Weston."

My face must have registered my surprise.

"Don't look so flabbergasted, mate. 'E says good things about you."

"When—when did you speak with him?" I gasped.

"Just yester-evenin'. We was sharing a jug at the Muddy Duck."

"You were drinking with Billy at the Black Swan? Last night? But the landlord said . . ."

"Aye, well! Old John Rhodes ain't goin' to be a-tellin' to a stranger, now is 'e?"

I nodded understandingly. No, the landlord wouldn't be telling everything to an out-of-towner such as myself. But I still did not fully understand.

"You are telling me that you and Billy Weston have been drinking together? But the very reason I'm here is to make sure that he doesn't do you any harm. He was bent on trying to kill you, believing you responsible for Nell Burton's death!"

Ben nodded his head; the matted hair stuck out at odd angles as he scratched at it. "We talked about it. Even 'ad a bit of a tussle afore we got sorted out."

"He realizes you couldn't have been responsible?" I asked.

He continued to nod. "We was both torn up over it."

"I heard something about you saying that if you couldn't have Nell then no one could have her."

He continued scratching his head and for some reason went to shaking it negatively rather than nodding. "That was when I was thinking as 'ow Bill was stealing 'er away.

But then, when she got topped, well . . . what was I to do? No purpose to it then, was there?"

I had to agree. It seemed my task was complete. I presumed that Billy Weston, having discovered the truth, had by now returned to London. I should do the same. It had been something of a wasted journey. Well, perhaps I could still get back in time to see Jenny on Sunday.

"Thank you, Ben," I said. "I'm glad the reason for my trip proved to be in vain. I'll bid you good day." I turned to leave.

"What you goin' to do about it, then?"

I turned back. "What do you mean?"

"Billy says as 'ow you're goin' to find 'oo killed Nell."

"If we possibly can, yes." I saw that his eyes were red and realized that it might be that he had been crying. "Mr. Abraham Stoker, together with Scotland Yard, is on the case, Ben. Mr. Stoker can be tenacious."

He looked puzzled.

"He will keep on until he finds the killer, Ben."

He finally straightened up and swung a leg over the low fence rail, hopping on over to stand beside me. He smelled strongly of pigs.

"I—we—want to 'elp."

"I beg your pardon?"

"Billy and me. We want to 'elp catch 'ooever killed Nell."

I left my room, bag in hand, and made for the stairs down to the main level. I had plenty of time before the Friday morning train out of Langley Mill. It felt good to be heading back to London after such a fruitless two days. As I passed the one other room at the inn, the door opened. I looked around and found myself gazing into the eyes of Billy Weston.

"Billy!"

"Mr. Rivers!"

"What are you doing here, Billy? I thought you'd be halfway back to the Lyceum by now. And I had no idea you had been staying at the same tavern as me."

He shook his head, and his face turned a bright red. "I sure am sorry, Mr. Rivers. I should 'ave listened to you and Mr. Stoker. I guess my temper just got the better of me. I was just so . . . so torn up about Nell."

"It's all right, Billy. I understand."

"Do you think Mr. Stoker will let me 'ave my job back? I mean, I didn't mean to leave no one in the lurch, like."

"Well, we'll have to see about that. But I think you'll find Mr. Stoker to be a very fair and understanding man. I can make no promises, mind. But I will speak up for you when we get back."

"Thank you, Mr. Rivers. Thank you, sir." He still looked worried. "But . . . I mean, Ben and me, we was thinkin' that maybe we could 'elp in finding 'oo it was what done for our Nell."

"Yes," I said. "I spoke with Ben. He did seem upset."

"We both are. 'Im and me, we 'ad a long talk, and now, with Nell gone, well . . . It just don't seem right that 'ooever done it should get away with it, you know?"

"Yes, I do know, Billly. That's why Mr. Stoker and I— and don't forget the police as well—we're determined to catch whoever it was."

"So, can we 'elp, then?"

"Help? Track down the murderer?"

He nodded.

I thought about it. Mr. Stoker had told me to do whatever I felt needed to be done, while I was away. He was content to leave things up to my better judgment, he had said. He had even given me some extra money—a few sovereigns—in case I needed it.

I set down my portmanteau and stood thinking for a moment. Billy watched me, seeming to understand that I was contemplating something that would affect him. Finally, I looked at him again. I explained to him about the other murder; the one in Liverpool.

"You mean, someone else was done in like Nell was?"

I nodded. "Another young woman, Billy."

"But . . . I mean, 'ow can this be? What's going on?"

"Exactly," I said. "But we do believe the two murders are connected, so if we can solve one we can possibly solve them both. I did go to the Warrington site—that's where the second murder took place—but I really didn't have enough time to get every bit of possible information. Now, how would you and Ben like to help by asking some questions for me? It would mean going to Liverpool, or just this side of Liverpool. It's only a short journey from where we are now. About seventy-five miles."

"I—we—don't 'ave no money, Mr. Rivers. I 'ad to borrow some to get 'ere in the first place."

"Don't worry about that, Billy. The Lyceum—Mr. Stoker—will take care of the expenses. We just need you to go there to save us from doing it." I pulled out my half hunter and consulted it. "I don't have a lot of time if I'm to leave for London. Do you think you can get hold of Ben and the two of you could meet me at the railway station? Then, before I leave, I can tell you exactly what we need."

"Yes, sir, Mr. Rivers!" Billy reached behind him and pulled the door closed. He preceded me at a fast pace down the stairs and took off along the High Street as I left the Black Swan.

Twenty minutes later I was standing on the platform with a carriage door open beside me. My portmanteau was already in the train, up on the shelf over the seats. Billy and Ben stood attentively in front of me as I carefully went over all that I knew of the Liverpool/Warrington murder.

"Now, when you get there you are to make contact with the vicar of the local church, a Reverend Prendergast. I'm sure he will be able to help you find accommodation. You can tell him that you are following up on the information that he and I found. Mention Reverend Swanson; that should jog his memory."

"Swanson. Prendergast and Swanson." Billy repeated the names, as did Ben. I hoped that between the two of them they'd get it right.

"I want to know all you can uncover about the group he and I discussed; the evil group that we believe was active there."

"All aboard!" The guard moved along the short train, slamming closed any open doors. He waved for me to get inside. I did so but lowered the window and leaned out to finish talking to the two boys.

"All aboard!" the guard repeated as he climbed into the end car, leaned out, waved his green flag, and blew his whistle. The engine gave a toot and started to haul the train slowly out of the station. Billy and Ben trotted alongside as I gave last-minute instructions.

"Get any names you can of members of the group," I shouted. "See if the vicar knows who they are and where they might be."

The boys broke into a run to keep up.

"Remember, this will all help find Nell's killer. Get names if you can. Anything and everything you can learn!"

Billy and Ben had reached the end of the platform. I shouted to them but finally had to pull back into the carriage and close the window. Well, I had done what I thought was best. We'd have to see if it bore any fruit.

I settled down onto the seat. How nice if I was truly going straight back to the Lyceum, I thought. But no! With a heavy heart I knew it was not to be. Before I had left London Mr. Stoker had suggested I might return by way of Oxford, to see just what it was that Reginald Robertson was up to. Was he just blowing hot air, or did he have some plan to install himself as Britain's premier Shakespearean actor . . . perhaps drawing on his old grandmother's knowledge of witchcraft?

Oxford is the seat of one of the most ancient and celebrated universities in the whole of Europe. Lying amid picturesque environs at the confluence of the River Cherwell and the River Thames, it is surrounded by an amphitheatre of gentle hills. It has approximately forty thousand inhabitants and is the county town of Oxfordshire. The university comprises twenty-four colleges, many of them richly endowed by royalty and notable private persons. I never had the temerity to aspire to attend such a prestigious establishment myself—the Hounslow Masonic Institution for Boys was quite sufficient for my needs—yet I could appreciate those who did, and I stood in awe of the wealth of knowledge that was available in that one small town. I have never even been to Oxford before, but I had certainly read about it in many publications.

The station of the London and North Western Railway lay on the west side of the town. The King's Arms hotel, where I was to spend a night or two, sent an omnibus to meet arriving trains, so I did not have to worry about getting to my lodging. The King's Arms was at the corner of Park Street and Holywell Street and, I was happy to see, was across the road from a small and relatively inexpensive restaurant. After checking into the hotel I took my lunch at a table beside a large window and looked out at the passing world.

It was a fine April day such as one finds only in England . . . or so I have always been led to believe by the poets, at least. The sun, although lacking any great warmth, shone down from out of an almost cloudless blue sky. It was the sort of Friday that encouraged one to turn his back on all thoughts of winter and look ahead to spring and summer with a smile on one's face.

I enjoyed a large helping of Kentish capon pudding, with white sauce, followed by blackberry and apple pie with Devonshire cream, all washed down by a fine sherry. This last was something of a luxury for me, but it was such a beautiful day and I felt so good that I decided to indulge. Besides, I felt some small recompense was due me for being repeatedly dragged out of London and sent off to gather information from the ends of the earth . . . well, from Liverpool first, from Derbyshire, and now Oxford.

As I sat nursing my glass of wine and gazing out at the assortment of ladies and gentlemen, tutors and scholars, hurrying along the pavement past the window, I slowly brought my mind back to the matter at hand: Reginald Robertson. The Oxford Grand Theatre was a small theatre compared to many found in towns of comparable size. Most such establishments bore the name Theatre Royal, but presumably the inconspicuous edifice on Oxford's Fellowship Street was not quite bold enough for that title, even as a sobriquet. Enquiry at the King's Arms' concierge had brought me the information that the Oxford Grand was not too grand at all. It seated less than eight hundred patrons on three levels. In contrast, the Lyceum held more than three times that number. Mr. Robertson's Players had been in residence for two years but, according to my source, consistently with audiences far from capacity. All the more reason why it seemed strange that Mr. Robertson felt he was the heir apparent to the title of Britain's premier Shakespearean actor.

I finished my wine, paid the bill, and took to the pavement. The restaurant waiter had given me directions to Fellowship Street, and I enjoyed the weather and my surroundings as I made my way there without hurrying. A hurdy-gurdy player was entertaining a small group of grubby children and two or three adults at the first street corner, and I paused awhile to enjoy the melodious sound before continuing on my way.

Unlike the ever-vigilant Bill Thomas at the Lyceum, the stage door keeper at the Oxford Grand was not at his post when I entered the theatre. Admittedly there was no performance until that evening, but he still should have been at his post to regulate visitors. I finally tracked him down to a gloomy alcove in the nether regions, where he was making a pot of tea.

"Cuthbert Wellington," he introduced himself, barely looking up from the steaming water he was pouring into an old Brown Betty teapot. "Though most people call me 'Welly.' What was it you was wanting, then?"

"I'm up from London, Welly," I said. "Harry Rivers is the name. Stage manager at one of the West End theatres." I thought it best not to mention the Lyceum by name, given Mr. Robertson's strong opinions. "I'm just visiting the area and thought it might be nice to look in and see how things are done in the provinces."

"You've picked a good example," he said, putting the lid on the teapot and then settling a cozy on it. "You care for a cuppa?"

I was glad he seemed to have some sense of pride in the Grand. He was a short, wizened-faced man with scraggly gray hair, a wispy bit of a beard, and a large hump on his back. He made me think—not unkindly—of a character from a pantomime; perhaps Rumpelstiltskin. His eyes were very dark, almost black, it seemed.

We settled on a couple of dirty, well-worn, upholstered armchairs, each of us with a mug of steaming tea in his hands. I think my host was glad of the company. I looked around and, in the gloom, made out old playbills drawing-pinned to the walls. There didn't seem to be any recent ones; all were from twenty or thirty years ago.

Suddenly a young boy, about fourteen years old—just a few years older than Miss Terry's son Edward—popped into the tiny room and dropped down cross-legged on the floor.

He had a dirty face and tousled fair hair that had a reddish tinge to it, making me feel a certain affinity to him. He grinned at me but said nothing.

"This here's Rufus," volunteered Welly, without enlarging on the boy's position or duties. "You want a cuppa, Rufus?"

"Nar. Just 'ad a ginger beer."

"Suit yourself. Now, where were we?"

"I was going to ask you about Mr. Roberston's company." I said. "How is it?"

He shrugged. "It's working," he said, noncommittedly, and slurped his tea noisily. "I've been here a goodly number of years and seen 'em come and go. This one's all right, I suppose."

"I have heard that Mr. Robertson is a fine interpreter of the works of the Bard."

Again he shrugged. "Don't watch it myself. Stick to the stage door area, and my little rest room here. I hears 'em clapping and sometimes laughing." He looked up at me, a smile on his face, and winked. "Mostly at the comedies."

I smiled back. I sensed I might be able to draw him out. "I'll bet you have a wealth of stories you could tell, eh, Welly?" I sipped my own tea, trying to look appreciative despite the tiny amounts of both milk and sugar that had been available.

"You could say that." He nodded, and then glanced about him as though to be certain we were alone. "Theatre's always a place of superstitions, but then you'll know that being in the business yourself."

"Indeed." It was my turn to nod. "What? Do you have ghosts here, then, or something like that?"

"Only in that *'Amlet*, eh, Welly?" put in Rufus, his grin widening.

"Witches is more like it," said the older man, his face suddenly serious.

"*Macbeth*?" I asked.

"Oh, more real than that," said Wellington. The boy

stopped grinning and looked anxiously at him. "Now don't you go getting scared, Rufus. We've talked about this afore. What did I tell you?"

"You said it weren't real," the boy replied.

"That's right. Leastwise, no more real than most of what he plays around at."

"He?" I asked. "You mean Mr. Robertson?"

Again the humpbacked man had a quick glance around. He lowered his voice a little. "He don't make no secret of the fact that his grandmother were a witch . . . and he makes good use of that, from all accounts."

I sat quietly for a moment, so as not to frighten him off the subject. A dozen questions buzzed around in my head. Eventually, after another drink of tea, I said, "He does 'witch stuff,' whatever you call it, then, Welly?"

"You know 'e does!" put in Rufus.

"Shh!" Wellington again looked all about him, and his voice dropped even lower so that I had to sit forward to catch what he was saying. "Every time there's a full moon, he goes below stage at midnight and him and two or three others get together and . . . do things!"

"We've spied on 'im!" cried the boy.

"Shh!" The hunchback looked quite alarmed. "Now you just bite your tongue. You know what I've told you."

"Sorry, Welly."

"Next week, just seven days from now, it's a full moon. He'll be at it again then, believe me," said the older man.

I drank the rest of my tea. "What exactly does he do? What's the purpose?"

"Purpose? To be the best of 'em, I reckon. And I won't say he's not trying to do away with the others. That's why he does the sacrifices."

Chapter Eleven

Before I had a chance to ask about the sacrifices we heard footsteps coming along the passageway, from the outside stage door.

"Lor' but that's probably him!" cried Wellington. "Quick, Rufus, get out Mr. Robertson's teacup in case he wants a drop."

The boy scampered around to a cupboard, brought out a fancy, delicate Staffordshire bone china cup and saucer, and placed it reverently in the center of the otherwise messy tea-making area. No sooner had he done so than a face appeared around the doorpost. I presumed it to be Reginald Robertson himself. He was of medium height—nowhere near the imposing six feet two inches of the Guv'nor—with dirty blond wavy hair framing a young face bare of beard or mustache. His eyelids drooped as though he were perpetually bored. His clothes were fine, at the height of fashion, and he carried gloves, top hat, and cane. A diamond—albeit small— glistened in his cravat. His eyes immediately alit upon me.

"We have a visitor, Wellington?"

His voice, slightly high-pitched, sounded equally bored. After making the observation he lingered no longer on myself but glanced at the Brown Betty.

"Ah, tea! My usual. Two lumps. Just a hint of milk. Three digestive biscuits. Get the boy to bring it to my dressing room."

He turned away, and we heard his footsteps move off along the hallway.

The hunchback jumped to his feet and swiftly poured the requested tea. "Here! Look lively now! Don't go slopping it into the saucer."

Rufus swung into action, opening a biscuit barrel and extracting three biscuits, which he dropped onto a plate matching the cup and saucer. Gathering up all, he had gone in a trice.

Wellington breathed heavily and then poured himself another mugful of tea. He didn't offer me any more, but it looked as though that was the last of the pot.

"So that's the would-be-great Reginald Robertson?" I said. "Not the friendliest of people, if I may say so."

" 'Friendly' is not a word known to Mr. Robertson," replied Welly, lowering himself once more into his arm-chair. "He must've thought you was a mate of mine or he would have had you thrown out. Come to think of it, he was in a remarkably good mood, seems to me."

"Was he now?" I murmured.

I stayed awhile longer but had no opportunity to return the doorkeeper to the subject of witchcraft. I did, however, seem to strike a friendship, if only temporary, and promised to stop by again the following day.

I was fortunate to find myself dining at a table next to a second-year student of Christ Church College, known among its members as "The House." The undergraduate's name was Claude Baird-Parker. He was dining alone, as was

I, and suggested we get together for company. I was quite agreeable to the idea and moved across to sit opposite him.

"Can be a bit of a bore at times," he said, tucking into the roast beef and Yorkshire pudding we both settled upon. "A chap likes to stay independent and not get caught up in one or other of the cliques so prevalent around here," he said, helping himself liberally to the horseradish sauce.

I nodded and murmured some response that I hoped seemed to indicate that I knew what he was talking about.

"You've been through all this, I'm sure, old man, so you understand." He smothered mustard along with the horseradish onto his beef and nodded appreciatively as he sank his teeth into a forkful.

"You are in your second year here, is that what you said?" I asked. He grunted assent and went on chewing. "Forgive me, I'm not that familiar with Oxford," I continued.

He stopped and looked up at me, his eyes wide. "You're not a Cambridge man, are you, for heaven's sake?"

"No, no!" I hastened to assure him. "No, I'm . . . from the south. I have always admired Oxford."

"Can't be too careful," he said, as though Cambridge people were continually trying to insert themselves into the Oxford environs. He returned to his meal, carefully separating the Brussels sprouts from the peas and carrots.

I got the feeling that young Mr. Baird-Parker did not have a lot of friends. He had a mop of dark brown hair, worn overlong and brushing acquaintance with his shoulders. In contrast, a beard and mustache tried desperately to take hold of the lower section of his face but with little success. We ate in silence for a while.

"Christ Church," I said. "That is one of the larger of the colleges, is it not?"

"Probably the largest," he said, with some satisfaction. "Founded by Cardinal Wolsey in 1525." He sounded as though he was quoting from a college brochure. "Two hundred to two hundred and fifty undergraduates."

"You have a lot of great libraries around here, I understand." He nodded. "I was wondering how familiar you might be with something I recently came across?"

He raised an eyebrow.

I took a deep breath and hoped that I was remembering Mr. Stoker's pronunciation correctly. "*Walpurgisnacht*," I said.

The eyebrow lowered again, and he concentrated on dissecting the rest of the roast beef. "Isn't that at All Hallows' or something?" he said.

"I was told Beltane."

He looked about the tabletop and spied the gravy bowl. He treated himself to a generous helping of the dark brown liquid.

"Ah yes. The other half of the year."

"Excuse me?"

"Beltane and Samhain—or All Hallows' Eve—are two of the main festivals of the old pagan calendar. Yule and Lughnasadh are the other two."

"So . . . *Walpurgisnacht*?" I asked again.

"That's the German—well, West European—name for Beltane, or May Eve."

"And they have some significance?" I pursued.

"I did a paper on pre-Christian paganism and delusions of witchcraft a while back," he said. "They used to break down the year into the light half and the dark half, like the summer months and the winter months," he volunteered. "Beltane and Samhain were the two turning points."

"So *Walpurgisnacht* was the end of winter and the start of summer?"

He nodded, cleaning his plate and then pushing it away from him. "Important dates. Big ceremonies. Turn of the year, with sacrifice, death, and rebirth."

"What do you know of these ceremonies?" I asked.

"No one knows a lot," he replied. "It was a long time ago they indulged in all that nonsense."

"They don't still do them, then?" I asked.

He waved a hand. It seemed to me he was trying to imply that he knew more than he actually did know. "Oh, I'm sure in some backward areas of Europe there are peasants who still worship the Old Gods." He laughed without humor. "Not at all our sort of thing, old man."

"No. I suppose not," I agreed. We both sat back and awaited dessert.

"Did they do sacrifices at all of their festivals?" I asked, once we were settled with large helpings of gooseberry tart and cream.

Claude shook his head. "I don't think so. Just certain of them, as I recall."

"So it would be unusual for there to be, let's say, a ritual sacrifice at three consecutive celebrations?"

Claude put down his spoon and fork and studied me. I had come to recognize that for this undergraduate to stop eating was an unusual event in itself. "What are you on about, Harold? You seem to be more than just a little bit curious."

I decided to come clean. Without going into details, I told him a little of the investigations both in Liverpool and in London and of trying to be of assistance to Scotland Yard. His face was a picture. His lower jaw had dropped, and his mouth hung open. His eyes had grown wide.

"Scot—Scotland Yard?" he stammered. "You are with the police?"

"No! No, Claude," I hastened to assure him. "No, I am working in an entirely amateur capacity. It's just that, well, since these two murders occurred on these specific dates, I thought you might have access to knowledge, through your great college libraries, and to information I had not."

The slight flattery seemed to work. His mouth closed,

and he picked up his utensils and went back to devouring his gooseberry tart.

"I am but a lowly second-year student, Harold. Would that it were not so. You should speak with my tutor. I could probably arrange it."

"No. Don't worry," I said. "I have a well-versed mentor back in London who probably knows more than anyone. I was just curious, since I am here in Oxford, as to whether there was anything obvious that I had not thought about."

"Suit yourself."

Claude Baird-Parker seemed slightly miffed, as though by my questions I had offered something delectable and then withdrawn it. It couldn't be helped. An early evening conversation had got slightly out of hand, I felt. It was entirely my fault. Yet not sufficiently that I felt any need to apologize. We finished our meal with a demitasse of coffee apiece and, after a formal handshake, went our separate ways.

The following morning I again ventured around to the Oxford Grand. My thought was that sometime during the morning I might be able to speak to one or two of the company and get their thoughts and feelings on their leader. Cuthbert Wellington had mentioned that Reginald Robertson was planning a read-through of their next production, *Julius Caesar*. I was surprised they were already looking at a follow-up to *Coriolanus*. I wondered if perhaps they might draw larger houses if they extended the run of each production but then, on reflection, realized that it was probably only by presenting a variety of plays that they were able to maintain sufficient interest to fill the seats. Wellington seemed not unpleased to see me and installed me on a stool behind him, in his cubicle next to the stage door.

"They'll be in and out all morning," Welly explained, "so I've got to be up front. Don't you worry none though, Harry.

We'll squeeze in a pot o' tea later, you see." He gave me a wink and a nod of the head. As unprepossessing as his appearance most certainly was, I found Cuthbert Wellington to be a friendly personality.

"Where might young Rufus be?" I asked.

"Oh, he's about, trust me. He'll be here like magic when I brew the tea."

The outside door slammed, and I recognized Reginald Robertson's voice as he entered the theatre, his Yorkshire dialect evident despite his attempts to hide it. He was deep in conversation with another man, taller than himself, and they walked past the stage door keeper's cubicle without any acknowledgment of Wellington's presence, despite the hunchback's wishing them a good morning.

"I'm sure they've got a lot to discuss," Welly said, obviously aware of their ignoring him.

I grunted agreement. "Who was the fellow with him?" I asked.

"Lancelot Nightingale. You may have heard of him. He's in all the productions. I think he's down for the title role in *Julius Caesar*. Mr. Robertson will, of course, play Brutus."

One of the Guv'nor's favorite roles, I thought to myself. *Well, everyone is entitled to play whatever he believes is right for him.* "Tell me, Welly, if you would," I said out loud. "All this nonsense reported in the press. Does Robertson really think he's a better actor than Henry Irving?"

"Oh, he believes it, all right. Henry Irving, John Parselle, William Macready, Charles Kean, Beerbohm Tree . . . the lot! Yes, he truly thinks he is God's gift to the theatre; the Shakespearean theatre, at least."

"But surely these poor houses you have—you must have trouble paying the bills—and the terrible reviews . . . doesn't anything get through to him?"

The hunchback shook his head and gave the slightest of smiles. "He believes what he wants to believe and never mind the rest! Besides, his faith lies in his grandmother's old rituals."

"Magic?" I said.

He nodded, and then grinned. "Oh, you don't have to tell me, Harry! But you'd be surprised at how many people do believe that nonsense. I've known actors I looked up to, who I thought were more intelligent than most, I've seen them in fear and trembling, shaking like a tree in a thunderstorm when they thought they had inadvertently crossed Mr. Robertson."

"You mean, he rules here by fear?"

"That's about the length and the breadth of it. He does some of his mumbo jumbo, and everyone bows down to him. Crazy, isn't it?"

"It is indeed. Tell me . . . you mentioned sacrifices?"

He nodded his head. "Catches black cats and kills 'em. Terrible."

"Cats?"

Again he nodded.

An hour or so later I had managed to have a few words with three or four of the company, and then, as the play-reading proceeded on the stage, Wellington and I moved back to his cozy, if dimly lit, alcove and enjoyed a cup of his strong tea. As the hunchback had predicted, Rufus suddenly bounded into the space like a released jack-in-the-box.

"'Ere we are then, Welly! 'Allo, 'Arry."

"Here! That's Mr. Rivers to you, boy!" snapped Wellington.

"Sorry." The boy grinned at me, and I nodded that I was not offended by the familiarity.

"What do *you* know of Mr. Robertson's magical rituals, Rufus?" I asked.

The grin quickly disappeared, and he scratched his head, frowning at the ceiling as he thought.

"Don't know nothin' but what Mr. Wellington tells me,"

he said. "Though, o' course, there's always Mr. Robertson's 'Big Book' as 'e keeps in 'is dressing room."

"His 'Big Book'?" I repeated.

"You don't know nothing about that, young Rufus," snapped Welly. "That's just hearsay."

"What say?"

"Hearsay. Things that you've just heard other people saying."

"No, it ain't, neither, Mr. W.," Rufus protested. "'E's got a book. all right. I know. I seen it."

There was a sudden silence. Cuthbert Wellington had been vigorously stirring sugar into his second serving of tea, and his hand stopped, causing tea to splatter over the rim of the cup.

"What do you mean, you've seen it?"

"Just what I says. I seen it. In 'is dressing room."

"When were you ever in Mr. Robertson's dressing room?"

The young boy looked defiantly at the hunchback. "When there was that water leak what 'e complained about. You remember! Some pipe cracked, or something, last winter, and 'e claimed 'is 'ole dressing room was flooded." He sniffed. "Flooded, my arse!"

"Here! You watch your language, young man."

"Sorry. But it's true. You remember now?"

Wellington went back to his tea stirring and then sat down with the fresh cup. "Hmm. Yes. I do remember. But you weren't in there for long. Just had to move some things for him and then the plumber went in there."

"I was in long enough to see what I seen," mumbled Rufus, and he flung himself down in a corner.

"Exactly what was this book?" I asked, looking at both Wellington and the boy. "What did it look like? Was it open? Did you see inside it? Have you seen it yourself, Welly?"

The hunchback seemed reluctant to answer but finally did. "Long time ago I saw it. Didn't take much note of it at the time. Wish I had done. It's an old leather-bound book. Dark red leather. Looks real ancient. My guess is it was his grandmother's."

"I seen in it," volunteered Rufus.

Wellington looked surprised.

"You did? What was in it?" I asked, truly curious.

The boy shrugged. "Dunno. I can't read."

Welly and I looked at each other for a moment, and then we both burst out laughing.

"So much for the secrets of magic!" cried the hunchback, wiping a tear from his eye.

"What do his fellow actors think of Mr. Robertson?" I asked.

He gave me one of his noncommittal shrugs. "They're glad to be employed. Of course, there's Mr. Renfrew. He's very long-suffering."

"Mr. Renfrew?"

"Mr. Stewart Renfrew. He's Mr. Robertson's understudy. He's treated something cruel. I don't know how he puts up with it. One of these days he's going to fight back, don't you know it."

I raised my eyebrows. Welly took it as a sign of interest and continued.

"Robertson will pretend to have a sore throat . . ."

"Or a bad cough," put in Rufus.

"Mr. Renfrew will go on in his place and then Robertson will claim that he made a mess of the whole play and blame him for every bad review we get, even when they refer to Robertson himself."

"Is Mr. Stewart a bad actor?" I asked.

Rufus vigorously shook his head.

"He's much better than Robertson," said Welly.

Rufus disappeared shortly after that, and I didn't see him again until I was taking my leave. There was a train back to London in the late afternoon, and I felt that if I could be on it then I'd have all of Sunday morning to report my findings to Mr. Stoker, and I would be assured of meeting with Jenny come the afternoon. I thanked Welly Wellington for his time and his company, assuring him that any time I found myself back in Oxford I would look him up. I returned to my hotel and packed my bag.

I was at the railway station boarding the train when I heard a shout. The guard had blown his whistle, and the engine was blowing steam and spinning its wheels as it strained to start moving the carriages. I was leaning out of the window and saw a small figure that I recognized dart under the arms of the stationmaster, trying to check for tickets, and hare along the platform to where I was starting to move.

"'Ere, 'Arry!" Rufus gasped, thrusting a soiled newspaper-wrapped package up at me. "Take it. You can do summat with it, I'm sure."

As I took the package from him he twisted away, dodged the stationmaster again, and ran off out of the station yard. The London train bore me away, and I couldn't help smiling. I would miss both the hunchback and the waif.

As the train left Oxford and settled into a steady rattle over the rails, I sat back in the carriage, which I had to myself, and unwrapped the precious package. I gasped at what was inside. It was Reginald Robertson's grandmother's book of magic. Rufus must have stolen it out of his dressing room while they were all busy reading *Julius Caesar*.

Chapter Twelve

"So this is Reginald Robertson's grandmother's famous book of witchcraft?" Abraham Stoker sat at his desk looking down at the dark red leather-bound book that I had laid in front of him. "Your young friend took quite a chance, taking this from the man."

I nodded. "I know it, sir. And to tell you the truth, I'm somewhat worried for him. If Robertson finds out that Rufus took it, there will be hell to pay, pardon me for saying so."

"I agree."

Stoker sat back in his chair and fingered his beard. I was anxious for him to open the book, that I might listen to his appraisal of it, but he seemed in no hurry to do so.

"Have you contact with the boy?" he continued. "If harm should come to him, would you have any way of knowing?"

"Welly—Cuthbert Wellington—would, I'm sure, find some way of getting word to me," I said, hoping that what I said was true. "He seemed to take an almost paternal interest in the boy. I have no idea what the true relationship is between them, but he does seem to care."

"Hmm." Stoker nodded his head and then returned his attention to the book in front of him. He opened it, not at the beginning as I would have done, but in the middle. He then turned pages back and forth, investigating various entries at random before finally settling on the early pages.

"Much as I anticipated," he murmured.

"Sir?" I edged around behind him so that I could see what he was seeing.

The pages were covered with thin, spidery handwriting that wavered across them in irregular lines. Here and there short articles and paragraphs, on pieces of paper clipped from other books or periodicals, had been pasted in. Diagrams and formulas dotted the pages. Many were the inkblots and smudges.

"There is a great deal of folklore here," said my boss, tapping the pages with his forefinger. "Probably passed down from generation to generation. Along with that is much 'borrowed' material—to put it kindly—from such traditional works as *The Greater Key of Solomon* and *The Lesser Key of Solomon*, *The Arbitel*, *The Red Tree of Gana*, *The Heptameron*. Here!" He stabbed a crudely drawn illustration. "The ubiquitous Seal of Solomon."

"Looks a bit like that chalk drawing where we found poor Nell Burton," I suggested.

"Very similar, Harry. Very similar. Good."

I felt pleased. "But what does it all mean, sir?" I asked.

"What, indeed?" He ran his fingers through his beard and then scratched the top of his head. "Robertson's grandmother seems to have accumulated a hodgepodge of high and low magic. Now how much of it she understood, and could safely use, I don't know. And that must apply equally to Robertson. He has this inherited wisdom—and believe me, Harry, there is a great deal of true wisdom buried in here—but is he capable of allowing it to work for him?"

"Work for him?" I echoed.

The big head nodded slowly up and down. "Oh yes, Harry. A definition of magic says that it can cause events to bring about the very course that the magician desires."

I frowned.

"He can make things happen that he wants to happen," Stoker elaborated. "You remember, I told you something of this when we first found those chalk markings at the site of poor Miss Burton's murder."

I felt uncomfortable. "I remember, sir," I said. "But surely no man can really do that?"

Again he tapped the pages before him with his forefinger. "This is no more nor less than a book of instruction for that very ideal."

"So how would this apply to what Robertson is trying to achieve in the theatre?"

"If he knows what he is doing—*if* he can manipulate the forces that may be conjured—then Mr. Robertson could wield tremendous power not only over his own career but also over those other careers that he wishes to curtail."

"Mr. Irving's?" I was incredulous.

"Oh, most decidedly, Harry. Most decidedly."

Sunday afternoon came at last, and I hurried over to Grafton Street. Jenny was just coming out of number 15a as I got there, and with her on my arm, we proceeded in the direction of Grosvenor Square, our final destination being Hyde Park. It was a beautiful April day, with the sun warmer than we deserved and hardly a cloud in the clear blue sky. Jenny wore a cream-colored dress highlighted with pale green ribbons, and she carried a matching parasol. On her head rested a straw turban trimmed with dark green taffeta silk and quill. She looked a picture of loveliness, I thought.

I listened as Jenny related how her week had gone. I

sensed that she needed to speak of it in order to relieve any small tensions that may have built within her. There was nothing, apparently, of any great consequence, but she seemed to delight in sharing with me the many little crises of belowstairs life and the far fewer triumphs in the duties of a maid. Apart from her releasing any stress, I just enjoyed listening to Jenny's sweet, melodic voice and found myself with a wide smile of satisfaction as I beamed at all about me.

"But I prattle on," she said, with a small giggle. "Tell me about *your* week, Harry. How is Mr. Stoker?"

"He is well," I replied. "In fact, I have never known him as anything but well. The man has an iron constitution, it would seem." I went on to tell her, in general terms, of my visit to Derbyshire and then on to Oxford. She listened, enthralled, as I told her of Reginald Robertson, Welly, and Rufus.

"You lead such an exciting life, Harry," she said, her eyes sparkling. "Far more so than mine."

"Are there not moments to relieve the boredom?" I asked.

"Actually, now that I think of it, there are occasional little changes. That is the delight of working in Mr. Irving's home. For example, during the time you were away the American gentlemen came to lunch one day. Tuesday, I think it was."

"Mr. Booth?" I asked.

She nodded. "Yes. He and his manager—is that what he is?" I nodded. She continued. "I don't like that man. A colonel, they call him. He doesn't seem much like a military gentleman to me."

"Why do you not like him?"

"It's the way he looks at me," she said. "He seems to look me up and down whenever he sees me. He doesn't look at the other maids like that."

"Well, Betsy and Susan are nowhere near as pretty as you, Jenny."

She blushed and shushed me. "No, really, Harry. He *looks* at me. He doesn't just notice me or glance at me, as you would expect with a gentleman and a maidservant. I don't like it."

I didn't like it, either, but I didn't want to upset or worry Jenny. "I'll mention it to Mr. Stoker," I said. "But I suspect that he will just say you should feel flattered."

"Oh no!" she cried, her hand going to her throat. "No, don't say anything to him, Harry. Please. It's really nothing to make a fuss about. Probably just my imagination." She flashed me a smile. "I don't want Mr. Irving thinking I'm a blatherer. Just let it go. I'm sure it's nothing."

We entered Hyde Park through the Grosvenor Gate and strolled in the direction of the Serpentine. We were not alone in being drawn to the clear blue water on such a beautiful day. My plan was to take out Jenny on a boat on the Serpentine River, but every single one of the vessels was in use, so we strolled on over the bridge and into Kensington Gardens.

"Is this Mr. Robertson really able to harm Mr. Irving?" Jenny asked, as we walked through the beautiful greenery amidst the freshly blooming flowers.

I had a momentary flash of the big leather-bound book I had last seen sitting on my boss's desk.

"No," I said, perhaps a little too forcibly. "No, of course not." I laughed. "Why, he is just a young upstart Shakespearean actor trying to establish himself in the minor towns and villages. He has a loud mouth, and the Oxford local papers use his ill-considered utterances as fodder for their publications. I'm sure Mr. Irving pays him no heed."

"Yet you say Mr. Stoker had you visit there?"

Jenny was smart, I granted her that.

"Look!" I pointed to the south. "There's the Albert Memorial."

The ornate pavilion, over the seated figure of his late

royal highness, had been erected less than a decade ago, memorializing the queen's idolized husband. The figure sits facing south, toward the elaborately styled Royal Albert Hall. I doubted that Jenny had actually seen it before.

"Are you changing the subject, Harry?" she asked, with a smile.

As I had thought, Jenny was smart. We found a seat in the shadow of a weeping willow, and I told my beautiful lady friend the whole story. Suddenly I felt that I could best protect her—if, indeed, she needed protecting—by sharing with her all that was in my thoughts. She deserved to be treated as an equal, to my mind, and I intended to do that.

"Is there really danger from that book that Rufus stole for you?"

I didn't like the word "stole," and yet it was accurate. I shrugged. "At least the book is safer in Mr. Stoker's hands than in Reginald Robertson's. I'm waiting for Mr. Stoker to go through it and appraise it, Jenny. He knows all about those things. With that business a few weeks back, with that Peter Richland, Mr. Stoker proved to my satisfaction that he knew far more about these supernatural happenings than anyone else I have met."

She nodded. We sat in silence for a while. It was she who eventually broke it.

"What about Rufus, Harry? What will happen to him?"

She had hit on the very thing that had been worrying me; lurking at the back of my mind ever since I got back from Oxford.

"I don't know, Jenny. I must admit that I have a very bad feeling about this. Rufus was acting on his own, of course, when he decided to take the book. I think he did right in doing so. I think it needed to be removed from Robertson's hands, and if anyone can handle it and the power it may possess, that person is Abraham Stoker."

We found a small tearoom on the Kensington Road,

shared a pot of Earl Grey and enjoyed a scone apiece, and then I walked Jenny back to her place of employment. The day remained fine, but both our spirits had been dampened by thoughts of young Rufus. I determined to send word to Welly first thing the next morning to enquire as to circumstances at the Oxford Grand Theatre.

I nspector Samuel Charles Bellamy had not been in my thoughts for quite some time, but he seemed to have the knack of popping up and reintroducing himself at irregular intervals, just often enough to mentally throw me off balance. On Monday morning I knocked on Mr. Stoker's door and entered without waiting for his bidding, as was my wont. He liked to start the day by running over possible problems with me and letting me know of any upcoming changes to our plans. This morning, instead of finding the big man in his usual place, I was confronted by the policeman standing over my boss's desk and looking down at all that was on its surface. A quick glance told me that the witchcraft book was not in evidence.

"Inspector! What are you doing here? Where is Mr. Stoker?" I demanded.

Bellamy had not the courtesy to look embarrassed. Instead he peered at me with his beady brown eyes and pursed his lips.

"Mr. Rivers," he said, as though confirming my presence.

There followed a long silence. I finally cleared my throat and moved forward, trying to assert myself. "Does Mr. Stoker know you are here?" I asked.

"Oh yes. Yes . . . or so we presume. Your doorman said to wait for him."

I couldn't imagine Bill Thomas directing anyone, not even a Scotland Yard policeman, to enter Mr. Stoker's office without the big man's permission. But perhaps there had been some sort of miscommunication. I was saved from further rumination by the arrival of the man in question.

"Harry! Good morning." Stoker paused momentarily on seeing Bellamy but gave no further sign of query. "Inspector Bellamy. To what do we owe this visit?" He moved around, adroitly taking up position between the policeman and the desk. "Have you news of some import?"

Bellamy backed up slightly and then stood contemplating various old framed playbills hanging on the wall. He took his time answering.

"Nothing really new, from the Yard's point of view. We are aware, however, that your young assistant here has been running around the crime scene up north."

"Up north?"

"Warrington." He turned to face Stoker. "Oh, Inspector Whittaker keeps the Yard apprised as to what is going on up there, have no fear."

"But you knew I was going there, Inspector," I protested.

He shrugged. "To Warrington, yes. But we knew nothing about your going to Derbyshire and then to Oxford." He looked at me accusingly.

"Mr. Rivers's work in both those places—and especially in Oxford—was theatre business," said my boss icily. "I do not think it necessary to connect with Scotland Yard on all Lyceum affairs."

Bellamy gave a grunt that could have meant anything, and then started to change the subject. "We seem to recall telling you specifically *not* to go running off up north in search of your missing actor, but . . . no matter."

"He was just a scene shifter, not an actor," I murmured. He ignored me.

"We have reports that both that young man and the other one, Ben Gossett, have been poking about near the scene of the Elizabeth Scott murder," the inspector continued. "What, might we ask, has that to do with Lyceum business?"

"You will have to ask them, when and if you manage to connect with them," said Stoker. "And now, unless you have something of importance to impart, I'm afraid we have much work to do even if Scotland Yard has not."

"Importance?" Bellamy could be infuriating when he repeated what was said to him with no further comment. Mr. Stoker and I waited.

"We have been considering the suspects in these crimes," he finally said.

"You have suspects?" My boss looked surprised.

I was equally so. The police had made no mention before of any possible suspects.

"The various members of the theatre; the fellow actors," the inspector continued. "Perhaps there was jealousy involved. A lovers' triangle, not impossible. Bribery. Blackmail. All of these things need to be addressed and investigated. Any one of them could have led to the murder."

Stoker sat back in his chair and smiled. "Are you, then, desperate, Inspector? Is this the best you can come up with? That someone from the *Hamlet* cast was responsible for Miss Burton's murder, based on typical police domestic disputes? Have you no stomach for ritual slayings? Your ideation is amazing. Please feel free to speak with any one of the cast, crew, front of house, or whomever else you feel falls under your suspicion."

Bellamy remained standing, his eyes focused, unblinking, on my boss. "Perhaps you can tell me a little of the main actors?"

"The principals?" Stoker gave one of his long sighs of resignation. "Let me see. You are familiar, of course, and I believe have already spoken with Mr. Irving and Miss Terry. Miss Grey, who plays the Queen, is one of the principals, as are Anthony Sampson, Guy Purdy, and Arthur Swindon."

"And your views on this lady and these gentlemen?" The inspector's notebook suddenly appeared in his hands, and he quickly found a blank page and prepared to start scribbling as Mr. Stoker spoke.

"I don't know what you would consider pertinent, Inspector. All are hardworking actors who take their job seriously. To the very best of my knowledge, none are involved in lovers' triangles, petty jealousies, or blackmail. But you will have to arrive at your own conclusions after speaking with them. Just do not interrupt any of the performances, please, or you will incur the wrath not only of Mr. Irving but also of myself. And that, I can assure you, you do not want to do. Good day, Inspector."

Bellamy stood a moment undecided, then put away his notebook, turned, and went out without a word.

"Should I have told him the truth, I wonder?" said Mr. Stoker, partly to himself and partly to me. "That Miss Grey would like to play Ophelia but will never be of that age again. That Mr. Sampson would like to play the Queen. Mr. Purdy is most interested in our young callboy, and that Arthur Swindon is only ever just sober enough to go on. Hmm. Somehow I think that would not have advanced the inspector's investigation one jot."

I chuckled. "You sum it up very well, sir, if I may say so."

Bram Stoker settled into his chair and made himself comfortable. He picked up a sheet of paper, glanced at it, and then put it down again. It was time to get back to business.

"Harry, I have learned the name of the man that Colonel Cornell wishes to be part of our company. It is a Mr. Seth Hartzman."

The name meant nothing to me. I waited.

"As we were told earlier, Harry, the good colonel wants to install a face familiar to Mr. Edwin Booth. I presumed from that, that the person would be a member of Mr. Booth's own theatrical troupe, who had come across the Atlantic with him. Yet in the case of this Mr. Hartzman all

I have been able to discover is that he did *not* arrive here with Mr. Booth."

"Does the Guv'nor know about this, sir?"

Stoker shrugged. "It's not something he would concern himself with, Harry. He told the colonel it was fine to bring in one of Booth's men, but the Guv'nor is not going to worry about exactly who he is. He just wants to make Mr. Booth feel comfortable. My guess is that Mr. Edwin Booth does not, himself, know any of these details. In fact he may not even be aware of the colonel's request."

"It makes little sense," I muttered.

"Oh, I'm sure there is sense there somewhere, Harry. Some plan or scheme of the colonel's own, perhaps? I don't know. All we can do for now is to keep an eye on Mr. Hartzman and see where it may lead us. Although his presence is intended for *Othello*, when Mr. Booth is truly part of our family, this Mr. Hartzman will become part of our *Hamlet* crowd scenes immediately, to familiarize him with our operation." He gave yet another one of his deep sighs. "Now! Have we heard anything from Billy Weston, Harry? Are you expecting him back anytime soon?"

"I told them to find out anything and everything they could and then report back, sir," I said. "No time limit. They could turn up at any time."

He nodded. "I understand. All right." He reached behind him and lifted a pile of dusty scripts to reveal the witchcraft book secreted underneath. He placed it in the center of the desk. "Now have a look here, Harry. I've been through this grimoire, and there are some very interesting items contained in it."

I scurried around to stand behind him, peering over his shoulder as he opened the book. He had slipped *Hamlet* playbills into the volume at various points to mark pages. He opened at the first of these.

"See the figure, Harry? Crudely drawn, I grant you, but accurate nonetheless."

I looked down at the figure, not really knowing what I was studying. I could see that it was much like one of the chalk designs found at both Nell Burton's murder site and at Elizabeth Scott's.

"Exactly what is it, sir? What does it mean?"

"It is the sigil for Belial, a king in the hierarchy of demons as recorded by Fromenteau in the early sixteenth century. Belial is second only in importance to Lucifer himself. According to Fromenteau, Belial can bring about promotions of all sorts, but . . ." He paused dramatically. "But he does demand sacrifices be made to him."

I was silent for a moment, trying to absorb what he said.

"Can you explain a little about this, sir?" I asked. "I've heard of Lucifer, of course, but this Belial. Who is he, exactly? What's this all about?"

Stoker waved me to take a chair. "Of course, Harry. I'm sorry. I was forgetting you know nothing of ceremonial magic. Let me explain." He settled back in his seat and gazed up at the ceiling for a moment before starting to speak. I could imagine him lecturing at a college, though he did occasionally look directly at me when making a point.

"As I told you shortly after we found the site of Miss Burton's demise, magicians—true magicians—would, in the Middle Ages, conjure perceived spirits in order to bring about what they desired. They conducted elaborate rituals that had to be performed with care. Generally, they were for such mundane things as acquiring knowledge of herbs, speaking in tongues, fortifying buildings, or revealing buried treasure. But on occasion an especially ambitious follower of this Art Magical would reach out in a major rite to bring about such an audacious act as would demand, from the spirit concerned, a sacrifice . . . animal or even human."

I gulped. I remembered Mr. Stoker implying this when

we found Nell Burton's body, but it hadn't really sunk in at that time.

"So, the magician would be trying to get something specific, but in order to bribe the spirit he would have to kill someone?" I said.

"Precisely, Harry. And I like the word 'bribe.' That is exactly what it was."

"And you think that Reginald Robertson was behind these two murders?"

"I find it interesting that Mr. Robertson is trying to establish himself as the premier Shakespearean actor in these British Isles, and now here we find that he holds a book containing the magical rites that could lead him to accomplish that, regardless of his actual competence on the stage."

I gasped. "So Reginald Robertson murdered Nell and Liz Scott!"

Stoker was silent for a very long time. Then he said, "No. I don't think that he did. I think that was beyond his amateur attempts. I think there is someone much cleverer and very much more dangerous behind those deaths."

He got up and moved toward his Indian clubs. Time for his workout, I thought. I beat a hasty retreat.

Chapter Thirteen

I had spent much of Monday trying to get my mind around the idea of people performing elaborate rituals to bring about the appearance of demons and entities of various kinds, most of which, it seemed to me, were thoroughly unwholesome. Mr. Stoker pointed out how dangerous the practice was, and the fact that many a would-be ceremonial magician had ended up in Southwark at Bethlem Hospital, better known as Bedlam, or at the more recently established Colney Hatch asylum.

"One wrong move, one incorrect intonation, and the demon can swoop in and seize the very reason of the would-be conjurer," Stoker had said. "Yet such are the promised rewards of this odious practice that there is no lack of those who would attempt it."

To my mind, no magical carrot would ever tempt me into the insane asylum. My head was buzzing around these ideas when I entered my office Tuesday morning to find

Miss Edwina Abbott awaiting me. As always, she was clutching her precious tarot cards.

"Yes, Miss Abbott?" I said.

"I'm sorry to bother you, Mr. Rivers, but there is something that I think you ought to know about."

"Oh?"

"Yes, sir. Of course, it's not really my place . . ."

"Miss Abbott! What is it?"

"It's that person as Mr. Irving had us take into our crowd scenes. Mr. Hartzman."

"What about him?"

"Well, sir, it's difficult to put a finger on it . . ."

"Try, Edwina."

"Yes, sir, Mr. Rivers. Well, he seems to stir things up, if'n you know what I mean."

"Stir things up?"

"Yes, sir. The greenroom used to be a nice place where we could all relax a bit between scenes, but now it seems there's always arguments going on there. Mr. Hartzman is forever criticizing Mr. Irving and the way he acts; and I mean, him being the Guv'nor and all . . ."

"But surely no one listens to him, do they?"

"Well, sir, I'd like to say not, but there's a few of the new ones—who just came in for *Hamlet* and as wasn't in the Lyceum for other productions—well, some of them certainly *listen* to him."

She looked anxious, as though uncertain whether or not she should have said anything at all.

What was going on? Was this just some petty little squabble among the extras? There would be no good reason for the colonel to knowingly bring a miscreant into the Lyceum. It was not for me to question the Guv'nor's arrangements, nor even to look askance at the colonel's employees, but I did have concern for the Lyceum cast and crew. A happy theatre means a successful production. A successful production means profits for the Lyceum. Profits for the Lyceum bespeak a happy theatre. It was a continuous circle. I would brook no interference from outsiders.

"Thank you for letting me know, Miss Abbott. I will take it from here. I will ask Mr. Stoker to have a word or two with the person concerned."

"Should I do anything, Mr. Rivers?"

"Just keep an ear open, if you would, please? If there should be anything that seems truly out of line, that is showing it might cause a real disruption of the production, then let me know right away. I will appreciate it, Miss Abbott."

Intermittently since 1705 there had been a so-called Beefsteak Club in London. The first of these had been started by an actor, Richard Estcourt, championing beef. It had developed into a very private club where the members— mainly actors plus a few politicians—wore a uniform of blue coat and buff waistcoat with brass buttons. The buttons bore the symbol of the club, a gridiron motif, which was also found on their cuff links. The steaks were served on hot pewter plates, together with baked potatoes and onions. Porter and port were served, as was toasted cheese. Nothing else was offered. After eating, the table—one long table at which all guests sat—was cleared and the evening given over to revelry.

After a checkered existence, the Beefsteak Club had finally disbanded in 1867, but Mr. Irving had decided to revive it just a year or so ago. It met sporadically, usually late in the evening after a Lyceum performance. Mr. Stoker was an enthusiastic member, and he had even been instrumental in inviting myself as a guest on occasion. I had always enjoyed the excellent steaks served, not to mention the porter.

Today my boss informed me that there was to be a Beefsteak Club that very evening and that he would take me along as his guest. The occasion was to make Mr. Edwin Booth a member of the club. I suspected that Colonel Cornell would also be inducted. As a guest it meant that I did not have to wear the blue jacket uniform as all the regular members did. Such a jacket would be presented to Mr. Booth as part of his initiation.

The room was one that had been used for such club meetings for many years, when the original Beefsteak Club was still in existence. It was part of the Lyceum Theatre, though tucked away at the back where it had some privacy. The room had its own kitchen, of course, and Mr. Irving's personal cook prepared the meal. When I was told of the evening's activity I took the opportunity to pass along Miss Abbott's concerns to my boss.

"We have a useful young lady there, Harry," he said. "It's good to have someone watching out for the Lyceum's interests like that."

I agreed. "So, what are you going to do, sir?" I seldom questioned him on his intentions, but I was curious as to exactly what could be done.

"It's a delicate situation, Harry. As you know, the Guv'nor agreed to this arrangement in return for the colonel's coaching in matters to do with the Freemasons. I hate to upset any balance there may be. And of course, it could just be Miss Abbott's overactive imagination. You know how extras can get into mischief when they are confined in the greenroom overlong."

"She did seem very credible," I said. "And apparently she was not alone in her feelings about what was ensuing."

Stoker nodded his head. "I understand that, Harry. No, I'm not trying to evade the issue. I think that tonight's meeting of the Beefsteak Club might be an ideal time to speak to the Guv'nor about this issue . . . if I can find the

right moment. I'll see if I can't get some sort of an adjustment or at the very least get his blessing on me speaking to
the man directly, without slighting the colonel."

I was content to leave it in Mr. Stoker's capable hands and
went on about my business for the rest of the day. It has
been said that the lot of a theatre stage manager is never a
dull one. So it turned out to be this day.

The Tuesday performance is usually relatively quiet. The
house is invariably about three-quarters full, whereas we
have full houses for the rest of the week. Exactly why that
is, I don't know. This evening the play got off to a solid
start, and audience reaction seemed to be good. I made a
point of passing by the greenroom as often as I could, but
all seemed quiet there.

It was as Act Three got under way that I became aware
of a problem near the stage door. I hurried back to find Bill
Thomas arguing with someone. Bill is not a big man, but
he is quite capable of keeping any riffraff out of the theatre.
I found him out of his cubicle and standing glaring down at
a slight figure in front of him who seemed intent on moving
into the main part of the theatre. I started forward and then
stopped short.

"Welly?"

The short figure's head jerked up, and he wheeled around
to face me. It was my old friend Cuthbert Wellington, from
the Oxford Grand Theatre. His grizzled face broke out in a
wide-toothed grin.

"Harry!"

"It's all right, Bill," I said. "I know this gentleman."

Bill grumbled and growled and muttered something
about people being more polite if they wished for cooperation, then he returned to his seat and his *Sporting Times*.

"Come back to my office, Welly," I said. "We can talk
quietly there, yet I can still keep an eye open on what's happening onstage."

When we were safely settled I asked the one question that was uppermost in my mind. "Is everything all right, Welly? Has anything happened to young Rufus?"

The hunchback's face grew grim. "You've hit the nail on the head, Harry. Aye, it's the boy I've come about. I wouldn't bother you for the world—I know you've got your own theatre to run—but I'm afeard that something bad has befallen him."

"What makes you think that?"

"It were the day after you left." Welly's big face was lined, his eyes wide and red rimmed. "Mr. Robertson was in a foul mood. It seems he'd lost his precious book; his grandmother's one." He looked at me intently. "You know the one I mean?"

I nodded.

"Tell me, Harry, did the boy steal it and give it to you?"

What could I say? Again I nodded. "He did, Welly. He thrust it into my hands just as the train was pulling out. I didn't realize what it was that he had given me until after I had left Oxford and was on my way back here. I would never have let him give it to me if I'd known."

"I'm sure." He gave a long sigh. "The boy has a mind of his own." He shifted in his chair and shook his head slowly from side to side. "Oh, I don't doubt that the wretched book is in far better hands with you than it was with Mr. Robertson. But that doesn't help young Rufus."

I sat forward in my seat. "Tell me, Welly. What has happened? Is he all right?"

"Somehow I don't think he is, Harry. And it sure grieves me. Robertson stormed about the Grand for an hour or more—he has a fearful temper—but he seemed to suspect Rufus from the start. He nearly grabbed the boy at one point, but Rufus darted away under his very arms and skipped out of the theatre. We haven't seen him since."

"But he could be safe, couldn't he?"

The hunchback looked even more miserable and again slowly shook his head, scratching at his wispy beard. "The next morning Mr. Robertson came into the theatre still mad, but saying that at least he'd seen to it that 'the wretched arab' wouldn't be any more trouble. I asked him what he meant by that, and he said, 'Don't think no more about it, Welly. Just don't go expecting your young friend to show up here again . . . or anywhere, for that matter.' It gave me the creeps."

My heart skipped a beat. It did indeed sound as though Robertson has done some mischief when it came to Rufus.

"I was wondering . . ." Welly looked hopeful. "I mean, you've got a good head on your shoulders, Harry. More so than me, I don't mind saying. Is there any chance . . . ? I mean, if you could just come up to Oxford again for a quick visit, like? I'm sure it wouldn't take long for you to find out exactly what has happened to Rufus."

His eyes were so pleading, as was his whole face, that I could say only one thing.

"Of course, Welly. Of course. I'll have a word with Mr. Stoker this evening. We have to go to a special meeting after the house closes. I'll have a word with him then. I'm sure there will be no problem."

"Oh, *thank* you, Harry. You've no idea what a relief that is."

I held up a hand. "I've done nothing yet, Welly. Save any thanks for finding the boy safe and well. Now . . . you have somewhere to stay?"

"A rooming house down the road. Don't you worry about me none."

"Then I'd suggest you go back there and get what rest you can. You may not get much more for a while. We'll meet up tomorrow morning and get on Rufus's trail."

Chapter Fourteen

I t was going to be a late night. Not that this was anything new. I frequently spent uncounted time after a performance checking props, making notes for discussion with Mr. Stoker the next morning, and even helping Sam Green repair and paint a piece of scenery that had been damaged during the play. But tonight was different. As I struggled into a clean shirt and impaled a stiff white collar onto the back stud, I almost salivated thinking of the rich steaks that would be served at the Beefsteak dinner. I did not have a lot of time. Both Mr. Stoker and the Guv'nor had the luxury of changing into their blue coats and buff waistcoats in Mr. Irving's dressing room. I had to rush back to my rooms on Chancery Lane, to make myself presentable.

I did not actually own evening dress. It was expensive, and in my case, it was seldom that it was called for. So, as on previous occasions, I had "borrowed" the appropriate attire from the theatre's wardrobe department. The majority of costumes there were Shakespearean, since that was Mr.

Irving's forte, but in the days when the Batemans owned the Lyceum, Mr. Philius Pheebes-Watson had presented a disastrous production of *Hamlet* in our modern-day dress. It was booed off the stage and attacked by the press as being "anti-English." A number of those "costumes" remained in our wardrobe department, and I felt it my duty to give them the occasional airing. I fixed my cravat, slipped into my frock coat, and hurried down the stairs, eschewing a topcoat despite the briskness of the evening.

I was relieved to find that I was not the last to arrive in the oak-paneled Beefsteak Room. It was usually a small, select group, but this evening it seemed that every seat would be taken at the long table. I immediately recognized the prime minister, Mr. William Ewart Gladstone, who was an old friend and admirer of the Guv'nor's. Mr. Gladstone was in his second ministry. He also served as chancellor of the exchequer (this being his fourth time in that position). One or two others of his cabinet I recognized, though I was not familiar with them all. Sir William Harcourt, the home secretary, was often pictured in the newspapers, as was the Earl of Northbrook, the First Lord of the Admiralty. Someone pointed out Lord Glenmont, a crossbencher from the House of Lords.

I was surprised to see Philius Pheebes-Watson, from Sadler's Wells, in attendance. He is now the lead actor at that theatre and has long been a rival of the Guv'nor's. There had been quite a tussle between the two theatres little more than a month ago when it was thought that someone from Sadler's Wells had tried to poison Mr. Irving. Apparently all was now forgiven, though I doubt forgotten.

Our own Anthony Sampson, John Saxon, Guy Purdy, and Arthur Swindon were huddled together in a corner, awaiting the call to be seated. I was surprised to see Swindon there since he had quite a reputation as an imbiber of alcohol. I seemed to remember Mr. Stoker intimating that the man would not be allowed to attend any further Beefsteak Club meetings after his performance at the last dinner. At that time he insulted a veteran actor visiting from Edinburgh and managed to fall over the prime minister's legs. It was a meeting that I had not attended. I noted that Swindon already had a tankard in his hand, which he was waving about as he spoke with his three cohorts.

"Ah! There you are, Harry."

Mr. Stoker materialized out of the throng surrounding the Guv'nor and Mr. Booth. I couldn't see the colonel but had no doubt that he was in attendance.

"Quite a gathering this evening," Mr. Stoker continued.

"Yes, sir. Distinguished company, as always," I replied.

At that moment Mr. Irving called the room to order and invited all—members and guests—to be seated at "the long table." There was a more or less orderly movement, though I noticed that Messrs. Sampson, Saxon, Purdy, and Swindon managed to be the first to sit. Happily they took seats at the far end and did not try to impinge upon the members and honored guests who habitually sat in the center area.

I recognized two waiters from Romano's, who had obviously been hired for the occasion, hovering in the background, waiting to start serving when given the cue by the Guv'nor. Not that I was ever able to dine at Romano's, but on more than one occasion I had been directed by my boss to deliver a note to Mr. Irving, who was there, reminding him of an approaching curtain time.

I found myself seated across from Mr. Stoker, who sat to the left of the prime minister. The PM, in turn, sat beside Mr. Irving with Mr. Booth on the Guv'nor's right. I saw that the colonel was on my side of the table, opposite Mr. Booth, with the Earl of Northbrook facing Mr. Irving. I was between Sir William Harcourt (seated beside the earl) and Philius Pheebes-Watson.

The aroma from the chateaubriand, baked potatoes, and onions was mouthwatering. The steak was to be served with a reduced sauce made from white wine and shallots, moistened with demi-glace and mixed with butter, tarragon, and lemon juice. I understood that originally the Beefsteak Club's steaks were plain and unadorned, but Mr. Irving's cook had recently started taking liberties, and no one had complained. I couldn't wait for the speech making and inductions to be over so that we could eat. But, catching my boss's eye, I tried to contain myself.

"When Captain James Cook sailed to the antipodes to observe the transit of Venus, he took with him a large number of casks of porter."

I swung around. It was Sir William Harcourt who had spoken. Although not looking directly at me, I presumed that the comment was addressed to me.

"Really, sir? I didn't know that."

He nodded sagely. "Porter is enjoyed around this globe of ours, thanks to such luminaries as Captain Cook."

I wasn't quite sure what to say. Porter was certainly one of the most popular drinks, and I myself was no slouch when it came to disposing of it. I saw that the vast majority of those sitting at the table were quenching their thirst with the black beer. I was about to make some comment about the porter when Philius Pheebes-Watson stuck his head forward and spoke across me to Sir William.

"I understand that porter is giving way to these newer ales. Milds and pale bitter ales. So I hear." Pheebes-Watson's Yorkshire accent was in stark contrast to the refined tones of Sir William Harcourt.

Sir William turned his head and glared at the speaker. "Where did you hear that, might one ask?"

Pheebes-Watson was taken aback. "Oh! There—there have been reports in the papers . . ."

"I saw nothing in the *Times*."

Pheebes-Watson shrank back again. Obviously Sir William was not to be challenged on the subject of porter. I couldn't help smiling. With a snort Sir William directed his ensuing conversation to the earl, sitting on his far side, completely ignoring Philius and myself.

"Well, I think we now know where we stand with Sir William." So saying, Philius Pheebes-Watson lifted his own tankard and drank.

I was not too happy at being cut out of any further conversation with the home secretary. It meant I was stuck with Philius, though happily Mr. Irving came to his feet at that moment, and all thoughts of conversing were put out of my mind.

"Gentlemen!"

The Guv'nor's "stage voice," as I liked to call it, resonated around the relatively small room, and all conversation died.

"Gentlemen, I welcome you here—members and visitors alike—to this our esteemed and historic Sublime Society of Beefsteaks. I venture to state that there is no other of its ilk in the whole of London, and we should feel ourselves blessed to be so intimately associated with it."

There were murmurs of approval, one or two mutterings of "Hear, hear!" by the politicians, and a general thumping of the table by several dozen pewter tankards of porter.

The hint of a smile touched Mr. Irving's lips. He nodded his appreciation.

"At our regular meetings here we enjoy the gastronomic delights prepared by our Mr. Cooke . . ."

Here he stopped and raised his glass—Mr. Irving was a port man rather than a porter aficionado—and all about the table did likewise with their glasses and tankards, acknowledging the somewhat red-faced, white-aproned figure of our chef.

". . . and we leave the verbal badinage until our appetites are sufficiently appeased," continued the Guv'nor. He gave a dramatic pause before continuing, the table hanging on his words. "This evening, however, we reverse that order. I ask you to hold rein on your appetites, gentlemen, if only for a few precious moments. For tonight we have the privilege, nay the honor, if I may so state it, of welcoming into our midst a new member. If only by reputation he is known to us all—especially we of the theatrical fraternity—as a world-class thespian who has made his mark across the waters of the broad Atlantic Ocean. I refer, of course, to our honored guest, Mr. Edwin Booth."

Applause, supported by more banging of tankards on the table, broke out around the room. Led by Mr. Stoker, we all came to our feet and decorum swiftly gave way to shouts and whoops of glee, if nothing else attesting to the potency of porter.

Mr. Booth himself, like all prominent thespians inured to such displays of approbation, stood and raised his own glass, turning first one way and then the other, inclining his head in acknowledgment and appreciation. As the applause died down and we again sat, the Guv'nor waved to Anthony Sampson and Guy Purdy, whom I saw now stood at the back of the room holding bundles of clothing. They moved forward, and I noticed that what they held were the buff waistcoats and blue jackets to be presented.

"Along with Mr. Edwin Booth," continued Mr. Irving, "I would like to welcome his manager, Colonel Wilberforce Cornell." There was a smattering of applause. "Both gentlemen are this evening inducted into our ancient and esteemed brotherhood, the Sublime Society of Beefsteaks. *Absit invidia*. Gentlemen!"

I felt hot breath at my ear. Philius's hoarse voice whispered, "Absent what? What's he talking about?"

I was loath to take my eyes off the proceedings but whispered back, "*Absit invidia*. It's Latin. It means 'may discontent be absent.' Or something like that." I only knew that courtesy of Mr. Stoker. "Shh!"

He sat back in his seat, grumbling about people not

speaking English. I thought of his pronounced Yorkshire accent and smiled.

Guy Purdy walked around the table to where the colonel sat, and then he and Anthony Sampson assisted the two guests of honor in exchanging their dinner jackets for the traditional buff waistcoats and blue jackets. When suitably adorned, they turned to face the Guv'nor.

"Gentlemen, I bid you welcome. Know that any time you visit our fair city you are welcome to join with your brother Beefsteakers and partake of the best that London has to offer. As a token and official insignia—insofar as any of our mutual enjoyment may be official—I would like to present to you a set of gold cuff links, which you will see are emblazoned with the gridiron motif that we have adopted as our emblem. By mutual agreement with the owners of the Waldorf Hotel restaurant . . ." Here he acknowledged an elderly gentleman with bushy white eyebrows, who merrily waved his tankard and smiled around at everyone. "I may advise you that by the simple act of shooting your cuffs and displaying these links, you will experience what many refer to as 'the royal treatment' at that esteemed establishment."

There were again loud cries of "Hear, hear!" and once again much banging of tankards.

Messrs. Sampson and Purdy did the honors of delivering the cuff links, which I noticed were in beautiful silk-lined presentation boxes, to Mr. Booth and the colonel, who graciously accepted them and lost no time in installing them in their cuffs.

"And now, without further ado, gentlemen, I think we have all worked up an appetite such that can only be abated with the introduction of our prestigious and—if I may wax poetical for a moment—almost apotheosized beefsteaks."

To shouts of glee, applause, and the inevitable table thumping by tankards, the waiters moved forward and began serving the meal for which we had waited so long. I ignored Philius Pheebes-Watson's grumbling about the delay and the quality of service and concentrated on my enormous pewter plate, barely large enough to contain the magnificent chateaubriand and baked potato. There was a conspicuous pause in the conversation, the chatter replaced by the clink of knife and fork and the sound of tankards being repeatedly drained and refilled.

I was aware of a wide grin spreading and setting on my face, as I gazed about me at the crowded table. Sir William Harcourt, the home secretary, nodded appreciatively and smiled at me, apparently forgetting and forgiving Pheebes-Watson's earlier faux pas. All was serene, and I felt at peace.

The port and the porter flowed freely, and more extensively as the night wore on. Perhaps I should say the morning, for I knew we would be greeted by the rising sun when finally emerging from the back room of the Lyceum Theatre.

With the meal over, the table was cleared and the participants, drinks in hand, rose and mingled freely. Those unable to rise sat and digested, imbibed more, or—in a few cases—slumped forward and rested their heads where their plates had been. I found myself chatting variously with an enthusiastic young actor down from Birmingham for a visit to "the big city"; a pale and painfully thin poet who couldn't stop talking about the quality of the steak we had enjoyed; and the hard-of-hearing politician, Lord Glenmont, who spouted platitudes regarding the Anglo-Afghan War and the war against the Mahdi in Sudan (I thought I recognized several quotes from the prime minister himself but couldn't be sure). I soon thereafter found myself fending off a loquacious scenery designer from the Drury Lane Theatre. He seemed to think that I might be able to help him gain employment at the Lyceum, despite my protestations that I had no part in any of the hiring.

As I eventually thought about seeking my bed at Mrs. Bell's establishment, I found myself in a corner with my back toward Colonel Cornell. He was talking, in his loud American voice, to a group of five or six bleary-eyed celebrants who seemed hypnotized by his accent. I delayed my departure if only to ascertain what information it was that he was imparting.

"The fella's a scoundrel! Back home we'd take him out and string him up!"

Somebody whimpered while another man chortled.

"If I had my shootin' irons with me . . ." continued the colonel.

"You have shooting irons—I mean guns?" asked the man who had chortled, in an unbelieving voice. He had the affected tone of an upper-class man who has limited time for "the little people." I later learned that he was Clarence, son of the Duke of Oxstone.

"Why sure! Two pearl-handled beauties. Forty-fives."

"B-but you don't carry them around with you. I mean, are they not dangerous?" asked the timid one.

The colonel decided to ignore him and went back to the meat of the discussion. "This Robertson fella needs putting in his place. He's an upstart and an incompetent."

I pricked up my ears. Was he talking about Reginald Robertson? I wondered. His following words left me in no doubt.

"The man's a ham; an incompetent pretender! He couldn't act his way out of a whorehouse in a mining town!"

There was a collective gasp from his small audience.

"Why, Mr. Booth could act rings around him with one hand tied behind his back."

"But surely . . ." began another man. The colonel cut him off.

"And would you believe the methods he uses to get ahead of the herd?" His voice had dropped an octave, and I leaned inward to catch what he was saying. "The man is not above cutting down any who get in his way, if you follow me." He looked around accusingly at the inebriated group of blue-jacketed Englishmen. I had turned slightly, the better to see and hear. What I saw was the colonel drawing a finger across his neck, in the time-honored gesture of slitting a throat. The timid man sat down heavily on the bench behind him, while the others drew closer together.

I was surprised when Mr. Booth's manager apparently recognized me. He pointed a finger at me. I couldn't help noticing a slight shake to it; perhaps he had overindulged in the porter himself?

"Mr. Barry—Larry—whatever, will bear me out. Won't you, boy? This Robertson is up to no good, wouldn't you say?"

All eyes turned to me.

"I—er—that is," I spluttered. I had no wish to be brought into the conversation, yet here I was suddenly the center of attention. "Are you speaking of Mr. Reginald Robertson, of the Oxford Grand Theatre?" I asked, just to be sure.

"None other." He waited for me to continue.

"Well . . . he has certainly made some ridiculous claims in the press. Unsubstantiated, I think we can safely say," I contributed.

"Pshaw!" A trace of spittle ejected from the colonel's mouth and landed on the lapel of his closest listener, going unnoticed. "The man is a scoundrel, let's make no bones about it. A scoundrel and worse!" His heavy eyebrows descended, and he swung his head from one side to the other, directing his dark scowl at all about him. "I am new to these shores, gentlemen, yet what I find here is not all that different from what I have seen in the dens of iniquity in my own country."

"Are you, then, familiar with dens of iniquity, Colonel?" I found myself asking, emboldened by my own imbibing.

His dark eyes bored into me, and I immediately regretted having spoken.

"Mr. Barry Withers," he started to say.

"Harry Rivers," I corrected.

"Whatever! Mr. Withers, you will see that my fears are justified. It may already be too late, but I fear Mr. Robertson's reign of terror is not yet over."

Reign of terror? What was he talking about? I looked about me to see where Mr. Stoker might be. He was on the far side of the room deep in conversation with the Guv'nor, Mr. Booth, the prime minister, and the Earl of Northbrook. No help there. In another corner I saw Lord Glenmont in a huddle with some people I did not know. When I turned back I found that one of the gaping gentlemen in our clique had insisted on bringing the conversation back to the subject of six-shooters and the excitement of the American West. Somewhat to my surprise, I saw Mr. Stoker detach himself from his group and cross to Colonel Cornell. After a few quiet words, my boss reached out and the two men shook hands. I took the opportunity to slip away.

Chapter Fifteen

I studied the face looking out at me from the mirror. It had the shock of ginger hair that I recognized, and the slightly protruding ears that I also recognized. What I did not recognize were the bloodshot eyes, with dark bags under them, the drooping eyelids, and the pasty face. Happily, the mirror did not reflect the throbbing inside my head and the parched throat as I tried to control a swollen tongue.

My half hunter, lying on the dresser, told me that it was well past my usual time of rising and that I needed to hustle. With a final glance at the stranger in the mirror I made a silent vow to reject any future invitations to carouse at the Beefsteak Club and set off to meet with Cuthbert "Welly" Wellington. Mr. Stoker had said that he would join us, though I didn't hold out much hope for him being there early. He and his wife, Florence, lived at number 27 Cheyne Walk, in Chelsea, together with their two-year-old son, Noel, and Stoker's younger brother, George. Stoker's normal and regular daily routine was to take the Cadogan steamboat ferry, which stopped a few feet from his front door, to Waterloo from whence he walked to the Lyceum. I was due to meet with Welly at ten of the clock. I really didn't expect to see my boss before noon.

Welly had taken a room at a small hotel on Russell Street. Alongside the hotel was a tearoom popular with the ladies of the Lyceum. I joined Welly at this establishment for a late breakfast and was surprised, if not amazed, to find Mr. Stoker there ahead of me.

"So you have finally emerged, Harry," he greeted me, the hint of a smile on his face.

"Good morning, Harry," said Welly, half rising from the table where they sat near the window.

"Don't get up, Welly," I said, slipping into the seat next to Mr. Stoker. "Good morning, sir. Yes, I have to admit it wasn't easy crawling out of bed after entering it only an hour or two before."

Welly looked from one to the other of us but refrained from asking questions. Instead he poured me a cup of tea from the pot already delivered to the table. "Thank you, gentlemen, both of you, for meeting with me."

"That is quite all right, Welly. May I call you that?" asked Stoker, stirring three lumps of sugar into his cup. Welly smiled and nodded. "From what Harry has told me I feel I know both you and young Rufus well."

"Ah! Rufus." Welly gave a deep sigh. "I am that worried about the lad." His face reflected his concern.

The waitress came and took our order. Welly declined to eat anything and sat nursing his cup of tea, looking sadly into its depths.

"Tell us the whole story," urged Stoker, spreading a thick layer of marmalade on a slice of toast he had taken from the toast rack in front of him. "Do not omit a single detail."

"Yes, sir."

"You can tell Mr. Stoker what you told me yesterday evening, Welly, if you would?" I said.

"Of course, Harry." He cleared his throat and then focused his attention on Bram Stoker. "The morning after Harry, here, had departed on the train, Mr. Roberston came storming into the theatre in an even fouler mood than he usually has, though perhaps I shouldn't say that, sir?" He looked anxiously at my boss, who gave a slight shake of the head and waved a marmalade-laden knife to indicate Welly should continue. "I suppose he's not *always* in a bad temper but, well, more often than not. Anyway, that morning he certainly was. And why? He started shouting that someone had stolen his book."

"His book?" asked Stoker.

"That thing he says his grandmother gave him. The book with all them magic spells and stuff. He treated it like it was a Bible, if I may say so?"

"So he had discovered that it was gone?"

"Yes, sir. He stormed about the theatre all morning, pulling open drawers, upturning boxes; he made a fine old mess. He was screaming that someone had robbed him, and he made no secret of the fact that he believed the thief was young Rufus."

As the hunchback leaned forward, the breakfast order arrived, and Welly took the opportunity to top up his teacup. I saw that my boss had ordered a mixed grill of fried eggs, tomatoes, bacon, kidneys, mushrooms, sausages, and potatoes. My own bowl of porridge paled by comparison, but there was no way my stomach could sustain such an onslaught after the previous evening's extravagance. Mr. Stoker waved his fork at Welly as an indicator that he should proceed.

"As I told Harry, here, sir, I firmly believe that the book is in far better hands now, though it were certainly wrong of young Rufus to take it and no mistake. But anyway, Mr. Robertson would listen to no one, and when he later spotted Rufus, he charged at him like a raging bull, he did. He nearly managed to grab the boy, but Rufus ducked under his arms, dove between his legs, and scampered out the door."

Mr. Stoker paused in his eating to nod several times approvingly.

"Mr. Robertson stayed mad, and I heard as how he gave a terrible performance onstage that night. Not that there was much of a house to witness it, anyway."

"Did you catch up with Rufus?" asked Stoker.

"No, sir. Never saw hide nor hair of the boy. Then the next morning Mr. Robertson came into the theatre but with a bit of a smile on his face. I wondered what was going on. I didn't dare ask him, but he volunteered the information. He said as how he'd seen to it that 'the wretched street arab,' as he put it, wouldn't be any more trouble. Then I asked him what he meant by that and he said, 'Don't think no more about it, Welly. Just don't go expecting your young friend to show up for a cup of tea anytime soon.' He was still mad, and from time to time throughout the day he cursed Rufus and kept searching everywhere he could think of in case the boy had stashed the book somewhere."

"And you haven't seen Rufus since?" asked Stoker.

"No, sir. Like I said, not hide nor hair." He took a long drink of his tea, which I thought must surely be cold by now. "It gives me the creeps," he said. "Then I thought of Harry and, after a few more thoughts about things, I just left the theatre and took the train down here."

"Quite right, Welly. Quite right," Stoker acquiesced.

"What do you think, sir?" I asked.

Mr. Stoker took his time answering. He chewed thoughtfully for some moments then sat back and looked hard at the hunchback.

"A systematic search must be undertaken, Mr. Wellington. We must obtain the services of as many of your local lads as we are able and put them to work tracking young

Rufus's last movements. Someone must have seen something; seen in which direction he went. Did he have any favorite haunts that you know about?"

"No, sir. He was always a very secretive lad. Not given to making friends easily, if you know what I mean? I don't even know where he lived. He was always slipping away, sometimes for days at a time."

"Did he have a regular job at the theatre?"

Welly shook his head. He went to take a drink from his cup but, finding it empty, pushed it away.

"He had just turned up one day, out of the blue you might say, and struck up a conversation with me. I liked him right away, and we would chat on this and that. It got to where he knew when I would be brewing a cuppa and he'd make sure to drop in about that time." Welly smiled as he recollected. "Nice kid. Not like many of them these days."

"So he wasn't actually employed by the Oxford Grand Theatre?"

"Lor' no, sir! I got to giving him a sixpence once in a while for doing odd jobs, and most others there got to know him and he'd run errands for them."

"I see." My boss's great head nodded up and down as he digested the information. He returned his attention to his breakfast, very soon wiping the plate clean with a crust of toast. Welly and I said nothing, waiting for him to speak.

Mr. Stoker looked up at the clock on the tea shop wall and then pulled out his gold pocket watch. He studied that before signaling the waitress for the bill. As he gave her some coins he looked at me.

"Harry, we must take some action. I cannot get away immediately, with the rehearsals for *Othello* ongoing, but I feel you must go on ahead of me and accompany Welly back to Oxford. I will join you as soon as I am able. You know what to do. Get a search party organized. You have money to pay them?"

I nodded. I always had something set aside in my office for emergencies.

"Good." He got to his feet. Welly and I both stood up. Mr. Stoker extended his hand to the hunchback, who seemed a little taken aback as he took it and shook it. "Have no fear, Welly. We are on the case. You can rely on Harry, here. I know I do. We'll find your missing boy. Now, if you'll excuse me, I must get on to my own theatre."

I sent a message to Jenny, just in case I shouldn't be able to make it back by the weekend, and I briefed the necessary people at the Lyceum, though things were moving like clockwork there. Finally, I went back to Mrs. Bell's and packed my valise. I had arranged to meet Welly at Paddington Railway Station. There was a train to Oxford by way of the Great Western Railway leaving at 1:37 P.M. The return fare was fourteen shillings, and I thought the least I could do was to also pay for Welly's one-way fare of eight shillings. I had learned that he had come rushing down to see me barely able to cover his Oxford-to-London conveyance.

I took the omnibus to Praed Street, the station lying between that thoroughfare and Bishops Bridge Road. I had arranged to meet Welly on the concourse, at the statue of Brunel, the designer of the imposing terminal, and was pleased to see him there ahead of me. He was gazing up at the huge glazed roof, supported by wrought-iron arches in three enormous spans.

"Ah, there you are, Harry," he said. He waved a hand over his head. "We've got nothing like this in Oxford. Must be very grand, living in a big city like London."

"It has its moments, Welly," I admitted.

We traveled second-class and had a carriage to ourselves. It seemed that early afternoon on a Wednesday was not a busy time on this railway line. There was the usual jostling and shaking as the engine got up steam and started pulling its load out onto the track. After just over fifty miles there was a brief stop at Didcot, where the Oxford branch diverges to the right of the main line. Didcot is a little town dating back to the Iron Age. The river there is known as the Isis and there are countless beautiful views to be enjoyed as the railway line crosses a fertile and pleasing area. Beyond Radley the line again crosses the Isis, with Bagley Woods on the left, and to the right there is a fine view of the city with its towers and spires.

"You see, Welly," I said, pointing, "you have much here that we don't get to see in the bustling metropolis of London."

"I suppose you are right, Harry. What is it they say about the grass being greener?"

Welly had said that he would love to have me stay with him while I was there, but regrettably he just didn't have the room in his small flat. I didn't press him on that and assured him that I would stay where I had on my previous visit, at the King's Arms hotel. If and when Mr. Stoker arrived, that would be his choice, too, I felt.

After checking into my room I returned downstairs to the lounge area. Welly had gone back to the theatre to see if there was any news of Rufus and was going to join me at the hotel for dinner. I settled into one of the comfortable chairs near the fireplace and picked up a copy of the local paper. The *Oxford Bugle* was a low-key publication reporting on local events. On page three there was another of Reginald Robertson's rants against the English stage and its failure to recognize his genius. The fact that it was on page three seemed to indicate to me that even in his hometown they were tiring of his tirades.

I was suddenly disturbed by a commotion at the front door. The voice of the landlord, Mr. Timothy Carstairs, boomed through the lobby and into the lounge. I got to my feet to discover Cuthbert Wellington and a group of ragged, grubby children advancing over the carpet in my direction. Mr. Carstairs protested at their dirty boots and general appearance.

"Welly! What is this? Who are these children?" I asked.

The hunchback grinned at me and totally ignored the protests of the landlord.

"Mr. Stoker said to get onto it right away, Harry. I've done what he suggested and rounded up several of the street arabs from around the Grand and thought you'd like to direct us on how to go about the search."

"So no word on Rufus, eh?" He shook his head. "It's all right, Mr. Carstairs," I said to the landlord who, with a glare at Welly and the children, returned to the inner room behind the front counter.

"No word at the theatre," said Welly. "No sign of Mr. Robertson. Curtain-up isn't till this evening so I thought— bearing in mind what Mr. Stoker said—that I should get things moving. I just can't sit around, Harry." His eyes were wide and appealing.

"You are right, Welly. I should have been onto this myself. I think the journey lulled me into a lazy place. Well done! Let's see what we can do."

We all marched outside, the children looking at me intently. I gathered them around me and explained about Rufus's disappearance.

"We are very concerned about the boy," I said.

"We knows Rufus," said the tallest of the children, wiping his nose on his sleeve. "'E's a good'un."

"Yeh. Everyone knows Rufus," said another one. There was a murmur of assent.

"Good," I said. "Well then, you are probably the best people to look for him. You know where he might go. Perhaps somewhere he might hide?"

"No one knows where Rufus goes," said a young girl dressed in a boy's trousers and shirt and with dirty blond hair sticking out at all angles from a filthy cloth cap pulled down over one ear. "'E don't talk much . . . but I like 'im."

"Well, you all have a better idea than myself or even Welly here. I want you to spread out and look everywhere. There's a shilling in it for the first one to find him, or sixpence to find where he has been, even if he's moved on from there. Report back to me here at the hotel or to Welly at the theatre."

They seemed to like that and ran off, singly and in pairs, in different directions.

"We'll see what happens, Welly," I said. "Thanks for getting things moving right away. Now, do you have to be at the theatre?"

"Best I be there for the performance tonight," he said. "I missed the last one, though I got someone to cover for me. But better not press my luck. Mr. Robertson would throw me out on my ear."

I nodded. "Let's have an early dinner, Welly. Perhaps by then there will be some news."

But there wasn't. We dined, and then Welly went off to the Oxford Grand Theatre and I settled hopefully in front of the fireplace at the King's Arms, with a tankard of porter to fortify me.

Chapter Sixteen

Mr. Stoker was as good as his word and arrived on the early train the next morning. After a late breakfast, he complimented me and Welly on starting the search.

"Do you think it might be possible to speak directly to Mr. Robertson, sir?" I asked. "After all, it was he who told Welly not to expect Rufus to show up again."

"Oh, I wouldn't advise that," said Welly quickly. "You don't know him like I do. That could set him off and no mistake!"

"I'm quite sure I am capable of handling the tantrums of one such as Mr. Robertson," said my boss to the hunchback. "But with deference to you, my friend, I will refrain. Besides, I doubt very much that he would have anything positive to contribute to our endeavor. If he really is responsible for Rufus's disappearance, he is most unlikely to give us any clues as to what he did to the boy. And if he is innocent of any wrongdoing, then he can provide little of substance to aid our search. No, I think we need to move ahead under our own steam, as it were, and we can confront the man if and when we have results."

Mr. Stoker proceeded to the local police station to alert them to the disappearance, while I started a round of questioning any who might have seen Rufus after he left the theatre. I started with cabdrivers and then extended my enquiries to news vendors, delivery boys, crossing sweepers, and the like. It seemed that the boy had made a clean getaway, disappearing into the jungle of main thoroughfares and cross streets around the Oxford Grand Theatre. Many admitted to being familiar with Rufus—his cheery grin had become well-known—but none had seen him within the last few days. I thought of how Mr. Robertson must have truly put fear into the young boy's heart to make him disappear so totally.

"We must not give up hope," said Mr. Stoker over dinner that evening.

Welly and I sat with the big man at a table in the hotel, the hunchback moving vegetables about on his plate but not eating. I must admit that I, too, had lost my appetite, though Mr. Stoker followed the line of thinking that the body must stay fueled if it is to operate at full capacity.

"Have we had any word from our search party?" I asked.

Even as I spoke, the grubby blond girl wearing the cloth cap bounced into the room, ducking under the arms of the landlord as he tried to restrain her.

"We've found 'im!" she shouted. "Come on! 'Elp get 'im out!" With that she turned tail and ran back out of the room.

We all three of us came to our feet and hurried after her.

There were others of the search party outside the hotel. They had come with the girl, but she had been quicker and got in to inform us and out again before they had even got through the door. We all trailed after the female figure who, still shouting, "Come on!" was now a distance ahead of us. I learned that her name was Charlotte, though everyone called her Charley.

It was a motley crew of breathless adults and grubby, excited children who finally came to a halt in a muddy ditch behind a half-built and abandoned housing project many blocks away from the theatre district. The evening was advancing and the light was failing, but we could discern a narrow drainage pipe disappearing into the ground. Stooping down, I was able to make out what looked like a bundle of rags stuffed down into the pipe.

"What do you see, Harry?" asked Stoker.

I told him.

"Is it our boy?" he asked. I couldn't help noticing that the missing urchin had suddenly become "our boy" to the big man.

"It's 'im!" chirped the girl, Charley. "I recognize 'is coat."

The figure did indeed wear a jacket with a particularly loud checkered pattern. The figure was not moving.

"Rufus!" Welly got down with his face into the end of the pipe. "Rufus, lad! It's me, Welly. Can you hear me?"

There was no sound and no movement.

"We must get him out," said Stoker. "Harry, can you reach him? Get a grip on his coat?"

As Welly moved aside I stuck an arm down as far as I could. My fingertips brushed the material but I was unable to make a purchase.

"We are wasting valuable time," said Stoker. He looked around at the sea of dirty faces. "Which of you children knows where we might find a doctor?"

The tall, skinny boy, who I had originally taken to be their leader, looked up and nodded. "Doc Schrock over on West Street," he said. "He's closest."

"Run and get him."

The boy was off like a shot, two other smaller boys chasing after him.

"Now!" Stoker surveyed the rest of the children. His attention focused on a boy in a turtlenecked sweater a size or two too small for him. "You, boy. What's your name?"

"Alfred," said the boy.

"Alfred, I think you may be Rufus's only hope."

The boy gasped, and despite the growing dusk, I could see his face redden. "Yes, sir."

"I want you to crawl into the pipe. It will be a tight fit, but I think you can do it."

"But what good will that do, begging your pardon, sir?" protested Welly. "He'll only get stuck as well and then we'll have two boys to get out."

"No, Welly." Mr. Stoker sounded reassuring. "He can't go in too far because Rufus is blocking the way. But he can go far enough to get a good grip on the boy's jacket. We can then haul out both of them by pulling on Alfred's legs."

There were murmurs all around. Some seemed dubious, but I could envision the strong possibility of it working. "Are you willing, Alfred?" I asked the boy.

He shrugged his shoulders. "I dunno."

"Garn!" Another boy chided him. "You won't get stuck. We can all pull on you."

"Yes!" cried Charley. "Come on, Alf! We gotta get Rufus outta there!"

The rest of them suddenly joined in the chorus. "We gotta get Rufus outta there!"

To his credit, Alfred got down on his knees and stuck his head, followed by his shoulders, into the end of the pipe. I had to admire him. I have a fear of confinement. I wouldn't have done what he was doing even if Her Imperial Majesty herself had been trapped in that tight enclosure.

When Alfred signaled that he was ready, we broke into

two groups, one on each of his legs, and started pulling. For a moment nothing happened, and then slowly, very slowly, Alfred's filthy, once-green trousers began to reemerge from the end of the pipe.

"Pull!" gasped the blond girl.

Suddenly we all fell backward as Alfred popped out of the opening . . . empty-handed.

"What happened?" asked Mr. Stoker, as we picked ourselves up.

"S-sorry, sir," said Alfred, breathing deeply. "I just couldn't keep a grip on 'im."

"Then get back in there!" snapped Charley.

Reluctantly, Alfred once again got down on his knees and inserted his head and shoulders into the pipe.

"Get a good grip this time!" shouted one of the boys. There were murmurs of agreement.

Once again we gathered at the projecting legs and, gently, started pulling. Bit by bit, inch by inch, Alfred's lower regions began to come back out of the pipe.

"What's going on here? Who called for me?"

I glanced up over my shoulder and saw a pale, thin figure in top hat and frock coat, clutching a black doctor's bag, standing with the tall boy beside him. It was Dr. Schrock. Mr. Stoker quickly told him what was going on.

"Is he alive?" asked the doctor.

After the briefest of pauses, Stoker replied, "We hope so."

"If he's not," said Welly darkly, "then I swear I will make Mr. Robertson pay for it."

It took all of ten more minutes to get Rufus out of his confinement. We all helped lift him up out of the ditch and lay him on the grass verge. We hovered around as the doctor examined him.

"He is breathing—though only just," was his final pronouncement. "Get him to my house right away."

It was as I traipsed along beside Mr. Stoker, who insisted on carrying the still figure of Rufus, that we learned that Dr. Schrock was actually a veterinarian.

"No matter," he said. "One animal is much like another, human or not."

It was a long night. Rufus was unconscious. Dr. Schrock said he was comatose. We had originally thought that Rufus had crawled into the opening to hide and get away from Robertson or Robertson's men, but it was looking more and more as though he had been caught and badly abused. We reached the conclusion that the boy had been savagely beaten before being stuffed into the pipe.

I spent the night sleeping on the floor at the doctor's house while Mr. Stoker returned to the hotel. Welly stayed at my side. The following morning, when Mr. Stoker came back, there had been no change. Half the children had also slept on the floor, though one or two—those who, presumably, had homes to go to—returned early, bringing pies and rolls with them, which we all fell upon gratefully.

"What is your prognosis, Doctor?" asked Mr. Stoker after the veterinarian had made yet another examination of Rufus. "And I ask you to be truthful. We will get nowhere if we beat about the bush."

Dr. Schrock nodded and then slowly shook his head.

"I have done all that I am able. And I hasten to add that I doubt any other man of medicine could do more. I may primarily be an animal doctor, but as I said last evening, we are all animals of one sort or another."

Stoker grunted in agreement. "Know that I hold you in the highest regard, Doctor. I thank you for your efforts. It seems we must all pray and send our healing thoughts and energies to this poor boy."

I saw that a number of the children had eyes red from

tears. Charlotte—Charley—stoically remained dry-eyed, though I could see that her movements were jerky and mechanical, as though her mind were elsewhere.

"Harry, I ask that you remain here, at least for the time being. Regrettably, I must return to the Lyceum. As you know there is much to do there that requires my attention. The Guv'nor leans on me a great deal, especially with Mr. Booth being there and with *Othello* opening night drawing ever closer."

"I quite understand, sir," I said.

"Get back as soon as you can," continued my boss, "but not before we have a more definite and stable condition for the boy."

It was to be another day before I was able to return to the Lyceum. I then walked into Mr. Stoker's office and slumped down on the chair in front of his desk. I had taken the milk train to get there, and happily, my boss was in his office early. He looked up at me, his eyebrows raised.

I said, "Rufus died."

Chapter Seventeen

It was Saturday afternoon—the matinee—and I had tried to get absorbed in the performance but found it difficult to concentrate without my thoughts continually straying up to Oxford. As I had told Mr. Stoker, Welly had taken it upon himself to see that Rufus would be given a proper burial and had seemed almost anxious to get me away and back to London. I was now concerned about the hunchback. He had not shown the emotion that I was sure was locked up inside him. I felt that he needed to get it out. But, with grim determination, he had assured me that all was well with him and that I should return to where I was needed. I could not argue. The first train to the capital had been at 4:30 A.M. that morning, and I made sure that I was on it. It stopped at every station along the line, picking up milk churns, and we finally steamed into Paddington Station at 8:15 A.M.

"Are we certain that Reginald Robertson was the one responsible?" asked a hushed voice.

I looked up from where I stood in the Opposite Prompt

corner, stage right, watching but not seeing the performance progressing. Turning, I saw Mr. Stoker in the shadows. I nodded my head.

"Everything seems to point to it, sir. He had chased Rufus, and he was the one who made the remarks about the boy not showing up again."

My boss stood there silently for several moments before moving off. I returned my gaze to the stage and tried to focus my attention on *Hamlet*.

Billy Weston was also far from my thoughts, yet he was what I needed . . . someone on whom to fasten my attention and to get my mind moving again along other lines. We still had to find out who murdered Nell Burton and Elizabeth Scott. I was therefore grateful and relieved when Billy showed up in my office shortly after the final curtain.

"You found the Reverend Prendergast, I take it?"

"Yes, Mr. Rivers," he said. "Nice enough for a vicar. Bit too preachy for me, but then I s'pose that's 'is job."

I smiled, for the first time in many days.

"Where's Ben?" I asked.

"He went back 'ome and I came down 'ere."

"Sit down, Billy," I said. "Tell me all about it."

It seemed that the two of them had not wasted any of my money. They had got straight to work and talked, over several days, with the Reverend Prendergast, and then, after that, with various locals in the area around where Elizabeth Scott had been murdered.

"What did you find?"

"Well, Mr. Rivers, the vicar had done some diggin' about, after 'e spoke with you, it seems. 'E said as 'ow 'e'd read over a journal—I think 'e called it—that the *old* vicar had kept."

"The Reverend Swanson," I said.

"That's 'im. Reverend Prendergast said as 'ow it was quite a eye-opener for 'im, was the way 'e put it."

I nodded. "That's good. I think the old vicar had more of

a grasp on what was going on in his parish than does this
new one. Certainly so far as the sort of incidents in which we
are interested. Go on, Billy. Tell me what you found."

"The vicar said as 'ow there was reports in the journal
about meetings of groups of people. 'E talked about them
gettin' together at certain times of the year and dancin'
round bonfires and stuff. Weird things. Creepy, I thought."

"Mr. Stoker is going to love this." I chuckled. "Just the
sort of thing he suspected, I think. Anything else, Billy?"

He started checking his pockets, looking for something.

"I got a list 'ere somewhere. The vicar let me copy it down.
Where is it?" He stood up, the better to dig into his trouser
pockets. "Ah! 'Ere it is." He pulled out a crumpled, grubby
piece of paper, together with a half sovereign and a number
of smaller coins. "Oh, and that's all the money we got left,"
he said. Sitting down again, he laid the scrap of paper on my
desk and repeatedly rubbed his hand over it in a futile effort
to smooth it out. Then he took it up and peered at it.

"What is it, Billy? A list of what?"

"Of the people as was jumpin' about round the bonfires. Let's
see, there was a Sadie Compton—was women as well as men, it
seems—and Ben Staples, 'Arry Westwick, Albert Pottinger,
Bessy Wheatly, Jacob Nugent, Matthew 'Iggins, Matthew
Epson, Sarah Winterbotham, Angus Wilson, and Cuthbert
Nightingley. That's all the names there was, Mr. Rivers, but the
old vicar said as 'ow there was others 'oo 'e didn't know."

I nodded. "Well done, Billy. This will be a big help. I'm
sure Mr. Stoker will want to pass this along to Inspector
Bellamy after he's had a look at it."

Billy sat back, looking pleased with himself.

"Have you been home yet, Billy? Had anything to eat?"

He shook his head. "No. I came straight 'ere from the
railway, Mr. Rivers."

I pushed the small pile of money back toward him.
"Well, take this and go and get yourself something to eat,"

I said. "Hold on to anything left over. If you need to go back to your rooms for a while, that's fine. Be back here before this evening's performance, and we'll both go and see Mr. Stoker and you can tell him all you've just told me. I'm sure he'll have some questions."

Billy Weston had no sooner gone than Inspector Bellamy slipped into my office space. Speak of the devil, I thought. I briefly wondered how he managed to move so quietly in those big policeman's boots.

"Mr. Rivers," he said, as though summoning me to a witness stand.

"Inspector Bellamy," I responded, refusing to be intimidated. "And to what do I owe this unexpected pleasure?" I stressed the last word, meaning it to carry a trace of sarcasm, but he seemed impervious to any such subtlety.

"We have been pondering the whole question of your young lady's murder," he said, positioning himself in front of where I sat.

"I would hope that you have," I replied.

"We are not prone to beat about the bush, so we must say that there would seem to us to be the elements of a conspiracy here."

"A conspiracy?" What was he talking about?

"Yes, sir. A conspiracy." He shifted his weight from one foot to the other and back again, fastening his beady little brown eyes on me.

"Concerning . . . ?"

"The murder of your young actress, Miss Nell Burton."

"What the devil are you talking about?" I cried, and came to my feet. Unfortunately, my lack of height did not give me the ability to look him straight in the eye, but I did the best I could.

"All this talk of ritual slayings and theatrical knives

belonging to Mr. Irving just doesn't make sense," he said. "This is a theatre. You people are actors. You present these dramas, and we do know that you have to practice them. We also know that in your practices things can go wrong. Horribly wrong! In this case, when things went 'off the rails,' as the current expression puts it, then you all conspired to present this ridiculous story of Satanist rituals and human sacrifices. You did your little chalk drawings and then claimed they are myth . . . mist . . ."

"Mystical?" I said.

"No, sir! No! It will not wash! We know better."

I was almost speechless. I wished Mr. Stoker were there. He would not have been at a loss for words, but he had gone to dine with Mr. Irving between performances. I had to handle this on my own.

What would Mr. Stoker have done? I felt that he would have tried to make the inspector see how ridiculous was his charge. I sat down and even managed to smile up at the imposing figure before me.

"Won't you sit down, Inspector?"

He remained standing and glaring down at me. I swallowed.

I raised my hand and extended my fingers. I began to count off points on them as I elucidated.

"Firstly, Miss Burton was more specifically an extra, not an actress in the general sense of the word."

"Did she or did she not appear on your stage in your play?" he demanded.

It threw me off balance a little, but I tried to ignore it. "You are correct on that score. In that sense, yes, she was an actress." I moved on to the next finger. "And yes, the murder weapon was a knife taken from this theatre and had indeed *once* been used by Mr. Irving. But as we explained some time ago, the Guv'nor had no knowledge even of the fact that the knife was missing."

The inspector said nothing but remained with his eyes fixed on me.

"At rehearsals—rehearsals, Inspector, not practices—nothing goes wrong."

"Nothing goes wrong? Then why do you need to practice?"

I swallowed. It was a good point. "Nothing goes wrong to the extent that you are implying. No actual knives are used in practice . . . I mean, rehearsal. We use prop knives; wood and rubber. Onstage we might use an actual blade, if the performance merits it, but then it is never, ever, a sharpened blade."

"It seemed to do a good job on your young lady's throat."

"Because it wasn't the blade we use in the play!" I cried. "In fact that particular knife is not used at all in *Hamlet*. It belongs to *The Merchant of Venice*. And anyway, if we staged all this, then why would we use Mr. Irving's own knife and implicate him?"

I could hear my voice getting higher and higher as I became more and more frustrated. I took a deep breath and mentally counted to ten.

"Inspector Bellamy, we have been over all of this. Mr. Stoker has been over it. If you want to go over it yet again then I suggest you speak directly to him. He is not here at the moment but . . ."

"The waste of police time is a serious offense, Mr. Rivers. There are penalties for such," he intoned.

"I would think that the waste of time when you could be out finding the murderer would be a much more serious offense, Inspector," I said through gritted teeth, my fingernails digging into the palms of my hands as I clenched my fists.

He stood staring at me for a long time before saying, "Yes. Well, that's as may be." Then he turned and walked away.

I sat seething for the longest time. How incompetent could the Metropolitan Police be? How could they possibly believe that we had manufactured all the evidence to cover up a blunder on our own part? How could they not see that Nell's throat had been viciously slashed? I sat there for a long time. My thoughts strayed once more to Rufus and to Welly. All seemed very bleak.

Chapter Eighteen

I t had been some time since I'd last spoken with Miss Edwina Abbott. Not that I had missed the young lady, but I remained fascinated by her tarot cards. Mr. Stoker seemed to have respect for their prognostications, so I tried not to dismiss them in too cavalier a fashion myself. As I passed the entrance to the greenroom during that Saturday evening's performance, I glanced in and, as usual, saw the girls all huddled about Miss Abbott as she spread out her pasteboards on a table. Seth Hartzman leaned up against the wall, watching them. He caught my eye and nodded in a not unfriendly manner. I paused, and he came over to me.

"Miss Abbott sure keeps 'em happy with those cards," he said.

"Has she read them for you?" I asked.

He shook his head. "Nar! I don't need no cards or such to tell me what to do."

"I don't think that's quite the idea of them," I said.

He shrugged. "I don't need the likes o' them."

I saw an opportunity. "What exactly is your connection with Mr. Edwin Booth?" I asked, as casually as I could.

"Booth? What about him?"

"How well do you know him?" I persisted.

Again he shrugged. "I don't, really. It's Colonel Cornell I know. It was him as got me this job." He looked back at the girls, still crowded around Edwina. "Not that I'm overjoyed with it."

"You have acted before?" I asked.

"Been in and around theatres some, yes."

That didn't exactly answer my question, but I let it go.

"Have you known the colonel a long time?"

He paused before answering, and I wondered if I had overpressed my luck and been too obvious in trying to get information out of him.

"We go back a way, yes. Here! Where's that callboy? It must be near time for us to go on again."

"Edward won't let you miss an entrance," I assured him. I thought to change the subject. "Are you looking forward to doing *Othello*?"

"I do what I'm told," he said, enigmatically. "Go where I'm told to go."

"It was Colonel Cornell who told you to do this and *Othello*?"

"He's a very busy gentleman. I don't get to talk to him a lot." He turned away, back to the others in the greenroom.

I passed on. It seemed that Mr. Hartzman was not causing any disruptions, and that was all I cared about. I moved up to the stage level and stood in the wings watching the play progress.

It was as Act Five, Scene Two, got under way that my calm was disturbed. The graveyard scene had gone well, with the Guv'nor's "Alas, poor Yorick" speech well received.

Saturday evening performances were always the best of the week, with a near-capacity house that truly seemed to appreciate the works of the Bard. Now we were into the last scene, approaching the death of Hamlet. I felt a tug at my sleeve and looked down to see Edwina trying to get my attention and mouthing words I couldn't quite hear. I backed farther away from the stage.

"What is it, Miss Abbott? You'll soon be needed for curtain calls, won't you?"

"Mr. Rivers!" Her voice, though hushed so as not to be heard onstage, had an edge of panic to it. "Mr. Rivers, they've gone. Vanished!"

"What have gone?"

"My cards, Mr. Rivers. My old aunt Jessica's pasteboards. Someone's stole 'em!"

I could understand her distress. I knew that the cards meant a great deal to her, not only for their intrinsic value but for the prestige that they gave her among her fellow actors.

"Are you sure?" I asked.

She nodded vigorously.

"You haven't just mislaid them?"

"No way, Mr. Rivers. I'd done a layout for Ruby Sticks and then, when we was called for the Mourners in the graveyard scene, I left them there in the greenroom. When I comes back, they were gone!"

"You're certain you left them there? You usually put them in the pocket of your skirt, don't you?"

"Yes, Mr. Rivers. But since I'd only just laid 'em down, I left 'em. Thought I'd come straight back to them."

"And you've looked everywhere? Perhaps someone tidied up? Put them away for you?"

"Put 'em where, Mr. Rivers? I've looked all over and asked everyone as was in the greenroom. No one has seen them. I've looked everywhere."

The play was drawing to a close. Hamlet was dead. The whole cast was gathering in the wings, waiting to go on for the several curtain calls we always had.

"Stay with it, Edwina. I'll check into it for you. We'll have all the extras gather in the greenroom before they take off their makeup. Leave it to me."

I tried to sound more confident than I felt. I stood by, ready to summon them all as soon as the final curtain fell. But when I peered out at the lineup taking their bows, I noticed that Seth Hartzman was missing.

I t was late and the theatre was almost empty when I discovered Edwina Abbott's precious cards. They had been stuffed into the hollow skull of "poor Yorick," which lay at the bottom of the "grave," which was in the trap on stage right. Most theatres have a number of traps. In *Hamlet* we used the one at center stage for the appearance of the Ghost of Hamlet's Father and the ones stage right and stage left for the graveyard scene. Lowered slightly, they enabled Hamlet to appear to leap down into the graves; one for Ophelia and the other for Yorick. It was quite by chance—on a whim—that I looked there, and I was glad I did. My immediate thought was that Seth Hartzman had stolen the cards and stashed them there. He would seem to be the obvious suspect. He had missed the curtain call and had not shown up afterward. He was missing from the group I assembled in the greenroom, and I had made a note to pass on that information to Mr. Stoker.

Miss Abbott had been most upset when I finally persuaded her to go home, on the assurance that I would continue searching. I was now glad I had not given up. She would be delighted at their safe return. Since the theatre would be closed the next day, I found a street urchin and gave him thruppence to take the tarot deck around to Mrs. Briggs's rooming house and deliver it to Edwina.

* * *

Sunday came at last. It seemed as though I'd been waiting a month, not a week, to see my Jenny again. It turned out to be a damp, dull day with intermittent rain showers that were unable to diminish our joy in each other. We walked leisurely to Hyde Park and sat on a newspaper I spread out on a park bench, under an overhanging weeping willow, with my umbrella keeping us as dry as was possible. It was the same seat we had occupied the previous Sunday.

I told Jenny all that had transpired since I had seen her last. I didn't dwell upon the contents of Reginald Robertson's grandmother's book of magic but concentrated more on the joys and delights of the Beefsteak Club.

"You are making my mouth water just talking about it, Harry," she said, looking up at me through long eyelashes.

I then had to tell her of Cuthbert Wellington's visit and our resultant rushed return trip to Oxford.

"I had a bad feeling about it, when you told me young Rufus had taken that book," said Jenny. "And you say Welly came all the way down to London because the boy had gone missing?"

I was reluctant to continue with the story but knew that I had to. When I had told Jenny of my original encounter with Rufus, her full heart had seemed to warm toward the boy. Now I had to tear it. I went over the visit by myself and Mr. Stoker, the search for the boy, and his eventual discovery in the drainage pipe. I tried not to dwell on the details of extracting him and of sitting with him in Dr. Schrock's home. But Jenny was made of strong stuff. She listened silently and then nodded her head slowly and sadly.

"It was meant to be," she said quietly. "A young life lost needlessly. So many promising children perish in this modern world. I sometimes wonder at the price we pay for what is hailed as 'progress.' " She turned her head to look up at me. Her eyes were moist. Involuntarily, I put my arm about her and drew her close. She rested her head on my shoulder, and we sat in silence for a long time.

It was not the day of joy and delight that I had been anticipating, being with Jenny again. Yet we were able to find warmth and comfort in each other's company. The rain let up, and we walked randomly about the great park, with Jenny hanging on to my arm. She told me that Colonel Cornell had visited Mr. Irving twice during the week, to coach him on matters pertaining to the Guv'nor's anticipated entry into the Ancient Order of Freemasons.

"You are not one of them, are you, Harry?" she asked.

"No, Jenny. I think that is more for businessmen and politicians," I replied. "People of note . . . and of substance."

"Would it not help you in your career?"

I shook my head. "I don't think in terms of a career, when it comes to my work in the theatre. Someone in Mr. Irving's position may well do, but I am more than happy just working with Mr. Stoker and tending the daily running of the Lyceum. No, Jenny, I don't think I need intrude on the Freemasons."

We ended up, as we usually did, at the little tea shop on Kensington Road, sitting at a table in the window and looking out at the rapidly drying pavement as the sun came out and shone down. I almost asked if Jenny was feeling better but was afraid it might then bring attention back to the loss of young Rufus. Instead, I asked after her aunt Alice, whom I had met at the end of March.

"Oh, Auntie is fine, thank you, Harry. She still talks of our outing to Kew Gardens."

"We must do it again sometime," I said.

Jenny beamed at me, as she poured our cups of tea. "That would be nice. Especially now the weather is so much better."

The rest of the afternoon passed quickly, and finally I walked Jenny back to Grafton Street, at the corner of Bond Street. After a quick look up and down the road, to make sure we were not observed, she gave me a quick kiss on the cheek and then hurried into the house, disappearing behind the black door. With a smile on my lips, I turned and walked away.

Chapter Nineteen

"Today starts the last week of *Hamlet*," announced Mr. Stoker when I entered his office on Monday morning. He stood grasping the lapels of his frock coat and looking down at the mess of papers on his desk, a frown on his face.

"Yes, sir," I said. "Something of a mixed blessing, I think."

"Indeed, Harry. Indeed." He gave one of his long, deep sighs. I thought that at that moment he looked very much like Mr. Irving, whom I know he truly admired. "Yes. The Guv'nor is giving a brief talk to the full cast and crew before curtain-up tonight. The usual thing, of course. Telling them not to get slovenly just because the run is almost at an end. We must close triumphantly."

"I don't think there's any fear of that, sir," I said. "It has been a very successful run."

"It has indeed." Another sigh. "No break for us, though, Harry, eh? The theatre will be dark for a short while, and then *Othello* is to open the second of May, as you know. We have little enough time to prepare. Rehearsals are going well, so I hear. Mr. Booth is a consummate actor who will complement the Guv'nor in every way. I believe London is in for a treat." He paused before continuing. "The *Hamlet* set is to be struck right after the final curtain on Saturday, and then the new set will go up. Costumes are to be finished and fitted. I will be kept busy with programs, playbills, and the like, not to mention priming the press on what awaits them."

"Speaking of the press, Mr. Stoker," I said, drawing the morning paper from under my arm and opening it on top of the accumulation on his desk. "Have you seen that Mr. Robertson is still holding forth? Another tirade against the state of the Shakespearean theatre today—with his usual digs at what he calls 'the old guard'—and demands that his genius be recognized." Stoker grunted. "Happily, the *Times* has seen fit to relegate it to a back page," I continued.

"Any further word from Cuthbert Wellington?"

I shook my head. "Welly seems to have faded away, sir. He wrote to tell me that he has given up his job at the Oxford Grand, after I don't know how many years, but he didn't say what he planned to do."

"Such a shame, that whole episode. Rufus's death was so totally unnecessary. A tragic loss. One can only imagine how Wellington must feel. I have no doubt, in my own mind, that Robertson was the culprit but what evidence do we have? None that would hold up in a court of law. Would that I had it in my power to bring about retribution. Karma will have its way, you mark my words, Harry. But regrettably we may not be around to see it."

I decided to broach something that had been bothering me, at the back of my mind, for quite a while.

"Reginald Robertson, sir. Do you think there really *might* be a connection between him and the ritual slayings of the two girls? I mean, now knowing that he is into rituals, spells, and all that . . . stuff of magic? I did notice that when Rufus was killed it was a full moon, and Welly had once commented that Robertson 'did things' under the theatre stage on such nights. Whether or not he got to Rufus that way, could he have done magic against the two girls, do you think?"

My boss was not as quick to dismiss the idea as I half expected him to be.

"The murders of our Nell Burton and Elizabeth Scott have not been far from my mind, Harry." He took off his coat and hung it on the stand behind him. Straightening his waistcoat, he glanced at his pocket watch and then sat down at his desk. He waved me to my usual chair. "Mr. Robertson does appear to have had the opportunity to do the deeds. His seeming determination to discredit the Guv'nor, and all who tread the boards in the metropolis, could seem to be reason enough for a demented mind to act in so violent a fashion."

"And the ritual part of it?" I asked.

He nodded, his great head moving slowly up and down. "Again, Harry, there would seem to be a distinct connection. From what we have seen of Mr. Robertson's granny's book, there is sufficient information there to imply—at the very least—that he might have employed the ancient arcane arts to better his position."

"With the sacrifices of the girls being part of his rituals?"

There was silence for a moment.

"You see, that is what bothers me, Harry. Oh, Mr. Robertson could easily have traveled to Liverpool for Miss Scott, or where was it?"

"Warrington, sir. Just outside Liverpool."

"Right. Warrington. It's not that far from Oxford. By the same token he could have run down to London, as Welly did the other day, for our Miss Burton. But what bothers me, Harry, is *would* he?" He sat back in his chair and gazed up at the ceiling. "Somehow I just can't see Reginald Robertson with the ability . . . no, the patience! The patience to put together and then carry out what would most certainly be a complicated and intense magical ritual culminating in human sacrifice."

He returned his attention to me, looking me in the eyes.

"It would be one thing for him to lose his temper and strike out against someone like Rufus, as we know he did. But the rest of it? I don't know, Harry. It just doesn't sit right with me."

I had to agree. "But if not him, then who, sir?"

"Ah! Who indeed? Well, Harry, if the evil forces at work—whoever they turn out to be—are following the ancient pagan calendar as we believe they are, then we have less than two weeks to find out . . . two weeks until they make their third sacrifice. Only a fortnight until May Eve. *Walpurgisnacht*, Harry!"

"What's this, Harry?"
"What, sir?"

I was running around getting ready for that evening's performance when Mr. Stoker stuck his head out of his office and waved a piece of paper at me. I changed direction and headed for him, following him back inside his room and closing the door behind me.

"Sit down, Harry. Here! I believe you left this on my desk for me to see?"

I glanced at it and saw that it was the list I had copied from the grubby piece of paper that Billy Weston had given me. I'd had Billy tell his story to Mr. Stoker and, at that time, had left the list on his desk. "Yes, sir. As I told you earlier, Billy got those names from the Reverend Prendergast. Apparently they compiled it from the earlier vicar's journals."

"I remember you mentioning it. But what I'm questioning is one of the names on the list. Here, see? Jacob Nugent."

I studied the name he pointed to. "Yes, sir. I noticed it was a Nugent, but I don't see any reason he'd be connected to Bart. I mean, we know that Bart was in prison when both murders were committed, so . . ."

My voice trailed off as a number of thoughts suddenly came to me. I looked up from the piece of paper to find my boss's eyes fixed on me, the hint of a smile on his lips. He raised his eyebrows in a question.

"You're right, sir," I said, feeling slightly chastened. "I should have checked it out."

"We are dealing with two terrible murders here, Harry. And the clock is ticking. We need to check out any and every instance that looks questionable." He sat back in his chair. "Yes, there is probably no connection between the two Nugents. One is in London and the other near Liverpool, for heaven's sake. *But . . .*"

The word hung in the air. I got to my feet.

"I have to finish getting ready for tonight's performance, sir," I said. "But first thing in the morning I promise I'll get onto this."

"Good man, Harry. I knew I could count on you."

As good as my word, Tuesday morning saw me leaving Mrs. Bell's establishment at the crack of dawn, fortified—if I could use that word—with an underdone kipper and two slices of burnt toast, all washed down with lukewarm, extremely weak tea. *I really should look for better lodgings*, I told myself for the one hundredth time. Yet Mrs. Bell was very convenient for the theatre, and the rent was reasonable. I jumped on an omnibus and headed for Scotland Yard.

"Inspector Bellamy?" questioned a corpulent sergeant, when I enquired for that gentleman. "I don't rightly know as 'ow 'e's in yet."

"Would you ascertain that?" I asked.

"And what did you want with Inspector Bellamy?"

"That is between that gentleman and myself," I replied, somewhat stiffly. I suddenly felt that the underdone kipper was not sitting well in my stomach.

"Well, keep your 'air on!" muttered the policeman, and he shuffled off down the passageway behind the enquiry counter. He returned and gestured with his thumb over his shoulder. "Yes. 'E's in." He busied himself moving papers back and forth on the countertop and proceeded to ignore me.

I walked back along the short corridor to Bellamy's office. The inspector sat at his disorderly desk, staring into a large mug of steaming tea. He looked up as I entered.

"And to what do we owe the pleasure of this visit, Mr. Rivers?" he asked, remaining seated.

"I have a question for you," I said. I pulled the list of names from my pocket and glanced at it. "Jacob Nugent," I said.

"What about him?"

"Are you familiar with the name?"

"Older brother of Bartholomew Nugent." He took a long drink of tea.

"Ah! So they *are* related?" I mentally thanked Mr. Stoker.

"Oh yes. As close as brothers can be. What about Jacob?" He leaned forward slightly and looked hard and long at me. "Is this something to do with our murdered actress young lady?"

I took one of the two seats in front of his desk. He obviously wasn't going to invite me to sit, so I presumed to do so myself. "We know that Bart was spending time in Newgate at the time of the murder, so we didn't think he could be involved," I said. "But I hadn't realized he had a brother."

"So you think that Jacob Nugent was connected?"

"I don't know, Inspector. That's what I've come to talk to you about. What do you know of the man?"

Bellamy took his time answering. He took another long drink of tea and set down the mug. Then he sat back in his chair and drummed his fingers on the desktop.

"As it happens, Mr. Rivers, we have had our eyes on Mr. Jacob Nugent ourselves."

I was surprised. "You mean, you think . . ."

Bellamy held up a hand. "Hold on, now. We are not saying he is a suspect in the murder. He is simply a person of interest at this time."

I sighed. "Of course! Yes."

"Mind you . . ." He stuck a pencil into his teacup and gave the liquid a vigorous stir, for no good reason I could see. The mug was already half empty. He sucked the pencil dry and sat staring into the mug. "Mind you, older brother Jacob is a shifty character and no mistake. We've had our eyes on him over a number of happenings but just haven't been able to connect with him. But he spends a lot of his time out in the suburbs and farther north, and out of our reach."

"That would, then, put him in the right location for the Elizabeth Scott murder."

"It's not impossible."

"Not like the younger Nugent," I suggested.

"You are right there, Mr. Rivers. Young Bartholomew goes in and out of Newgate Prison so much we have been thinking of installing a swing door."

I laughed out loud. Humor from Inspector Bellamy was the last thing I expected. Then I grew serious again. "Tell me, Inspector, do you think there might really be a connection between this Jacob and Nell Burton's murder? Mr. Stoker was only just saying that it would be quite possible for the man to have been at both the scene of Nell's murder and that of Elizabeth Scott."

The pencil clattered onto the desk as Bellamy dropped it. He looked at me sharply.

"Mr. Stoker said that?"

I nodded.

"Hmm. It does seem that on occasion—on occasion, mark you—Mr. Stoker does have an idea or two that might possibly be in the right direction."

I smiled at the inspector's reluctance to give my boss full credit for anything, but it was gratifying to hear him bend a little in Mr. Stoker's direction.

"What else did he say?" He picked up the pencil again and sat tapping it on the desktop.

"Isn't that sufficient?" I asked.

"For what? To arrest the man for murder? I think not, Mr. Rivers."

He was right, of course. "Do the two brothers see much of each other? I know that Bart is frequently locked up, but does Jacob ever see him?"

"That you would have to find out for yourself, Mr. Rivers. It's possible Jacob has paid a visit or two to Newgate to see his brother over the years, but I wouldn't know of it."

"Thank you, Inspector," I said, getting to my feet. I could see that I'd have to pursue this line of enquiry myself.

"Oh, by the way," Bellamy said casually, "you might like to know that we have crossed off your theatre cast and crew from our list of suspects." He drained the dregs from his teacup. "All just too full of themselves, it seems to me, to be interested in murdering their own kind."

Chapter Twenty

Not wanting to take any more time than necessary, I took a hansom to the gloomy granite building that was Newgate Prison. There I asked to see the chief warder but had to settle for the assistant warder, an officious gentleman no taller than myself but with a military bearing. He sported a fine black mustache, heavily waxed at the ends, and had black bushy eyebrows that seemed to meet over his beak of a nose. There were large bags under his eyes, and it looked as though he was in dire need of sleep, though his mind seemed sharp enough. His highly polished black boots gleamed under his uniform trousers.

"Nugent?" he snapped. "He is currently not in residence, though I doubt it will be long before his return." He stood ramrod straight behind his desk, apparently unwilling to bend enough to sit down.

"Yes." I nodded. "Yes, I know he's out. But I was wondering if you could help me with my enquiries regarding visitors he might have had while here?"

"Visitors? Hah!" He snorted and fingered the ends of his mustache. "Not many of those for any of our clients."

Clients? I thought.

"But they do—he did—have some?"

"No one is allowed more than five visitors a month. Many don't get that, and Bartholomew Nugent was one such. It was an unusual day when anyone came to speak with him, unless it was a solicitor. Is that what you are looking for?"

"No! No," I assured him. "No, I was wondering about regular visitors, not anyone connected with his arrest."

He pulled a large black leather-bound book from where it sat on the side of the desk, opened it, and flipped through pages while he spoke.

"Well, I can answer that right away, young man. He only ever got one interested party to attend on him. Name of Jacob Nugent, as I recall. Almost certainly a relative. He'd pay a visit on rare occasions, which seemed to suit young Bartholomew, it seemed to me."

I thought about that. Such occasional contacts didn't tell me much, but they did tell me that there was communication between the two brothers. Enough, perhaps, to allow them to plot and plan? Enough to show that both men were involved in the murders? I sighed. Why was it all so difficult?

The assistant warder stopped turning pages and then ran a finger down a column of names in the book.

"Ah! Here we are. Nugent. Yes, he did have one other occasional caller. Name of Higby. Don't ask me who he was; we don't keep that sort of information. Only came once or twice. There! That's it!" He snapped the book closed. He had obviously finished with me.

"Thank you, sir. You've been of help," I said. He looked down at my proffered hand as though I had presented a kipper. I withdrew it, turned, and sought the exit.

* * *

"Harold, dear boy!"

Without turning, I knew who hailed me. It was Guy Purdy, the only one who called me Harold. I recall that my father would occasionally use that form of address, and when he did, it invariably meant that I was in trouble. It's no wonder, then, that I am not enamored of the name Harold. Harry does quite well, thank you very much!

I stopped as I was about to enter my office, turned, and forced myself to smile at the old actor. Guy Purdy had been with Mr. Irving as long as the Guv'nor had been at the Lyceum. Mr. Purdy was of the old school, and even with my untrained eyes I could see that he tended to overact. Overly dramatic gestures, grimaces, projected voice that bounced off the upper levels of the theatre. He was too old for most of the young parts but applied his makeup heavily in an attempt to compensate. He had an eye for the young lads in the business, so I'd heard, though he'd always behaved himself at the Lyceum.

"Is there something I can do for you, Mr. Purdy?" I asked.

"Not a thing, dear boy. Life smiles down upon us despite the final curtain approaching for young Hamlet. 'Our revels now are ended,' as the Bard informs us."

"Yes. Well, some of us still have lots to do," I replied pointedly. I moved to go into my office, but he stepped forward, close to me.

"A word in your ear, dear boy, if I may?"

A dozen thoughts flew through my head, but I nodded and ushered him to the one seat in front of my desk.

"You are to play Cassio, in *Othello*?" I asked. I understood from Mr. Stoker that there had been some rivalry between Guy Purdy and John Saxon for that role.

"That I am, dear boy, that I am."

"So is there a problem?" I asked. I looked at his sagging chin and the bags beneath his eyes. He would certainly never play Romeo again, if he ever had. His dyed brown hair was growing thin, and his eyes were dull and listless.

He looked uneasy. "I have heard rumors—and don't we all, in the theatre, Harold? Indeed, the theatre would not be the theatre without the underworld of rumors to fuel . . ."

"The point, Mr. Purdy!" I interrupted. "I really do have a great deal of work to get through. Here it is Tuesday already. *Hamlet* may be in its final week, but, as you well know, there is a tremendous amount of preparation to be accomplished before the second of May and the opening of *Othello*."

"Of course, of course, dear boy. And far be it from me to slow the wheels of progress in that direction. No, Harold. It's just . . ." He jogged his chair a fraction closer to my desk and glanced quickly over his shoulder as though to be sure that no one was within earshot. His voice hardened. "I have heard rumors that John Saxon is trying to talk the Guv'nor into switching roles with me. Saxon is cast as Roderigo, a bit part compared to Cassio, in my opinion." He sounded bitter. "John Saxon does not have the presence for such a role as Cassio . . ."

Once again I interrupted him. "Mr. Purdy. You know as well as I do that when the Guv'nor has cast a play, he is not going to rethink the roles."

"But you have the ear of our esteemed Mr. Stoker. He, in turn, has the ear of Mr. Irving."

"It makes no difference," I said. "And you should be well aware of this, after all your years of working with Mr. Irving."

"I ask merely that you enquire as to the possibility—and I do say *possibility*—of circumventing John Saxon's ability to approach our esteemed Guv'nor on this point."

A thought suddenly struck me. "Who was it told you of this possible change?"

Again the quick glance over his shoulder.

"'Tis no matter." He stood up. "I should have known better than to come to you with this."

I, too, came to my feet. I hated dissention in the theatre, as I knew Mr. Stoker did. "Mr. Purdy, this is important. I must insist that you tell me who is spreading these rumors."

"Ah, dear boy! There you have it. Rumors! It is as I first stated." He shrugged his shoulders and forced a stage smile. "We should ignore them. They do us ill. 'Rumor of oppression and deceit, / Of unsuccessful or successful war, / Might never reach me more!' Who was it said that?" His brow wrinkled.

"I have no idea," I said, my patience at an end. "Now, unless you want me to pass your fears on to Mr. Stoker, would you be so kind as to tell me who told you that John Saxon was trying to take your part?"

He sank back down into the chair at the thought of me passing on his uncertainty to my boss.

"It was that new young lad. What is his name? In the chorus. Seth, I believe it is. Seth Hartzman. I once knew a Hartzman, in a little theatre up in Yorkshire . . ."

"Seth Hartzman told you that John Saxon was trying to talk the Guv'nor into giving him your role?" He nodded. "Did you not think to ask Mr. Saxon himself if that was what he was doing?"

"Dear boy, one does not like to confront one's friends in such matters."

I sighed. "Leave this with me, Mr. Purdy. I am certain there is no truth in the rumor, but I will pursue it and let you know. Now, is there anything else?"

"An interesting lad, young Hartzman." The old actor settled back a little more in the chair, now that his problem was in my hands. "Yes. He tells me he has crossed the broad Atlantic and viewed our brethren who tread the boards in such far-flung venues as New York and Philadelphia. Most interesting."

"Seth Hartzman has been to America?" It was my turn to sit down again, my interest piqued. I had been told that Hartzman had not arrived here with Mr. Booth and the colonel, so I had assumed he had not come from America, but I had not considered that he might have traveled to that country prior to that. And indeed, why should I have thought it? "What did he say about it? When was this, do you know?"

Guy waved a flabby hand. "Lifetimes ago for all I know, dear boy. No, he just happened to mention it as we chatted. Why? Is it important?"

It was my turn to wave a dismissive hand. "Don't worry about it, Mr. Purdy. You get on with learning your lines, and I'll attend to behind the scenes."

The old actor nodded, came to his feet, and made a dramatic exit from my office. He had intrigued me. Mostly with his talk of Hartzman having been to America but also with the whole episode of Hartzman suggesting to him that there was a problem with the *Othello* casting. Was this newcomer determined to cause conflict within the Lyceum ranks? Why would he do such a thing? I determined to have a talk with him.

"Ten days until Beltane, Harry!" Wednesday morning I was greeted by my boss's somber call. It wasn't often that he reached the theatre ahead of me, but this morning I found him there and at his desk when I entered his office.

"I thought you were counting the days till *Othello*'s curtain-up," I responded.

He looked grave. "So I am. But is not the prospect of a third sacrifice of an innocent young woman of even greater urgency?"

"Of course it is, sir. I didn't mean . . ."

"I know, Harry. I know. We have two events, each in its own way of great import. The one we can control; the other is in the hands of the gods, it would seem."

"Have you heard anything new from Inspector Bellamy?" I asked. I had already filled him in on what I had learned on my visit to Newgate.

He shook his head. "Nary a word. Not that I expected Scotland Yard to resolve anything. They do try, I sometimes believe, yet are wont to stumble over their own not insignificant feet."

I looked at a half-drunk cup of what I recognized as one of Bill Thomas's strong cups of tea, resting at the edge of his desk.

"How long have you been here, sir, if I may ask?"

Stoker rubbed the back of his neck. "What? Oh, I could not sleep, so I came in early. Quite a change, I don't mind admitting. You are usually the early bird. Not that there seem to be any worms for either of us to catch."

I pulled the *Times* from under my arm, opened it, and spread it across the lower part of his desk. I flipped through the first few pages, glancing at the headlines to see if there was anything of note. I almost missed an article halfway down one of the right-hand pages.

"My goodness me!" I exclaimed.

"What is it?" asked Stoker.

"Look at this, sir." I read it aloud:

Well-known actor found dead in his own theatre.

Shakespearean actor Reginald Robertson, moving force behind the Oxford Grand Theatre, on that town's Fellowship Street, was found dead in the early hours of yesterday morning. His body had been stuffed into a costume hamper discovered at the rear door of the theatre. Cause of death has not yet been announced. Fellow actors and theatre staff are being questioned by the local police. Scotland Yard has been called in.

Mr. Robertson had proclaimed himself "the next Henry Irving"—alluding to the London actor/manager of the Lyceum Theatre—and was planning a national tour. Mr. Stewart Renfrew, Mr. Robertson's understudy, stated that the Oxford Grand Theatre would continue after what he termed "a fitting time of mourning," and that he, Mr. Renfrew, would assume the principal roles.

"The next Henry Irving indeed!" cried Stoker. "What about the present Henry Irving? Here! Let me see that." He turned the newspaper around to read it.

Our eyes met.

"What do you think, sir? Could it possibly be Welly?"

There was a long silence.

"Let us not jump to conclusions, Harry. And let us hope that the police don't jump to any, either."

"Welly did seem to have accepted Rufus's death, last time I saw him," I said. "Though I was somewhat concerned that he appeared to have suppressed his emotions."

"He left the employ of the theatre, did he not?"

"Yes, sir. He said that he needed some time alone, to adjust."

"Did you sense any sign of antagonism toward Robertson?" Mr. Stoker persisted. "And goodness knows, he had sufficient cause to hate the man. But was there any hint of a need for revenge, do you think?"

I thought long and hard. I shook my head. "No, sir. That wasn't the Welly I had come to know. He was a loving and extraordinarily forgiving man."

"I sensed the same."

I remembered something. "At the Beefsteak Club meeting, sir," I said. "You may recall that I afterward spoke to you of Colonel Cornell's remarks about Mr. Robertson. He said, 'This Robertson fella needs putting in his place. He's an upstart and an incompetent.' I remember that quite distinctly."

My boss nodded but said nothing. We sat in silence for a while. Finally, Mr. Stoker closed and folded the newspaper.

"Well, this does take Reginald Robertson off our list of suspects for the two murders," I suggested.

"Does it, Harry? All it does is remove him from any list of suspects for the upcoming sacrifice. But we cannot just sit back and see whether or not that now takes place, can we? Robertson may or may not have murdered our Nell Burton and Elizabeth Scott—though, as I've said before, I don't think he did—but I'll still lay odds that there will be that third sacrifice in ten days." He stifled a yawn, clenched and unclenched his fists, then stretched his arms up in the air and shook them. "Reginald Robertson, by all accounts, antagonized most of the people with whom he came in contact. I don't think we need place Welly at the top of any list of suspects . . . at least for now, Harry. And as for the colonel's remark, well . . ." He left the sentence unfinished.

"I agree, sir." I moved to the door but then paused before going out. "But whether or not Welly was responsible for Mr. Robertson's death, I do think that he will be affected by it, don't you? I'm sure the police will put him high on their list. Don't you think he may need help?"

"Probably, but not necessarily ours, Harry." He looked at me, his eyes surprisingly soft and gentle. "You have a big heart, Harry. I admire you for it. But just look at the calendar. We have two crises rapidly approaching. I think that we can let the theatre business—the opening of *Othello*—proceed at its own pace. All seems to be under control there, other than the usual bits and pieces of any new production. No, I think we need to focus all of our energies on finding the killers of Nell Burton and Elizabeth Scott and, hopefully, in doing so, prevent the killing of some other unfortunate young lady."

"Yes, sir!"

I t was between houses that day when I happened to bump into Seth Hartzman. He had apparently just got back to the theatre after taking a quick meal, as most of us did, between the matinee and the evening performance. I immediately broached the subject of his upsetting Guy Purdy with wild rumors. He didn't deny it; merely tipped back his head and laughed.

"The old fool! No, don't pay it no never mind, Mr. Rivers. I was feeling bored and just playing with the old mummer. Not much else to do around here."

I shook my head. "That won't do, Mr. Hartzman. This theatre runs on mutual respect and harmony. I've a good mind to report this to Mr. Stoker."

It didn't seem to faze him. "Yes? Well, you do what you think you have to do, Mr. Stage Manager."

His attitude was in contrast to the relatively congenial exchange we had had in the greenroom the previous Saturday. Though I reminded myself that he had then gone on to fool around with Miss Abbott's tarot cards. He was a difficult person to judge. For the life of me I could not see where he fitted in with Colonel Cornell. I contented myself with a final warning.

"Just keep your pranks to yourself and out of the Lyceum," I said.

He waved a nonchalant hand and turned away, ambling off in the general direction of the backstage area. I had more important things on my mind and hurried off to my office space.

I had hardly been sitting at my desk ten minutes when I heard, "It's the Chariot, Mr. Rivers!"

Edwina Abbott's voice echoed off the walls. It was shriller than I had heard from her before. It was approaching curtain call for the evening performance, and I didn't have a great deal of time.

"Calm down, Miss Abbott," I said as she burst into my office. "Now I know these cards mean a great deal to you, but, quite frankly, I do feel you get carried away by them. In fact, I would like to ask you to refrain from . . ."

"The Chariot, Mr. Rivers!" She was not to be reined in. "I was in the dressing room with the other girls and someone—I think it might have been Bess Monroe, though I can't be sure—said to pull a card for the ending of the run. You know, just to see if we was to go out in a blaze of glory, as they say. So I spread out all the cards, facedown o' course, and we all—every one of us—decided on which one card to turn over. Just one card. It was the Chariot!"

She made the announcement as though revealing the long-sought answer to a riddle. I tried to humor her. "The Chariot, eh? And what exactly does that signify, Miss Abbott? Will we, then, be finishing *Hamlet* to resounding applause and numerous curtain calls? Or will that final curtain simply drop down and stay down?"

She was standing facing my desk with the pasteboard in question held up for me to see. It depicted a crude two-wheeled chariot drawn by two prancing horses, one white and one black. The figure at the reins wore a crown and held a scepter. He had a determined look on his face, I thought.

"This is a driving force, Mr. Rivers. Unstoppable!" She emphasized it. Her finger jabbed at the two horses. "There is both good and evil here. The chariot is rushing forward and there ain't nothing we can do to stop it!"

"I see. And I can see how that applies . . . I think. We are rushing toward the end of our *Hamlet* run. There is certainly no stopping that. I don't know about your 'good and evil,' but in all other respects I don't think your card shows anything untoward. Certainly nothing to get excited about . . . is there?" It suddenly struck me that Miss Abbott did seem to have a knack of seeing things in her cards that I did not.

"Good *and evil*, Mr. Rivers," she said. "And there is a figure of some importance at the reins, guiding them. Someone in charge."

I took the card from her and examined it. The figure certainly did look grim, but surely that was merely the whim of the artist? I had a thought. "Is it possible to draw another card and learn more of this person?"

Without a word, she drew the deck from her pocket and fanned the cards, holding them out toward me and indicating that I should choose one. I put down the Chariot card and studied the proffered pasteboards. I hesitantly ran my finger along their backs—back and forth.

"Just pull out whatever card feels right to you, Mr. Rivers," she said.

The trouble was that none of them "felt right." What if I should pull something terrible? I had memories of the windmill struck by lightning that she had turned over once before. And the heart stuck through with swords. But time was getting on. I had work to do. I stabbed my finger onto one card and pulled it free. Obviously, it was just going to be the luck of the draw. Not really significant. Edwina took the card from me and turned it faceup.

"The Hanged Man," she said, her voice little above a whisper.

Chapter Twenty-one

I had scarcely sat down at my desk on Thursday morning when Mr. Stoker appeared. He had on his overcoat and top hat and stood drawing on his gloves. "Harry, I need you to accompany me."

"But . . . will we be back in time for curtain-up, sir?" I asked, getting to my feet and quickly stacking the papers on my desk.

"It is of no consequence. The curtain has risen countless times throughout this run. This very successful run, I might add. I'm sure it will do so again. Alert Sam Green to cover your duties should we be detained, and put on your coat, Harry. We have work to do."

"Where are we going, sir?" I saw that the carriage was moving northwest, out past Ealing and heading toward Uxbridge. Mr. Stoker had hired a four-wheeler rather than a hansom, so I knew that we were going farther than just the outskirts of the city.

"I had a disturbing yet possibly enlightening night, Harry," said my boss. The sun had come out, and he had removed his hat and sat with it resting on the seat in front of him. "Not a dream, for I was in full possession of my faculties. Tell me, did you notice the gentleman, Lord Glenmont, at the Beefsteak dinner last week? He was the crossbencher associated with the prime minister's party."

I thought back. It was less than ten days ago. There had been so many dignitaries I wasn't sure that I could recall them all. I certainly remembered Sir William Harcourt, the home secretary, since he had sat close to me. And there was the Earl of Northbrook. I ran their faces through my mind. Yes, there had been someone sitting farther up the table. I vaguely remembered hearing his name mentioned by the Guv'nor at some point.

"Was that the constantly smiling gentleman with the round face and dimples?" I asked. "I was struck by his youthful-looking face despite the mass of white hair on his head. Clean-shaven, I believe?"

My boss nodded. "That was he. Constantly smiling is a good description, Harry. Not particularly notable; keeps his head down in the House. When I started thinking about him, I realized that not a lot is known about Lord Glenmont."

I wondered where this was leading.

"No. Not a lot at all," Stoker continued. "Remind me to check Debrett's *Peerage* when we get back to the Lyceum, Harry. That will tell us all about his lordship."

"Yes, sir."

"I do recall, however, that an ancestor of his was a member of the original Hellfire Club of Sir Francis Dashwood. There's that name raising its head again! Indeed, I very much think that he became somehow associated with the

American Benjamin Franklin. Franklin, you know, visited this side of the Atlantic Ocean on occasion and would participate in the Hellfire rituals when present. I personally think Franklin was a member just because he liked to be a part of anything and everything! Probably the wine and women rather than the devil worship, I wouldn't wonder."

I had heard of Ben Franklin. I knew that he had been ambassador to France for a decade and had paid many visits to England. I was somewhat surprised to learn that he had been an occasional member of Sir Francis Dashwood's group.

"Is there some connection between Lord Glenmont and our excursion this morning, sir?"

"There is indeed." Mr. Stoker peered out at the passing countryside. "The gentleman has an estate somewhere not far from where we now find ourselves. I would very much like to have a good look at it."

"So that's where we're going? To Lord Glenmont's estate?"

"Indeed. Knowl Estate, it's called. West of Maidenhead, alongside Knowl Hill, so I'm told."

He raised his cane and rapped on the rear of the driver's seat. The man on the box looked back over his shoulder.

"Yessir?"

"Driver, how close are we?"

"'Alf an 'our at most, sir, I reckon. Should be seein' the gates afore long."

"I want you to pull up a goodly distance from the entrance-way, if you would," said Stoker. "Just stop and await my instructions."

"Yessir." He returned his attention to the road.

"It all sounds most mysterious," I said. "Can you not tell me a little of what to expect, sir?"

He was silent for a while, obviously going over things in his head. Finally he looked at me. "I want you to cast your mind back to that Beefsteak dinner, Harry. That's what I was doing while lying in bed last night. For whatever reason

I seemed unable to fall asleep, and many thoughts kept running through my head.

"I was recalling what I know of the old Hellfire Club. They originally used to meet at Sir Francis's home in West Wycombe. As a matter of fact, their very first meeting was held in 1752 on *Walpurgisnacht*, so you can see how that date resonates. Then in 1755 they moved to Medmenham Abbey, or the ruins thereof. Sir Francis renovated the abbey, and underneath it he had a series of caves carved out. It's all chalk around that area."

I wondered where this was all leading but kept quiet and let my boss take his own time.

"But to return to Lord Glenmont. His Knowl Estate is close to Medmenham. At the Beefsteak dinner I happened to overhear his lordship talking with Colonel Cornell. It appears that a generation ago Lord Glenmont's father had similar caves carved out there—though on a much less pretentious scale. I thought that it might be worth paying them a visit, Harry."

So that was it. "You think that Lord Glenmont might be leading a modern Hellfire Club at his estate?" I asked.

Stoker chuckled. "No, Harry. No. Somehow I can't imagine such a cherubic-faced gentleman leading satanic rituals when not occupied in the House of Lords." Then he was silent for a moment. "However, having said that, I do not think we can always judge a book by its cover, as Miss George Eliot recently put it, so eloquently, in one of her own books."

I, too, had difficulty imagining the round-faced gentleman I had seen at the Beefsteak dinner involved in dark rites that included the slaying of innocent young women.

"What do you hope to find there?" I asked.

"I'm not quite sure, Harry. In all probability there is nothing at all. I certainly don't expect to find the chalk designs that were at the sites of the two murders, nor do I even expect to discover melted candles, bloodstains, or abandoned altars. No. As I say, I really don't know what to expect. It was just that on hearing his lordship mention the caves I felt a desire to see them for myself. To see just how similar they might be to those at Medmenham Abbey."

"Do you know why Lord Glenmont's father had them carved out?"

"I think that is part of what intrigues me, Harry. We know that the earlier Lord Glenmont, back in the last century, was one of Dashwood's followers, but I've never heard any hint of later Glenmonts treading that same path. I'm sure it will be something of a waste of time, but I have long since learned not to ignore my nighttime thoughts and dreams."

We sat back and traveled in silence for quite some time. The scenery was delightful, with spring growth thrusting forth and bringing back some color to the fields and hedgerows. There were flat meadows close to the river with occasional tree-covered hills and with the church spires of tiny villages reaching up to greet the now warming sun.

We were really not that far from Oxford, and my mind went to Welly and where he might be and what he might be doing. I wondered if the police had yet made a connection between him and the murder of Reginald Robertson. I refused to believe that there was any direct link, but I could certainly see how the mind of Scotland Yard might stitch things together. My mind also dwelt for a moment on Rufus, of course. I still couldn't quite get over the tragedy.

I must have dozed off in the warm sun and from the jogging of the carriage. I was awakened when Mr. Stoker called out to the driver to stop. I looked about me but saw nothing to indicate that we had arrived at any particular point. The country road wound on into the distance, rising and falling on gentle hills. But my boss seemed to know where we were. We both climbed down from the carriage, and I spent a minute or two stretching the stiffness out of my limbs.

"Come, Harry," he said, waving the carriage away. "We will walk on to the estate gates. No need to announce our arrival."

"Why the secrecy, sir?"

"Not exactly secrecy, Harry. Let's just call it caution, shall we?"

I suspected that my boss desired to have a look at the caves he had mentioned but did not necessarily want his lordship to know of his interest. I'm sure Lord Glenmont was not at home, anyway, but surely someone would be at the house. We walked less than a quarter mile before we came to the entrance to Knowl Estate. The thick hedgerow had given way to a stout wrought-iron fence that, in turn, ended in tall gates set in stone pillars surmounted by heraldic beasts. A broad drive curved off and away between stately beeches.

"Do we just walk up the driveway, sir?" I asked.

"It would seem to be the best way to enter, Harry. Come! I have a feeling we won't have far to go. Let us just keep over to the side, under the shadow of the beeches."

It was very pleasant walking, though I wished I had chosen better shoes for the hike. This was not something I had been prepared for. We advanced along the gravel path, and sure enough, just around the first curve, we came upon a side spur that led toward what appeared to be a folly; an ancient-looking ruin projecting above the trees. It may well have been an actual ruin—there were a few of those about the county—but I suspected it had been carefully designed and constructed, probably by one of the earlier Glenmonts. As we drew closer I saw that it was set at the edge of a small lake, also in all probability man-made.

"As I suspected," murmured my boss. He stopped to admire the structure.

It gave the impression of being the façade and crumbled

walls of a small stone church or chapel. Mullioned windows bare of glass faced out to the lake and on the side closest to where we stood. Blocks of stone lay as though a tower had collapsed and fallen toward the water.

"See here, Harry." Stoker pointed at the ground as he started to walk on. I could see what he indicated: the grass was pressed down as though more than one person had passed that way. There was not enough wear to constitute a footpath, yet obviously this mock ruin was not totally abandoned.

We followed the trail to where part of the pseudo-ancient wall formed an impressive entranceway, reminding me somewhat of the north porch of Salisbury Cathedral. Side by side, Mr. Stoker and I peered in and saw steps descending into darkness.

"I believe we have found the entrance to the Glenmont caves," murmured my boss.

"So what do we do now, sir?"

As if in answer to my question, a voice from behind us said, "Turn 'round slowly and no funny stuff!"

We did as bid. Facing us, with an over-and-under shotgun pointing in our direction, stood a squat fellow dressed in a worn Norfolk jacket, with gaiters encasing his lower legs. His boots were muddy. His face was tanned from years of outdoor life, and I presumed him to be some sort of gamekeeper for the Knowl Estate. I glanced at my boss, but he seemed unfazed by the shotgun.

"What you doin' rootin' about 'ere? This 'ere's private property, don't yer know?" To emphasize his position he cocked the gun, still keeping it trained on us. I swallowed.

"Is that not a Williams and Powell Simplex 10 gauge?" asked Mr. Stoker.

"Eh?" The gamekeeper's brows drew together, and he looked perplexed.

"My father had one of those," continued my companion, and he started forward.

"'Ere! Just you wait a minute." The man waved the barrels of the gun.

Stoker held out his hands toward the weapon and continued to advance, a smile on his face. "Deucedly handy little thing, my father always thought. Used it for pheasant back in Ireland. May I see?" He reached out and took the gun from the man's unprotesting fingers and eased the hammers back down. He ran one hand along the barrels. "Damascus. Very nice." He looked the man squarely in the eyes as he handed back the gun. "I see you keep it in good care. Nicely oiled. Well done."

It seemed that the man could not take his eyes off Mr. Stoker's face. His voice was much subdued when next he spoke. "'Oo are you?"

Stoker removed his glove and extended his hand. The man ignored it. "Oh, I'm sorry. Stoker is the name. Bram Stoker. And this is my good friend Mr. Harry Rivers."

I raised my bowler hat as though I'd been introduced to someone on the streets of the city rather than having been rescued from a challenging gamekeeper in the depths of the country.

"What you doin' 'ere?" the man asked.

"Perhaps his lordship failed to mention that we might stop by," said my boss, turning back to admire the folly behind us. "We had been together at a dinner last week, and Lord Glenmont made mention of what he had here. I found it most interesting." He turned back to the gamekeeper. "And you are . . . ?"

"'Igby. Bill 'Igby. 'Is lordship's gamekeeper." He had the decency to raise his hand and tug at the dirty hat on his head. "Sir," he finally added. He seemed quite disconcerted by Mr. Stoker's demeanor, which I could well understand.

"Good," said my boss. "Good. Well now, Higby, don't let us keep you from your rounds. You must have much ground to cover. Fear not, we can fend for ourselves. Off you go then."

Thoroughly disconcerted, the gamekeeper turned away, slipping his shotgun into the crook of his arm, and with several backward glances walked off into the woods abutting the folly and disappeared.

I gave him time to move out of earshot. "That—that was incredible, sir," I said. "I can't believe you simply talked him out of it."

"Oh pshaw! The man would never have shot us, Harry. He just didn't know it, that's all."

Chapter Twenty-two

On the journey back to town I told Mr. Stoker of my thoughts and concerns about Welly. It wasn't easy to get him out of my mind. It felt like abandoning him.

"I applaud your concerns, Harry. I, too, have had thoughts in that direction. But one thing at a time. Beltane, or *Walpurgisnacht*, fast approaches, and we must, at all costs, ensure that no third ritual slaying takes place."

"Yes, sir. I know."

"You are probably wondering what was the point of our excursion today."

"I did rather wonder," I admitted.

"It was not pure idleness on my part, or simple curiosity. I am more convinced than ever that these terrible crimes are connected to the misguided actions of individuals caught up in the perceived romance of Sir Francis Dashwood's Hellfire Club. It's amazing how that simple little group of so long ago still stirs the minds of individuals of a certain type.

There have been many resurrections of the concept since Dashwood's passing. Most have been by the younger crowd, looking for excitement and with no true dedication to evil. Certainly with no intention to actually harm another. Yet even one or two of those have got out of hand in the heat of the moment."

"So you are saying that these murders may not have been intended, sir?" I was puzzled.

"These two in particular, Harry? Oh yes, they were intentional. No question about that. No, what I am saying is that many members of these latter-day Hellfire Clubs—how I loathe the name—are no more than gatherings of idle-minded persons who imitate true satanic rites in order to titillate. Yet there are certain less altruistic beings that take advantage of these people; who steer them in a direction they had no intention of taking. They it is who are the true Satanists. They it is who commit the most heinous crimes for their own purposes."

"And that is what has happened here, with Nell Burton and Elizabeth Scott?"

He nodded. "So I believe, Harry. Some powerful and knowledgeable leader has taken his followers over the edge in what they thought was mere dabbling and used their energies to bring about an end that he had been working toward all along. Once they have taken that step, then they cannot go back, and this leader is in a position to command their complete allegiance and to ensure that they do all of his further biddings."

"But who would do such a thing?" I asked.

"Who indeed, Harry? Who indeed?" Mr. Stoker gave one of his long sighs. "That person is the one we must determine before the end of this month. He—or she, for it is not unknown for a woman to lead such rituals—must be apprehended. Today I wanted to see for myself the caves of Lord

Glenmont. I doubt that they will be used in the upcoming ceremony, but I needed to be fully aware of their location and availability just in case."

"Why wouldn't they simply use the original caves at Medmenham?" I asked.

"Those have long been boarded up," said Stoker. "Too many people broke into them and abused them, spreading red paint and the like to simulate blood. A shame, for they are historical, whatever their original purpose."

"So what now, sir? Now that you've seen the Glenmont caves, what is our next step?"

"Back to London to try to track down this leader. Thanks to you and young Billy Weston we have a list of suspects; persons who may well comprise the bulk of the congregation for these rites. I have prevailed upon our Inspector Bellamy to attempt to locate them and detain them for questioning, though I do not hold out a great deal of hope in that direction."

"We do know one of them, sir," I said. "Jacob Nugent."

"That we do, Harry. And the inspector has already had the man into Scotland Yard for questioning."

"And?" I sat on the edge of my seat, expectantly.

"As we might have expected, young Nugent has a fine alibi for every instance we could think of."

I slid back in my seat again and watched as our four-wheeler entered the outskirts of the big city.

"But we will not leave it there, Harry."

I turned to my boss expectantly.

"We are certain, from that list of names, that Jacob Nugent is entangled somehow. Scotland Yard is keeping a close eye on him and on his movements. If nothing else, there is a good chance that Mr. Nugent might lead us to someone more directly involved."

The trees and hedgerows slowly gave way to houses, first well spread out and then increasingly closer together. The soft dirt road became a hard-topped street, which quickly showed signs of its constant use. I spotted crossing sweeps, hurdy-gurdy players, newspaper sellers, and pie men and knew that we were almost home. It had been an interesting excursion but one I could have done without. We arrived back at the Lyceum in good time for the evening performance.

"We can't get anything out of the minx, so we thought your Mr. Stoker might have a better idea of what sort of questions to ask her."

It was Inspector Bellamy. Seeing him at the Lyceum was not my idea of a good way to start off Friday morning. I had just left my boss's office and almost bumped into the man as I headed back to my own desk. Behind the inspector I could see a police constable with a firm grip on the arm of a young woman. She had bright red hair, a mirror image of my own, although hers was understandably long and in ringlets. The woman was not shoddily dressed, though her fawn jacket was well-worn at the collar and her walking skirt much tattered at the hem from constant contact with the pavement. She wore a fur felt walking hat sporting a fancy quill. The hat, I thought, was worn at a roguish angle, so I was not entirely disconcerted when she winked at me. She had piercing green eyes and, in other circumstances, might have been thought attractive.

"Who is this young lady?" I asked. "Mr. Stoker is not casting for the next play."

"Out of our way, Mr. Rivers. This is police business. We are not in the habit of providing young women to work your theatre. This is part of our investigation."

"Oh, I see." I turned back to Mr. Stoker's office door and tapped on it. "In that case I'm sure he'll see you."

"Come!" My boss's voice emanated from within, and I opened the door and told him who was there.

"Show him in, Harry. Let us not hinder the Metropolitan Police in the course of their enquiries. Ah, Inspector! Please come in. And who do we have here?"

There was not a lot of room in Mr. Stoker's office, but I did not feel inclined to leave; I was far too intrigued. I edged over to the far wall so that the inspector, the constable, and the young lady could all enter and close the door. The inspector sat down on the chair facing Mr. Stoker but left the others standing.

"Miss Sarah Winterbotham," said Bellamy, waving a hand in her direction. "On your list, if you recall. We picked her up in Piccadilly just yesterday afternoon and have been trying to fit her into your murder scene."

"I'm sure I don't know what you're talking about," said the woman, looking about her at the playbills on the walls of the office.

"Now then. None of that." Bellamy barely glanced at her before returning his attention to my boss. "She does not have an alibi for either of the murders . . ."

"'Ere! I told you. I don't know nothing about no murders!"

Bellamy continued without looking at her. "No alibis. No recollection—or so she says—of what she was doing at those times. No one to vouch for her or her movements. We thought perhaps you might have more pointed questions to ask her, sir."

Mr. Stoker sat back and studied the young lady. He smiled, which seemed to surprise her. I think she was expecting my boss to browbeat her, as did the police.

"And what is your name, young lady?"

"We've told you that . . ." exploded the inspector.

"Shh! Please, Inspector." Stoker kept his eyes on the young woman, nodding encouragingly. "And by the way, may I compliment you on your hat? It is very becoming, especially with the entrance of spring all about us."

I kept my eyes on Miss Winterbotham. It was fascinating to see how Mr. Stoker's few words calmed her. She had come into the office—had been almost dragged into it—and was perhaps understandably antagonistic. But I saw the hint of a smile tug at the corners of her mouth.

"You like it? It was me mum's. She only wore it on 'igh days and 'olidays. Got lots more life in it yet."

"I can see." Stoker's head nodded. "Charming. Tell me, Miss Winterbotham, speaking of holidays, isn't there one coming up in a few days? What is it . . . ?" He paused as though trying to think of it.

"Beltane," she provided. "My favorite. Springtime, ain'it?" She looked defiantly at the inspector, as though half expecting him to deny the approaching season.

"Ah yes." Stoker's head again nodded. "Beltane. That's it. So much nicer than Imbolc, wouldn't you say? All that coming out of the winter and yet still frost biting at our toes."

She laughed. "Ain't that the truth."

"Mr. Stoker, sir." Inspector Bellamy could remain silent no longer. "We didn't come here to discuss the weather. All this going on about belting and bolting, or whatever. Can we not get on with finding out what this woman knows? I need not remind you of the importance of this. After all, it was your acting young lady . . ."

My boss held up his hand, stopping the inspector in midsentence. "Inspector, please! You have your methods. Methods that you openly admit have produced no results. I have mine. I would suggest that you leave this young lady with me for the rest of the morning. Young Harry and I will take her to an early lunch, and then I will attend upon Scotland Yard and apprise you of the results."

"Leave her with you? We can't afford to let our constable lallygag about here all morning. He's got other duties he needs to get to."

"I'm not asking you to leave your constable here, Inspector. Mr. Rivers and myself are well able to escort Miss Winterbotham."

Inspector Bellamy spluttered and argued, but eventually, as I knew he would have to, he and the police constable went out, leaving the young lady with us. Stoker smiled at her and indicated the chair that the inspector had vacated.

"Won't you please be seated, Miss Winterbotham? I apologize for the crudeness of our Metropolitan force. Harry, would you see if Bill has got his kettle on? A cup of tea might not go amiss."

"You let her go?" Inspector Bellamy was incredulous. "Don't you know how lucky we were to find her in the first place? You were the one who alerted us to that list of people, and we managed to strike lucky and get hold of one of them. And now you go and let her off the hook?" His mouth hung open, and his eyes were wide.

Mr. Stoker sat down, placing his top hat and gloves on the inspector's desk and laying his cane across it. He settled back in the chair and fixed his eyes on the policeman. I tried to be as unobtrusive as possible and eased myself down into the only other chair in the office.

"And what would you have done with her, Inspector? Thrown her into a jail cell perhaps? Beaten her? Tortured her?" He laughed. "I jest . . . I hope. But seriously, I do believe that Mr. Rivers and myself obtained all available information from Miss Winterbotham. To have forcefully retained her would have served no purpose. But to set your mind at rest, I did prevail upon one of my ever-helpful young street lads to keep an eye on her movements and to alert me in certain circumstances. It will not be a major task to apprehend her again should it really become necessary."

The inspector harrumphed and moved papers about on

his desk. "All the same, we do wish you had consulted us in the matter." He paused before also sitting back and looking Mr. Stoker in the eyes. "So what great information did you learn? Something more than the weather through the year, we would hope."

"That initial little exchange that you witnessed actually gave me a great deal of information. With just a couple of questions I got Miss Winterbotham to acknowledge that she is fully aware of the pagan calendar; that she recognizes the names of the ancient feast days. The days on which, if you recall, Inspector, the first murder took place and the third might. Imbolc, or February Eve, and Beltane, or May Eve. How many ordinary citizens would know that? How many young ladies of Miss Winterbotham's class would be conversant with those terms? No, Inspector, we have ascertained that this young lady in particular is indeed a member of the group we seek and she, in turn, could well lead us to the others."

Chapter Twenty-three

Mr. Stoker's hope that Miss Winterbotham would lead us to others of the satanic group bore no fruit immediately, but I had learned to be patient when one of my boss's plans started to fall into place. He had arranged for a number of street urchins to keep an eye on the young lady, taking turns in following so that she would never see the same face behind her.

Meanwhile the good inspector's men did manage to discover another of the group. Mr. Albert Pottinger had, in effect, been sitting out in the open all the time. He was the proprietor of an apothecary shop in Watford, a small town northwest of the city. It seems it was quite by chance that one of the sergeants attached to Scotland Yard, a Sergeant Ames, was visiting an aunt in Watford and was sent in search of laudanum for that lady. Directed to the shop, he fell into conversation with the man behind the counter, not revealing his own profession. He discovered that the store-keeper was a collector of ancient recipes and herbal cures for little-known maladies and was interested in ancient magical practices. The sergeant was struck by the unusual name of the proprietor and suddenly remembered that name being on the list that Inspector Bellamy had distributed. He arrested the man and dragged him back to Scotland Yard. Under Inspector Bellamy's questioning, Mr. Pottinger reluctantly admitted to being one of a group that occasionally gathered in Warrington and elsewhere, though he denied any connection with devil worship or knowledge of Elizabeth Scott's murder.

The inspector arrived at Mr. Stoker's office early Saturday morning mainly, it seemed to me, to crow about the capture.

"Our Sergeant Ames—one of our finest, I might add— immediately recognized the man and lost no time in bringing him to justice," he said, his thumbs tucked into his waistcoat pockets and his chest thrust out.

"Justice?" asked Mr. Stoker. "For what? It seems you have yet to actually connect him to any murder. Although I applaud your sergeant's rapid response, I fear it will mean but little unless you can follow up on the man's admission of having been in Warrington."

The thumbs came out of the pockets, and the inspector looked hard at my boss and frowned. "Yes, well . . . that remains to be seen. We don't think it will be too hard to establish the connection. Not under our questioning."

"And just what have you learned so far?"

"He has no alibi, sir! No alibi at all. He is unable to account for his movements at the time of either murder. We are holding him at Scotland Yard for the time being." He lowered his head and glowered at Mr. Stoker. "We will not be releasing this gentleman into your custody, Mr. Stoker. He will stay safely with us."

"I am sure he will quickly feel at home there," said my boss. "Now, if you have no further news of any substance . . ."

"Just one more item." Bellamy pulled out his tattered

notebook and flipped through the pages to the item he was looking for. "Mr. Cuthbert Wellington . . ."

"Welly!" I shouted out. I couldn't contain myself. "Oh, I beg your pardon, sir," I said to Mr. Stoker. "I was just over-excited to hear mention of him."

"Quite all right, Harry." He addressed himself to the inspector. "So! What news do you bring of Mr. Wellington, Inspector? I understand you had been wanting to talk with him ever since the passing of that upstart actor in Oxford."

"Indeed we had." He consulted his book. "Mr. Wellington surfaced down in Brighton where, it appears, he has found employment at a small theatre there, the Brighton Alhambra on the King's Road."

"Wonderful," I murmured. The inspector ignored me.

"It would appear that he was well ensconced there at the time of Mr. Robertson's passing. Not that there is any further concern on our part, regarding that particular gentleman's death."

"Oh?" Stoker looked surprised. "Pray tell, Inspector. What other news are you keeping from us?"

Bellamy looked pleased with himself, having information that my boss did not have.

"At the Oxford Grand Theatre, under more of our effective questioning, Mr. Stoker, we were able to elicit a complete confession from . . ."—another quick glance at his notebook—"Mr. Stewart Renfrew, the late Reginald Robertson's understudy. It would appear that Mr. Renfrew had long been aggravated by that gentleman and one evening he decided he would take it no more and hit Mr. Robertson over the head with a metal bust of Julius Caesar."

"A bust of Caesar?" I said.

"Apparently a stage property of some kind."

Mr. Stoker grunted. "Yes. Well, we have had our own problems with understudies in the past. They do seem an unstable lot. So is that it, Inspector? May we now be allowed to get on about our daily business? Or would you like to chat away until curtain-up for this afternoon's performance?"

With the trace of a smile on his face, Inspector Bellamy left, and Mr. Stoker and I got back to the business of the Lyceum.

I t was between houses that I got the terrible news. The worst news I have ever received in my life, it seems to me.

"Mr. Rivers, sir."

I was hurrying along to the prop room and did not want to be delayed. There was little enough time to accomplish all that was required. I glanced back over my shoulder.

"What is it? I'm in a bit of a hurry."

"It's me, sir. Timmy."

"Timmy?" The name didn't immediately mean anything. I stopped and turned around. It was the young boy from Mr. Irving's residence. "Timmy! What are you doing here? Are you looking for Mr. Irving? His dressing room is up the stairs. Here, let me show you the way."

"No, sir. No. It's you as I was told to find, sir."

I was puzzled. Then a thought struck me. Perhaps Jenny had to get an urgent note of some sort to me. Perhaps she wouldn't be able to meet me tomorrow. My heart sank at the thought.

"What is it, Timmy? Did Jenny send you?"

"No, sir. It was Mrs. Cooke what told me to come and find you. But it's about Jenny. She's gorn and disappeared, sir."

I would swear that my heart stopped beating for a moment.

"What do you mean, she's disappeared?" I spoke sharply. More sharply than I meant to.

The boy shook his head. "I dunno. Mrs. Cooke says to tell you. Jenny was sent out to get summat at the shop yesterday and she never come back."

"What do you mean, she never came back?" I could feel

panic growing in my stomach. I involuntarily grabbed the boy by his arm and jerked him around to face me.

"Ow!"

"Sorry! I'm sorry, Timmy. But . . . Look, let's go and find Mr. Stoker. Come with me."

We hurried along to my boss's office, and I threw open the door without even bothering to knock. As I burst in, I knocked his Indian clubs from where they stood close to the door. I scrambled to retrieve the heavy objects and looked about me. The office was empty.

I t was a good ten minutes before I located the big man. I then had Timmy repeat what he had told me.

"The first thing is not to panic, Harry."

That was easy to say, I thought, but not so easy to do. "But what can we do, sir?" I felt wretched.

I sent Timmy home with a note to Mrs. Cooke advising her that I had alerted Mr. Stoker and he, in turn, had advised Mr. Irving.

"What are the possibilities?" asked Stoker. "Does she have any relatives nearby? Might there have been some emergency that she had to attend to?"

"There's only her old aunt who lives in Bermondsey, though I don't know the exact address. The last I heard, Aunt Alice was in fine fettle. But if Jenny had gone there, surely she would have advised Mrs. Cooke? She wouldn't simply run off."

"Hmm. Agreed. It does seem unusual. Still, I think I will send one of our men off to Bermondsey to locate the old lady, just to be certain. Meanwhile, you and I will do a little police work, Harry." Stoker got to his feet. "Come. Let us proceed to where Miss Cartwright was last seen and begin our own enquiries."

I gave Sam Green what details I could remember of Aunt Alice Forsyth and where she lived and saw him off as he left to try to locate her. Then I hurried after Mr. Stoker as he exited the theatre and summoned a hansom. At a fast trot, we made our way to Mayfair and to Grafton Street. The big black-painted front door opened as we drew near it. Timmy was looking out for us, and he ran up the stairs to alert the housekeeper the moment we stepped out of the cab.

"I take it Miss Cartwright has not yet returned?" My boss's voice echoed up the stairway as Mrs. Cooke's short, stocky figure appeared at the top.

She quickly put her hands up to check that her hair was secure in its bun and then shook her head. "No, sir. Not a sign of 'er. Never done this afore. She 'ad run out to the milliner's for me, to get me some thread, and just never come back."

"And this was yesterday, Friday?"

"Yes, sir. About teatime it was, so I didn't really notice Jenny 'adn't returned till close on six of the clock, sir."

My boss had ascended but a short way up the stairs and stood, holding the banister rail and speaking up to the housekeeper at the top. I stood uncertainly just inside the front door, which remained open.

"And this milliner is located where, Mrs. Cooke? Precisely."

"Number 63 Bond Street, sir. We always goes there. Mr. Irving says . . ."

"Yes. Thank you, Mrs. Cooke." Mr. Stoker turned back down and waved me ahead of him. "Lead on, Harry. Around the corner to Bond Street. Thank you, Mrs. Cooke," he called back over his shoulder as we went out and closed the door behind us.

It wasn't far to the milliner's shop. The ladies behind the counters at Mrs. Hazlett's Millinery and Mercantile all looked up as the bell tinkled when Mr. Stoker threw open the door.

"Which of you is Mrs. Hazlett?" he asked, his eyes sweeping the shop.

There were a number of lady customers, all of whom were obviously surprised to see two men invade what they

surely thought to be their territory. I heard one or two murmur but was unable to catch what was said. A petite, dark-
haired lady, smartly dressed and wearing a fashionable hat
sporting a tall peacock feather, excused herself from a cus-
tomer and advanced upon us.

"I am she. May I ask who enquires?"

Stoker removed his hat and gave the slightest of bows.
"Forgive our intrusion, madam, but we are here on urgent
business. Is there somewhere we may speak?" His eyes ran
across the other ladies whose faces were all locked on us.

To her credit Mrs. Hazlett wasted no time. "Ladies,
kindly proceed with your business. Gentlemen, won't you
please follow me?"

She led the way back behind the counters and beyond the
fitting rooms to a small office. There was a large table, rather
than a desk, in its center, with a variety of rolls of cloth
spread about together with a peaked-brim bonnet of wired
buckram on a stand. It was covered in silk taffeta and deco-
rated with feathers. She swept a clear space on the table and
turned to face us.

"Now, gentlemen. What is so urgent that you must interrupt the working of my establishment?"

Mr. Stoker wasted no time. "We are seeking a young
gentlewoman who has disappeared, madam. She was last
known to have visited your shop. It was late afternoon yesterday. I am informed that she was here to purchase some
thread for her employer."

"Can you describe her? We have a varied clientele. We are
a not unpopular purveyor of hats of the latest fashion
together with a wide assortment . . ."

"Forgive me, but time is of the essence," said Stoker,
holding up his hand to stop her. He turned to me. "Harry,
be so good as to give this lady a full description of Jenny."

I did so.

"A little over five feet in height, you say? And with brown hair and eyes?"

I nodded. "Yes, madam."

"At that hour of the day we did not have a great many ladies in the shop, but as it happens I have good reason to remember the lady you describe," said Mrs. Hazlett.

I thought my heart might burst through my chest. "You do?" I gasped.

"Easy, Harry," said Mr. Stoker. He addressed the milliner. "Pray tell all you remember, madam. It would be of great service to us. The young lady in question has disappeared, and we are most anxious to locate her. Anything you can tell us will be gratefully appreciated."

"The young lady you mention had barely entered my shop when the door swung open again behind her and a rather large, rough-looking gentleman followed her in. He threw his arms around her waist and, as he dragged her back out of the door, shouted something at me that sounded like, 'My willful daughter. She just won't obey me.' The young lady seemed most surprised and started to scream, but the man hustled her outside and into a waiting cab."

"Sir!" I cried, turning to Mr. Stoker.

"Easy, Harry," he said, for the second time. "Mrs. Hazlett, we are indebted to you. Can you tell me in which direction the cab proceeded?"

"Why, toward Piccadilly, I believe."

"Ah! Piccadilly, eh? I'm sorry, Harry. I'm afraid there's no way we'll be able to track it. Piccadilly, as you know, is the veritable hub of London. They could have continued in literally any direction from there."

"But surely, sir . . ."

"Are you aware of just how many cabs ply their trade in the city, Harry? And of how many pass through Piccadilly within the space of just one hour?" He shook his head. "No,

Harry, direct pursuit is not to be the order of our day. Come! Let us return to the Lyceum."

"There must be something we can do, sir," I protested as we rode back to the theatre. "I can't do nothing. Perhaps Sam Green will have found Aunt Alice. Perhaps . . ."

"Easy, Harry. One step at a time. We will, of course, advise Scotland Yard and the good inspector, but there is one thing you should keep in mind."

"Sir?" I felt the slightest hope from my boss's reassuring voice.

"If, as we both must suspect, young Jenny has been taken to play the part of the next victim for the Hellfire group, then we can rest assured that she will be held in good state until that appointed night. They will not harm her—in all probability will treat her well—until they need her for their shameful rite on the eve of May. That is yet a week away. We can accomplish a lot in a week, Harry."

I did, indeed, feel some small consolation from that thought. Mr. Stoker was right. For some strange reason I had had a certain dread at the back of my mind that my Jenny might be the chosen one; that she would somehow be spirited away by these demons. There was no logic to my fear. Why would Jenny be chosen, out of all the young women in London? And yet I had felt very strongly that there was a connection of some sort. I shared my thoughts with Mr. Stoker.

"I think you are right, Harry." His big head nodded with the motion of the hansom passing over the cobbled street. "I blame myself for not acting on such a supposition in a more timely manner. Nell Burton was one of our own. If, as I suspect, this whole trio of rites is being aimed at the Lyceum and—as I am becoming more and more certain—at our Henry Irving, then it would make sense that there would be a strong connection between the victim and their center of focus."

"But Elizabeth Scott had no direct connection with us, sir," I said. "She was a simple flower seller, not even in London, never mind part of the Lyceum."

"Very true, Harry. And I have my own theory as to why she became the first victim of these tragedies. Ah, here we are. Let us get back inside and to my office. I find I think best in my own milieu."

We both descended from the cab and hurried back inside the Lyceum to prepare for the final performance of *Hamlet*. The theatre was full.

Chapter Twenty-four

Saturday night saw *Hamlet* go out in a blaze of glory. The Guv'nor took ten curtain calls and could have squeezed several more out of the enthusiastic audience if he had wanted to. Everyone seemed delighted. Mr. Irving took the principals out to a very late dinner at Romano's. Mr. Stoker was invited but declined. His mind was on other things.

The next day was a most unusual Sunday. It had been a sleepness night for me. There was to be no meeting with Jenny that afternoon. Yet the day started like a regular weekday morning . . . I went in to the theatre and met with Mr. Stoker in his office.

"I've been thinking, sir," I said. "The Nugents. Just where do they fit into this whole scheme of things?"

"I've been trying to sort out that myself, Harry. They are both obviously involved in some way, and I think I might have it fathomed. Tell me again the name of the second man that Newgate Prison said would occasionally visit Bart Nugent."

I had to turn to my notebook for that. I'd come to realize that there were some things Inspector Bellamy did that were worth copying. I now wrote down any and all items I might possibly forget. I'd always kept such a workbook for my theatrical duties, but now I kept a second one for the many diverse happenings that seemed to bubble up all about me in the blink of an eye . . . tarot cards, railway timetables, directions thither and yon, and many, many names. Even with the notebook I found it difficult to keep the names in any sort of order. I had to record what each name was associated with and how I had encountered it. I now ran my finger down a page and stopped under the Newgate Prison heading.

"William Higby," I read out. "The assistant warder said that he only visited Bart once or twice."

"And what was the name of Lord Glenmont's gamekeeper? He of the double-barreled shotgun?"

I turned a page or two then turned back.

"I'm sorry, sir. I didn't make a note of that. Should I have done?"

"I can tell you, Harry. It was Bill Higby."

My mouth fell open. "It was? Was there any connection between the two Higbys?" I asked.

"There were not two Higbys, Harry. Just one—I'm certain of it. The gamekeeper was the man who visited Bart Nugent in prison." Mr. Stoker sat back in his chair and looked pleased with himself.

"Well I'm . . . I'm speechless," I said.

My boss looked even more pleased with himself. "I knew I'd heard the name before somewhere, when Lord Glenmont's man said it. I just couldn't place it right away."

"So why did he visit Bart?"

"It was clever and it tells us a lot, if my reasoning is correct, Harry."

"It does, sir?"

"It most certainly does. You know, of course, that we had

242 · RAYMOND BUCKLAND

two young ladies murdered. One up north near Liverpool and the other right here in London. Both were ritual slayings. Ergo, both required a number of participants. Now don't you think it would be a very large coincidence if there just happened to be operating two separate and distinct Hellfire groups—for want of a better name? Don't you think it much more likely that it was in fact two parts of one single group responsible for both deaths?"

I nodded. It was persuasive.

"Two parts of a whole," he continued. "And consequently a need to coordinate their actions."

"So, how . . . ?" I started to say.

"The leader, or the spokesman, for the northern half—Jacob Nugent—would report to his brother Bart, in Newgate Prison, on a visiting day. Then the spokesman, or coordinator, for the southern half—William Higby—would collect that information from Bart on another such day and take it on down to his group. Bart would act as go-between, being useful despite his confinement. The two groups could thus coordinate their actions to get together for the third big event . . . the *Walpurgisnacht* slaying."

"So Jacob Nugent is the leader of the northern half . . ."

"Not the leader, to my mind, Harry. The leader is the mastermind behind it all, and I do not think either of the Nugents so capable. Most certainly not our gamekeeper, either. No, Harry. They are merely pawns in this mighty game of chess."

"Why didn't both murders take place in the London area, sir? Why pick a young woman up near Liverpool?" I had been wondering this for some time. "Surely then there would have been no need for coordinating and go-betweens."

Mr. Stoker nodded his head slowly as though thinking things through. "Good question, Harry. I do have a vague sort of idea that is still germinating. It seems ridiculous on the face of it, but then so do many things about murder when first contemplated."

He did not elaborate, and I knew he would not do so until he was more certain of things. I asked him what he would like me to do.

"I know you want to keep busy, Harry, and I think it best you do. There is nothing calling for your immediate attention here at the Lyceum today, now that *Hamlet* has taken its final bows. Starting tomorrow we will be deep into *Othello* rehearsals, but this afternoon I would like to suggest that you call upon Lord Glenmont."

"Call on him, sir?"

"Not literally, Harry. I still hesitate to associate that gentleman with the satanic group, though I have not scratched him off my list. I think it more likely that the true mastermind is taking advantage of his lordship. But we cannot take anything at face value. I'd like you to make enquiries at the House of Lords, and at his lordship's club, to get some idea of Lord Glenmont's movements at the times in which we are interested. Perhaps even see if you can discover if his lordship has any special plans for May Eve? I, myself, have things to do."

"Yes, sir!" I jumped to my feet. Here was something I could immerse myself in, however temporarily, to take my mind off thoughts of Jenny being held and possibly abused. "I'll get onto it right away."

There was little information I could extract at the House of Lords. I could not even gain access there. The Palace of Westminster, of which it is a part, is closely guarded, and I had to do some fast talking in order to speak with the steward of the palace, Sir Gregory Ford. I was lucky to find even him there on a Sunday.

"The crossbenchers are under no obligation to sign in or

out," he told me. "They are invariably on hand when there is a vote expected or even for strong discussion, but the very fact of their being crossbenchers precludes any obligation on their part. I am not even sure that Lord Glenmont has been here at all this week. Now if you will excuse me?" He bustled away, looking about him as though searching for someone.

I returned through the great gates of the palace and started walking down Great George Street toward St. James's Park. It was turning into a beautiful day, and my mind kept straying to thoughts of strolling with Jenny around that park or Hyde Park. I tried to put such thoughts out of my head. Mr. Stoker had warned me that to dwell on Jenny's abduction would do her no favors and that I needed to keep my brain active.

I cut across the park, walked along the side of St. James's Palace, and came out at the junction of Pall Mall and St. James's Street. My destination was number 60 St. James's Street, the home of Brooks's, the leading Liberal club for gentlemen. I had learned from Debrett's that this was the club favored by Lord Glenmont. When the House of Lords was in session many of the politicians lived in their respective clubs, traveling home only at the weekends. The accommodation at such establishments is without parallel, and the cuisine is nothing but excellent. Baedeker claims that the wine and viands at the West End gentleman's clubs attain excellence unequaled by the most elaborate and expensive restaurants. Who, in his right mind, would want to go home? I thought, my mind briefly visiting Mrs. Bell and her cold kippers and lukewarm tea.

I knew that I could not hope to gain entrance to Brooks's, being neither a member nor a member's guest, but it was not admission that I sought. It was information, and a Sunday seemed the ideal day to acquire it.

A commissionaire was to be found at the entrance to all such gentleman's clubs. He was usually a retired army ser-

geant major; big and burly enough to keep out any undesirables yet educated enough to be able to converse intelligently
with the members and their guests. At Brooks's I encountered Sergeant Major Oliver Martingale, formerly of the
Coldstream Guards. His dress uniform gleamed in all the
right places; his boots and belt reflected the sunlight; and
the paired brass buttons of his jacket dazzled the eyes. His
bald pate gleamed to match the boots, and I briefly wondered if he polished that, also. It wasn't difficult to get into
conversation with the commissionaire, there being little
coming and going at Brooks's on this Sunday.

"I don't think there's a man in England who does not
look twice, and with pride, at the uniform of the Coldsteam
Guards, Sergeant Major," I said. I sensed rather than saw
that he pulled himself up a little straighter and thrust out
his chest.

"Crimean. Waterloo. Napoleonic Wars. Wilhelmstal.
Siege of Namur." He counted them off as though he had
fought in all of them, though I happened to know that the
siege had taken place two hundred years ago. Still, it was by
such benchmarks that a soldier defined his regiment.

"Amazing," I murmured, sufficiently loudly for him to
hear and appreciate my awe. "Surely you must find this gentleman's club a far cry from your past glories."

"Oh, you would be surprised at some of the goings-on
I've witnessed 'ere," he said, leaning in toward me in a con-
fidential manner.

I raised my eyebrows and tried to look surprised.

"Many of them as is supposed to be gentlemen fall far
from the mark, to my 'umble mind, when they've got a drink
or two in 'em." He pursed his lips and nodded his bald head.
"Wouldn't have done back at the regiment, I can tell you."

"No, I'm sure not," I agreed.

In no time I was able to bring the conversation around to
certain members of the club, Lord Glenmont in particular.

I expressed my particular interest in that gentleman and his movements, implying a desire to discuss certain investments with his lordship. By then the sergeant major was much more relaxed, and I could tell he seldom got to be at ease and to just chat. We quickly came to be on first-name terms. I soon learned that his lordship was one of the few members for whom he had any respect.

"Never seen 'is lordship falling down drunk, 'Arry, which is more than I can say for most of 'em. 'E always bids me good day and stops to comment on the weather. Nice old gentleman."

It transpired that the sergeant major kept a register of the members' comings and goings together with any guests that they admitted.

"You must see some very important people come and go, Oliver," I said.

"Just feast your eyes on this," he said.

We stood in the foyer of the club, at the foot of the marble staircase that curved away up to the main club rooms. The book lay open on the desk where the commissionaire normally sat. He flipped a page or two back and pointed to the signatures of the prime minister and various well-placed members of his party. Just then a carriage bearing a discreet coat of arms on its door pulled up at the club entrance.

"No rest even on a Sunday!" said the sergeant major. "'Old on, 'Arry. I'll be right back." He tugged his uniform jacket straight and marched across to open the doors for the party descending from the carriage.

I wasted no time. I quickly turned the pages in the book, back to the date of Nell Burton's slaying. I ran my finger down the signatures. There was no sign of Lord Glenmont's name. I turned back farther.

"What you looking for, 'Arry?"

With a start I realized that the sergeant major was back

beside me. I couldn't believe I had not been aware of his heavy boots marching across the foyer. I glanced down at the thick carpet.

"I can't believe some of these names, Oliver," I said. "Lord this and Earl that. Did I see a duke in there?"

"Could well be," he smirked. "Could very well be."

"No, sir," I said. "I could see no indication that Lord Glenmont went out from his club at the time of Nell Burton's murder. Apparently he was in residence there at the time. Does this mean he's clear of any involvement?" I stared at Mr. Stoker to see his reaction.

"We cannot jump to any hasty conclusions, Harry," he said. We were back in his office late on Sunday afternoon. "I must admit, I find Lord Glenmont a bit of a puzzle."

"Sir?"

"Everything seems to indicate that he really is all he seems to be . . . a benign elderly gentleman with a smile for everyone. But is that truly him, or is he a consummate actor—good enough for the Lyceum family—who is secretly the mastermind of this terrible satanic group intent on destroying life?" He shook his head. "I just don't know, Harry."

"But you have your suspicions, sir?" I urged. "You always have your inner feelings. Your grandmother's senses?"

"I don't know who you've been listening to, Harry. I'm sure I would never lay claim to such paranormal abilities."

I stifled myself. Mr. Stoker could be almost laughable at times, I thought. I kept a straight face. "Any second thoughts then, sir?"

He pursed his lips and tapped the side of his nose with his forefinger, gazing off into space. "I must admit that I am inclined to take his lordship at face value. I think he may well be an unwitting link in the chain. I think it possible that others have made use of him without his knowledge. But time alone will tell, Harry, and we cannot sit around and wait for that time to pass. Come!"

He got to his feet and reached for his overcoat on the mahogany clothes tree.

"Where are we going, sir?" I asked.

"Out!" came the enigmatic response.

The hansom deposited us outside a small, cheap hotel in Belgravia. I followed my boss as he surged up the steps and into the foyer. A tall, thin lady with a lantern jaw and what I believe is described as a hatchet face stood from where she sat behind the counter. Her black eyebrows rose in questioning mode, though she said nothing.

"Mr. Seth Hartzman?" said Stoker. "I believe he is one of your guests? Is he presently in residence?"

"I am unable to divulge any particulars of my guests . . ."

"Is he in residence?" thundered my boss.

The eyebrows rose even higher. "Sir!"

Stoker slammed his hand down on the counter and looked the lady squarely in the eyes.

"This is no time for shilly-shallying, madam! Mr. Hartzman. It is imperative that I speak with him."

To her credit, the lady looked straight back at Mr. Stoker without flinching. "As it happens that particular guest of the hotel is not in residence at this time, sir. He left yesterday evening with his bag packed. It was my understanding that he would not be back for several days, though he did request that we hold his room."

"Damnation!"

"Sir, I must ask that you leave this establishment immediately."

I was surprised at my boss's outburst. It showed me, in no uncertain terms, that he was more emotionally involved with the approaching ritual, and the fate of my dear Jenny, than he cared to say. He raised his hat to the lady.

"My apologies, madam. I forget myself. It is certain circumstances that bring unexpected pressures." He looked briefly at me. "Come, Harry. Let us take up no more of this good lady's time."

I trotted after him as he swept out of the hotel.

Chapter Twenty-five

"Now where, sir?"

A light rain had started to fall, and I felt we should do rather more than simply stand in the middle of the pavement looking up and down the street.

"Damnation! I should have acted yesterday, when I knew our man was still here. I should have confronted him before this. I blame myself."

"Our man?"

"Hartzman. He is the key to much that is going on, Harry. We need to track him down and have a heart-to-heart talk with him."

"I hesitate to suggest it, but would Inspector Bellamy be of any use here?" I said. I turned up my coat collar.

Mr. Stoker pulled out his gold watch, looked at it, and then thrust it back in his pocket. "It's a Sunday and late in the afternoon. I very much doubt that the good inspector will be at his post right now. But let us not forget him, Harry. Perhaps we can squeeze him in tomorrow?"

"I'll make a point of it, sir," I said.

"Good. Then don't keep me here in this rain any longer. Let us repair to an eatery for some tea."

We found a tea shop open on Wilton Crescent, though it looked as though they were preparing to close for the day. We took a table in the window, and the waitress bustled about bringing us tea, sandwiches, and pastries. Mr. Stoker inspected the assortment of savories. Apparently satisfied, he sank his teeth into one of the sandwiches and sat back while I poured the tea.

"I had alerted Inspector Bellamy to Hartzman a while ago," he said, gazing out of the window. "If he had only acted at that time, instead of putting it off, we might have apprehended the young man. Now he may have to institute a search."

"What is it you think you'll discover about him, sir?" I asked, stirring a lump of sugar into my tea.

"I'm not certain. I have one or two theories but nothing firm as yet. I intend to do some further digging tomorrow morning, while you are busy with the inspector."

"Mr. Hartzman should be at the theatre this week for *Othello* rehearsals," I said. "Wasn't that the reason the colonel wanted him in the cast, so that he could be a part of it when Mr. Booth was onstage?"

"That was the suggestion, yes."

I thought he sounded unsure.

"You think there may have been other reasons?"

"Once again, time will tell, Harry. Now eat up and let us allow these poor people to close the shop and go home."

On Monday morning we received a note from Scotland Yard saying that Inspector Bellamy would be obliged if Mr. Stoker would come by. He didn't mention me, but I presumed to accompany my boss. When we got to the Yard we found Bellamy in conference with another police officer.

I immediately recognized him as Inspector Whittaker of the Warrington police. How could I forget that short, bald-headed official with the receding chin? I thought. I didn't see his baton in evidence, but I was sure it was in the room somewhere. I wondered what brought him to London all the way from Liverpool.

"Come in, gentlemen," said Bellamy, and he waved us to two chairs set out beside the one occupied by Inspector Whittaker. He made no comment on the fact that I had accompanied my boss, but that there were two chairs ready showed that he was not altogether surprised.

"Your note intimated that there was some urgency," said Mr. Stoker.

"If we are to abide by your prediction of an upcoming murder, sir, and if this ties in with your missing young lady, yes, there is indeed urgency." He moved a bulky file into the center of his desk and opened it. "We have had the good inspector, here, dig back through his files to the murder of Miss Elizabeth Scott. He has been good enough to bring those files with him to Scotland Yard, at our request." His eyes settled on Mr. Stoker's face. "We felt it would save time if you were present while we went through them since you have, on previous occasions, managed to put a somewhat different perspective on things."

I thought it very magnanimous of Inspector Bellamy to admit to Mr. Stoker's brilliance. I grinned. If Bellamy saw the smile, he ignored it.

"But surely you have already been through these files with a fine-tooth comb?" Stoker looked surprised. "Have you, then, discovered something new and of note?"

Inspector Bellamy looked uncomfortable.

Whittaker knitted his brow. "It was a complete . . ." he started to say, but Bellamy cut him off.

"What our colleague is trying to say, is that the Scott murder occurred at a time when the Yard was going through changes. Our predecessor was retiring, and we were just starting to take the helm. There was some, er, mismanagement, perhaps . . ."

Inspector Whittaker could contain himself no longer. "The Yard made a complete mess of things! That ridiculous Inspector Watson—thank the gods he did retire—he came in and took over what was most decidedly *our* case. The first good murder we had had in years. Just snatched it right out of our hands! Then the fool goes and retires and the new man . . ." Here he had the grace to incline his head to Inspector Bellamy and nod. "Well, no doubt . . ."

"We were pushed into this with no preparation," pleaded Bellamy. "Too many cases suddenly thrust upon us. It's no wonder the murder did not get the full and complete examination that it deserved."

"You are saying—'admitting' might be the more accurate word—that the Elizabeth Scott murder was not properly examined?" Mr. Stoker sounded amazed.

"Oh, it was all done properly," pleaded Bellamy. "It was just that we didn't have the time or the manpower to look into it as thoroughly as we might have done."

"And wouldn't allow the Warrington force to work it," grumbled Whittaker.

"Water under the bridge," muttered Bellamy. "Water under the bridge."

"Properly done but not thoroughly done." Mr. Stoker sat forward and turned the file around so that he might read it. "Well, no matter, gentlemen. We are here now, and let us get on with it." He turned to Whittaker. "Inspector, would you be kind enough to give me a complete rundown on the case from your point of view? What have you learned, both from your original, if sparse, investigations and from your subsequent perusal? Harry, you might take notes if you would."

Over the next four hours the three of them worked their

way through the large file, the two inspectors bickering from time to time but being brought to order by Mr. Stoker. To my mind the only really new information was the fact that although locally there had been the occasional "juvenile high spirits"—it seemed that Inspector Whittaker thought along the same lines as did the vicar—there had never been any real problems in the area until the beginning of this present year. Then suddenly there seemed to be a number of previously unknown people, "undesirables," as the inspector termed them, who appeared in the area around Warrington and then as quickly disappeared right after the murder of Miss Scott.

"You say that you were not familiar with many of these malcontents?" asked Stoker.

Whittaker shook his head. "I was born and raised in Warrington, Mr. Stoker. Certainly we have changed over the years. Being so close to Liverpool, it's no wonder. But I have never seen such an influx of strangers in so short a time. It is a small community, so a dozen strange faces suddenly appearing can be disconcerting. I had mentioned this to the original Inspector Watson, but he seemed to have thought it insignificant. He did not even record my remarks."

"And you say these new faces disappeared as quickly as they had come?"

"To the best of my knowledge."

"Exactly what time period are we talking about?"

"From the start of the year up until the first week of March. Only about eight or nine weeks."

"But what we find of especial interest, Mr. Stoker," said Bellamy, "is the name of one of those persons. Hartzman. Seth Hartzman. The gentleman you are looking for, I believe?"

Mr. Stoker pursed his lips and fingered his beard. "So our Mr. Hartzman was definitely on the scene at the time of Miss Scott's murder. Very interesting."

"More than simply 'on the scene' as you put it, sir," said

Whittaker. "It is my belief that he was some sort of leader, or organizer, of these interlopers."

"Why do you say that?"

"One of the problems that we had was the burning of bonfires. They built and lit one the night of Miss Scott's murder. Hartzman was noted as organizing the building of it. It was at the opposite end of the village and was what drew our attention away from any activity we might otherwise have observed at the old windmill. Then a second, admittedly much smaller, bonfire was lit on the night of . . ." He dug into the file on the desk. "The night of the twenty-first of March."

Stoker's head slowly nodded up and down.

"Pagan holidays, sir?" I ventured to ask.

"Oh yes, Harry. Imbolc, the night of the sacrifice of Miss Scott, and then the spring equinox, Ostara, the sacrifice of our own Miss Burton. Bonfires often featured as the focal point of pagan festivities; not that this group is necessarily pagan. The fire represents the sun. Even today, in various remote parts of England, bonfires are lit—usually on hilltops—to celebrate all the old feast days."

"But why would they build a second bonfire in Warrington when that particular sacrifice was taking place in London, sir?"

"Merely a token to indicate the continuation of the rites, Harry. An indication that both sacrifices were connected. Inspector Bellamy! Do you have any evidence of a similar large bonfire being lit in your bailiwick on the night of Miss Burton's murder?"

"We get lots of fires around the city, sir, all the time."

"I am talking a large bonfire, Inspector. Of the Guy Fawkes variety, but far from the fifth of November and without the fireworks."

Inspector Bellamy had to call in a sergeant, whom he instructed to check on my boss's suggestion. In no time the sergeant returned with the news that yes, there had indeed been an unusual bonfire on that night. Not especially large but definitely unusual. Bellamy relayed the details to us all.

"On the river, not far from the warehouse where we discovered the body of your Miss Burton," he said to Mr. Stoker. "Right on the water, a flat homemade raft was set adrift and floated downriver. There was a large pile of kindling, driftwood and the like, piled on the raft, and it had been set alight. It took the Thames River Police by surprise, we can tell you."

"I am sure it did," murmured Stoker. "I'm sure it did."

"So we had bonfires up north and down here," said Inspector Whittaker. "What of it? What about the people? What about this Hartzman you seem to know?"

"I am certainly of the opinion that Hartzman is a key figure in all of this, even in the two murders," said Mr. Stoker. "But I still do not believe that he is the ringleader, the mastermind. I have my suspicions, but am not yet ready to point the finger. We need to look into this a lot closer."

The meeting came to an end, and Mr. Stoker and I departed Scotland Yard, heading back to the Lyceum. There was much to do there, with *Othello* rehearsals proceeding apace and with scenery and props to be attended to.

I was startled to be addressed by the Guv'nor himself, at the end of rehearsal. He stopped by my humble office on his way out of the theatre.

"Mr. Rivers. I suppose we have no further news regarding our missing young lady?"

"No, sir. I'm afraid not."

"Such a shame. Young Jenny is very much missed back at my rooms, and I understand that you have a special interest in her?" He bowed and tut-tutted, sadly shaking his head.

He glanced up again. I noticed that he never actually looked at me. I couldn't help thinking that it was as though he were playing a part onstage. Not overly dramatic yet just not natural, to my mind. Still, I was grateful that he was even aware of myself and Jenny.

"Miss Terry and I have spoken of this on a number of occasions recently. Our thoughts and prayers are with you both, young man. Together we will pull through this trial."

"Yes, sir. Thank you, sir," I said. I really didn't know what to say.

"Yes, we are all most concerned." It was Colonel Cornell who had spoken. I was surprised to see that Mr. Edwin Booth and his manager had come up behind the Guv'nor. They were all on their way out of the Lyceum at the end of rehearsal.

Still sadly shaking his head, Mr. Irving moved on, and I was left once again with thoughts of my Jenny in the hands of the satanic abductors. I felt very depressed. The Guv'nor's words had not cheered me at all; in fact quite the opposite. I reached for my coat and made for the Druid's Head and a pint of porter.

John Martin, the tavern keeper, gave me a cheery wave, but I barely responded. I sank down onto a bench at a table close to the fireplace. The fire was low, the day having been quite warm for the time of year. A tankard brimming with beer appeared almost magically at my elbow, and the serving girl asked me if I'd like anything to eat. I didn't feel like facing Mrs. Bell's offerings so I settled on a piece of pork pie and some cheese. But I was not really hungry, and when it arrived I just toyed with the food.

"Not like you, Mr. Rivers, from what I've heard. Everyone always says that you are bright and cheerful all the time."

I looked up to see Miss Abbott smiling at me from across the table. I waved for her to sit down.

"What are you doing here, Edwina?" I asked.

"We were at rehearsals. They were doing the crowd scenes this afternoon. I sometimes drop in here for a quick bite before going back to Mrs. Briggs's. Tilly Fairbanks said she might look in as well, though she had to do something first."

I felt a little better just by virtue of having another member of the Lyceum family with me. I managed a smile.

"Let me buy you supper, Miss Abbott," I said.

"Oh no, Mr. Rivers. There ain't no need for that. I just saw you sitting here and you looked so sad that I had to say something. Now, I can be on my way."

She started to get up, but I stopped her. "Stay, if you would, Edwina. I must admit, I could use a bit of company."

"No news, then?"

"No." I signaled the serving girl to come and take her order. "But Mr. Stoker says to be patient. He seems to know how things will play out, and I trust his judgment."

"Would you like me to read the cards, Mr. Rivers?" She reached for her reticule.

Again I stopped her. "Not right now, I don't think, Edwina. But thank you."

"Oh, by the way . . . I never did thank you properly for finding them, when they was lost last week."

I waved a dismissing hand.

"No, really, Mr. Rivers. You've no idea."

I looked up.

"You see, I'd thought of looking under the stage myself," she continued. "Though goodness knows how they would have got there. But when I went down there—just out of the light, you know, and was groping around trying to find my way—suddenly someone grabbed me."

"Grabbed you?"

"Yes, sir. They must have been waiting, I'm thinking. P'raps that's why they took the cards in the first place. To entice me down there, if you see what I mean?"

I was beginning to. "What happened? Tell me every-thing."

She shrugged. "I was lucky. I threw out my arms and just happened to feel a big piece of wood, or something. I grabbed hold of it and swung it back over my shoulder. I think it must have hit the man on the head. I don't think it did any real damage, but it was enough to make him let go for a second. I dropped the wood and ran out of there as though the devil were at my heels!"

"You were indeed lucky," I said. "You should have reported this, Miss Abbott. You should have let me know."

"I know." She hung her head. "But then I suppose I got caught up in something else, and by the time I was back at the theatre next morning I'd really put it out of my mind."

I wondered who it might have been. Was it just one of the stagehands looking for a little nonsense with Edwina, or was it more than that? Perhaps someone's first attempt to get the next ritual victim? Failing, they went on to take my Jenny.

We sat in silence for a while. From time to time Edwina would look back toward the door, obviously wondering if her friend was coming. The serving girl brought her bread, cheese, and a pickled onion, together with a half pint of ale. We chatted about the way *Othello* was shaping up and what we thought of the American Mr. Booth. Eventually Tilly Fairbanks appeared, and, draining my porter, I left the two of them by the fire.

Chapter Twenty-six

Rehearsals started early Tuesday morning, as they had since the end of *Hamlet*. It felt good to hear voices echoing about the stage area and to hear people hurrying here and there, trying on costumes and exchanging banter. Mr. Irving was strict when it came to directing those onstage but slightly more lax with the rest of the cast backstage, so long as their talking did not interfere with the rehearsal.

I had dealt with some minor crises—a broken spear and a misplaced helmet—but felt that all was on course and flowing as it should. Just before the lunch break Bill Thomas stuck his head around the corner of my office space.

"Harry! There's a young feller up front with a message for you. Says he was told to give it to you personally. Wouldn't even let me bring it to you."

I looked up, surprised. "Thanks, Bill. I'll be right there."

I got up and followed his stocky figure as he returned to his domain just inside the stage door. A scruffy young street urchin stood by Bill's window. He grinned when he saw me.

"You Mr. Rivers then?" he asked, and he wiped his nose on the sleeve of his tattered jacket.

"I am. Who sent you?" I had a sudden hope that it was a message from Jenny's abductor, but that was soon dashed.

"Sergeant Major Martingale. 'Im as is at the gentleman's club on St. James's Street." He dug into his pocket and pulled out a grimy piece of paper. He had the grace to hold it against the wall and rub his hand over it a few times to get rid of the creases before handing it to me.

"Thank you," I said.

"'E said as 'ow you'd see me all right." He looked anxious.

"Of course." I dug into my own pocket and found a six-pence, which I gave him.

"Ta, guv." He turned and quickly disappeared out of the door.

The note said that the sergeant major had just acquired certain information regarding the gentleman I had been enquiring about, and that he'd be happy to pass along that information if I should care to look in at the club. I applauded the commissionaire for not using any names in his note, nor revealing any other details of my quest. I decided to go over to St. James's Street right away. The Lyceum wouldn't miss me for a while. Besides, it was almost lunchtime.

I was tempted to look in at the Druid's Head and get something to eat first but decided that anything however loosely connected to Jenny's disappearance was more important than my midday meal. I took a hansom to the club.

"Ah! There you are, 'Arry. I thought as 'ow you'd be interested." Sergeant Major Oliver Martingale was in his gleaming uniform, his boots as highly polished as ever. His face was cheery and his smile infectious. He was sorting mail into individual boxes behind his desk, by the club's front entrance. "Just a minute. Got to get these billet-doux into their right boxes." He pronounced it "billy-doos."

"No rush, Oliver," I said. "I thank you for thinking of me."

He finished his task, saluted two gentlemen who came down the staircase and hurried out, and then turned to me. Although the lobby was now empty, he glanced about him as though to be sure we were alone and then dropped his voice to a conspiratorial level.

"Your Lord Glenmont, 'Arry. Thought you might be interested to know that 'is nibs 'as apparently got some plans for this coming weekend."

I was immediately alert.

"The gentlemen usually let me know if they are going to be in residence over the weekend or if they are going 'ome to their wives and children. Just so's I can know in case they get unexpected visitors like."

I nodded and waited for him to continue.

"Well Lord G. said that 'e's leaving late Friday and may not be back for a few days. Just thought you'd like to know, 'Arry."

"Yes. Yes, indeed. Thank you very much, Oliver." My mind was racing. Did this mean that his lordship was going back to Knowl Estate to be on hand for the ritual sacrifice? I needed to share this with Mr. Stoker. "Thank you, Oliver. This really could be important." I slipped a whole sovereign into his waiting palm. He gave a wink and a nod, and I hurried out.

On the ride back to the Lyceum I ran over possibilities in my mind. Could this possibly mean that Lord Glenmont was the mastermind we had been looking for? Was this confirmation that the ritual would take place at the caves on Knowl Estate? If so, could we get there without being seen and be successful in rescuing Jenny?

My mind galloped on at high speed. Before I knew it the cab pulled in to the curb in front of the theatre. As I paid the driver and got out, I determined that I needed to pay another visit to the caves and study the lie of the land.

I ate a quick lunch at the Druid's Head before going back into the theatre. As it happened, when I did go in Bill told me that Mr. Stoker had left with the Guv'nor and Mr. Booth and had said that he wouldn't be back today. That settled it, I thought. A sure sign that I should run out to Knowl Estate by myself and make a thorough investigation before reporting everything to my boss. But it was not to be immediately. Miss Connelly, the wardrobe mistress, cornered me with some concerns about Cassio's costume. As I had on numerous previous occasions, I tried to point out to her that my duties as stage manager did not extend to wardrobe. But again, as usual, she completely ignored that and carried on with her concerns. I sighed and tried to deal with them. One thing led to another until I realized that I wasn't going to be able to get to the caves today. I determined to get up early and leave first thing in the morning. With no current production, I did not have to meet with Mr. Stoker in his office first thing. I could see him, and have much more to report, later in the day.

Wednesday morning was cold, and there was a steady drizzle of rain. I felt damp and miserable as the four-wheeler took me out of the city, but I was determined. As on the last time with Mr. Stoker, I had the cabdriver drop me off a short distance before the entrance to the estate. I looked carefully all about me—wondering if Sergeant Major Martingale's habit had now become mine—and then hurried forward to the estate gates, my coat collar turned up and my bowler hat pulled down over my ears. Another quick look around and then I was off down the driveway, keeping well under the outstretched limbs of the beech trees and grateful for their shelter. I doubted that there would be anyone traveling the driveway, but I was keenly aware that the gun-carrying gamekeeper could be anywhere, and the last thing I needed was to come face-to-face with him again. I did not have Mr. Stoker's confidence and aplomb when it came to dealing with such people. On that visit we had not actually entered the caves, due to the gamekeeper's diligence, but I determined to rectify that omission this time.

I soon came upon the folly and carefully skirted it, making around to where I could see the steps down into the caves. Huddled under a large bush, I took my time ensuring that no one else was about. What I wanted to do was what we had not been able to do on the previous visit. Namely, to actually go down into the caves and see how extensive they were. It was feeling rainwater seeping down into my shoes that finally made me make my move. The rain had not given up; if anything it had increased its intensity. Trying to keep low, and with a hand holding on to my hat, I dashed across and down the steps.

I had thought to bring a bullseye lantern with me; one that we had in the property room. It held a candle, rather than having the more usual oil reservoir and wick. I struck one of Bryant & May's safety matches and lit the candle. It felt good to be out of the rain, though it was still cold. I shone the lantern about me.

A bullseye is also known as a dark lantern. This is because it has an inserted sliding cylinder of metal that has a hole cut out at the front. This hole allows the light to pass through to the bullseye glass, which then magnifies the illumination. But it is possible to rotate the metal cylinder so that the light can be gradually cut off until it has completely been hidden. The wick will keep burning because of the chimney on top of the lantern, which allows a flow of air. The cylinder may then be rotated again to open up to full light.

The cave entrance was made of flint and chalk mortar, and then there was a short brick-lined passageway before coming to the inner rough chalk walls. Not far into the passage the walls had been expanded to make what amounted to a small room. With large nails hammered into the walls in lines, I assumed that this was a robing room, or similar, the nails being to hang the robes. Beyond, the passage or tunnel continued. It advanced for some way, though it was not easy to judge the exact distance, before coming to a very large room. This, I guessed, was the main space. A section of it in the center had a higher floor than the rest, making it a small stage. Presumably this was the actual ritual area.

There was little beyond the ritual room. I was disappointed. I recalled Mr. Stoker speaking of the ongoing passage in the original caves of Sir Francis Dashwood. I had been told that they included a wine store, a buttery, a banquet room, and two or three other rooms of varying sizes. Here there was a continuation of sorts, but the passageway quickly became quite narrow, and the roof was low enough to cause me to stoop. The short section ended with a pile of chalk rubble on the floor; rocks large and small.

I was about to turn around and retrace my steps when I froze. I heard footsteps. Someone was coming my way, humming tunelessly as they came. Who could possibly be here? I wondered. It had to be the gamekeeper. Surely no one else would be in this underground cavern? Frantically, I looked around. Where to hide? There was nowhere. I did the only thing possible. I blew out the lantern and dropped down flat on the ground behind the small mound of loose rock.

The heavy footsteps got closer, and a glow showed that whoever it was had a lantern. It didn't emit much light, just enough to show the way. The steps stopped just before entering the low-ceilinged end section where I was. The person seemed to stand and look around. The humming continued. Then the lamp was put down on the ground, and I heard a sweeping sound.

I took a chance and peered up over the chalk pile. It was indeed the gamekeeper, William Higby. Apparently, he had brought a broom with him and was now sweeping the floor of the main area. Thankfully, he didn't seem at all interested in probing the darkness at the very end of the tunnel where I was. I carefully eased myself up into a less cramped position.

He swept for ten or fifteen minutes, pushing the dirt into the area where I sat. I had to cover my mouth with a handkerchief to keep from sneezing. After the first few minutes he gave up humming, which was a small mercy, it seemed to me. But then he started an equally tuneless whistling.

It was obvious that the gamekeeper was cleaning the area because someone was expected or because the place was to be used for some purpose. It didn't take a genius to guess that the purpose was almost certainly the ritual murder of my beloved Jenny. If attacking the gamekeeper could have prevented that, I would not have hesitated, but I knew he was only a small cog in the wheel. I bided my time. I determined to get away from there and to take back to Mr. Stoker all that I had learned.

As I sat back and gazed around at the ghostly white of the chalk walls, I became aware of a dark fissure or alcove that ran down from ceiling to floor close by where I lay. Once aware of it, I couldn't keep my eyes off it. I strained to make out more definitely what it was. Perhaps the equivalent of a cupboard dug into the chalk? A storage niche of some sort? I couldn't wait for Mr. Higby to be finished with his task and to go away.

The man dithered around for a long time after he had finished sweeping. I don't know what he was doing. Preparing the place in some way, presumably. Eventually, however, the tuneless whistling stopped, and the light grew dim as his footsteps shuffled away. I waited what I thought a reasonable time before groping in my pocket for my matches and relighting my bullseye. I immediately focused it on the dark gash in the wall, coming to my feet and moving forward to it.

I thought at first that my guess of a cupboard was correct, but then I saw that the recess went much deeper than that. It wasn't very wide but was wide enough for me to squeeze into. I felt a cool breeze on my face. With a thrill I realized that it was a way out, a back entrance. Exit, I suppose, would be the more correct term, but I was not about to quibble on semantics. I pushed through toward the freedom of the outside world.

Once outside I lost no time in making for the main road. I had no idea how long I had been trapped inside the cave, but my watch indicated it had been more than two hours. I cursed the gamekeeper for his leisurely sweeping. I had asked the driver of my four-wheeler to come back and pick me up within the hour. I broke away from the shelter of the beech trees and ran out to the road. There was no sign of any transportation. I grew concerned.

After waiting another half hour, just on the off chance that the cabbie would check back, I started the long walk back toward the last village we had passed through. My shoes were still damp and not made for walking. Happily, the rain had stopped, but I was not a happy man. I plodded on.

I had walked well over a mile before I saw a carriage in the distance, coming toward me. It was not the one I had used, for I saw that this was a different driver. Since it was going in the direction of Knowl Estate I knew it was no good trying to beg a ride, so I stepped to one side to let it go by. I was surprised when it stopped opposite me. The figure inside the carriage leaned my way, and a hand beckoned me forward. I hurried across the road and looked up. I'm sure my jaw gaped open when I saw who was inside.

Chapter Twenty-seven

"I do find you somewhat predictable, Harry," said Mr. Stoker, sitting back and gazing out at the passing countryside as the carriage trundled along the country road. "I enquired around the theatre when I got in this morning, and no one had seen you. Bill Thomas told me of the message you had received late yesterday, mentioning a gentleman's club on St. James's Street. I guessed that it was Brooks's and that you had been summoned there by your friend the commissionaire. It was obvious, to me at least, that this was to do with the comings and goings of Lord Glenmont, so I immediately tied your disappearance to a desire to revisit the Glenmont caves. Am I correct?"

I had been overjoyed to see my boss smiling down at me from the carriage. He always seemed to turn up when I most needed him. I now sat with my sodden bowler hat resting on the seat opposite me and my hands thrust deep into my pockets.

"Yes, sir. Thank you, sir. Very perceptive of you, if I may say so."

I went on to tell him of my adventures and of the game-keeper's domestic chores within the caves.

"Getting things in order for use in the immediate future, would you say, Harry?"

"Yes, I would. That was my thought. I'd stake anything on the caves being the place where they are planning on having their ritual."

His big head nodded. "Mmm! Yes, I have to agree with you. It seems most probable. The only real clue we have, so far, as to the exact venue. Well done, Harry. A little presumptuous of you to go running off like that, all by yourself, but commendable nonetheless."

"Thank you, sir. So what are we going to do?"

"Ah! What indeed, Harry?"

Mr. Stoker could be very annoying at times, I thought. Surely we could now go rushing in and rescue Jenny. I said as much.

"Rush in where, Harry? To the caves? But you know yourself that they are empty. There will be no activity there—if indeed that is the site to be used—until Saturday night. Another three days. We know that Jenny is not being held in the caves. You have seen as much yourself. So why would you have us go rushing in there?"

He was right, of course. But it just felt so frustrating to sit there and do nothing. We were almost certain that the ritual would take place in the Glenmont caves, but as Mr. Stoker said, we still did not know where Jenny was. It was going to be a long ride back to the Lyceum.

Somewhat to my surprise, I had a good night's rest after my excursion to the Knowl Estate. I had half expected to toss and turn all night. After a quick, if somewhat inadequate, breakfast, I was out and along to Mr. Stoker's office bright and early Thursday morning. He was already there.

Since the start of *Othello* rehearsals my boss had been coming into the theatre extremely early for him. It still caught me by surprise.

"Good morning, Harry. Sit down. We have much to discuss."

I did as he bid.

"Lord Glenmont."

I waited.

"All we have so far is circumstantial evidence."

I started to speak, but Stoker held up his hand.

"Consider it, Harry. In fact, all we know is that his lordship will not be going into his club for a few days and that his gamekeeper has been sweeping out the old caves under the Glenmont folly. Now, what would Inspector Bellamy, for example, make of that?"

I again opened my mouth to speak, only to be silenced.

"Yes, I know your opinion of Inspector Bellamy, and I'm not about to dispute that. But the point is, Harry, that we don't have anything definite to link Lord Glenmont to this bunch of would-be Hellfire ghouls. Nothing!"

"We can't sit and be idle, sir!" I cried.

"Of course we can't. And we are not going to. No! There is a great deal that we can do. Top of our list, of course, is to try to locate where your Miss Cartwright is being held."

"Yes!" I nodded vigorously. "But where do we start looking? You've pointed out that she isn't in the caves themselves. Just supposing that Lord Glenmont *is* behind all of this, have you any idea where he would keep her? Do you think that Knowl Hall is a possibility?"

"I think it well worth investigating, Harry. We must leave no stone unturned."

There was a tap on the door, and it was thrown open. We were surprised to see the Guv'nor standing there, with Miss Terry close behind him. We both came to our feet.

"Sit, gentlemen. Pray, sit."

The pair came into the room. Despite what Mr. Irving said,

I stood and offered my seat to Miss Terry. She gave me one of her wonderful smiles and sat down with murmured thanks. I was sorry I didn't know where my boss kept his cushion.

"What can I do for you, Henry?" asked Mr. Stoker.

"You can bring us up to date on our missing young lady, for a start, Abraham. Both Ellen and I have an interest in what happens to our Lyceum extended family, for I do see my own household staff as part of that kin."

Mr. Stoker started to do that, telling of my excursion the previous day. While he did so I slipped out and found another chair, which I carried into the office. With a brief nod, the Guv'nor sat down. I closed the door behind me and leaned back against it, listening to what was said.

"So where do we go from here?" asked the Guv'nor, when Mr. Stoker had finished. He echoed my own earlier question.

"Young Harry and I were just discussing that and pondering the possibility of Miss Cartwright being detained at Knowl Hall itself," said my boss. "Though I have no idea how we might ascertain that."

"Well now, I might be able to help there," said Miss Terry.

We all looked at her in some surprise.

"Oh yes." She laughed, her musical laugh, shaking her head. "Don't look so astonished. As it happens I do know Lady Glenmont reasonably well. She and I have both been present at the Great Spring Show for the past two or three years. The Royal Horticultural Society's Show is held at the society's garden in Kensington, as you may know."

"Is it not a little early for that?" asked the Guv'nor.

"For the show itself, only a week or so," agreed Miss Terry. "But Lady Glenmont is on the committee, and she and I are always involved in preparation work. As it happens we were both at a meeting less than a fortnight ago."

"Not to make light of your horticultural interest, my dear," said Mr. Irving, "but where does this lead us, might one ask?"

She smiled patiently and patted him on the knee. "You were wanting to know whether dear Jenny might be detained at the hall, Henry. I could go there and try to find out for you. Lady Glenmont would be delighted to receive me, I know. I could go with questions about the coming flower show. Believe me, I could do a little 'looking around' while I am there, if that would help?"

"Wonderful!" Mr. Stoker and Mr. Irving both spoke together. Miss Terry smiled at everyone, and I felt a warm glow in my stomach.

"I shall go first thing in the morning," said Miss Terry. "For now, I must leave you gentlemen. I have a costume fitting I must attend."

"We need to decide upon a plan of campaign."
After Miss Terry departed, the meeting moved to the Guv'nor's dressing room, where he felt more comfortable. I perched on the edge of an upholstered chair with my notebook open on Mr. Irving's makeup table. He and Mr. Stoker relaxed on a comfortable-looking tripartite sofa on which, I understood, the Guv'nor would occasionally stretch out and relax between acts.

"It certainly looks as though the upcoming ritual is to take place in the caves below the folly, whether Lord Glenmont is aware of it or not," said Mr. Stoker. "So we have to plan our actions for that location. Now, young Harry has discovered a rear entrance to the caves, which solves what I had seen to be our biggest stumbling block . . . how to gain access to the ritual."

"Well done, Mr. Rivers," murmured the Guv'nor. I felt myself blush, which was ridiculous when I thought about it. "And this entrance is easy to find?"

The blush evaporated, or whatever blushes do. I suddenly realized that in making my escape from the caves I had rushed away without marking exactly where the entrance was located. I vaguely recalled that there was a large bush partially hiding it and that there was an oak tree close by, but other than that I had no idea.

"Of course," said my boss, glancing at me. "Right, Harry?"

I mumbled some brief response and kept my head down over my notebook. Surely, I thought, I'd be able to spot it when I returned there. How difficult could it be?

"I would like to join you on this," said the Guv'nor, surprising both Mr. Stoker and myself.

"But—but this could be dangerous, Henry. This is no staged play . . ."

"Nonsense! I'm fit. Have to be for what I do. No, I intend to be a part of this rescue attempt. It's the least I can do. After all, the young lady is in my employ."

There was no arguing with him. Personally, I thought that the more of us there were, the better, since there were apparently quite a number of the Hellfire people. I made so bold as to say as much.

"Aren't there close to a dozen of these people?" I asked. "Perhaps we should even recruit some of the stagehands, sir? I know Sam Green would be happy to lend a hand."

"And Edwin, too, I don't doubt." Mr. Irving was becoming enthusiastic. "The colonel also, perhaps . . ."

"No!"

I was surprised at the force of Mr. Stoker's rejection of that last suggestion. The Guv'nor looked surprised as well. Mr. Stoker hurried on. "Don't ask me why right now, Henry, but I would rather not include Mr. Booth's manager, if you don't mind." He turned to me. "But I like your idea, Harry. Yes, let's ask Sam Green to join us, and perhaps a few others, though we may have to restrict our numbers due to the limited room. Is there cover for us when we get into the caves?"

My mind went back to my crouching behind the small pile of rocks.

"Very little, I'm afraid. We may have to be strung out back through the entranceway, ready to rush in when you give the command, sir."

"What is the order of the program?" asked Mr. Irving.

Stoker shrugged. "We don't know, and cannot know. We can only surmise. It is going to be an extemporaneous performance for our side, I'm afraid."

"There is that raised section in the center of the main cave that I told you about, sir," I said. "Presumably that's where they'll have Jenny. Do we just rush in and rescue her as soon as they bring her in, or must we wait for some special time?"

"I know you are cognizant of these arcane rites, Abraham. Tell us the probable order of things."

Mr. Stoker pursed his lips and squinted his eyes as he thought. Slowly, he started to share those thoughts.

"It is my belief that the celebrants will be the first to fill the cave, probably distributed around in a circle. Possibly some of them will have designated tasks, such as the lighting of candles and of incense, the purification of the area, and the like. The introduction of the intended sacrifice— our Miss Cartwright—will follow with all due ceremony. You will need to brace yourself, Harry, and restrain yourself from doing anything foolish. She may be bound and gagged, or she may simply be drugged so that she is at least semipliant. She may not walk in of her own accord but may be carried in and laid on the sacrificial altar."

"Good heavens!" murmured Mr. Irving.

"She will be well guarded," continued Mr. Stoker. "We will have to carefully time our attack . . . and make no mistake, this will be an attack on our part. The celebrants will be in a somewhat drugged state themselves, from the incense, possibly wine, and the whole ecstatic glow and euphoria of the occasion. But they will be quite capable of defending what they see as their 'property.' They will not tolerate having reached that peak of emotion only to see their sacrifice snatched away."

"What about weapons, Abraham?"

"Weapons?" Mr. Stoker's eyes opened wider and he sat up straight. "Yes, Henry. Yes, you are right. We may well need some sort of weapons, though I doubt the general congregation will be armed. Although . . ." He broke off as various thoughts obviously passed through his mind. "Hmm. Yes, I suppose there is always the possibility that each of the celebrants may carry a ritual knife of some sort. Still, such tools are usually purely ritualistic and not meant for mundane use."

"You mean, they wouldn't use them to fight us?" asked the Guv'nor.

My boss didn't look comfortable. "Such would be the case in any normal situation, but here . . . well, we just don't know."

"Why not clubs of some sort, sir?" I suggested. "I couldn't imagine myself crossing blades with someone, but I will willingly break a few skulls to rescue Jenny!"

"Well said, young Harold!" cried Mr. Irving. "I would rather look forward to crossing swords with someone, but I can see that in such a confined space that might not be the best weapon of choice. Yes. I think you have the right idea. Cudgels it should be!"

Chapter Twenty-eight

Friday was a blur for me. Happily, I was very much involved in the rehearsals for *Othello*. Come what may with the Glenmont caves ritual the next day, we were all fully aware that opening night for the play was on Monday. Everything had to be ready at the Lyceum for that event. Saturday afternoon would be the first costume rehearsal and Sunday the final dress rehearsal. The whole theatre could not come to a halt because Jenny was missing, even though there was every indication she could well become a murder victim.

Inspector Bellamy was very much in evidence, thanks to pressure from Mr. Stoker, who asked him to call. He was apprised of our plans for invading the caves—tut-tutting at the fact we had kept it all from him until this point—but he promised the support of a number of police constables.

Miss Terry returned from Knowl Hall quite late in the afternoon and found Mr. Irving, Mr. Stoker, Inspector Bellamy, and myself gathered in the star's dressing room.

"What news, my dear?" asked the Guv'nor. "Did you discover any sign of our missing damsel?"

Miss Terry smiled, sat, and semi-reclined on the sofa while the gentlemen stood admiring her.

"I can tell you, with absolute conviction, that poor Miss Cartwright is not being held at Knowl Hall."

"How can you be so certain?"

"After the appropriate amount of gossip about the upcoming horticultural extravaganza, I admired Lady Glenmont's wallpaper."

"I beg your pardon?"

Even Mr. Irving's jaw hung open briefly, though he closed it faster than the rest of us did ours.

Miss Terry laughed. "Yes. I used it as a way to get into talk of furnishings. I told her that I loved to look at other people's ideas for decoration in order to get ideas for decorating sets onstage. She was delighted and took me on a tour of the house . . . beautiful residence, I might say, Henry. You should get Lord Glenmont to take you around sometime."

"And there was no sign of Miss Cartwright?" pressed Inspector Bellamy.

She shook her beautiful blond head. "None whatsoever," she said. "And I was not altogether surprised."

We all looked at her questioningly.

"Marjorie—Lady Glenmont—told me that first thing tomorrow morning she and her husband are leaving for Sandringham. I was lucky, and honored, that she made time for my visit. The Glenmonts will be spending a few days as guests of His Royal Highness, Edward, Prince of Wales. There is a strong possibility that Her Majesty may be there as well, according to Marjorie. She is quite excited."

"So Glenmont is going away," said Mr. Irving.

"Which means he can't be leading the group that will be in his caves," concluded my boss.

"We are back to the beginning," I muttered.

The inspector looked from one to the other of us. More specifically, at the other three. As usual, he ignored me.

"Where does this put us?" he asked.

"In the same place," replied Stoker. "In the Glenmont caves. Just because his lordship won't be there—it seems highly probable that he is not involved after all—that doesn't mean that there will be no activity in his caves. Harry, here, was there a day or two ago and saw the preparation."

"And anyway, it is the only clue we have, is it not?" asked the Guv'nor.

My boss agreed. We were all silent for a while.

"By the way, I've canceled my Freemasonry initiation," said the Guv'nor. "That was set for tomorrow evening."

"Canceled it, Henry? But you were so looking forward to that. You went to a lot of trouble preparing," said Miss Terry. "What happened?"

"Well, *this* happened!" The Guv'nor spread his hands to indicate all of us. "This need to rescue our young lady. You surely don't think that, even for such a momentous occasion as my initiation promised to be, I would abandon my family?"

"Oh, Henry!" Miss Terry's eyes glistened with tears.

I felt a lump in my throat. So often I had thought Mr. Irving to be unfeeling and even unaware of the rest of us. Now here he was making his own very powerful sacrifice on Jenny's behalf. I was humbled.

"The colonel, of course, tried his best to talk me out of it," he continued. "But I remained firm. A new date can be set, I am sure. What we have to do is far more important."

"Did you tell the colonel your reason for canceling?" asked Mr. Stoker.

"I didn't go into details, Abraham, no."

"Good," murmured my boss.

The inspector pulled out his pocket watch and made a great show of looking at it. "Well, we have much ground to cover if we are to prepare for this assault tomorrow. At what time do we assemble?" He addressed Mr. Stoker, apparently acknowledging my boss's leadership. "We take it we need to be in position well ahead of the Hellfire group's arrival?"

"I don't think so," said Stoker, which brought a surprised look to the inspector's face. "My thought is that they may be there from early evening. Who knows? The ritual itself will not take place till late evening . . . I'm sure they have in mind a midnight sacrifice. But they would not want to arrive en masse, especially since his lordship doesn't know of their intended use of his property. And they won't know that he won't actually be at the residence, I'm sure. So they will in all probability arrive in ones and twos, slipping onto the property and making for the caves. If we tried to be there ahead of them it would mean being in place and staying securely hidden for many hours."

The inspector grunted. "Hmm! We can't see our men sitting quiet for that long!"

"Exactly," agreed Stoker. "So my suggestion is that we get there after all the ritualists are safely tucked into the caves."

"But won't there be guards? Watchmen?" asked Mr. Irving.

"I don't think so, Henry. Probably our ubiquitous gamekeeper, but I feel fairly certain he will be alone."

"We can easily overpower him, if we need to," I said.

Stoker nodded. "Exactly. Then we will quietly enter by way of the rear entrance, we four leading the way, and lie low until I give the signal to attack. Unlike the Hellfire people, we can all arrive together, though assembling some distance from the estate. We will then advance cautiously and quietly slip in to take up our positions."

"And they will be?" asked the inspector.

"What do you mean?"

"Exactly where will our positions be? We haven't been there before."

I moved forward and unfolded a large sheet of paper I had prepared. I spread it out on the makeup table.

"I've made a rough sketch map of the area," I said, as they crowded around me. "Here is the main entrance to the caves, in the folly. And here"—I pointed—"is approximately where I remember the rear entrance to be."

Inspector Bellamy opened his mouth to say something, but I quickly continued.

"There is a large bush by the entrance and an oak tree not far from it. The rows of beeches that line the driveway are not far away, and there are plenty of other bushes and underbrush, so there is a good amount of cover. I will determine the exact entrance and wave my handkerchief. Mr. Stoker and Mr. Irving will join me, followed by you, Inspector, together with your men and our stagehands."

"I would suggest that some of the men gather at the front entrance," said Mr. Irving. "I would imagine that when we break up their meeting, they will move to escape by the way they went in."

"We'll be there to arrest them," assured the inspector.

"And where do I come in?"

We all looked up as Miss Terry rose from the sofa and came across to look at my hand-drawn map.

"You don't, my dear," responded the Guv'nor. "We are not going to risk your lovely neck in a possible melee."

"But I have to play some part!" she protested.

"If I may suggest a most important part?" said my boss.

"Please do, Abraham." Mr. Irving looked at him hopefully.

"We will have to leave here in the afternoon; it is a number of miles away. Tomorrow afternoon is the costume rehearsal. Perhaps Miss Terry might take charge of that, thus freeing you to be with us, Henry?"

"Perfect!" cried the Guv'nor. "And I will urge Edwin to stay also. I have no wish to risk the neck of our American guests, either."

Miss Terry sighed and then looked around at each of our faces, finally breaking into a smile. "If it will contribute to the cause, gentlemen. Very well."

I slept very badly Friday night, though probably much better than did my beloved Jenny. She must have known what lay in store for her, and she had no way of knowing if help was at hand or far, too far, away. I skipped breakfast, telling myself that I would eat a good lunch to compensate. But by lunchtime I had absolutely no appetite at all. I did, however, force myself to take some small repast at the Druid's Head so that I would be somewhat fortified for what promised to be a long evening reaching late into the night.

The Guv'nor organized some rehearsing before the main costume rehearsal was scheduled to start, and the theatre became a hive of activity. But after an early dinner break—at which I again ate very little—Sam Green and some of his men slipped away and gathered outside the scenery bay doors. The Guv'nor, Mr. Stoker, and myself quickly joined them. We were all dressed in black. We had ordered two four-wheelers, which stood at curbside, and we climbed into them.

"What are we waiting for, Abraham?" asked Mr. Irving, as we sat and looked about us.

As if in answer, three more carriages came around the corner carrying Inspector Bellamy and the men from Scotland Yard. Mr. Stoker acknowledged their arrival and then gave the signal for our cabbie to set off.

There was very little conversation on the journey. Each of us had our separate thoughts of how the night would play out. The caravan of carriages passed through Ealing, Greenford, and Uxbridge. As evening drew on, the sun sank down, and night slowly descended upon us. By the time we reached Beaconsfield it was quite dark.

My mind ran over possibilities of what might take place

in the caves. There would be some sort of a ritual, I knew. Exactly what, I had no idea; Mr. Stoker had given no specifics. He had spoken of the possibility of singing and some sort of dancing, though I couldn't imagine the dancing with which I was familiar taking place in a dark cave, as part of a secret rite. But what did I know? I did know that at some point the leader of this infernal group would approach my beloved, who presumably would be laid out on some sort of altar. There would come the inevitable as he raised a knife . . . dagger? Sword? I had no idea. But I did know that I had to do something!

I could see myself running across the darkened space, thrusting aside drunken revelers, striking out at all who tried to stop me! I would . . .

"Harry!"

Mr. Stoker's voice broke into my fantasy.

"Try to relax, Harry. I know what must be going through your mind. Let us just stay with our plan and do nothing rash."

He was right, of course. I looked down at the heavy cudgel I had brought with me. I had dug it out of the properties under the stage. It was heavy, but not too heavy for me to wield and break a few heads, if necessary. I smiled and tried to relax. I saw that the Guv'nor had followed along similar thoughts to myself and had a hefty walking stick with a heavy-looking silver knob to it resting alongside his seat. Somewhat to my surprise I saw that my boss had dragged along one of his Indian clubs; the sort he unconcernedly tossed about his office when exercising. He handled them easily, but I knew them to be extremely heavy. I had once tried to lift one. It must have been all of fifty pounds. I sat back and tried to relax for the rest of the journey.

Chapter Twenty-nine

Despite the blackness of the night—it was well past the new moon but still almost a fortnight to the full—I was able to locate the big oak tree that I had remembered. Standing with my back to it, I peered in the direction from which I thought I had originally approached the tree. I was able to make out the dark shape of what I assumed to be the very large bush by the cave entrance. I carefully made my way forward to it.

At first I thought I was mistaken. I seemed to remember coming out from the cave through a wide section that opened up to the outside world, but I couldn't see such an obvious passageway. However, the more I looked around the bush, the more certain I was that I was at the correct spot. I risked partially opening the light control on my bullseye lantern just enough to see more clearly. I immediately saw that I was in the right spot. I signaled Mr. Stoker, who had remained by the oak tree. He came across to me, followed by the Guv'nor.

"This is it, sir," I said. "You have to squeeze in between

the bush and this rock, but then, as you slide around the rock, you'll come to the way in."

"Good. Well done, Harry." He turned and waved to the inspector, who quickly joined us. I repeated my instructions, and he nodded. I was pleased that he didn't immediately try to take complete control of our little operation.

"We suggest that one person—perhaps your Mr. Rivers here, since he is familiar with the layout—might slip in and see how things are going," said Bellamy. "When he thinks that it's getting close to what we believe you folks term 'showtime,' he can let us know and we'll all follow him back in."

"Actually 'curtain-up' is more appropriate, Inspector," said Mr. Irving, "but no matter."

"I think I will go in along with Harry," said my boss. "I might have a better sense of the progress of any ritual. I can then send him back out to alert you at the best chosen time. When I give the word, Inspector, you can sound your whistle."

"Agreed. I will have some of my men posted along by the main entrance so we can descend on them from both ends."

As Mr. Stoker and I drew closer to the inner sanctum of the Hellfire Club, the sound of the proceedings grew in volume. My nose wrinkled as it was assaulted by a burning of pungent incense. The rock walls had a deadening effect, so that the drumming and chanting that we discovered did not reverberate off the walls as I had imagined they might. I was glad to find that there was sufficient sound to cover any slight noise our shoes might make as we edged in and settled down behind the rock pile. We had brought our respective cudgel and club with us and laid them carefully on the ground. Mr. Stoker eased forward to where he could look out at the activity, and after a moment I joined him. Dressed all in black, we must have been virtually invisible to anyone looking in our direction from the main area.

The rhythm for the dancing came from a hand drum being beaten by a young man and from the clapping and foot stamping of the revelers. They chanted some monotonous phrase that I could not make out. They seemed well foxed, and I saw that there was plenty of ale available from a firkin set up against one wall.

Mr. Stoker pointed out the gyrating figure of Miss Sarah Winterbotham, her red hair loose and flying, its color obvious even in the diminished light of the cave. I was glad that I had thought to wear a black knitted hat pulled down over my own head. Some of the dancers were dressed in ritual robes, but many were in ordinary everyday clothes. There seemed no real order to them.

"I am happy to note that the participants do not appear to be armed," murmured my boss. "As the third of this trio of sacrifices, I imagine the rite is mainly celebratory. They must believe this to be the climax of whatever cursed sorcery they are attempting. Ah!" He gave a sharp intake of breath, and I leaned over to see what it was that had drawn his attention. "I did not notice the presiding figure at first, Harry. Look. Seated there in the shadows."

I was surprised to see a large and ornately carved chair against the far wall. It had not been there when I last visited, and I suspected that it had been dragged down to the caves from the main house when it was found that his lordship was not at home. On the thronelike seat was a figure dressed in deepest purple. He—or she, for I was aware of Mr. Stoker's earlier comment that the group might well be led by a woman—had his face covered by a mask. The façade was like the head of a bird, with a ravenlike beak. Standing close behind the throne was a second masked figure wearing black robes with scarlet trimmings, his face that of a cat.

"Note the altar, Harry," whispered my boss. "It is about to be crowned with the sacrifice. Hold firm now, Harry! The time is not yet ripe."

It was as well he had warned me, for suddenly there was a break in the dancing and two men came into the main area half carrying a figure in a white robe. I knew at once that it was Jenny, and despite Mr. Stoker's warning, I started forward. But a firm grip on my shoulder stopped me.

"No, Harry! Don't put her in any greater danger. Just stay calm and wait."

I gritted my teeth and clenched my fists. I dug my nails into my palms in an effort to control my anger and the desire to wrest my Jenny out from the hands of these demented beings. We watched as they brought her forward to the raised dais in front of the throne. Jenny must have been drugged, or partially so, for she offered no resistance and lay still when they placed her, unbound, on the table that had been set in the center of the stage. The two men stepped back, and all was silent as the masked figure arose from the throne and stood looking all about the crowded cave.

He was tall. Taller than I had thought, seeing him seated. He stepped forward and up, to stand beside the comatose figure. I shuddered when I saw that he held, down at his side, a large curved dagger whose blade caught the light of the flickering candles. The man said nothing but repeatedly looked around at the silent throng. The second masked figure also moved forward but did not step up onto the dais.

"Stand by, Harry!" Stoker's voice was in my ear. "I think now's the time to get out to Bellamy and have him blow his whistle. Then get back here as fast as you can."

I needed no urging. I rushed out, not now caring whether or not I made any noise. Apparently I did make some, for I heard a shout from behind me, back in the cave proper.

I got to the exit, and for the first time in a year I was pleased to see Inspector Bellamy, his ponderous figure hovering just inside the passage.

"Now, Inspector!" I shouted. "Blow your whistle and get your men in here!"

I didn't stop but spun around to rush back to Mr. Stoker.

Behind me I heard the police whistle sound and be repeated and relayed off through the trees and brush.

As I got back to our alcove I saw Mr. Stoker with his arm drawn back and holding the heavy Indian club. Looking past him, I saw the purple-clad figure raising the wicked-looking knife and holding it above the still, white-robed figure of Jenny. Mr. Stoker's arm came over, barely clearing the cave ceiling, and the club turned end over end as it flew across the intervening space.

The club smashed into the arm holding the knife, and club and dagger crashed to the ground. A roar of pain and anger came from the tall figure. He tore the mask from his face. To my great surprise it was Colonel Wilberforce Cornell, Mr. Booth's manager.

As Inspector Bellamy, Sam Green, and other men came rushing in from outside, I scooped up my cudgel and joined my boss as he charged into the main cave. Swinging my club from side to side, I brooked no interference as I made straight for where Jenny lay. As I approached, I saw the black-and-red-clad figure had retrieved the dagger. He, too, ripped the mask from his face, and I saw him to be Seth Hartzman. I swung my cudgel into his face, fearing to not connect with his arm if I tried for that. I felt it hit solidly and was aware of his shout. But now, tossing the club away from me, I threw myself down on top of Jenny's still figure, shielding her body from any other attempt at sacrifice.

I realized that all about me was chaos. Men and women screamed. Police whistles blew, resonating throughout the caves. I thought I caught a glimpse of the gamekeeper, wrestling with one of the Lyceum men. Sam Green was wielding a mallet and doing considerable damage. Mr. Henry Irving, great Shakespearean actor that he was, stood up on the seat of the thronelike chair and with his walking stick hit any head that came within range, while reciting the Act Three,

Scene One, speech of *Henry V* at the top of his voice: "Once more unto the breach, dear friends . . ."

But then my attention was caught by Mr. Stoker. He stood toe-to-toe with Colonel Cornell. The colonel had somehow managed to retrieve the dagger while my boss had similarly rescued his Indian club. They moved first one way and then another, fencing, feinting, each trying to gain the advantage. The colonel's monocle had long since gone, and his bald pate was scratched and bleeding.

Slowly the noise died down in the caves. I saw that the battle was over. Policemen were leading Hellfire members out and away. Soon there was only myself, the inspector, the Guv'nor—who had come down off the chair—and Sam Green to form a loose circle about the dueling duo. I perched on the edge of the altar table, my arm around Jenny, who clung to me and was very slowly returning to normalcy. I heard her murmur my name and my heart skipped a beat.

I think that the colonel knew there was no escape. He paused and looked at each of us.

"All of this to take down one man!" he cried. He glowered at the Guv'nor. "Mr. Booth is a far, far better actor than are you, sir! He is the best in America, and I am determined to see that he becomes the best in the world." He suddenly lunged forward and stabbed at Mr. Irving. The Guv'nor's years of onstage fencing stood him in good stead. He reacted immediately, though not quite quickly enough to escape completely. The dagger slashed down and tore into his arm before an almost equally immediate swing of Mr. Stoker's Indian club sent the colonel to the ground.

We took both Mr. Irving and Jenny up to Knowl Hall to be treated by Cook and others of the hall staff still in residence. I was determined not to let Jenny out of my sight. Mr. Stoker said that he would give Inspector Bellamy a hand with sorting out the gang of miscreants and ensuring that Colonel Cornell and Mr. Hartzman were sent safely off to Scotland Yard.

Chapter Thirty

It was Sunday morning before we were able to make any sense out of the *Walpurgisnacht* Hellfire debacle. Before starting the rehearsals—full costume was to take place that afternoon—I was ushered by Mr. Stoker onto the stage. I had been assured, before parting company last evening, that Jenny was safe and would spend a few days with Aunt Alice in Bermondsey. I was reluctant to be away from her but realized I couldn't stand at her side permanently. The conspirators had been apprehended, and everyone should now be safe. I was elated that Jenny had come to no real harm. She had not been abused nor treated badly in any way, just badly frightened and confused. I was so thankful and filled with joy.

Mr. Irving came onstage with his arm heavily bandaged. He did, however, seem to be in good spirits, pooh-poohing the attentions of Miss Terry.

"Everyone here, Abraham?" he asked, looking around.

I saw that a select group had been assembled. It included

Sam Green and the stagehands who had been at the caves with us, Edwina Abbott (I was surprised to see her included), Bill Thomas, Billy Weston, Miss Connelly, Mr. Edwin Booth, and Inspector Bellamy.

"I think this is all concerned, Henry."

"Good! Good." The Guv'nor cleared his throat as he did when preparing for one of his addresses to an assembled cast. This was a relatively small group, but he gave it his full attention.

"Firstly, I must congratulate all of you, and thank you, for your contributions to the events of last evening. What we were involved in was nothing less than a situation that might have been penned by the Bard himself. Shades of *Macbeth*, *Othello*, *Julius Caesar*, and many of the other tragedies. Yet by your efforts, a real tragedy was averted."

There were some murmurings among the stagehands, who stood with wide grins on their faces. I believe they had almost enjoyed the set-to with the Hellfire congregation.

"The subject of this unique event was, of course, a young lady in my employ; a young lady who had done nothing to be drawn into this nightmare. She was being used as a pawn to get to myself. I am sure she would wish me to pass along her own gratitude for your efforts." He gave a moment for that to sink in before continuing. "Much that transpired is still something of a mystery, to myself and I am sure to many of you. I would therefore ask our more knowledgeable theatre manager to run over the events and to explain, as fully as he is able, their sequence and reason. Thank you, Abraham."

He went to gesture with his arm, in Mr. Stoker's direction, but I saw him wince. Obviously his wound was more severe than "just a scratch," as he had dismissed it. Miss Ellen Terry must have caught his brief flinch and crossed to stand close beside him. He gave her the briefest of smiles as he took a step back and waved Mr. Stoker to center stage.

My boss was always reluctant to be the center of attention but, when forced into it, was well able to rise to the occasion. I had often thought that he could have made a more than adequate living as an actor.

"Where to begin?" he asked, of no one in particular. "You are all familiar with the tragic murder of our own Miss Burton in late March. Some of you are also aware of the earlier murder of a Miss Elizabeth Scott. The dates of those two events led me to surmise that there might well be a third murder attempted last night, and that was how it turned out. Happily, we were able to prevent that."

"Not to interrupt, Abraham," said the Guv'nor, interrupting my boss. "But you had made mention of being able to explain why that first young lady, so tragically taken, was not of the theatrical persuasion?"

"Indeed." Stoker turned to the figure on the far side of Miss Terry. "Edwin, you had said that you and the colonel arrived in Liverpool on the thirty-first of January."

"Two days late," agreed Mr. Booth. "Aboard the SS *Germanic*. As I think I told you, it was a very rough crossing."

"I believe that if you had arrived on time," continued Stoker, "it would have given the people concerned time to settle on someone directly connected with the Lyceum, in the London area and in time to become the first sacrifice. Your delayed arrival precluded that, and they had to settle on a young lady conveniently on the scene; the scene of your arrival."

"Forgive me," said Mr. Booth. "I am still somewhat in shock at this whole recent chain of events. Despite his being caught in the act, I am appalled to discover that my very own manager was the mastermind behind this series of murders." He looked around at everyone and then, more specifically, at the Guv'nor. "Believe me, Henry, I cannot apologize enough for what I have brought to your shores. I am in shock!"

Mr. Irving held up his hand—the uninjured one—and shook his head. "We are all in shock, Edwin. That Colonel Cornell should have felt so strongly is, perhaps, understandable, yet to take such drastic action . . ." His voice trailed off. The first time I think I have seen the Guv'nor at a loss for words.

"If I may ask, Edwin?" picked up Mr. Stoker. "Were you aware of the colonel's activity in the so-called Hellfire Club?"

"He never discussed it at any length, though on occasion he did make passing reference to it. I knew he was an active Freemason. I know that he also had a great interest in ancient magic and magicians. I seem to recall his mentioning Paracelsus, Merlin, King Solomon, and others. I also knew that there were one or two Hellfire clubs dotted about the New York and Pennsylvania area. A legacy of our Mr. Benjamin Franklin. Though I do believe that most, if not all, were simply an excuse for drinking and revelry."

"I agree," said Stoker. "As was the case on this side of the Atlantic, though these were more directly sired by Sir Francis Dashwood himself. Incidentally, I have some doubts as to the colonel's true attachment to the ancient body of Freemasons. I think it may have been a cover for his more frequent activity with the Hellfire group and as a connection with the practice of ritual."

"What makes you say that?" asked the Guv'nor.

"Simply that at the last Beefsteak dinner I made a point of shaking hands with the colonel, and he didn't seem to know the supposedly secret handshake of the Freemasons. But that is perhaps neither here nor there. I think he claimed to be able to coach you in matters Masonic in order to be able to exercise some sort of control over your activities."

"Where did Seth Hartzman fit into it, sir?" I asked. I had been wondering that for a long time. "We saw that he was acting as the second in command at the ritual last night."

"He was the key figure to connect the two sides of the

Atlantic," Stoker said. "We knew he had been to America. He admitted as much himself. But I took the trouble to check the passenger lists of the White Star Line's ships berthing here just prior to the arrival of Mr. Booth and the colonel. Hartzman arrived just two weeks prior to them, on the smaller SS *Celtic*. He had been primed by the colonel before leaving America, and his job was to organize the Hellfire group for the ritual on this side of the Atlantic. I believe that as time grew short he settled on the group in Warrington, since it was so close to where the colonel would land."

"And why did he become a part of our crowd scenes?" I asked.

"Possibly so that if all else failed he would be on hand to attack the Guv'nor directly."

"Not by any magical method, you mean?" asked Mr. Booth. "But why not just do that anyway? Why not simply murder Henry if he felt it necessary to get rid of him, rather than go through all this magical rigmarole?"

Mr. Stoker gave one of his long sighs. "I think the main reason was that to murder Henry would have led to a murder investigation, almost certainly by Scotland Yard. It would produce a trial and all that attends that scene. Whereas to bring about the Guv'nor's death by magical means—if indeed that is possible—would result in a mysterious death, certainly, but no obvious killer, no crime scene, probably no recriminations."

Inspector Bellamy finally spoke up. I had almost forgotten that he was present, which was very nice.

"We would like to point out, gentlemen, that Scotland Yard is most definitely implicated now, and we can promise that those involved—*all* of those involved—will be brought to justice."

"But are all of those poor people who were in the caves truly guilty?" asked Miss Terry. "Were they not simply part of the scenery, as it were?"

294 · RAYMOND BUCKLAND

"We must view them as accomplices to the murders, ma'am. That is the law."

"In effect, tricked into it, in my opinion," said my boss. "But I am sure that all will be sorted out at the trial."

"Please, sir?"

I recognized the voice of Edwina Abbott. "Miss Abbott," I called. "You have a question? Won't you please step forward?"

She did so, and Mr. Stoker gave her his full attention.

"My cards, sir? I'd just like to say as how they was right in the end, then."

"Right?"

"You remember, Mr. Rivers. The Chariot and the Hanged Man."

My mind went back to when Edwina pulled cards to see if there was anything regarding the end of the run of *Hamlet*. She had drawn those two cards. "What about them, Miss Abbott?"

"I think I can answer that," said my boss. He acknowledged Edwina with a nod of his head and then addressed the assembly. "I believe that Miss Abbott has quite a talent for prediction, with her pasteboards. She did, as she has reminded us, pull two cards. One of these—the Hanged Man—speaks for itself in that both Colonel Cornell and Seth Hartzman will almost certainly swing for their parts in these heinous murders. But the other I find interesting. Won't you please tell us about the Chariot, Miss Abbott?"

Suddenly finding herself the center of attention, especially with both Mr. Irving's and Mr. Booth's eyes on her, she blushed and took a step backward.

"Come now, Edwina," said Mr. Stoker. "We are all friends here. We would be delighted if you would elucidate."

She gave a nervous cough and then stepped forward again, groping in her reticule as she did and producing her cards.

"It was like I told Mr. Rivers at the time. The Chariot is rushing forward with an important man at the reins. He is unstoppable."

"And he almost was," murmured Mr. Booth. "Important? I suppose being a colonel might qualify."

"There was good and evil there," continued Edwina.

I saw, in my mind, the image of Mr. Stoker battling the colonel. Good and evil indeed. And with people like my boss, I knew that good would always triumph.

"Is there anything else of which we should be made aware, Abraham?" asked the Guv'nor.

"Nothing of any great importance," Stoker replied. "But one small item that I found fascinating. Perhaps one or two others of you may do the same. Perhaps a reason why Colonel Cornell felt that this was the opportune time to make his play to depose the Guv'nor and install Mr. Booth as premier Shakespearean actor. It was, or is, the year. This year."

"What do you mean, this year?" asked Mr. Irving.

"It is 1881. A magical year. According to numerology we have 1, 8, 8, 1. Add those together—1 + 8 and 8 + 1. That equals 9 + 9 which, in turn, equals 18. 18 is 1 + 8 which again equals 9. The number 9 has always been regarded as a magical number, and so this year of 1881 is very much a magical year. Nine, by the way, is regarded as a fire sign; emotional, active, and impulsive. I think we have seen all of that."

"Lot of what someone called rigmarole, if you ask us," said the police inspector. "We think that we will stick to our crimes and criminals and leave the magic and mathematics to others."

"Gentlemen! And ladies," cried the Guv'nor, his gold pocket watch in his hand. "Fascinating as all this may be, *tempus fugit*! Tomorrow sees the opening night of *Othello*. We are honored to have Mr. Edwin Booth with us and know that this will be as successful a production as was *Hamlet*. But to doubly ensure that success, we must now break up this verbal autopsy and focus our minds and efforts on a good dress rehearsal. I know I can count on you all." He waved his watch. "It is the time for some repast. Take a good lunch, for we may not manage another break for some hours. I want to see you all, plus the rest of the cast, in makeup and costume onstage here by two of the clock. Thank you."

He turned and swept Mr. Booth and Miss Terry ahead of him as he left the stage. The others broke up and headed out of the theatre and toward the Druid's Head.

"Come, Harry," said Mr. Stoker. "The Guv'nor gives good advice. Let us take a good meal. Tomorrow is the start of another life."

"Happily, one that will include Jenny in it, sir," I said promised myself that for much of the morrow I would f myself in Bermondsey and would do everything in power to make up to Jenny for all that she had been for to endure. Life was indeed starting afresh.